AF447649

DIANA GARCÍA

Paradise Loss

First published by dgmk squared @paradiselossbook 2023

Copyright © 2023 by Diana García

All rights reserved. No part of this publication may be reproduced, stored or transmitted in any form or by any means, electronic, mechanical, photocopying, recording, scanning, or otherwise without written permission from the publisher. It is illegal to copy this book, post it to a website, or distribute it by any other means without permission.

This novel is entirely a work of fiction. The names, characters and incidents portrayed in it are the work of the author's imagination. Any resemblance to actual persons, living or dead, events or localities is entirely coincidental.

Diana García asserts the moral right to be identified as the author of this work.

First edition

ISBN: 978-9968-03-299-5

Cover art by Luísa Dias

This book was professionally typeset on Reedsy.
Find out more at reedsy.com

For Matthew, my champion.

Contents

Acknowledgement

I want to thank, first and foremost, my husband, Matthew J. Koschara, who has championed my dreams and my writing from the moment we met. I could not have completed this novel without the moral support from all the strong women in my life who include, but are not limited to, my grandmother, Vennel (may she rest in peace), my mother, Kay, my aunt, Fran, my mother-in-law, Kris, and my dearest friends. I extend my heartfelt gratitude to the New York Public Library, Sistema Nacional de Bibliotecas (SINABI Costa Rica), the Chapel Hill Public Library, the Carrboro Arts Center and Jeremy Hawkins for his Novel Writing Workshop; the Chapel Hill-based Novel Gazers writing group that provided the feedback and support I needed to work through the initial drafts; the North Carolina Writers' Network and Luísa Dias for the cover design. I am indebted to Quince Duncan's short stories and to the recorded oral history of the people of the Talamanca coast entitled, *"What Happen"*, by Paula Palmer, as well as to all the journalists out there who risk their lives to report on the facts.
I count myself fortunate to have (had) you all in my life and to be a recipient of your thoughtfulness, care, and kindness. Finally, a mi tierra, Costa Rica, ¡siempre te querré!

1

Guatemala - February 1997

"Are you headed to Tikal, too?" the tall, elegant man standing next to Anja asked. With his afternoon shadow, he was the best put together tourist she had met on her trip so far. And his accent, Anja noted, was unmistakably Austrian.

"Yes," she replied, looking up at him with a bemused smile. "Would you care to sit together? You're from Vienna, right?"

Meeting Gustav on the line for the Mayan Temple Tour was not quite what she had hoped for, but they had nonetheless hit it off right away. With his wavy dark hair and his aquiline nose, he had reminded her of Fabian, her best friend in high school. Fabian had moved to Berlin not long after they had graduated and was happily settled down with a former East German he had met not long after the Wall fell. She, on the contrary, had not been so lucky in love.

Anja had, as fate would have it, made a name for herself with her moody, luminescent abstractions and was fortunate to be represented by a small but respected gallery specializing in unusual prints and gouache paintings. At the age of thirty-seven, however, she had encountered a block of fuck-it-all indifference and had found herself more and more staring blankly at the mottled paper in front of her. Her studio flat in the bohemian quarter of Basel no longer offered up the muse of inspiration she so desperately needed since what had once been an edgy, working-class neighborhood had turned into a gentrified bubble too soft to offer up any meaningful resistance.

To make matters worse, her circle of friends and acquaintances had tightened in recent years, and though she had felt at ease living in Switzerland—the thin veil of neutrality allowing her to set aside the hefty weight of her German past—traveling was the only way she knew how to meet new people. A good part of her hoped this trip might also offer the potential for a romantic tryst since she had long ago sacrificed any semblance of a relationship for the sake of her art.

Anja spent a dizzying day with Gustav, admiring the towering Tikal temples, while he, a good foot taller than she, had listened to her teenage tales of growing up in the small-minded village of Rheinfelden not far from the Swiss border. Getting back on the bus, she turned the topic of conversation to him, confident she had gained his quiet trust.

"I have to say, I'm impressed that a Viennese would be open to exploring such a wild place," she said, as she looked at his elegant hands. "You don't really strike me as the adventuring type."

"No, I'm not," he smiled. "Not usually."

"So, let me guess, you're a musician?"

Gustav narrowed his eyes.

"How did you know?"

"First of all, you hold yourself like a conductor, and with a name like Gustav, well—"

At this, they both laughed out loud.

"It was fated, obviously," he said, his olive-complexion reddening. "And you? I sense we're kindred spirits where the arts are concerned, though you've told me almost nothing of what it is that you do."

"I paint," she said. "Nothing figurative."

"I knew it," he replied, flashing her a mischievous grin. "We make the perfect pair."

Anja laughed.

"For a Kandinsky, yes, but why is it we're both traveling alone?"

He looked around at the pale faces surrounding them.

"Are we? It's as if we've come over here with a built-in magnet. I've already met most of these people in the past month, with the lovely exception of you, of course. Where on earth have you been?"

"Aren't you the charmer," Anja said, feeling comfortable enough to gently elbow him. "But you're right. We end up forming these little groups of convenience, huddling together, too timid to go off the beaten track. We fantasize about discovering the secrets of the Maya, or some such nonsense, and in the end, we're just queuing up for the next attraction."

"Still, we should give ourselves *some* credit," Gustav said. "It's a far cry from Euro Disney."

Anja rolled her eyes.

"Can you imagine? At least in the jungle we don't have to contend with the crowds."

"And we have *this*," Gustav said, as he gestured toward the cathedral-like light piercing through the canopied forest.

Anja nodded.

"Your senses are immediately inundated, a kind of harmonious cacophony, don't you think? The birds screeching. The monkeys howling. Beneath it all this continuous whirr of the most ungodly looking insects, and the moment you move your feet, you add to the discordant symphony with the crunching of layer after layer of dried leaves. Every bit of it is stunningly palpable."

"Assuming you're not too worried about stepping on a snake, that is."

Gustav smiled.

"I almost did yesterday morning. One slithered across the path in front of me. I've never felt so terrified and at the same time so alive. I felt sorry for the poor thing afterwards. I'm the one who startled him."

Anja glanced over at him and smiled.

"So, tell me again why it is we're traveling alone?"

Gustav contemplated the gray upholstery of the seat in front of him for a moment.

"It's hard when your work consumes you. People get jealous of it. Just as much as another person."

"I couldn't agree more," Anja said. "My first live-in boyfriend was a painter, too, until he grew resentful of the fact I was landing exhibitions. He started to tear down my work in a strange way, trying to compete. I swore off dating other artists, but then the man I went out with after that couldn't fathom I had an actual career. When things started to get serious, he told me I needed to cater more to *his* schedule, as if I was somehow just dabbling in art until he came along. You can well imagine what I said to him."

Gustav chuckled in sympathy.

"It's never easy."

"And you?" Anja asked.

"Apart from the occasional affair, I don't think I've fared much better. But then again most of the men I meet aren't looking for anything long-term," he added, glancing at her sideways to gauge her response.

"It must be hard when you're so beautiful," she replied.

Gustav laughed and nudged her back.

"Like you said before. We make a perfect pair."

Anja traveled with Gustav through the rest of Guatemala, a refreshing change from the young backpackers with whom she had crisscrossed the Yucatán and Belize on the public bus. Most had been North American students in their early twenties including a few from Europe and Australia, and while she did not share much in common with them, the thrifty travelers were quick to compare notes on how best to negotiate border crossings or gain access to some of the lesser-known Mayan sites. She had found comfort in these temporary alliances, especially when confronted with the foreignness of an uncongenial and, at times, deceptive Latin American bureaucracy. Up to now she had mostly avoided the men her age, some of whom were on the prowl for under-aged locals, the unfortunate shadow side of Latin American travel.

In Gustav she had met her ideal traveling companion as they made their way through the *pueblos* and rain forests in search of inspiration, whether captured in an unusual jungle howl or the ostentatious plumage of a rare bird mirrored back in an enigmatic, indigenous pattern.

On the long and bumpy journeys, they would talk about their lives, about art and politics and the books they loved, and when they couldn't keep their eyes open anymore, invariably one head would rest on the shoulder of the other, the platonic boundaries between them comfortably fluid now much like what she had shared with Fabian. In the evenings they took their meals in the small family restaurants they would find near whatever hotel they would decide to book for the night, often choosing for the sake of convenience to share a room.

"My mother collapsed just a week before I was supposed to start at the art academy," Anja told him that first night over dinner. "An inoperable brain tumor. My father was already sick with cancer though he said nothing about it. I had no choice but to defer my studies, and when she passed away, it was his turn to be nursed."

Anja cast her eyes across the dark waters of *Lago Petén Itzá*, the shallow waves reflecting silver crests.

"He was an amazing person, my father," she said. "He worked all his life at the local brewery, but he always told me, 'Anja, follow your heart'.

"I remember sketching and painting to pass the time by his bedside, and how he would smile when I showed him my work. After he died, I couldn't wait another second to get out of that miserable town, and when I got to Basel, I poured myself into painting."

Gustav took a sip from the chilled wine the young waiter had just served them.

"I can't say I was ever that close to my parents," he said. "Like you, I was raised in a conservative village, and there were three of us growing up, two boys and one girl. Of course, my parents *must* have known, but nothing was ever said. The piano was my friend and confidant. I was good enough to receive a conservatory scholarship, so as soon as I finished school, I never looked back."

"Do they come and visit you?" Anja asked, once the waiter had handed them menus and lit the candle at their table. He had glanced up only once to catch Gustav's eye.

"Now and then for the occasional concert. But to be honest, I think we're all glad to have some distance between us. My sister married a local. Got pregnant right away. And Gregor, my older brother, followed our dad into the family business. They're too busy these days doting on grandchildren to worry about my private life."

"It must be a relief in some ways."

"It is and it isn't. In Vienna I have my friends, people my parents would likely not approve of. It remains an unspoken thing. I visit them for the holidays, but apart from that, our worlds don't mix."

The waiter returned so they took a moment to finalize their selections. Standing stoic and silent, he rewarded them with an enthusiastic "*con gusto,*" when they finished placing their order in Spanish, a broad, handsome smile spreading across his taut, bronze face.

"And no steady boyfriend?" Anja asked, once the waiter had walked away.

"I don't have time for it. For a while I was dating an older man, and I was keen to settle down, but I couldn't put up with his constant jealousy, the need to control my every move. It got in the way of my work. After that I just opted for a simpler approach, and I prefer it."

"Don't you get lonely?"

Gustav chuckled.

"It's not such a hardship for me. In many ways I've spent most of my life alone."

Just then the waiter brought out their filleted fish with a side of *yuca con hierba mora.*

"I wish I could say the same," Anja said, looking curiously at the yuca hash sprinkled with bits of black nightshade. "As much as I enjoy my work, I can't fathom living alone the rest of my life. I've realized that the painting just isn't enough, and at the moment it isn't anything. That's why I'm here. To try and stir things up again."

Gustav nodded as she took a tentative bite. Surprisingly, the flavors were quite subtle and refreshing. They ate in silence for a while, enjoying their meal as they listened to the waves lapping on the tranquil shore.

Anja could not help but think further of the difficulty of trying to find love in her late thirties. Life had already revealed to her an endless variety of dysfunctional relationships, and it no longer seemed possible to look at a prospective mate without a built-in sense of skepticism or doubt. It was precisely this world-weary view that had so often led to a stalemate in her relationships, with neither party wanting to "invest" further unless some unknown sign was made apparent. Usually, the exact opposite would happen. The mundane and annoying habits of the other would reverberate like the echo of some past depression. An internal alarm would sound calling out for "more space," but it was precisely this vast emptiness that left Anja feeling somehow less than fully alive.

"Call me as soon as you get back," Gustav said, giving Anja one last embrace before parting ways with her at the Guatemala City airport.

"And you're absolutely sure you're done here?" Anja asked, not wanting to let go.

Pulling back to hold her at arm's length, Gustav smiled at her.

"I'm looking forward to seeing your new paintings," he said, kissing her on the forehead, his grace and confidence conferring just enough strength to get them through the farewell.

Gustav's absence was palpable. It reflected itself in Anja's increased irritability at having to manage travel through Central America on her own. She could feel the weight of her loneliness bearing down on her again in the days that followed. The time spent en route to Tegucigalpa passed her by in a depressing blur. Lush countryside was broken up by poor, litter-infested hamlets. Rural inhabitants dressed in soiled rags stood by roadside trenches overflowing with garbage. Witnessing such depravation alone without the solace of another was almost too much for her to bear.

Anja would drift in and out of sleep to escape these visions. Upon waking, she would daydream about the past or future, dwelling on the brief moments of rapture she'd experienced with the few men she had hoped would become more than transient lovers.

She would indulge these memories but only up to a point. Fantasies about the future were the only ones that propelled her forward, especially on the days when weariness might otherwise grind her down and pin her to her bed with a paperback as her sole companion.

And then, of course, there were her frets concerning motherhood. In this respect she was certainly not immune to the biological clock ticking away despite her hollow attempts to claim otherwise. If she wanted to descend into the depths of misery, all she needed to do was add a dollop of childbearing envy. After all, wasn't a child the ultimate act of creativity? Could she truly experience all that art could convey without becoming a mother? Without bearing her own, she could only attain a part and not the whole of what her body had pledged with the—some would say cruel—randomness of her female birth.

As she peered out of the windows and watched the landscape blur into a kaleidoscope of leaves sprinkled with reds, violets and yellows, she thought about the ease with which she and Gustav had spent their days together, with rarely an awkward moment between them. Anja could almost imagine spending the rest of her life with him, if their meeting had not, once again, proved too good to be true.

2

Costa Rica - March 1997

The bus driver turned up the volume on the tinny salsa station, and Anja let out a sigh. She pulled off the embroidered tunic she had picked up in Guatemala and then fanned herself with a travel brochure. The heat had spiked without warning as they lurched down into the Caribbean lowlands, catching her and the other half-asleep passengers by surprise.

They had driven three hours over the treacherous Braulio Carrillo mountains and had not even reached Limón yet. It would be a good half hour or more to get to Caway after that. A few precious seconds of cool air breezed past the sliding glass window, but Anja could already feel the sweat gathering beneath the folds of her cotton skirt, the only thing keeping her bare legs from sticking to the worn plastic seat.

Traveling with Gustav earlier, Anja had not paid much attention to the heat, but now as she bumped shoulders with the woman next to her, she was overwhelmed by the stifling, sticky air, stale with sweat. When she had arrived at the station at 5 AM that morning, early enough to purchase an assigned seat, she was surprised to see so many passengers who had joined the queue late willing to pay for standing room only. Now, with so many armpits exposed, Anja asked herself if perhaps standing was not the better choice. To make matters worse, a traffic jam was starting to form on the narrow, two-lane highway, and the diesel fumes from the long-haul trucks were wafting in.

Anja wondered if the journey was worth the hassle, but the Swedish woman she had met at the hostel in San José had sworn the beaches were a hidden gem. Under normal circumstances her excitement would have overcome her fatigue, but after weeks of bumpy, Central American bus travel, she was at her breaking point.

She leaned her gray-streaked curls against the windowpane and watched as row-after-row of evenly spaced banana plants blurred past like a low-lying forest, their stalks bundled in blue plastic beneath gargantuan, fanned out leaves. She thought about her parents and how with childlike joy they would recount the taste of their first banana not long after the end of the Second World War. If only they could have seen where their cherished fruit was grown, assuming they could have tolerated such unbearable heat.

Twenty slow minutes later Anja spied an array of shipping containers—Hamburg Süd, Maersk, Hapag-Lloyd—signaling their entry into the Port of Limón. The city itself appeared as a rusty patchwork of corrugated roofs looming large over crudely built homes, the walls painted in a kaleidoscope of vivid colors: orange, red, green, yellow and turquoise. The poverty was even more apparent here than in San José, but something about the Day-Glo colors and the slow, determined gait of the locals spoke of a defiant type of joy. This was still Costa Rica, but the Rasta banner—superimposed with Bob Marley's contemplative silhouette—hung more prominent than the blue, white and red stripes of the national flag that bore a coat-of-arms too reminiscent of the Republic's colonial past.

At the downtown terminal, the bus driver pulled in for a 20-minute break, their first after an almost four-hour journey down the mountains. Squinting, Anja shook out her legs and stepped out into the noonday sun. Her experience just a few days earlier on the Pacific had been one of intense, arid heat, but here she could feel the weight of the air's moisture blanketing her in a layer of perspiration.

She took in her surroundings and was surprised to see an above ground cemetery situated on a small hill across the street. The tight cluster of white, bathroom-tiled tombs perplexed her with their opposing sense of garishness and restraint, as if the two forces were locked in some eternal stalemate. Anja attempted a rough translation of the hand-painted lettering written across the arched entranceway.

"Jesus says, *os aseguro?* He that guards my word will never die."

In a flash she recalled the verse in German, a fading relic from her Confirmation days. She shook her head and turned her attention toward the rest stop.

It would be a while before she had another opportunity to relieve herself, so stepping inside the dark confines of the *cafetería*, she queued up behind the line of women waiting to use the lavatory. Anja found the public toilets in Costa Rica better maintained than in the other countries she had visited on her Latin American journey. Though the fixtures were quite often old or corroded, it was clear they were on a regular cleaning schedule and included paper, if not in the stalls, then at least available for purchase from whoever might be manning the entrance. The only thing lacking were hand towels, so Anja learned to make do with just a flick of her hands.

Back in the dining hall, a dense aroma of simmering stews and rices reminded Anja that she had not eaten since breakfast. She chose the shortest concession—the bus would be leaving any minute—and found herself standing in front of a petite, indigenous woman whose smooth face and clear eyes made her look remarkably young. Anja would have mistaken her for a teenager if not for her matured and motherly figure.

"*Un agua, por favor,*" Anja said, before pointing to an unknown pastry. "*Y estó?*"

"*Es un patí,*" The woman said, in a sweet but almost silent voice.

"*Un patí?*" Anja furrowed her brow. "*Es dulce?*"

"*No, es con carne picante. Una especialidad caribeña. Muy rico.*"

Anja doubted the wisdom of eating strange meat, but the growling in her stomach soon prevailed. "*Okay, eine,*" she said.

The woman looked at her confused.

"One. I mean, *uno, por favor.*"

What she really wanted was another cup of coffee but there was no time.

Cradling the fried pastry in a piece of square tin foil, Anja boarded the bus again and sat down. The seat adhered to the back of her arms as she leaned back, but once the bus careened into motion, now free of its standing passengers, the airflow from the wide-open windows helped to clear the oppressive heat that had built up during their stop.

The pastry, as it turned out, was quite good. It reminded Anja a bit of the *talas kebabi* she had eaten the year before in Istanbul. Funny that. People had warned her not to travel alone in Turkey, but she had found the men far more respectful to women there than in Latin America, where catcalling was considered a form of praise. Staring out through the dusty glass once more and feeling a bit melancholic, Anja kept her eyes trained on the horizon as the bus turned onto a much narrower, two-lane road. Through a marshy clearing, she could see the steady, lapping waves of the Caribbean Sea until the lowland jungle rose up again to obscure her view.

Thirty minutes later she was jarred awake by the bus pulling into an unmarked lot. Unsure of where she was, Anja stood to ask the driver.

"*Sí, es Caway,*" the man said, waving at her impatiently to get off the bus. Most of the remaining passengers would continue to Puerto Viejo.

With effort, Anja yanked at her backpack lodged tight in the miniature compartment overhead. She stuffed her folded up tunic into the front mesh pocket and then walked as fast as she could down the narrow aisle as people on either side leaned in to avoid getting bumped. The few passengers who had exited ahead of her—locals by the look of it—were already making their way down an intersecting dirt road. Not knowing where to go, Anja followed them.

She was dripping with sweat by the time she entered the center of town. It had a dusty, outback feel despite the flourishing green jungle surrounding it. She passed a small *Banco Nacional* on one corner, its barred and tinted windows reflecting an image of her hunched over with exhaustion. Across the way, the red cross insignia of the *Farmacia* made her feel reassured. Was it the resemblance to the Swiss flag, she wondered? At any rate, it made her laugh to think of this rural village in comparison to her hometown of Basel.

There was not much to Caway at all, apart from this tiny commercial thoroughfare and a couple of residential streets that radiated out on either side. The houses, compared to Limón, were painted in less vibrant hues and for the most part, looked no less the worse for wear. Only a few young men lingered on the street, laughing and teasing one another as they jostled a soccer ball back and forth. She spotted a couple of tourists making their way to the beach, but everyone else who was out seemed to be running errands though at an even more relaxed pace than in Limón.

From what she could make out, there were at least a couple of stores selling both groceries and basic supplies. Otherwise, the town was made up of small bars and restaurants scattered up and down the khaki-colored street. The aquamarine blues and greens of a large mural covering the side of the *Reggae Bar and Restaurant* immediately called out to her, so she went inside to buy herself a well-deserved drink.

In contrast to the blinding sun outside, the wood-paneled dining room with its wide-open windows appeared cool and dark. Overhead, the blades of two large fans rotated in slow motion, and though it did not *feel* any cooler, the welcoming shade at least suggested a slight drop in temperature. At this hour, the dining area was empty apart from a young couple studying their guidebook and a tan and wiry blonde man who sat at the bar. He was talking to the dreadlocked bartender who looked over at Anja and gave her a welcoming smile.

She took off her backpack and leaned it against the bar before dropping herself into one of the adjacent stools.

"*Una cerveza Imperial, por favor.*"

The bartender looked at her amused.

"Welcome," he said in English. Anja felt her cheeks flush. "Hot out there, yah? One cold *Imperial* at your service."

The blonde man next to her chuckled as he turned to look at her with a bright, toothy smile. "*Deutsche, nicht wahr?*"

Up close she could see the gray hairs in his moustache.

"*Ja,*" Anja said, lifting her bottle and smiling back. Despite herself, she was relieved to hear her native tongue.

"And what brings you to paradise?"

"Does one need a reason?"

The man laughed.

"No reason. Just that there aren't many people who know about us here."

"I'm on a three-month holiday," Anja told him, watching as he took another sip from his Pilsen. "Making my way down to Peru. And you? Have you been here long?"

"Twenty years."

She felt oddly drawn to him—this uncharacteristic German—far too happy in his threadbare shirt. The only sign of his European heritage was in the worn leather sandals he wore with socks pulled up to his calves. He was not tall yet he exuded a casual manliness, his hands and face leathered by the sun and work. There was something magnetic about his complete sense of ease here.

"You must have arrived when you were very young," Anja said, looking astounded.

"I still am."

The bartender looked at them and laughed.

"Andreas, he was born here. It just took him a little longer to learn how to speak is all."

They were sharing an inside joke, no doubt at her expense, but Anja had to admit she was enjoying herself.

"So, what was it like then?" she asked. "Has it changed much?"

"It was Eden," Andreas said, his impish smile as wide as his thin, bronzed face.

Anja looked at him with skepticism.

"So, you were "born" in paradise and never left. Impressive. That must have been some time in the mid-70s."

Andreas nodded.

"Things were different back then," he said. "It was still banana plantation. Not like now, with all *dem* tourists."

He chuckled.

"Banana plantation? That doesn't sound like Eden. Do you work for one?"

At this Andreas guffawed before saying something to the bartender in

Creole.

"William here, his great-grandfather, he worked the plantations."

The bartender nodded.

"My grandfather's father came from Jamaica to work the Canal. Then he followed the green gold all the way to Caway. He worked most of his life for *Mamita Yunai*."

"*Mamita Yunai?*" Anja asked looking over at Andreas.

"United Fruit Company," he said.

"Your family have lived here a long time."

"Yes," William said. "My mother's people fished and farmed here long before the English and Americans came and built the railway. They used to sail from Bocas every season to hunt the turtle grounds up near the large reef and then they settled here."

"And the Spanish, where were they?"

"Way back then the Spainman still kept to himself up in the highland valley while my mother's people traded with the Miskito and the Talamanca Bribri. And then the big ships started to come. The pirates first, and then the Americans with their big steam engine. They started to make the banana plantations and contracted with the men in San José to build the railroad."

"So was this still Costa Rican territory?"

William shrugged.

"Only when the Costa Rica president shipwrecked on The Bluff and asked to buy that pasture off Ole Smith, did they put us on their map and carve up the land. Still, they did not give us citizenship until 1948."

You're quite the historian, William," Anja said. "And the mural outside, was it painted by a local artist?"

William looked at her and beamed.

"Do you like it?" he asked.

"Yes, it's beautiful."

"Thank you," he said. "I painted it for the hawksbill turtles who lay their eggs out by Caway Point. Do you see the tree I painted by the side of the door there?"

Anja turned her head to look more closely.

"That's the Caway tree that grows out by the point. In Spanish they call it *sangrillo.* I painted it blood red for the color of the sap."

"So the town got its name, from a tree?" Anja asked.

"Yes, the Miskito Indian call it *cawi,* and from that we say Caway."

"Impressive."

"You live here long you hear *dem* ole stories," William said. "Too bad they don't teach it in school."

"And what do they teach?" Anja asked.

"What the government in San José wants. The public school, they teach the Spanish way. Only in recent times do they talk about *our* history."

"So, you speak Spanish as well?"

"*Sí, claro,*" William said, walking out from behind the bar to see to a couple perusing the menu. "But we don't let the children forget where we come from."

Anja nodded her head.

"And you—Andreas is it?"

"Andreas Freyer at your service," he beamed.

"Where do you fit in if you don't mind my asking? I'm Anja. Anja Reinhold."

"It's nice to meet you, Anja" Andreas said, holding her gaze just a few seconds longer than usual. "It's a funny question. Caway is my home. I knew it from the moment I arrived."

"What I really mean is what do you do here? I'm guessing from what you said before that you don't work on a banana plantation."

"Oh, that." He laughed again. "No. I own a restaurant and some *cabinas* up the road from Black Beach, about two and a half kilometers from here."

"Well, as it happens I'm looking for a place to stay."

"Yes?" Andreas said, his eyes sparkling. "It's a bit rustic."

"As long as it's not in the sun, that's not a problem. I prefer the beach in the morning or the late afternoons, but this midday heat I would rather avoid."

"It's the fair skin," Andreas said, stretching out his dark arm. "Stay here long enough and you'll look just like me."

Anja laughed.

"I'm only staying for a week."

"Plenty of time to enjoy the shade in my garden, then. But why not stay a little longer?"

"Believe me, I'd love to stay as long as I like, but I have to make it to Lima before my flight home."

"So why not change your ticket?" he asked.

"You make it sound so easy," Anja scoffed.

"What's holding you back? Your family?"

"No, my work. It's not like I can just pack up my bags one day and be done with it."

"It worked for me," Andreas said.

Anja narrowed her eyes playfully.

"Yeah, well, I'm not so sure I quite believe you."

Andreas shrugged his shoulders before finishing his beer.

"There's only one way to find out."

"Only one way to find out what?"

"Whether you really want your life to change."

At this Anja laughed.

"I wouldn't know where to begin. Can't I just blame all my troubles on men?"

"Depends on which one," Andreas said. "If you want the prize, you've got to be willing to risk a broken heart. There's no way around it."

"You can say that again," Anja said, as she finished her beer.

"Well, you can tell me all about it over dinner, but we'll have to leave soon so I can open my restaurant."

"Ok," Anja said, shifting to get at her wallet.

Andreas waved to William who was coming behind the bar again to pour drinks for his new guests.

"Just put it on my tab," he said, before picking up her backpack as if it weighed nothing.

"Thank you," Anja said. "But that wasn't necessary."

"First drink is always on me. Did you get this in Antigua?" he added, catching sight of her tunic.

Anja looked at him puzzled.

"How did you know?"

"I recognize the pattern," he said, his gait surprisingly buoyant. "In one of my former lives I used to sell textiles. Just follow me, and I'll tell you more."

3

Caway - March 1997

Even with Andreas carrying her heavy backpack, Anja could still feel the weight of the tropical sun on her shoulders as they stepped out of the Reggae Bar and into the afternoon heat. Lucky for her, Andreas seemed more than happy to accommodate her languid pace.

They turned left at the end of the main road where they could hear the steady crashing of waves veiled by a thick curtain of trees and foliage, a refreshing reminder of what the beach would have in store. On the other side, a lonely cement sidewalk stretched for a quarter kilometer framing a row of sun-bleached, wood-paneled houses. With hardly a car in sight, they chose to walk in the street instead, closest to the jungle-cast shade and where they could catch a glimpse of the rolling, turquoise sea.

Now and again a few cyclists pedaled past, some balancing bags of groceries or a small child on the handlebars.

"*Irie*," Andreas said, waving as two boys with hair knots raised their hands in a solemn salute. The younger one stood perched on the extended rear axle pegs while the other pedaled.

Andreas seemed to know everyone here, exchanging *pura vida* greetings left and right. It was a promising sign that the locals liked him, Anja thought, and a relief that she wasn't out of her mind to follow him to his out-of-the-way residence.

They passed a few more modest homes and hotels – the plots between them growing wider and further apart. Only one car drove past them, raising a slight cloud of dust on the road.

Finally, a stretch of glistening, black sand opened in front of them revealing the white crested waves pounding against a palm-lined beach.

"Wow," Anja said, drinking in the breeze. She remembered the Swedish woman's words, *You'll have a piece of paradise all to yourself.* "How is it that there's hardly anyone here?"

"This is Black Beach," Andreas said, smiling. "But the one closest to me will take your breath away. You'll see."

Andreas said little as they continued their walk, the sea view now eclipsed by a dark thicket of trees and blooming hibiscus that provided just enough shade to take cover.

The intense heat advised a bare minimum of exertion, but it gave Anja plenty of time to take in the lush surroundings. She could see why Andreas had fallen in love with the place at first sight. It was just the right amount of remote and wild to tantalize most adventure travelers. But to settle here? She wondered what it was that kept him from moving on.

Anja noticed that only a handful of roads intersected the one they were on, indicating that this was indeed just a small hamlet in the middle of the jungle. For quite some time the crossings disappeared altogether, until another one emerged. A few meters beyond that, Andreas turned left into what appeared to be a grove of trees, though in fact it was the unmarked entrance of his property. An almost perfectly concealed, open-air structure emerged out of nowhere, reminiscent of a Swiss Family Robinson treehouse with a steeply pitched tin roof barely visible through the overgrown canopy above.

"Here we are," Andreas announced, holding open the small wooden gate at the entrance. "My tropical palace."

"How does anyone know to come here?" Anja asked. "It's almost invisible from the road."

Andreas laughed. "Word of mouth. I prefer living *in* the forest, and not off of it, if you know what I mean."

"Yes, well, you've certainly achieved *that*," Anja said, feeling a slight flutter of concern.

Leading her up two wooden steps, they entered the restaurant. A large communal table, a typical German *Stammtisch*, was segregated from the main dining room that opened up through another threshold further to the right. Directly in front of them a padlocked solid metal grate painted a bright yellow covered an interior window.

The entire framework—neither oval nor rectangular, but rather free-form in its angles and curves—was made of beautiful dark woods that had been lovingly planed and varnished like the tables and benches occupying it. The ceiling was high with steep overhangs to keep the sun and rain from penetrating, yet it was surrounded on all sides by greenery: Andreas' garden.

"How did you find this place?" Anja marveled.

"I didn't find it," Andreas said, chuckling. "I built it. This was all jungle before, and I try to keep it that way as much as possible."

Anja looked around in disbelief. "How long did it take you?"

"Ten years, on and off. I bought the land first, and the trees I cut to clear space are the ones I used for the construction. I didn't have much cash, so it was slow going at first. I would work until the money ran out. Then I would go back to Europe, sell textiles, do odd jobs here and there, until I had enough to come back. When I finished the restaurant, I stayed for good, building the *cabinas* one by one. The one you'll stay in was the very first and is attached to the main building here."

"And where do you stay?" Anja asked.

"I have an entire apartment right above your head," he said, pointing up. "Are you thirsty? Let me open up the kitchen. Take a seat over there, and I'll get us a beer."

Anja settled into an upholstered bench on the far side of the *Stammtisch* while Andreas removed the padlock and pulled the grate down from the window. The open-air kitchen lay fully visible from where she sat, and to the right and back of it, she could see a wooden staircase leading up to the well-concealed apartment above.

"*Imperial* or *Pilsen?*" Andreas asked, looking through the kitchen window as he slid-open a refrigerated chest.

"*Imperial.* So when do you open?"

He laughed.

"Whenever the next customer comes in," he said, pulling out two bottles of beer. "Most days I start serving food at around five or six. Some nights I have a lot of people. Some nights not. It all works out though, and I have a woman who comes in to help. Hyacinth. She'll be here soon."

Andreas handed her the *Imperial* and took the *Pilsen* for himself. "*Prosit!*" he said, touching his bottle against hers with a resounding clink.

Anja returned the sentiment before asking, "Is Hyacinth the cook?"

"No, no," Andreas said, shaking his head. "I do all the cooking here, but Hyacinth takes the orders and helps in the kitchen when I need another pair of hands. It's a small operation, but I may need to hire someone soon. Two new lodges just opened up, and I'm getting more customers than I can really handle."

Anja arched her brow. "You must be quite the cook then. I'm looking forward to dinner."

"It's my coconut sauce," he said, lowering his voice playfully. "A secret recipe passed down from one of the masters."

"I take it there's no Bratwurst on the menu then?"

"When in Rome," he said. "But you know, if I came across a nice bratwurst with mustard, I wouldn't turn it down. With a piece of German bread. M-mmm!"

"So, you do get homesick after all," Anja said, triumphant.

"For my mother's cooking, yes, but for Germany no. Caway is my home now."

For a moment Andreas' face took on a shadow of seriousness.

"There's still too much war in Europe, the war going on in people's heads. Most Costa Ricans just want to live in peace. They don't care if their lives aren't perfect. It's hard work, yes, and not much money to show for it, but the reward is here." he said, touching his heart.

Anja drew in her breath. She wasn't used to men expressing their emotions with such candor. A part of her was awed by his ability to turn his back on his own culture and to make such an unwavering commitment to a less than perfect place. But what both aroused and alarmed her, was that he had taken this leap without a care for what it meant for his future.

Anja had often fantasized about leaving Europe, moving somewhere where life was less complicated. Where she could focus on her art and not the politics behind it. But could she do it? She had met expats before who ran businesses abroad, but they generally brought their homelands with them in the form of imported comforts. They would assimilate as needed, but never completely, and, of course, they always had the option of going home if and when things went wrong. This was clearly not the case for Andreas, who claimed Costa Rica was now his own. Had he really done so willingly?

Looking around it was clear material objects and refined comfort were not important to him. He had chosen to live as close to nature as possible, and in this harsh environment that meant letting go of possessions that required guardianship and protection. The jungle offered no such guarantees. Here the heat and humidity would decay all things sooner than later.

"So, you don't have any regrets at all?"

"I have no time for regrets," he laughed, taking their empty bottles back into the kitchen. "That's what makes it *pura vida!* I better show you to your *cabina* now."

"Good idea," Anja said. "I could definitely use a shower before dinner."

Andreas picked up her backpack and Anja followed him once again down the steps. Taking a sharp turn to the right, they walked down a small, dirt path around the restaurant until they came to a dark wooden door that faced the back garden and where a wooden gazebo with a latticed roof offered up a prismatic refuge from the sun.

"It's lovely back here," Anja said, admiring the well-manicured trees and flowering bushes given just the right amount of space to bask in some individualized attention.

"My secret garden," Andreas said, sounding content. "On a clear night you can gaze up through the gazebo and admire the stars."

Hmm, Anja thought, *perhaps an invitation for later?*

Andreas unlocked the door. Enough light came in through the window so that Anja could make out a double bed with mosquito netting. Andreas switched on a bare bulb overhead. The room was painted a vibrant blue and contained a simple nightstand with a lamp and fan as well as a wooden chair. A door to the back led through to a small water closet with a shower stall. It was rustic as advertised but kept clean and well-maintained.

"Will this do?" Andreas asked, his brow furrowed. "If not, there's a larger cabin just down the path."

"No, it's perfect," Anja said. "I intend to spend most of my time in the garden."

"I'll let you settle in," Andreas smiled, handing her the key. "When you're ready, come upstairs and I'll make you a meal that you won't forget."

Anja took her time showering. The tight stall didn't invite lingering, but she lathered up her shampoo and conditioned her curls, a habit she had grown lax in practicing of late.

A rush of hopeful desire had quickened her pulse, making her feel light and sensuous as she applied a delicate lotion against her skin, imagining Andreas' touch. With care she chose a white-embroidered sundress and the intricate coral and silver earrings she had picked up in Oaxaca. She pinned her curls back with two beaded combs, the ones Gustav had chosen for her in one of the Guatemalan outdoor markets.

Refreshed, Anja stepped back out into the garden and into the soft, gray light of the setting day. Immediately the scent of sunbaked jasmine greeted her senses so that she had to stop to breathe it all in. The air was still warm, of course, though no longer oppressive, and she felt a lightness in her step as she walked back down the path toward the restaurant, staring up between the trees at the pink and violet streaked sky bleeding into indigo the higher up she looked.

Walking around the bend, Anja was taken aback by an Afro-Caribbean woman of ample curves standing near the threshold, her close-cropped hair revealing the soft, caramel tones of her beautifully rounded face.

"Good evening," the woman said, her smile broad and serene, her voice cool. "You must be An-ya."

"Yes," Anja laughed. "Word gets around. You must be Hyacinth."

"The one and only," the woman said, taking Anja's hand in hers. With a slow and inquisitive movement, she turned Anja's palm to face open.

"I can see what he says is true," she added, looking into Anja's eyes before directing her toward the set table. Unsure of what to say, Anja followed her.

"Please sit. Andreas is preparing something special for you."

The imposing *Stammtisch* was set for one person with a clear view of both the restaurant and the kitchen. Catching Anja out of the corner of his eye, Andreas raised an eyebrow and gave her an approving nod before turning his attention once again to a large frying pan.

Anja settled into her seat and took a sip from the chilled wine in front of her. She watched as Andreas cooked and hummed along to a radio station playing hit songs from the 60s and 70s broadcast through a small set of speakers mounted on the eaves.

Hyacinth, meanwhile, was ambling back and forth between the dining room and kitchen, attending to two large tables of English-speaking guests who were carrying on an animated discussion of the animals they had spotted earlier in the national park.

The words floated past Anja as she continued to scan the dining room, the wine already doing its part to relax her. On the far side of the room, next to the side entrance, she spotted a thin, middle-aged woman with mousy hair also sitting alone. Dressed in a drab and formless sundress she was immersed in a thick paperback and only looked up to take a sip from her beer or to tap the ashes from her cigarette.

Definitely German or Scandinavian, Anja thought.

Since the woman's body language and unblinking stare made it clear that she wasn't there to socialize, Anja soon forgot about her, her eyes focusing instead on Andreas' and Hyacinth's movements. She marveled at the synchronicity between them, hardly having to exchange a word with one another as they worked. Anja wondered if they had a history together, though if they did, it wouldn't explain Hyacinth welcoming her in the way she had, like a proud and protective sister.

At any rate, it was obvious Andreas was trying to court her and that

Hyacinth was in on the plan. No man had ever cooked Anja a meal on a first date, let alone one that wasn't confirmed as such. But there was no need to say anything. To Anja their gravitational pull felt as natural as breathing.

No, all she needed to do was wait patiently for Andreas to finish, a promise implicit in the occasional glances he stole away from his work to smile at her. Hyacinth, meanwhile, plied her with more wine and a plate of perfectly grilled shrimp.

"The best I've ever tasted," Anja said, raising her glass to Andreas, before turning to look out at the last glimmer of light in the darkening garden.

Table by table the guests departed starting with the thin woman who got up after finishing her beer. Just as she was about to slip out the side entrance, Andreas yelled after her from the kitchen.

"*Mach's gut, Gertie!*"

"*Ja, Ja,*" the dour woman replied, dismissing him with a back-handed wave. *German after all*, Anja thought. *Another ex-pat?* In this day and age, it was odd to encounter two of her countrymen still clinging to their lost, hippie days. Had they really found what they were looking for here?

With the dining room cleared, Andreas was free to come out of the kitchen. He carried out two plates and sat down next to her at the setting Hyacinth had laid out for him.

Anja looked down at the whole red snapper staring google-eyed from its bed of fragrant coconut rice.

"Is the way to a woman's heart through her stomach?"

"Don't let him steal your heart *too* soon," Hyacinth said, smiling as she walked past with a beer in her hand. To Anja's disappointment, she took a seat at the makeshift bar, catty corner from the *Stammtisch*.

"You mentioned you sold textiles," Anja said in German, focusing her attention back on Andreas. "Did you go to culinary school as well?"

Andreas chuckled, his mouth full of food.

"Yes, the Culinary Academy of Caway. CAC."

"I'm asking seriously," Anja said.

The fish, much like the shrimp, was perfectly prepared.

Andreas waved his hand, dismissing the thought.

"I picked up a few things, but when I first arrived here, I made friends with an old fisherman. He would take me out on his boat sometimes in exchange for some carpentry work. His wife, she's the one who really taught me how to cook. I would watch her prepare the fish when we got back, and she helped me make my first coconut sauce. Showed me which ingredients I needed to use."

"William's grandmother?" Anja asked.

"The very same. I would have starved without her, mostly eating out of tins."

"And do you still see them?"

"He passed away some years back. Dolores, she lives with William's sister and mother now, so I see her when I go to Limón."

"Is there anyone in town you don't know?" Anja asked, remembering their walk.

"You live here as long as I have, you better know everyone. And if you don't, you can be sure they know something about *you*."

They both laughed.

"That's the small village life I couldn't wait to get away from," Anja said.

"Was it really that bad?" Andreas asked.

Anja nodded, jutting out her jaw, her brown eyes widening.

"My parents resisted the Nazis' madness. But the town itself was head deep in it. Of course, every single one of them would deny it now. Meanwhile, you can well imagine what festers behind closed doors. Particularly in a small town."

"I grew up in Dortmund," Andreas said, preparing a forkful of rice. "Red Army and all that, but still, I know what you mean."

"Growing up in a large city, don't you get tired of all the small-town gossip?"

"Pffft," Andreas said, swallowing. "It's not like Germany. Sure, people talk, but not in a malicious way. Mostly it's just for a laugh. It's live and let live here."

Anja furrowed her brow and took another bite of her fish.

"So what was it that made you leave Germany the first time?"

Andreas looked up, his eyes shimmering.

"The Rolling Stones."

"The Rolling Stones? As in the band?"

"Yes! I went to their 1967 concert in Amsterdam. After that, I never went home."

"Ah, yes. The Summer of Love," Anja said. "How old were you?"

"Eighteen. I had my dog with me and bought a used, gray VW bus I made into my home. We went all over Europe together traveling the festivals. France, Italy, Denmark. I would do odd jobs here and there for food and gas money. I was free to roam as I liked. If I'd stayed in Dortmund, I'd still be stuck in a factory somewhere, and I'm no good in a cage."

"So how did you end up here?" Anja asked, casting a sidelong glance at Hyacinth who was walking toward the kitchen.

"I saved my money and in '76 bought a plane ticket to San Francisco. I had a friend who'd moved there. He took me to some crazy parties, and after a couple of weeks I bought another VW bus and camped my way down the California coast. Once I got to Mexico I just kept driving until I hit the Pan-American Highway. Went to a language school in Antigua. That's why I recognized the pattern on your *huipil.* Guatemala is where I decided to start buying textiles. Things I knew I could sell back in Germany."

Hyacinth walked past them again, this time empty handed.

"*Buenas noches,*" she said, her voice sweet but all knowing.

"*Gracias, Hyacinth,*" Andreas said, looking over his shoulder. "*Duerme bien.*"

"Yes, thank you," Anja said, watching as Hyacinth disappeared down the steps and into the forest as if it was her own. Anja couldn't imagine walking home alone in the dark at this hour, but at least now she had Andreas to herself.

Picking up where their conversation had left off, she asked, "The Pan-American Highway. I thought it ran along the Pacific, no? How did you end up here?"

"When I got to San José, I heard about the train that could take me to the Caribbean. Back then it was the only way to get over the Braulio Carrillo mountains. I left my VW with friends thinking, why not make my first shipment out of *Puerto Limón*? I didn't realize I would be spending an entire day leaning out of a wooden boxcar window," he chuckled.

"We'd go rattling past the *cafetales*, the coffee farms, and then over the mountains and down this steep river gorge. When I got to Limón people said, go see the beach at Caway! I hitched a ride with a *bananero* and fell in love with it right away. The beaches, the people, the forests, they were untouched! I put a down payment on my small patch of Eden here, and that was the beginning of Quixote's."

"So that's what you call this place. Why am I not surprised?"

Anja couldn't help but admire Andreas' wit. Not to mention his dogged determination.

"Wasn't it dangerous, though, cutting down the trees, with all the poisonous snakes and plants and whatnot?"

"I learned the hard way, yes. But my friends here, they taught me what to look out for."

"And you don't miss the easy life in Europe? Not even a little? I'm not so sure I could get used to this heat all the time."

Andreas shrugged.

"Maybe every now and then when the sun gives me a headache. But life isn't just about coffee and cake at four and Sunday afternoon walks with the family. Not for me anyway. Sometimes I think those customs only came about to keep families from tearing each other apart. To keep them sane from the drudgeries of everyday life."

"But you must have a routine here, too," Anja said, pushing away her empty plate.

"Sure, but it's mine, not someone else's. Plus, I can take it easy whenever I want. The only one who pays the consequence is me, and I know the price I'm paying."

Anja cocked her head to one side.

"So, you've never wanted a family of your own?"

"I got married to a woman here. We have a son together, but the relationship didn't last."

"So, you're divorced," Anja said, surprised by the abruptness of her tone.

Andreas flinched as a slight shadow crossed over his face.

"Yes. She met someone else. Another German in fact. He promised her a life I couldn't give her. The one I didn't want."

"I'm sorry to hear that," Anja said.

"There's nothing to be sorry for. The only regret I have is that she took our son with her when she left. I didn't see him again for far too long. I should have stopped her, but I didn't."

Anja couldn't help but place her hand on top of Andreas'.

"Where did they go?"

"Berlin," Andreas said, looking off into the distance. "I thought she would see the error of her ways and come back. But she didn't. Not for five years. She had to learn the hard way."

Anja frowned, trying to decipher what he meant.

"Do you see your son now?"

"Yes, when I go to Limón. That's where they live now. He comes here, too, during school breaks when he's not spending time with his friends. He's twelve now. It won't be long before he'll want to go off on his own."

Anja felt a pang of sadness hearing about Andreas' son. He wasn't quite as "free" as she'd imagined after all, but then again, there was always a catch at their age, so there was no point in wishing otherwise. The important thing was that he was willing to be open about it. He could easily have said nothing at all.

Just then a pounding piano-bass thrum took over the airways.

Anja began to nod her head, her mind drawn to the invasive rhythm.

"Do you like this song?" Andreas asked, his face breaking into a jester's smile.

Anja met his now gleaming eyes with a laugh.

"Who doesn't?"

♫ *"Don't you worry 'bout what's on your mind, oh my!"* ♪

"Then let's dance," he said, extending his hand out to her as he stood up.

♫ *"I'm in no hurry I can take my time, oh my!"* ♪

Why not? she thought as she allowed him to pull her up from her seat.

She was taller than Andreas, but that didn't stop him from spinning her around the empty floor space, swinging her through his arms and round and round in the dining hall.

Her heart was racing when the song ended and when Andreas drew her in close to him. Their first kiss tasted like the sea, the one they had both been waiting for all this time.

4

Caway - Spring 1997

Anja woke up the next morning to a loud symphony of bird calls and booming monkey howls. Partly covered by a crumpled bed sheet, she looked out through the gauze of mosquito netting that covered Andreas' four-poster bed.

"*Guten morgen*," he said. "How did you sleep?"

He was already sitting up beside her, smiling down at her groggy form. She managed to mumble something back before he jumped out of bed, laughing.

"Not a morning person, eh? I'll go and make us coffee. Feel free to shower up here if you like."

Still disoriented, Anja took her time to look around. The queen size bed she was in was at the back of the loft-like space with an airy view of the dusty sun beams penetrating through the balcony. A large, wooden worktable occupied the right side of the apartment, and next to it, a leather couch and chair carved out a sitting area in front of the sliding glass doors.

Anja couldn't help but admire the open design. She felt sheltered but at the same time part of the surrounding jungle thanks to the large windows that framed the space, a complete contrast to the small, dark *cabina* where her belongings lay abandoned for the night.

"Are you enjoying your time in Caway?" Andreas asked, once she'd ambled down the stairs, her hair still wet and glistening.

Andreas handed her a steaming, white mug.

Anja flashed him a playful smile.

"If things keep up like this, you'll have to find me a plot of land so I can stake my claim."

"I'm more than happy to share," he replied, revealing his own, mischievous smile. "I quite like your company."

"Likewise," she said, breathing in the irresistible aroma of strong, black coffee as a glimmer of yellow and red caught her eye through the kitchen window.

"Is that a heliconia?" she asked, stepping in for a closer look.

She could see the morning dew still clinging to the hanging inflorescence, each painted red and yellow leaf stacked one above the other in a neat, geometric bundle. The chance to study and draw these unusual, flowering plants was why she had traveled to the Latin American tropics in the first place. The moment felt almost too good to be true, but for the fact she could still feel the pulse of satisfied desire coursing through her.

"I know it's none of my business, but were you and Hyacinth ever an item?" Anja asked.

She was sitting next to Andreas at a small table on the balcony. Business was slow for a change, leaving time for them to eat a cozy, candle-lit dinner upstairs.

Andreas put down his fork and smiled.

"No, but what makes you ask?"

"I don't know. You seem so comfortable together. I just—"

Andreas leaned in to twirl a loose lock of her hair.

"Are you jealous?"

"No, not at all," Anja blushed. "More curious than anything."

"Well good," he said, nuzzling her neck before leaning back in his chair.

"You have no reason to be. Hyacinth and I, we get along because she likes to keep her life private. I don't pry or ask too many questions, and that's why she prefers working here. Me, I don't like to talk while I work, and she gets that. She does her thing, and I do mine, and that's the magic."

"I can see that," Anja said. "You're an easygoing boss."

"Boss," he chuckled, pulling out a pack of cigarettes and offering her one. "I never see myself that way."

Without thinking, she took one, succumbing to her social smoking weakness.

"So, spit it out," he said, as she took her first, long drag. "I can still see those question marks popping around in your head. What's tugging at you?"

Anja laughed as a cloud of billowing smoke enveloped her.

"Is it that obvious? I'm no good at hiding my emotions."

"That's what I like about you," Andreas said. "You're like an open book. Fiery at times. I wouldn't want to get on your bad side."

"The men from my past couldn't agree with you more," Anja said. "I've had no luck when it comes to relationships. Unlike you, it's made it difficult *not* to ask."

"So, ask away," Andreas said. "I've got nothing to hide."

"OK, then. Here's the big one: do you ever miss your ex-wife?"

"Oh-oh," he said, his face morphing into a comedic grimace.

Anja shook her head.

"You don't have to answer. I'll be gone soon enough, and maybe it's better to keep things the way they are. But if I'm honest, that's the one thing I don't get about you. How you can still be so easy-going after all you've been through."

"Life's a state of mind, Anja. I feel sad about what happened, yes, but life isn't living when you're full of regret. I fell in love with *an idea* of who she was: a proud, beautiful Afro-Caribbean woman. I thought this and that about her, about her character, her loyalty. I was living in a fantasy that just wasn't true. When the mirror cracked, that's when I realized I must live my own life and not what I imagine about someone else's. I'm still friendly enough with her. She's the mother of my child, so I haven't got much choice. But I can see her for who she is now. What's sad is how much I wanted her to be someone she just wasn't meant to be."

"I can relate to that," Anja said, letting out a smoke-filled sigh. "I fell hard for my first boyfriend. He was an artist, too, and I was sure we'd conquer the world, until the jealousy set in. Problem is, the non-artists don't like my 'non-conforming ways'."

"Lucky for me," Andreas said. "Their loss is my fortune."

Anja smiled. "For as long as I'm here, yes."

Andreas locked her in with his eyes.

"And your parents?" he asked.

Anja bowed her head. A feeling of déjà vu struck her. Hadn't she already talked about all of this with Gustav? She drew in a deep breath and recounted her story for a second time.

"They led ordinary, working-class lives," Anja added, casting her eyes into the blue flame of the candle. "But they were far from ordinary.

"They bought us books, taught us to appreciate music. And my father was always inventing clever games for us to play. Not once did they try to keep me from becoming who I am. Once they died, the art academy was all I had left, so I poured every bit of myself into it."

Contrary to what she had intended, their romantic dinner for two had devolved into a heart-felt confessional.

Andreas reached out to touch her forearm.

"I'd like to see your work sometime."

"I'll send you pictures when I get back," Anja said, her eyes watery. "What's funny is that before I came here, I had run out of inspiration. I had buried myself in work for so long that I lost the spark. But being with you, spending time in your garden, I can feel it coming back."

"Stay as long as you want then," he said, leaning in for a kiss. "I'm not going anywhere."

"What do you think?" Anja said flipping through the colorful, pastel-laden pages of her sketchbook where she had drafted a few designs for Andreas' restaurant and cabinas. She was sitting in what was now her spot at the *Stammtisch.*

"I like them a lot," Andreas said, looking over her shoulder. "That last one puts me in mind of the garden, with the leaves, birds and letters all intertwined like that."

Two weeks had turned into three, and having exhausted the nearby attractions, Anja had offered to paint Andreas a few signs he could display near the bus depot and at the intersections near town.

"That's the one I prefer, too," she said, looking over at him as he settled into his seat. He had brought over a knife and cutting board and was holding a small bulb of garlic in his hand, ready to begin his coconut sauce making ritual. Anja had watched him before, his painstaking process both maddening and endearing as he slowly and meticulously cut each clove in half to remove the green germ at its center.

"Why do you do that?" she asked, knitting her brow. "Why not just chop it all up?"

"This," Andreas said, holding up a green shoot as if he'd caught a culprit red-handed, "makes the sauce taste bitter. Plus, it gives you gas."

"I never knew that."

"*Liebe Anja*," he smiled. "I'll stick to the cooking. You stick to the drawing."

"You've got a deal, although I'm going to need to go into Limón to pick up some supplies, and while I'm at it," she said, pointing to a stack of poorly mimeographed paper menus. "I could revamp those as well."

"Consider yourself in charge," he said. "I can't pay you what you're worth, but I'll gladly provide you with room and board."

Anja laughed. Not once had she slept in the *cabina* downstairs. "You definitely can't afford me," she said, reviewing her work. "In Basel, this would easily take care of my rent for at least a month."

"Too rich for me," Andreas said, shaking his head. "For that, I at least have my garden."

"Speaking of your garden, I saw that skinny woman walking through this morning."

"Gertie?" Andreas' asked, quick to hide his concern. "She was away for a couple of weeks. You remember that Canadian couple that likes to eat in the corner over there? She sold her house to them."

"So, where does she live now?"

"Oh, she still lives there. They're only down here a few weeks out of the year."

"Wait a minute. You're telling me she sold them her house but still lives there?"

"*Ja.* Not a bad deal, eh? It works out for all of them."

"I suppose so. But what about her belongings? Don't they mind?"

"Gertie doesn't own much. And anyway, she sleeps outside on the veranda."

"What?" Anja asked, shaking her head as if she'd misheard.

"Yeah, she doesn't like being cooped up indoors. As for the furniture, she sold that to them as well. That way they have everything they need when they come down to visit."

"Ok, tell me more. Have you known her for long?"

"Well, yes, ever since she moved here about four years ago. She bought the land off of Ole Mr. Buchanan. His son built the house for her."

"How odd to want to sell it then. I have to admit she doesn't strike me as friendly at all."

"*Ach,*" Andreas said, waving off her comment. "Gertie's like a sister. I'll introduce you when she comes over. Just don't take it personally if she doesn't want to talk. She's just a very private person."

"I'll try not to have too many expectations then," Anja said. "Not much you can do about family, I suppose."

On the morning Anja was scheduled to depart, she woke up to Andreas propped up on his elbow, gazing at her through the light of the budding dawn.

"Is everything OK?" she asked, her eyes still half-closed.

"Sleep is a waste of time if you're still planning to go."

"C'mon, now. Don't make this harder on me than it already is."

"Alright then," he said, pulling the sheet aside and jumping out of bed. "Let's go for our walk. I want to show you something."

Anja threw on her clothes and then followed Andreas down the stairs. He didn't say much as they walked down the road toward *Playa Grande,* now a part of their morning ritual, but he did hold her hand which wasn't like him. He stopped when they got to the end of the sandy path leading to the shore, where they had a clear view of the pink-blue sky majestic above the incoming tide.

"What is it?" Anja asked.

"You do like it here, don't you?" he asked.

"Yes, but—"

"Then marry me," he said, kneeling down on one knee in front of her before placing a thin, gold band in the center of her palm.

She looked at him, then at the ring refracting the early sun's light.

"I know this life doesn't compare to the one you've got back in Basel," he said. "And you don't have to answer right away. I just want you to think about it. You could come back and paint for a while—I'll set up a studio for you—and you could help with the business. You've already made things so much better as it is. But I sure could use the company, Anja, and I think you must already know how much I love you."

Anja's eyes began to well up.

"And you really want this?" she asked, not sure she could believe him.

"You'd be preventing a mess of a broken heart," he said, clasping together her shaking hands. "At the very least, say you'll come back when you can."

He was looking at her in such a way that she knew she could not refuse him.

Her eyes veered toward the flood of waves crashing on the shore, mimicking the loud pounding in her chest.

"This is the craziest thing I've ever done," she said. Through her tears, she started to laugh out loud knowing she had no choice but to take the risk.

"The answer is yes, but don't you dare ever make me regret it."

"It's a tall order," Andreas said, as he stood and pulled her toward him, his clear blue eyes piercing straight into her heart. "But I'll see what I can do."

5

Switzerland - Spring 1997

Patrice walked up to Anja in the main gallery of *La Sauvage Moderne*. "You're looking well," he said, genteel as ever in his blue tailored suit. His waves of silver hair—though thinning—were perfectly coiffed.

Anja ran her palm down a wrinkle in her skirt.

"This is quite the coup," she said, referring to the Frankenthaler woodcuts occupying the white, grey walls of his gallery. She had spent the last half hour immersed in their pulsating fields of color, and though she generally found Frankenthaler's style too free-form—too lax—for her taste, she could not help but appreciate the power inherent in her work. Patrice, on the other hand, was a lifelong admirer.

"Isn't it?" he replied, before leaning in to kiss her cheeks. He then turned and waved his hand indicating she should follow him inside his glass-enclosed office.

"Please, sit," he said, pointing to one of the Le Corbusier chairs surrounding the expansive glass coffee table where they had so often reviewed her new sketches and paintings. As she settled into the smooth leather seat, he poured her a fragrant cup of Earl Grey and offered her a Favarger praline decorated with an intricate gold leaf design.

"I wouldn't have thought it, but the tropical sun suits you," Patrice said.

Despite his age, he bore his demure manner with impressive poise.

"It does," she said, trying to sound confident. "So much so, that I intend to go back as soon as possible."

"Your message implied as much," he replied, meting out his words. "Am I to expect a new direction in your painting?" He took a careful sip from his white porcelain cup before returning it with care to the saucer he had balanced in his right hand.

"To a certain degree, yes," she replied. "I think you'll be pleased with where the new work is heading. It's a logical progression of what you've come to expect, but with a more vivid palette."

Anja had worked with Patrice for five years now and knew how to appeal to his more conservative temperament. Still, she felt out of her depth now, unsure of the hidden meaning lurking in his response.

"I'll look forward to seeing it," he said, his thin lips bending up at the corners. "The question is, when and where? I know these far-flung excursions of yours are necessary, but I will admit I was shocked to hear you are planning to relocate. And for how long, did you say?"

The alarmed look he gave her could hardly be mistaken.

Anja cleared her throat. "I'm not sure," she said. "All I know is that I'm following my gut, and that I'll have nine new paintings ready for you by summer's end."

"I'm not worried about *that*, my dear," he said, placing the teacup and saucer on the tabletop. "Your output has always been, shall we say, more than satisfactory. What I'm more concerned about is your welfare."

Anja's rounded brows immediately shot up.

"You're starting to sound like my father, Patrice. I'll be in safe hands, I promise you. Plus, I think you would appreciate Andreas' artistry. He's an outdoorsman, yes, but a connoisseur of the arts in his own right."

"Hmm," Patrice replied, lowering his eyelids for a moment. "I have no doubt he exudes a certain... appeal. I just wonder where these new currents will take you."

"I appreciate the concern, but you more than anyone knows that nothing is ever lost for art. It's 'the receptacle of all experience' you once told me."

"In my line of work that is certainly the case," Patrice said, the fine lines of his forehead ever so slightly creased.

"I just hope, for your sake, that your sacrifice will be worth it."

He paused to take a long look at her, his crystalline eyes steadfast in their unblinking appraisal.

Anja couldn't help but glance down at the ring on her hand. Andreas' ring.

"Well," Patrice said, standing with only a hint of effort. "I won't keep you long, my dear. I know you have a lot to prepare. Just promise me not to lose sight of your work."

"I won't," she replied, watching as he opened the door for her. It suddenly dawned on her she might not see him again. As she crossed the threshold, she leaned in to kiss him on the cheek.

"As always, I bid you a safe and fruitful journey," he said. "We'll look forward to receiving your parcels. And this time don't forget to write. We'll want to know how your new life unfolds."

"I will," she said, her eyes softening to take in his support and affection.

He leaned in to kiss her cheeks once more before turning back toward his desk, allowing Anja to take leave of the gallery on her own.

That night and every night, Anja called Andreas as she continued to pack up her attic apartment.

"It's machete day," he said.

She imagined him beneath the shade of the *pejibaye* palm in his garden, smoking a cigarette after thinning out the overgrowth. Living in the jungle meant he was never without work.

"I don't know how much more of this I can take," she said, looking despairingly at the stacks of painting supplies jammed into the recesses beneath the gabled roof.

"How did I manage to collect all of this? I keep throwing things out, giving stuff away, and somehow there's still more than I can fit into my travel trunks."

Andreas laughed.

"As soon as you're here you'll forget you ever had it."

"I would welcome a bout of amnesia right now, with the exception of you, of course."

For a few seconds neither one of them spoke. Anja could feel their longing reverberating through the phone, though at times she could not help but wonder if what they had was just another figment of her imagination run wild.

"Another night alone means another day closer to seeing you," he said, as if reading her thoughts.

Anja had placed but one condition on her return to Caway, and that was to meet Andreas' mother who still lived in Dortmund. Despite an ocean's distance between them, Andreas still doted on her, a fact that made Anja more than just a little nervous.

Meeting his mother, Anja thought, was an insurance policy, a way to check her sanity before immersing herself in Andreas' world. And though she had been avoiding it up until now, the night before her train ride up, she finally called Gustav to let him know about her plans.

"It's a huge gamble," he said, giving voice to the unspoken doubts that would creep in like phantoms during the agitated nights she spent alone in her apartment.

"Yes, I know. But it's not like my career is keeping me warm at night."

"Oh, but it does," Gustav said. "It keeps you fed, independent and doing the work you love. Not many people can say that. And you really think this Andreas can give you more?"

It pained her to hear the slight sliver of venom in his voice.

"For Christ's sake, I'm not giving up on painting, I'll just be working somewhere else for a change. Next to someone I love."

"You honestly think moving away from one of the art capitals of the world won't damage your reputation? After all you've invested in making a name for yourself?"

"You more than anyone knows I've had it up to here with the art world. It's a business like any other. An investment or a bit of background decoration for some corporate banker's wall. In music, at least, you perform the ineffable.

It's not like that with painting. At least not anymore.

"Anyway, unlike you, I don't have a trail of admirers to turn away each night," she added, trying to lighten the mood. "Not that I'd know what to do with them if I did. This is the real thing, Gustav. And I know what you're thinking, 'my God, it's only been a couple of months!', but it's not like the times before. Or anyone else for that matter."

Gustav paused just long enough for her to detect a softening.

"Well, then I'm happy for you," he said at last.

"I am, too, Gustav. For once in my life, I am, too."

Anja took the six-hour train ride up to Dortmund the next morning, nervous as a schoolgirl. Would Mutti approve of her, she wondered? Seconds later she berated herself for even having such a thought. Since when had such a thing mattered to her? No, what worried her was that they would have absolutely nothing to say to one another.

But like her son, the mother was a welcoming soul who embraced Anja the moment she walked through her door.

"Anja, my daughter-in-law to be, how nice it is to finally meet you," she said, her laughter-filled spirit and irrepressible energy belying her now seventy years of age.

Lieselotte, whose means were as modest as her son's, led Anja into her apartment. She had made the few pieces of furniture she had warm and inviting by covering them with an array of her crocheted quilts and doilies not to mention her hand-embroidered pillows. And she had baked no less than three cakes for her arrival, all lovingly displayed on her dining table with a thermos full of coffee waiting to be poured.

Eating and drinking more than her fill, Anja answered as many questions as she meant to ask, until Lieselotte finally led her to the couch, so they could go through the family albums.

"I want you to know that Andreas' father was a good man," she said, pausing when they reached a photo of her late husband to place a strong, but weathered hand on top of hers.

"He hated the Nazis. Our lot here, we all did. Our sympathies were more with the Reds. Of course, you can't say that anymore,"she laughed.

"Still, Werner had no choice but to fight. And like so many others, he was captured by the Russians. He picked up a lung infection while he was in the camp. And when he came home, he was a shadow of his former self, struggling just to keep alive. The coughing was terrible, I tell you. But not a single complaint.

"I'd lost my whole family—my parents, my sisters—during one of the air raids. I had no one left but Werner and our oldest girl, Katrin, who was five. Andreas was born the following year, 1951. And let me tell you, we had nothing, but nothing! Werner worked as hard as he could for us just to put a few scraps of food on the table.

"Andreas was only four when he collapsed. After that, it was just me and the children. I worked two jobs so I could send them to school. We didn't see much of one another in those early years. Still, I made sure they never forgot their father.

Children, they need to know where they come from, Anja. And with those monsters, my God! Well, I wanted to make sure Katrin and Andreas knew their father wasn't one of *them*. To this day, I'm proud they both know that hatred is not the answer. And let me tell you, the poor have known that far longer than anyone else. When you have nothing, you learn to get along with others, whether you're Jewish, African or anything else for that matter."

Anja could see Mutti's resilience and compassion had rooted itself firmly in her son. Their continental divide wasn't due to some irreconcilable difference, some hidden darkness, as Anja had secretly feared, but was rather the boldness of the matriarch reflected in her offspring.

"And what did you think when Andreas left home?"

Mutti smiled and her eyes lit up.

"Andreas was only five when he took his first journey alone. Without telling me, he rode the tricycle I had just gotten him to the neighboring town. When he didn't come home for his lunch, Katrin and I went out looking for him. I was worried sick, let me tell you. But when the sun set, he rode into the courtyard as if nothing had happened.

'Baba, where were you?!' I asked. 'Why didn't you come home for your lunch?' 'I went to Eving, Mama. I just followed the signs.'"

Mutti laughed out loud, her eyes vibrant with tenderness.

"Ach," she said, wiping her broad white cheeks with the backs of her hands. "After that there was no point in keeping him home. The *Wanderlust* was already in him."

"Hallo!" Anja called out, feeling giddy and triumphant. "Is anybody home?"

She had just arrived at Quixote's in a worn-down pirate cab loaded down with two large steamer trunks and a suitcase full of clothes. Leaving all but her backpack at the gate, she ran up the front stairs of the restaurant, hoping to find Andreas in the kitchen.

"So, you made it back after all," Gertie said, looking up from her seat at the far end of the *Stammtisch*, a novel in one hand, a cigarette in the other.

"*Ach*, Gertie, I didn't see you," Anja said, trying to hide her disappointment with a nervous laugh. "Is Andreas around?"

Anja had forgotten about Gertie's tendency to show up unannounced at the communal table with a beer she had just taken from the refrigerated case.

"He's fixing a toilet in one of the *cabinas*," Gertie said, before lighting another cigarette from the one she had just finished. "Did he know you were coming today?"

"Well, of course," Anja replied, her teeth clenched. "But it's not like I could tell him the exact time I would arrive."

"M-hmn," Gertie said, already peering down at her book.

"Do you mind if I join you for a drink?"

"It's your home now, no need to ask me."

"No, I suppose not," Anja said, walking into the kitchen to help herself to a cold beer. "I just didn't want to cramp your style with too much excitement all at once."

Gertie glanced up for a moment, annoyed.

"There's not much you could do that would surprise me."

"Is that so? Well, I'll see what I can manage all the same."

"Suit yourself," Gertie said, turning her attention back to her book.

Anja had tried to win Gertie over before but had failed in each attempt to exchange more than a few sentences. She realized now that any additional effort would be pointless. Gertie was not one to talk, other than with Andreas, who was unusually guarded when it came to revealing anything about Gertie's past.

And their unlikely friendship provoked Anja's discomfort even more. What on earth had brought this skinny, wrinkled creature to Costa Rica in the first place? It was clear from her outward appearance and demeanor that she had somehow given up on life. Her blonde-grey hair—self cut in a haphazard, fringed bob—hung limp and unattended, and her daily uniform seemed to alternate between two, possibly three, drab and threadbare sundresses that drooped shapelessly from her limbs in the same manner as her skin.

From what Anja had gathered, Gertie spent her days either reading or doing puzzles. In the evenings she would have a different paperback in front of her—whether in English, German or Spanish, a work of literature or a trashy novel—it did not seem to matter. She would gobble them up as if they were her only sustenance. And in fact, the only food Anja had ever witnessed Gertie eating was the burger and fries that Andreas would prepare for her once a week, one of the culinary treats for which he was locally famous. Apart from that, Gertie appeared to subsist solely on beer and cigarettes.

Anja's curiosity ached to know more about this unsympathetic woman who had nonetheless endeared herself to Andreas. But no doubt sensing in her uncanny way the satisfaction it might give Anja to know more, Gertie refused her at every turn.

6

Near Augsburg - Fall 1956

It was a cool, gray, September day outside the Eulenweg Primary School, the clouds moving as fast as the second hand on Frau Baecker's watch. As was her habit, the matron kept a vigilant eye on her first-grade class, most of whom were running from one end of the playground to the other, screeching with frenzy during a game of tag.

Only on occasion would Frau Baecker glance over at Gertie and Udo who were huddled over their marbles not far from the school's entrance.

"We're playing for keepsies," Gertie said, kneeling in her red gingham dress over the crude chalk circle she had drawn, her long, blonde hair pulled back in a messy braid.

Udo, practically swimming in his far-too-large *lederhosen*, pushed up the ridge of his horn-rimmed glasses. "You have to play the blue-green onionskin," he said.

"No way. I've only had it for one day."

"But my father gave it to me! You have to let me try and win it back."

"Fine," Gertie said. "But not today, ok?"

"Ok," Udo sighed, pushing up his glasses once more.

They each poured out the contents of their muslin bags, selecting with care only those marbles with which they were willing to part. With precision Gertie then arranged the target ones into a cruciform inside the circle, alternating one from each stash.

Not wanting to waste a precious moment of play, Gertie knuckled down with her favorite shooter, a yellow core with a rainbow swirl, and calculated her aim before flicking her thumb, watching as the purple polished globe she had set her sights on rolled outside the chalk lines leaving her shooter safe within bounds.

"Ha, that's the one I've been waiting for," she said, looking up triumphant.

Gertie and Udo had so perfected their game of ringer that the other children would no longer play with them. Instead, they would poke fun at them from a distance, muttering their childhood derisions reserved for tomboys and misfits.

Lost in their own world, however, Udo and Gertie were for the most part deaf to their insults, choosing instead to preserve their energies for working the marble playing field with an ever-increasing exactitude.

Glancing at her wristwatch, Frau Baecker yelled out a five-minute warning.

"Do you want to come over after school today?" Gertie asked, taking up her aim. Udo had just lost his turn by a hair's breadth.

"I can't," he said, looking glum. "I have a piano lesson. Maybe tomorrow."

"We can play for the onionskin," Gertie said. "I promise."

But the following morning Gertie was not at school. And when Udo asked Frau Baecker about her whereabouts, she shot him a stern look.

"There's been a family misfortune," she replied, her lips pursing together into a fine line.

Udo knew better than to ask anything else.

"Christian, you're late," Gertie said, her arms crossed as she stood outside the school's wrought iron gate. "Mutti said 12:30 and no excuses this time!"

"Alright already," her brother replied as he rolled his eyes and walked past her. "It'll be fried potatoes again, so who cares if we're a few minutes late."

"Still, I don't like it when she gets upset," Gertie said, struggling to keep up the pace as he walked ahead of her on the sidewalk. With his curly blonde hair, Christian was a good head taller than Gertie, and unlike her, quite popular with his fourth-grade mates. Most days, she had no choice but to entertain herself until he finished talking to them and was ready to walk her home.

"She's always upset," Christian said. "Besides, it's not like she's got somewhere to go or something to do. She'll just go up to her room when we're finished eating like she always does."

Gertie knew as much so there was not much point in arguing with him. At any rate, they were walking fast so by her calculations they would arrive on time.

Within fifteen minutes they had reached the outskirts of Hochzoll and had turned onto Speyer Street where they could see the steep roof of their white stucco house.

"Last one in is a rotten egg," Christian yelled, as they broke into a sprint. Without fail, Christian's long stride meant he was once again the first to throw open the imposing oak door that guarded the entrance.

"Mutti!" he cried out, yanking at his leather laces. Despite his impatience, he made sure to place his shoes in the rack beneath the stairwell before putting on his house slippers and shuffling down the dark-paneled hall smelling ever so faintly of the sickening pine cleaner their mother adored. On his way, he passed the shuttered entrances of the sitting and dining rooms, and with both arms extended, pushed through the swinging porthole door into the only heated room in their house.

Entering the kitchen, Christian was surprised to find the back door left open. It was not like their mother to waste any heat from the cast-iron stove, and even more puzzling was the sight of four, half-eaten and congealed porridge bowls from earlier that morning sitting unattended on the large, farmhouse table where they took every meal.

"Mutti?" he called out again, as a wave of uncertainty flooded over him. He debated climbing the dark, creaky stairs to see if she had locked herself in her room again but instead stepped out into the garden.

Outside, the clouds had grown dark and heavy with rain, and a few drops were starting to fall. Seeing that the wooden cellar doors were also left open, Christian ran toward them. He stepped down the cold cement stairs and was relieved to see a dim light radiating from the exposed bulb that hung from the top of the unfinished basement.

"Mutti, it's starting to rain," he called out, certain his mother was just gathering up potatoes to bring upstairs. Not hearing a response, he walked down further, greeted only by a waft of pungent and mildewed air.

Christian could not see his mother until he reached the bottom step.

And when he did, he could not fathom the sight of her, her body drooping like a heavy sack, her head limp and sagging. A thick rope was wound around the wooden beam above her like a spool while beneath her the kitchen step stool was knocked over on its side.

The horror of seeing her like this paralyzed him, depriving him of his voice and breath.

"Christian! Mutti! Where are you?" he heard Gertie calling from the garden above.

Waves of fear and panic engulfed him. Eyes gaping, he scanned the harrowing apparition for a sign of life, some movement, but found nothing. Somewhere deep, in the dark and narrowing void of his mind, he knew he had to keep his little sister from coming down the stairs.

"Mutti?"

Gertie's voice reverberated against the dank walls with a slight echo. She was standing right above him, peering down.

Christian's voice thundered with a crack.

"Don't come down!"

"But why?" Gertie replied, her obstinate response heightening his panic.

A sudden jolt of energy unleashed him from the spot, sent him hurtling up the stairs and pushing his sister back outside. In the yard, the rain pelted down on them.

"What is it?" Gertie asked, alarmed to see her brother's face gone so pale.

"Just go and get inside now," he said, shoving her towards the back door.

Propelled by the storm and her brother's insistence, Gertie did as she was told. Only upon reaching the threshold did she turn to watch as Christian struggled to close the heavy cellar doors.

"What's going on?" she asked as he sprinted back toward her. "Where's Mutti?"

Christian slammed the door before turning to face her.

"You're scaring me," she said.

Christian braced his hands on Gertie's shoulders, as tears flowed down his cheeks.

"She's dead."

Gertie looked up at him, her eyes widening with fear.

"Stop it," she cried out at last, hitting her small fists against his chest, working them into a rage. "Stop it!"

"It's true," Christian said, not halting her torment. "It's true."

"No. NO, NO, NO, NO!"

Taking short, jagged breaths, Christian wrapped his arms around his sister, holding her tight. "We have to call the police," he said.

All he could hear in response was her muffled cry against his chest.

"And you have to promise me you'll stay right here, ok?"

He was holding her at arm's length now. "Please?"

Feeling a palpable tightening across her chest, Gertie nodded.

Adelina Obermeier's burial took place quickly and quietly in the *Ostfriedhof* municipal grounds and was limited in attendance to what little remained of her family: her husband, Werner, their three sons, Thorsten, Uwe and Christian and their youngest, Gertie.

Stunned by the suicide—their father would no longer even say her name out loud—not a word was spoken at the funeral as they watched her casket being lowered into the ground.

To cope with the loss, Werner hired a local widow in her fifties to do the family's cooking and washing, a joyless woman who like him was not prone to wasting words. Frau Trautheim, as they called her, wore long, utilitarian grey dresses and carried out her work in a fastidious, and equally dull manner, making sure to place a warm meal on the kitchen table promptly at 1:30 PM when Thorsten and Uwe arrived home from school and at which time Gertie and Christian were called downstairs to join them. She would depart each day the way she entered, through the back door, leaving the table set with fresh slices of bread and cold cuts for the evening meal, and reheating a portion of the mid-day leftovers for Herr Obermeier, just minutes before he was due to walk through the door.

"And what did you learn today?" their father would ask the boys in lieu of a greeting once he was seated at the head of the table. Werner's life had been consumed by his work as a mechanical engineer in service to the former aviation manufacturer, BFW/Messerschmitt, and he considered it his obligation to ensure his vocation lived on through his sons. Upon hearing a response from either Thorsten or Uwe, or on a rare occasion, Christian, he would find a way to elaborate on some specific mathematical principle or pepper them with questions related to either physics or chemistry, sometimes using a recent occurrence as a catalyst for the evening's impromptu lesson.

Werner, of course, had not consciously sought to educate Gertie in this vein, but since he did not see the point of discussing anything else at the table, Gertie's scientific inculcation—along with that of her brothers—began at an early age. Werner's direct conversation with her was otherwise limited to making sure she had taken care of the household chores assigned to her.

One crisp, November evening the doorbell rang as they were busy eating their meal.

"Are you expecting someone?" Werner asked, looking sternly at each of his children. The disturbance had interrupted him mid-sentence as he was explaining a key mechanical principle related to torque.

"No," Thorsten replied, as the others shook their heads in silence.

"Well, go and see who it is," he said, gesturing to Gertie in an offhand way before turning his attention back toward the boys.

With a sense of apprehension, Gertie pushed herself away from the table and made her way down the darkened hall. Their family was not accustomed to visitors, and even in the years before her death, their mother had chosen to lead a life of self-imposed isolation. They had no close family friends, and the older boys tended to go over to their schoolmate's houses as opposed to inviting anyone over, so the rare visitors who came were usually work colleagues of their father who would make an appointment well ahead of time.

Gertie took a deep, bracing breath and pulled the door handle down.

To her relief it was none other than her playmate, Udo.

"What are you doing here?" she asked.

"*Servus*, Gertie," he said, casting his brown eyes down. His glasses slid down the ridge of his nose, and with his index finger, he pushed them up again. "I came to say good-bye."

"Oh," Gertie said. "But why?"

Standing in her doorway, Udo looked even smaller than usual, with his long and broken shadow stumbling down the stairs.

"My mother is taking us to Berlin," he said, daring to look up at her with watery eyes.

"But for how long?" Gertie asked, her thin brows, bunching together.

"I don't know. She said we might not come back at all."

But your family is here, why would you move away?"

"My father's family, yes, but not my mother's. She says we can't stay any longer, that we have to go straight away."

Looking into his eyes, Gertie mirrored his alarm. Udo was not like the other children at their school. In his own quiet way, he had stuck by her by still playing marbles in the courtyard, and not repeating what the others said behind her back. Now, for some inexplicable reason, he too was being taken away from her.

"Can you wait here for just one minute?" she asked. "Please?"

He gave her a solemn nod as she turned to climb the gloomy staircase behind her. In the wake of her absence, Udo could hear the bellowing of a deep muffled voice droning on behind closed doors.

After what felt like an eternity, Gertie emerged from the shadows holding out her hand.

"Take this with you," she said. In her palm was her prized swirl shooter.

"Are you sure?" Udo asked, his eyes doubling in size.

"Yes," she replied. "That way you won't forget me. But you have to promise not to trade it. Not ever."

"I won't," Udo said, letting her place it in his hand. "I promise."

Rolling it between his finger and thumb, he lifted it up to the light above the doorstep, admiring for some seconds the spectrum of color refracting through the glass. Then, fishing in his pocket, he pulled out the blue and green onionskin he had won back from her a few days back.

"This is for you," he said, handing it to her. "So, you can remember me, too."

"Thank you," she said, her voice wispy like a far-off wind.

They looked at each other a few moments longer, both lost in the confusion of an unwanted parting. Then remembering the time, Udo shifted onto his heels. "I have to go," he said.

Gertie nodded. "Good-bye then."

"Bye, Gertie," he replied, as she watched him descend the stairs. By the time Udo reached the road all she could make out was his silhouette beneath the fading glow of the streetlamp.

Not much remained of Gertie's childhood and adolescence beyond a blur of years filled with somber reproach. Spells of melancholy alternated with bouts of school lessons and homework that allowed her to at least corral her disjointed thoughts and provided her with some relief from the flood of more painful emotions. The family stigma had limited Gertie's capacity for making new friends, so she kept to herself during the school day making a point not to say much apart from what was needed to keep her participation scores high. As time progressed, her classmates assumed she was either extremely shy or unforgivably ambitious, so for the most part they were happy to just ignore her.

The double shock of her mother's suicide followed by her only friend's sudden departure left Gertie in a state of isolation from which it was difficult to recover. Her only solace was the silent affection Christian would bestow upon her, either squeezing her hand in the kitchen or patting her on the back in the evenings as they climbed the stairs to go to bed.

Out of the four children, Christian was the most visibly affected by Adelina's death. Whereas the others had doubled-down on their pretense of not showing any outward response—continuing with their daily routines as if what had happened had no sway over them—Christian, who had always been the most outgoing and social, grew progressively pensive and mute.

His teachers and schoolmates were quick to notice the drastic change, and though for a time his closest friends remained loyal in their attempts to engage him, they no longer recognized the charismatic boy they had once known. In time, they allowed him to fade into the background, their attempts to include him in some game or activity once too often declined.

In his withdrawal, he began more and more to resemble his young sister, and though he complied with their father's decree not to mention Adelina, the way he sometimes looked into Gertie's eyes acknowledged without words the mutual suffering they shared in the wake of her sudden departure. Whereas in the past he had felt burdened by their mother's delegation of the caretaking responsibilities, after her death, Christian grew more protective of Gertie, quietly aligning himself with her by helping with the household chores or standing up for her when their father voiced his displeasure regarding some household mishap. More often than not, however, he would choose to disappear for hours at a time, only joining the family at appointed meals.

The fog of unspoken grief dictated by their father's example hung over the family, so that they each embraced the external distractions of work and study. In a crippling way, the approach worked well enough for three of the four children when it came time to make their own way in the world and to attempt a form of assimilation, at least where external achievement was concerned.

Christian, however, was not so inclined. After his eighteenth birthday, he chose instead to follow his mother's example by hanging himself in the basement the day after the completion of his *Abitur*, his final secondary school exam.

Gertie was not the one who found him. It had been their father this time, who rising early on that Saturday morning was the first to go into the kitchen, and like his youngest son so many years before, had found the back door curiously left open.

In the three weeks that followed, a sickening silence prevailed over the household. The only words exchanged were between Thorsten and Uwe, who seeing their father's shock manifested, took it upon themselves to take over the management of the household since along with her condolences, Frau Trautheim had announced her resignation.

"I'm afraid my old back just can't take the hours anymore." she had told their father.

Deep inside Gertie knew there was something perverse about the family's continued denial. After Christian's death she wept herself to sleep each night, still making sure to cover her mouth with a pillow so that her father or brothers might not hear her uncontrollable sobs. She resented being like them, at times wishing she was sensitive enough—honest enough—to follow in Christian's path. But the survivor in her, mirroring their father's uncanny resilience, would not allow it.

Gertie understood and felt Christian's despair. And yet, a part of her had never been able to forgive their mother for abandoning them nor did she have a clear understanding why Adelina had made this choice. For as long as Gertie could remember, their mother had been inconsolable despite the family's good fortune. At times she suspected it might have something to do with their father, but apart from his emotional inaccessibility, Gertie was not able to pinpoint any other fault that would have driven her to kill herself. He had not abused Adelina, and after her death he had continued to provide for his children's material and educational welfare.

All Gertie knew was that Adelina had taken Christian away from them, and that through their own unspoken complicity, they had all played a part.

Three months after Christian's death, Gertie threw herself into her schoolwork once more. She was determined more than ever to get out of the family house and to make something of her life. If not for her own sake, then for some nebulous Good for which her young heart still managed to hope if only to honor her dead brother's memory.

She attended to the increase in housework having over time devised novel efficiencies for making short shrift of her responsibilities, but for the most part, she devoted herself to studying, a habit her father approved of assuming her chores were done. She knew her natural inclination toward the sciences pleased him on some level, even if he did not explicitly acknowledge her aptitude. At the same time, she was more than aware of his conservative position regarding women, and that only Thorsten and Uwe were expected to follow in his footsteps whereas she was expected to attend to the house.

So it came as a shock in the fall when—after graduating from the local *Gymnasium*—Gertie packed up her bags. Unbeknownst to her father and brothers, the Technical University of Munich had accepted her application to pursue a degree in a much different field than theirs, that of computational informatics.

7

Munich - 1968

The timing and conditions for Gertraud Obermeier's familial abscission could not have been riper. The year was 1968, Gertie was nineteen, and the world was in revolt against the war in Vietnam and against the oppression of those stuck on the lower rungs of society: women, workers, immigrants and people whose skin was darker than white.

Adding to the intrigue , Gertie's coming of age coincided with the tumult rising within Germany itself. As the post-war generation began to pick at the ill-concealed scabs of their forefathers' silence—poking fingers into the shattered mirrors of self-reflection—they attempted to identify what in the culture had led to the perpetration of the most heinous crimes ever imagined.

History was up for grabs, but foremost on Gertie's mind was finding a room where she could sleep at night after her days spent studying at the Technical University. Fortunately, on enrollment day, she had spotted a hastily written note taped to the TU's message board: "Room to let. Immediately available. Schraudolph Street 30, 5B."

Within 15 minutes of walking, she was sitting at a tiny kitchen table in a converted flat at the very top of the stairs of a worn-out, pre-war building. Across from her a bearded, and roguishly handsome young man—his long, dirty-blonde hair pulled back in a ponytail—was looking at her expectantly.

"So, Gertraud, all we're really asking is at least one month's notice if you plan to move out."

Gertie glanced over at Simone, the tall blonde with lilac-tinted sunglasses who was casually leaning against the edge of the kitchen sink.

"My course of study will take at least four years," Gertie said. "And my stipend is guaranteed as long as I keep up my grades, so that shouldn't be a problem."

"Fantastic," Simone said, lighting up a cigarette. "As long as you're not planning to run off to India any time soon like our last flatmate, we're all set. And don't worry, we're relaxed around here. Apart from making sure we can cover the rent, Gerhardt's obsession with the dishes is about as square as things get."

Gerhard rolled his eyes.

"You'll have to forgive Simi's occasional lapses in judgment. She seems to be under the impression that little green men do the cleaning around here. Let me show you around the flat."

Gertie followed him out of the kitchen and down the long hall that joined together not only the bath, but three small bedrooms in quick succession, each one facing the inner courtyard where the airy canopy of a tall birch still allowed enough sunlight to penetrate the high-ceilinged space. At the very end of the hall, a large, window-filled living room looked out on the quiet residential street below.

"It's perfect," Gertie said, looking again at the long, narrow rectangle with a single bed that would make up her room. "I only have one suitcase. How soon can I move in?"

Simone glanced over at Gerhardt and smiled.

"You can move in now if you like. We'll drink a beer to seal the deal."

Over the next few months, Gertie learned to play the role of mediator between her new roommates, both of whom studied at the prestigious Ludwig Maximilian University down the street. They were each agitators in their own way, with Simone, the sociologist, rejecting any sort of gender-specific housework or tidiness and with Gerhardt, the historian, incapable of abiding household disarray in spite of his anti-totalitarian politics. Gertie often chose to just resolve their invented conflicts on her own—by doing the dishes or replacing the toilet paper—and for her efforts she was rewarded by their unspoken gratitude and loyalty. Although they both found Gertie's academic pursuits incomprehensible and dull, they admired her pioneering choices. Gertie, in turn, was happy to find some support at home since the men at her university—by far in the majority—tended to scoff at her inclusion, exuding outright hostility whenever she bested them in their coursework.

Living with Simone and Gerhardt, for the most part, proved ideal. In time, Gertie grew to admire not only Simone's carefree beauty but her unflinching feminism. Through the course of many a beer-fueled, late-night discussion, not to mention the sit-in protests that Simone insisted they attend, Gertie learned to embrace herself as an independently minded woman, already a feminist at heart.

From Gerhardt she learned about the hushed-up political and judicial malfeasance of the post-war period as West Germany raced toward NATO integration and capitalist retrenchment, not to mention the retooling of animosity toward the now common enemy, the USSR. It was interesting, indeed, how quickly foes became bedfellows when strategic resources were at stake.

Gertie, meanwhile, following the progression of global and national student protests, formed her own quiet opinions with respect to women's rights and the removal of former Nazis from key positions of power. The hypocrisy of a quickly buried past was not lost on Gertie, particularly in the form of Denazification, a bureaucratic, pencil-pushing process that allowed a quick return of the social status-quo in order to facilitate Germany's *Wirtschaftswunder*, or economic *miracle*. Although Gertie did not possess any hard evidence of her own family's involvement in the National Socialist Party, the unresolved shadows of the past resonated deep within her. With a newly discovered sense of righteousness, she was determined not to turn a blind eye, though what she should focus on, she was not exactly sure.

A year after Gertie moved into the Schraudolph Street apartment, Gerhardt and Simone gave into the irresistible pull of the opposite with the unintended but unavoidable consequence of making Gertie feel like an outsider in her own home. To give the couple more privacy, Gertie began spending more and more time at the library and eating her meals in the university cafeteria, a rather uninviting and gray post-modern structure that, apart from the floor-to-ceiling glass windows that faced out on the wide avenue, resembled a bunker.

On an equally gray fall day filled with rain showers, the dining hall was packed with students and professors alike scrambling to keep dry between lectures. Gertie, who had jostled her way through the crowd with a lunch tray, could find only one seat remaining, and that, too, was occupied by an overflowing book satchel whose oblivious owner was balanced on the back legs of a chair, his upper body braced against the narrow window frame.

"Do you mind if I sit here?" Gertie asked, directing her question to the lean, dark-haired young man otherwise concealed behind the open pages of the *Süddeutsche Zeitung*.

"Not at all," he replied, with a deep, melodic voice.

He lunged forward to reclaim his satchel, however, the front legs of his chair crashed down faster than he could anticipate, knocking over the bag and spilling its contents out onto the floor.

A swell of male laughter rose up around them, as Gertie placed her tray on the table and knelt down beside him to help collect his things.

"I wouldn't normally bother you," she said, her cheeks flushed as she handed over his belongings. "But there's really nowhere else to sit."

"Don't mention it," he said, joining her on the floor and in the process brushing against her shoulder. His off-kilter, wireframe glasses did not match his otherwise sharp and handsome features that included a set of piercing blue eyes set above a square jaw.

"I'm the one who should apologize," he said, closing the bag and motioning toward the now empty seat. "I tend to lose sight of what's going on around me."

"Thanks," Gertie said. The intensity of his stare made it difficult for her to focus. Something about his eyes triggered in her an uncanny sense of déjà vu.

"I'm Klaus," he said. "Klaus Tischler."

"Gertraud," she replied, glancing up. "But you can call me Gertie."

Klaus smiled at her.

"It's nice to meet you, Gertie."

"Likewise," she heard herself mumble.

He watched her for a few moments as she used her fork to probe the daily special buried somewhere beneath a sea of brown gravy and otherwise hemmed in by a protective mound of mashed potato.

"There usually aren't too many women in here," Klaus said.

Without moving her head, Gertie looked up from her plate, her fork frozen in mid-air.

"I mean, that must be difficult," he added.

"Difficult?" Gertie asked, not knowing what to make of his attention.

"To be in the minority," he said, as she chewed her food in uncomfortable silence.

"Well, since you bring it up. Yes, it is."

Klaus allowed a few moments to pass before proceeding with more care.

"So, what do you study then?"

"Informatics."

"Interesting," he replied, doing his best to sound flattering.

Gertie narrowed her eyes at him.

"You really think so?"

"Of course! How fast we can process information is increasingly key to everything we do. No doubt about it."

"I'm glad you agree," she said, sinking her fork into the slowly disappearing muddle. The tone of his voice had made her relax somewhat. "Most people don't really understand what I'm doing. My family included."

Klaus chuckled.

"Well, most people aren't like us, are they," he said, his eyes lighting up.

Gertie returned his statement with a blush and a smile. It was the first time she had felt any camaraderie at the university, and it felt particularly intense since she detected a growing attraction between them.

Klaus, no doubt sensing her discomfort, feigned a return to his reading so she could finish her meal.

When it appeared she might be getting up to leave, he looked over his paper once more.

"*2001: A Space Odyssey* is showing at the Arena," he said.

"Oh, yes. I've been meaning to see it."

"How about tonight, then?" he asked. "Afterwards, we can get a beer at the Paulaner."

Unsure she had heard him correctly, Gertie gawked back in response.

"C'mon, don't keep me waiting. What do you say?"

"Shall I meet you there?" she asked, overwhelmed by a second wave of uncertainty.

"Yes. 8 PM sharp."

He did not take his eyes off her until she nodded back in response. Smiling, he picked up his paper once more and continued reading.

After her last lecture, Gertie rode her bike back to the apartment. Fueled by excitement, she raced up the four flights of stairs, opened the door and began yelling for Simone. Simone, unaccustomed to hearing Gertie's voice raised, rushed out of her room in a panic.

"What's the matter? Are you alright?"

"No, I have a date tonight," Gertie said, flailing her arms as if she had caught fire.

Simone stared at her blankly for a moment and then burst out laughing.

"What's so funny? You have to help me, Simone. What should I wear? What do I do with my hair?"

"My God. First you scare the life out of me, and then you're this worked up about a date? So, who is this lucky fellow?"

"Klaus," Gertie said, shaking her head with agitation.

"But Klaus who?" Simone asked, ignoring Gertie's fidgeting.

"Does it matter? A student in physics. What should I wear?"

Simone laughed, then gazed at her with exaggerated suspicion.

"You must really like him if you're giving a second's thought to how you look. That's so unlike you."

"Easy for you to say, you look gorgeous just getting out of bed. Now, c'mon, you know I'm hopeless when it comes to these things."

"If he's asking you on a date, he must like you as you are. It's not like you did anything special this morning."

"Please don't make this more difficult for me. Please?"

A feline smile spread across Simone's face.

"This Klaus must be something else. And physics, who'd have thought. They do say Einstein was quite the ladies' man," she added, making Gertie blush.

"Will you just please fix this? I don't have much time."

"Ok, c'mon then," Simone said, beckoning Gertie into her room.

"First, you'll need to borrow one of my minis. If you're trying to seduce this Klaus, then you'll have to go for the jugular with those cute legs of yours. He won't know what hit him."

"Whatever you say. Let's just get on with it."

"Don't worry, this won't take long. For a silent type, you're quite attractive as it is."

Simone handed her a skirt and blouse combination to try on and then pulled her over to the full-length mirror in front of her dressing table.

"Now, we just need to do something with your hair," Simone said, standing behind her with a brush. In the end she twisted Gertie's straight blonde hair into an elegant knot.

"Do you have a diaphragm?"

"Simone!"

"Oh, come on. Don't act like such a prude."

I'm not a prude, it's just..."

"Just what?" Simone demanded, pulling open a drawer to pick out a lipstick and eyeliner.

"I just don't think it will come to that."

"Then why on earth am I doing all of this?" Simone said, waving the make-up around in her hands. "Don't kid yourself, Gertie. You know you want it, so take it. Just don't get knocked-up in the process. Believe me, that's the last thing you'd need."

And Gertie did want it, didn't she? But she had never had it. And despite touting an intellectualized version of Simone's *make love not war*, she felt awkward about her complete lack of sexual experience especially when all her peers seemed rife in comparison. At any rate, it felt premature to assume her date would lead to anything more than a welcome night out.

Wearing a striped miniskirt and beige overcoat, Gertie arrived at the Arena five minutes before eight o'clock, looking like a book-worm version of Twiggy, her lids heavily lined and only slightly obscured by her cat eyeglasses.

Klaus, who had also arrived early, was leaning against the building's stucco façade next to a film poster for Werner Herzog's *Lebenszeichen*. Wearing a brown leather jacket, he had a self-rolled cigarette in one hand and a paperback in the other.

"*Guten abend*," Gertie said, in a soft-spoken voice.

Klaus looked up from his book and blinked.

"Gertie?"

"I hope I'm not late," she blurted out, suddenly alarmed.

"No, not at all. You look fantastic, by the way. I almost didn't recognize you."

Gertie blushed in response.

"Shall we go in?" he added, opening the door.

The gleam in his eyes was so magnetic that Gertie felt too woozy to respond.

They made their way through the crowded theater and before too long settled into their mid row seats. As the lights dimmed, Klaus stretched his arm along Gertie's shoulders at which point she allowed the weight of her upper body to melt into his as if it was the most natural thing in the world.

After the film they walked together along a tree-lined path animated by the briskness of the clear November night and their impressions of the film. Not far from the Paulaner Biergarten, Klaus stopped in his tracks to stare up at the star-filled sky.

"Do you think we'll make it up there someday?" he asked.

"You mean the two of us?"

"Well, if not us, per se, the common man."

"Sure, but if you ask me, we have our work cut out for us down here."

Klaus laughed and then peered into her eyes.

"Are you always this pragmatic?"

Gertie shrugged her shoulders and smiled.

"But say you could go up there, would you do it?"

Gertie paused for a moment.

"Yes, but only if I didn't have to come back."

Klaus drew her close beside him and then pointed up.

"Do you see where the three stars align in quick succession?" he said. "That's Orion's Belt, and that bright nebula beneath it is his hunter's sword. Now, over there is the Big Dipper, and if you follow that line extending from the edge of the bowl...you see that bright star there?"

"Yes."

"That's Polaris, indicating north, so no matter where you are in the world, you can always find yourself, just by looking up."

"It's spectacular," she said, leaning into him as she continued to gaze up. In his arms and admiring the night sky, she felt at home and at peace.

"Gertie?" Klaus said, tilting his head down to look at her.

"Yes?"

"May I kiss you now?" he asked, putting his hands around her narrow waist.

Gertie could feel her cheeks flush, but instead of responding, she lifted herself on tiptoe and put her arms around his neck.

The next morning Gertie woke up in her room, for once not alone. Klaus had accompanied her home, and in the comfort of her bed, she had discarded her virginity in exchange for the pleasure Klaus had aroused in her. To her surprise, he was remarkably attentive and gentle, and in the next few weeks, Gertie made up for her lack of experience by spending almost all her time with Klaus. When they were not in bed, they often studied together in his studio apartment, exchanging ideas as they lounged on opposite ends of his worn leather couch. Gertie's upbringing had more than prepared her to engage in theoretical discussions regarding physics, pleasing Klaus to no end since he much preferred her company to that of his competitive classmates.

Overall, their state of bliss lasted through the fall of 1969 and well into the winter. Gertie had never experienced such happiness, and she wondered why—upon discovering such pleasure at the hands of another—more people were not as elated as she. Their relationship deepened to the point that Gertie felt no need to speak of it. What was the point of discussing the future when she was living the present as a dream?

The winter, however, was not so kind to Simone and Gerhardt. Without Gertie around to act as mediator, their romantic interlude devolved into a state of constant bickering.

"It's getting tedious with just Gerhardt and no one else around," Simone said, during one of Gertie's sporadic visits to do her laundry. "Why don't you bring Klaus over sometime?"

"But I thought you two wanted more space," Gertie said, sitting on the edge of the tub and taking her clothes out of the frontload washer.

Simone sighed.

"We were getting along for a while, but it's just not the same without you. You seem to have the magic touch for keeping Gerhardt from becoming such a drag."

"You mean I'm good at cleaning up after the two of you."

Simone laughed.

"No, not just that," she said, as she followed Gertie into her room so she could hang the wet clothes on a wire rack next to the window.

But when it's just the two of us here, it's a bit suffocating. Gerhardt's too serious, and it's just more fun when you're around."

"Gertie and fun, two words I've never heard you say in the same sentence. Are you sure you don't have me confused with somebody else?"

"That's just it. You have a sense of humor, and sometimes Gerhardt forgets he has one, too. At least with me. You're better at bringing it out of him. He enjoys your wit.

"Come," Simone said, when Gertie had finished her chore. "Have a drink with me."

In the kitchen Simone dried off two glasses and put them on the table in front of Gertie, before pulling out a bottle of schnapps from the half-sized refrigerator that doubled as a cutting surface.

"What we should really do is throw a party," she said, lighting up a cigarette. "*Weiberfastnacht* is coming up, so what better way to clear the testosterone-filled air than a night of women calling the shots?"

"I don't know," Gertie said. "I'm not really cut out for hosting parties."

"Oh, come on, it'll be fun. We'll decorate the place, get dressed up. Plus, you know the boys secretly like it when we take charge. I'm sure you've tested out that theorem with Klaus, am I right?"

"Simone, do you ever not have your mind in the gutter?"

"Gutter?" she smiled. "Now surely I've raised you better than to think *that*."

Gertie rolled her eyes.

"Any excuse for flaunting your emancipation," she said, before turning her gaze toward the window and the skinny birch stripped bare of all its leaves.

"Sure, why not? The winter's been long enough as it is, and it'll be a nice break from studying for exams."

"Well, cheers to that, my friend," Simone said, raising her glass.

Women's Carnival Night, fell on a Thursday that year, February 5th. Simone, with Gertie's help and that of two other girlfriends, Petra and Annika, managed to turn their drab student flat into an alluring parlor with an intriguing twist.

At 8 PM, their guests began to arrive in their *Weiberfastnacht* costumes, the women attired in seductive dress and the men wearing old ties to be cut off at the appointed time. The invitations had made it clear that any man crossing the threshold was fair game once the scissors came out, and the novelty of it all had sent an electric current through the evening, with each player eagerly adapting to the roles assigned as if relieved not to have to make an original effort either way.

With the free flow of alcohol lubricating any lingering inhibitions, the young women soon enough began to tease out with greater daring the limits of their newly assigned power.

Simone knew, as a student of human behavior and the orchestrator of this particular social experiment, that for the party to succeed, it was essential to cultivate just the right amount of tension before allowing the scissors of irrevocable choice to make their debut, since a premature disclosure could result in a disastrous, anticlimactic ending. Fortunately, by eleven o'clock the initial rounds of mingling had produced the more obvious, paired constellations.

"When are we going to cut the ties?" Annika whispered into Simone's ear just a tad too loud. "Thomas keeps going on about an exam tomorrow morning."

Annika's face was flustered from too much alcohol, and her hair knot had come undone. Meanwhile, her cloying attempts to attract the clean-cut young man who stood at the end of the hall seemed on the verge of fizzling out. He was shifting his weight from one leg to the other and stealing glances toward the door.

Simone gave her a knowing nod and then turned her attention toward Gertie who was making her way toward the kitchen.

"Gertie, would you be a dear and go down to the cellar storage to get more schnapps for our guests?"

"Sure," she said, not giving it a second thought.

As soon as Gertie was out the door, Simone began distributing the scissors surreptitiously, and having already calculated how the chips would fall, and since courtesy dictated that as hostess, she make the last choice, she knew precisely where to stand.

With the shears distributed, the current in the room sizzled. Everyone stood on the edge of curiosity casting sidelong glances to see whether their inebriated assessments would prove correct.

"Ladies, you may cut your ties now!"

Annika, already holding on to her man as if he were on a leash, initiated the tie clipping. Not to be outdone, the other women followed suit making their own selections resulting in a flurry of activity and self-conscious giggling on all sides.

Simone waited only one second after hearing the last snip to turn her full attention to Klaus who had unwittingly, and rather drunkenly, placed himself in a corner no doubt waiting for Gertie's return.

"Klaus, I guess that leaves just you and me, " Simone said, swiftly slicing through the thin fabric of his tie. And without a moment's hesitation, she grabbed the shortened noose around his neck and marched him toward her room.

When Gertie came back upstairs loaded down with a canvas bag full of liquor, the apartment exuded a calmness that belied the festivities she had left behind. Jefferson Airplane was still playing on the HiFi, but the conversational noise was noticeably subdued. As Gertie hastened down the long hallway, she passed a short young man with dark features who—catching her eye—arched his eyebrow in a beckoning way.

Ignoring his gesture, she continued down the hall. As she entered the large living room it became painfully apparent that she had missed the cutting ceremony as there were two couples in advanced stages of embrace on either end of the sofa.

"Klaus?" Gertie called out meekly as she placed the bag full of bottles on the floor. But the moment his name passed her lips a sinking feeling in her chest informed her that she would get no response, and that her temporary absence had opened the door for someone else to benefit from his affections on this now dreadful night of table turning.

Walking back down the hall and finding the door to her bedroom closed, Gertie hesitated. She felt an unwillingness to open it and see who might be occupying her space, so instead she opted to leave the party altogether. Grabbing her coat and hat from the hallway rack, she closed the door behind her and ran down the stairs into the crisp, moist air.

Once she could look up at the sky, Gertie inhaled deeply, only then realizing that she had been holding her breath since the moment of her terrible recognition. Seeing the stars above her, she was able to calm herself enough to start breathing again.

"But now what?" The thought of Klaus in someone else's arms pained her.

It was not so much jealousy she felt but rather a sense of abandonment not unlike what she had experienced after learning how her mother had died.

The moment she had heard Christian speak those horrific words into the phone's receiver, she had felt the house closing in on her, as if it would trap her inside and never let her go. She had promised Christian not to leave his side, but, unable to help herself, she had run out of the house gasping for air, leaving him alone inside that suffocating house to wait for their father and the police to arrive. When they later found her crouching beneath the apple tree in the yard, she refused to go back indoors, only relenting sometime after midnight when she could no longer keep her eyes open.

She had done the same thing after Christian's suicide. Night after night she had taken her duvet and pillow out to the back yard so she could fall asleep under the semi-open roof of the garden's small gazebo.

Not knowing what to do with herself, Gertie walked through the streets of her Munich neighborhood until she reached the nearby Alter Nord Cemetery. Prior to the war, it had been an active burial ground, but since its closure in 1945 it functioned primarily as a municipal park in the *Maxvorstadt* district. At an all-night kiosk across from the entrance, she purchased a pack of Gauloises. Gertie had on occasion smoked Klaus's cigarettes but had not bought her own until now.

Finding an empty wooden bench at the edge of the park, Gertie sat down, pulled out a cigarette and lit it. She breathed in deeply allowing the nicotine to penetrate the full expanse of her lungs as she looked up, the stars brighter now that she had removed herself from the city's reflecting glare.

It was cold, but not windy, so in her thick winter jacket and hat she was well-insulated to withstand the elements. She slumped her body down on the bench so that she could rest her head on the back of it and still watch the night sky above her, smoking one cigarette after the other and imagining that the burning ember was somehow helping to keep her warm.

Her mind kept wandering back to what had transpired and how foolish she had been to think she was up to the task of swapping partners. She had known even as she agreed to help Simone with the party planning that she had no interest in sleeping with anyone else. And even as she had convinced Klaus that whatever happened would be ok—that she was as emancipated and self-assured as Simone—the truth was that all she wanted was to make her roommate happy without acknowledging the potential cost. She had allowed herself to be swept up by Simone's allure and charisma, letting her personal discernment fall by the wayside.

She had only herself to blame for her predicament, and although spasms of jealousy coursed through her at the thought of Klaus kissing another woman—images she quickly quelled as soon as they began to emerge—she knew she had no right to be angry with him. He was simply complying with the rules of the game.

And Simone? Well, Simone was Simone. She knew what she wanted. And deep-down Gertie knew that this was Simone's intent all along. That she had purposefully sent her out on an errand so that Gertie would be forced to demonstrate her allegiance for all that Simone espoused, and who better to taste the spoils of war than her mentor?

The realization upset her more than she could fathom, but at the same time she had walked into this trap with her eyes wide open. Now there was nothing to do but wait for the fallout. Would Klaus lose interest in her? Would he choose Simone's bed over hers?

Going back to her own flat was out of the question, leaving Klaus' empty studio, for which she had a key, as her only refuge.

Reluctantly, she forced the dead weight of her body against the bench to reanimate to a standing position, wishing all the while that she could just bring out her duvet and curl up in a ball instead.

The reckoning proved not as painful as expected, at least not for Gertie. After letting herself into Klaus' apartment, she drank what remained of an open bottle of vodka, sunk into his bed and pulled the covers over her head. She did not stir again until she heard him come in late the following morning.

"Gertie?" she heard him call out as he closed the door behind him. "I wondered where you had gone."

She could hear the remorse and agitation in his voice.

She pulled the covers down to look at him, trying to read the expression in his eyes.

"Did you?"

"Of course," he exclaimed, walking towards her, nervous and expectant, despite his visible fatigue. He looked pale and strung out.

"I was downstairs getting schnapps for Simone. When I came back up, everyone had disappeared, so I left."

"I'm so sorry. Honestly. I didn't know what to do. It all happened so quickly, and I'd already had so much to drink, and—"

"It's ok," Gertie said, sitting up in bed.

He looked up from the floor, his hair disheveled and glasses askew.

"Are you sure?" Klaus asked.

"Yes, but if you don't mind, I'd rather not talk about it. Unless you think it's necessary."

Klaus sat down next to her on the edge of the bed.

"Unless you think it's changed things between us," she added.

He looked at her curiously.

"No, why would it?"

Gertie shook her head.

"Simone is so attractive, and—"

"Gertie. Simone is not my type, believe me. And she's far too complicated for my taste. Anyone's taste, really."

His voice had recovered some of its lost confidence.

"That's a relief."

Klaus reached out for her hand.

"Then can we put this behind us?" His eyes were earnest, pleading.

"Yes," Gertie said, placing her hand on top of his.

For a few moments neither one of them spoke, letting the silence carry the weight of what they felt.

"I only have one question," Gertie said. "You weren't in my room, were you?"

Klaus shook his head no, flustered by the recollection.

Gertie squeezed his hand to reassure him.

"Is this going to make things difficult between you and Simone?" he asked, looking her over with a pained expression.

"Not if she doesn't want it to be. That's not to say I'm not upset and disappointed."

"Of course," Klaus said, his words trailing off.

He let out an exasperated sigh.

"You're right to feel upset. She wasn't playing fair last night."

"No, but at least now I know where I stand."

Gertie spent the next three days in Klaus' studio until the necessity of retrieving her clothes compelled her to go back to the Schraudolph Street apartment. She chose a time when Simone would normally be out, so she was surprised to find her in the kitchen with Gerhardt amid a heated argument.

Simone called out to her.

"Gertie, what a relief to see you!"

"I doubt the feeling is mutual," Gerhardt said, turning to look at Gertie who was standing in the threshold. "I was just telling Simone here that it's about time she moved out."

"Not on my account, I hope," Gertie said, taken aback.

"No, on mine," Gerhardt said, the steel edge of his voice unsoftened. "I think it's only fair she takes out the garbage for once."

"Nice one," Simone replied.

She was leaning against the window ledge feigning a cool countenance. She looked as composed and beautiful as ever apart from the aggressive tap she used to dislodge a cigarette from the pack she held in her hand.

"You knew exactly what I was about when we got together. But it's obvious you're not so much about equal rights as you claim."

She paused to let her words sink in and to flip open her Zippo with dramatic effect.

"Deep down you're just as much of a chauvinist as the rest of them." Then with a piercing intake of breath she added, "perhaps worse because at least the brazen ones wear it on their sleeve, while you just pretend to be someone you're not."

Gerhard turned to look at her, fuming so much that his nostrils flared.

"Your behavior has absolutely nothing to do with equality, unless you consider it a God-given right to be a deceitful, inconsiderate pig!"

"Fuck you, Gerhardt," Simone said, exhaling smoke in his direction.

Gertie could see the muscles in Gerhardt's arms and chest tensing.

"Why not ask Gertie here how it felt when you seduced her boyfriend?" Simone shook her head.

"She knew full well what the party was about. Didn't you, Gertie?"

Gertie stammered. She felt like a small animal caught between two sets of headlights.

"We even discussed the possibility beforehand. Not that it's any of your business. You and I never had an exclusive relationship, remember?"

"Thank God! I've never been more relieved to not be tied down to the likes of you. But that still doesn't give you the right to shit all over your friends, which is exactly what you've done whether you're willing to admit it or not. And since I'm the one who holds the lease, I want you out by the end of the week."

"Oh, that's it then, is it? Flexing your male dominance and throwing me out on the street? I've got rights, you know."

"Not here you don't," he said, savoring his declaration.

Simone waved her hand in the air then looked over at Gertie as if nothing was happening.

"Please talk some sense into him. You know it was all just in fun. We talked about it."

"I really don't want to get in the middle of this," Gertie said. "What happened, happened. I just want to put it behind us."

"See?" Simone said, smiling in her triumph.

"You're not in the middle of anything," Gerhardt said, looking at Gertie with concern. "I want her out, and that's the end of it."

"But surely Gertie has a say. You're always claiming majority rule, Gerhardt, you fucking hypocrite."

"If you could ever bother to listen, Simone, Gertie said she's abstaining. Though why she'd let you off the hook so easy, I don't know. And it doesn't matter. The lease is the lease, and according to the law, it's my say, so I suggest you start packing."

"But Gerhardt—" Gertie said.

"It's decided," Gerhardt said, looking at Gertie in astonishment. "Believe me, it's in your best interest as well as mine."

"In her best interest, my God," Simone laughed. "The patriarchal gloat just keeps oozing out of you. How on earth have you managed to keep it locked down for so long?"

"You've got until next Friday, Simone." Gerhardt said turning his back and storming out of the kitchen and down the hall. They could hear the door of his room slam shut behind him.

Simone broke the silence that followed by pointing toward the door.

"See what jealousy will net you? Take heed. You never want to get involved with a man like that. Before you know it, he'll try to control every aspect of your life."

Gertie shifted her weight.

"I can try to talk to him later if you'd like. When he's not so upset."

Simone cocked her head.

"You are a dear," she said, with an almost undetectable note of disdain. "And I do hope Klaus appreciates that about you. You know it was all just harmless fun, right? We're too young to be tied down. Otherwise, we'll just turn into the bigoted, judgmental barbarians of the past."

Gertie nodded reflexively. She questioned Simone's sincerity, but in her bewitching presence a part of her could not help but admire her strength.

"So, tell me," Simone said, lighting another cigarette from the butt of the one about to go out. "Who was the lucky guy that night?"

Simone was still scrutinizing Gertie and trying to gauge the extent of her harm.

"There was no lucky guy. I left."

"You're joking, right? But that was the whole point. Well, now I do feel like a cad. So, everything is alright between you and Klaus?"

Gertie looked up again, instinctively probing Simone's flawless face for a sign of deceit, but she could see nothing tangible in the clear, icy depths of her eyes.

"Yes," she replied. "Things couldn't be better."

8

Kirchheim - 1982

Exhausted, Gertie climbed the stone steps of her house only to open the door to a strange, high-pitched yip and the sight of Klaus' shoes and those of their sons' lying on the floor mat. Annoyed, Gertie unlaced her own leather oxfords, and stepping over the masculine pile, placed them in the shoe rack that stood opposite the door.

"I'm home," she called out, as a reverberating hollowness echoed down the hall.

Gertie hung up her coat, noted the absence of her mother-in-law's handbag in the foyer and then followed the sounds of her boys' giggling down the hall and into the living room. She opened the door and was surprised to see Christian, who had just turned ten, crouching on the carpet, holding a black Spitz puppy against his chest. His younger brother, Udo Jörgen, was kneeling beside him, trying to pat the dog on the head. Klaus, meanwhile, was sitting on the edge of an overstuffed chair, leaning over them and looking amused.

"What's going on here?" Gertie asked, directing her narrowed gaze toward Klaus who raised his eyes in brief acknowledgment.

"It's St. Nicholas Day, so I thought I'd surprise the boys with a puppy," he said. "They've just named him Rex."

Just then the pup stuck out its tongue causing the boys to giggle once more.

"He's thirsty," Klaus said. "I'll get him some water."

Klaus, who in the intervening twelve years had grown a beard and put on the heft appropriate for a man his age, got up to go into the kitchen.

Gertie followed on his heels.

"What's the meaning of this?" she asked in a low voice when they were well out of earshot. "We didn't agree on getting a dog."

"C'mon, now, where's your Christmas spirit? Didn't you see the boys' faces? They're ecstatic."

"But you know I don't care for dogs," Gertie said, her forehead furrowing. "And who do you think will clean up the mess he'll make? No, Klaus, they're far too young to take this on."

Klaus looked at her exasperated.

"But I don't want them missing out on this. My mother and I will make up the shortfall if they forget. You won't have to do a thing. And having a dog will teach them how to be responsible. That's the whole point."

After eleven years of marriage, Gertie and Klaus had, for the most part, learned to manage one another's expectations. Their professional lives afforded only limited time at home, so they defaulted to their strengths, Gertie in housekeeping and Klaus in looking after their sons' needs. Klaus had also grown up with a brother, and now that his widowed mother, Elke, had relocated to a sizable bungalow down the street, they had her to thank for any daytime childcare since she adored looking after her grandsons.

Gertie paced up and down their white galley kitchen.

"I don't know," she said. "What if they lose interest? You know how fickle they are about their games and toys."

Klaus turned his long, broad back to her as he took a shallow bowl from the side cabinet and walked over to the sink.

"It's different with dogs. They make their needs known. Plus, it builds character."

Gertie raised her thin, blonde eyebrows, bereft of any make up.

"Are you sure this isn't just about *you* wanting a dog?" she asked. She could feel her fists pressing against the tops of her hips as she tried to contain her frustration through sheer physical force.

"Does it matter? What's important is that the boys learn how to develop a caring and affectionate attitude."

"Oh, I see. So, this is about my lack of 'motherliness', again, is it? Was this Elke's idea?"

Unlike Klaus' mother, Gertie subscribed to a belief that children of a certain age should attend to their own needs and fears, and that parental obligation should be limited to providing a clean, safe environment. She had dutifully fed, diapered and cared for the boys throughout their toddlerhood and had instilled in them a capacity for understanding right from wrong, but in Elke's view, Gertie had—in an alarming way—distanced herself from her sons in recent years.

Klaus sighed.

"No, I didn't say that."

For his part, he was finding it increasingly difficult to mediate between Elke and Gertie. He was aware of his wife feeling "ganged up on," as she would sometimes claim, a fact he attributed to her almost complete lack of contact with her own family, a circumstance he did not fully comprehend but that relieved him nonetheless. At their wedding, he had found her father and brothers a queer and unsettling lot, and he was quietly glad that Gertie made sure to keep them all at arm's length.

The few interactions she did have with her family were over the phone or through a perfunctory exchange of letters. On a rare occasion she would travel to Augsburg, but she almost never took the boys with her or invited Klaus along, which was fine with him. And it was not as if her father or brothers demonstrated any keen interest in staying abreast of what was going on in their lives.

As he saw it, the burden and responsibility of maintaining a sense of family cohesion fell mostly to his side. And because of this, he could not help but sometimes sympathize with his mother's point of view. More often than not, *he* was the one who got up to allay their sons' childish disputes or provide comfort in the middle of the night after a bad dream.

It was not a question of whether Gertie loved her sons or not. That was never up for discussion. It was her inability—refusal really—to relate to their puerile natures, to see the world through their eyes, that Klaus found so infuriating at times. Gertie did not have any patience for their trivial spats and tantrums. Most of all, she could not abide their crying if she surmised the root cause was not some physical injury but rather an expression of feigned *neediness*. By her reasoning, their sons did not lack for anything, so what could they possibly have to cry about?

"Fine. So, without consulting me, you decided our sons were in immediate need of a dog, is that it?"

"I didn't come up with it on my own, Gertie, Christian asked for a dog for his birthday, remember?"

"Yes, and at the time I told you he was far too young."

"I had a dog at his age," Klaus countered. "My father and I would take him on walks together. They're some of the happiest memories from my childhood."

"Like I said, this seems to be more about your needs than theirs."

"No, it's about making our sons happy and teaching them a life lesson."

"And in your view, they are both up to the task of taking care of this animal?"

"Yes! We already talked about it. Go and ask them yourself."

Reentering the living room, Klaus took the puppy from Christian and placed it on the floor next to the water while Gertie motioned for the boys to take a seat on the couch.

"I'll admit I'm not happy about this," Gertie said, peering over at Klaus. "Your father should have discussed this with me first. But that aside, I want you to know this puppy isn't a toy. You can't just put him away when you get tired of playing with him. He'll need to be fed, walked and cleaned up after every single day. And he'll be both of your responsibilities, is that clear?"

Udo Jörgen and Christian, with their blonde bowl cuts and solemn blue eyes, nodded.

"You'll have to promise," Gertie said, her heart softening at their gaze.

Twin smiles spread across their faces.

"We promise, Mama," they said, barely able to contain their mixture of glee and relief. Having cleared the hurdle of her approval, they leapt out of their seats and bounded over to the euphoric Rex who wagged his tail in eager anticipation and made a puddle on the floor.

A week later Gertie was called into her sons' school for an emergency conference in the headmaster's office.

"Have a seat, Frau Tischler," Herr Schneider said, waving the back of his hand to a set of chairs opposite his oversized desk and scarcely bothering to look up from the sheaf of papers that lay in front of him. "Miss Schmidt will join us shortly."

Christian, a miniature replica of his father with an equally inquisitive mind, had, as it turned out, pulled the fire alarm just as classes were about to begin after the mid-morning break. It was a moment when most of the children were moving from the playground to their assigned classrooms, so confusion broke out as teachers frantically tried to corral them into some semblance of order so they could evacuate the building. In the disarray, a seven-year-old girl named Greta had fallen off the concrete steps, and in the process gashed her forehead just above her right eye.

Despite the initial shock, Greta had required only a few stitches and was otherwise fine; however upon facing questioning from the rather intimidating Herr Peters, two first-grade boys were quick to pinpoint Christian as the offender.

Herr Schneider, the headmaster, had wasted no time. A trim and stern-looking man with graying temples, he had marched Christian to the glass-enclosed anteroom of his office and had forced him to wait on a wooden bench under the strict scrutiny of his secretary.

As soon as Gertie had arrived, the secretary had jumped to her feet and shuffled both mother and son with exaggerated urgency into the headmaster's office.

Gertie had scarcely managed to catch a glimpse of Christian, before the steel edge of Herr Schneider's concentration made it clear it was better not to say anything just yet. Two minutes later, his teacher entered the room prompting Herr Schneider, with visible hesitance, to lay his reading aside.

"Now, Christian," he began, resting his elbows on the desk and touching his fingers lightly together. The boy looked up for a moment. "I think you know why you've been called into my office. Would you care to tell us why?"

"I pulled the fire alarm," Christian said, in a barely audible tone. He attempted a sidelong glance at his mother, but seeing her grim demeanor, he cast his eyes back down again.

"I appreciate your honesty, boy, now please wait outside again until I've finished talking with your mother and Miss Schmidt."

Sensing the magnitude of his transgression and the uncertain punishment that was sure to follow, Christian delayed in getting up from his seat, and then with a wary step, walked toward the door. Before exiting, he turned toward his mother with pleading eyes.

Gertie, with lips pursed, refused to look at him.

"Frau Tischler," Herr Schneider paused, as if waiting to garner her full attention. "I thought it best if Miss Schmidt and I discussed the disciplinary steps with you prior to our taking action."

"Of course," Gertie said, eager to express her own dismay. "I would just like to say that I am deeply disappointed by what happened. My husband and I will certainly be addressing this with Christian as soon as we get home."

"As you should," was Herr Schneider's curt reply. "I understand you work outside the home, is that correct?"

"Yes," Gertie said, surprised by the sudden change of topic. She took a moment to adjust her seat in the otherwise confining armchair.

"And who takes care of the boys when you are away?"

Gertie looked back at him with narrowed eyes.

"Their grandmother stays with them while we are at work."

"Would that be *your* mother then?" Herr Schneider continued.

"No," Gertie said, finding it difficult to conceal her agitation. "My husband's mother. Is this somehow pertinent? I thought we were going to discuss the school's disciplinary action."

"As you can well imagine, Frau Tischler," Herr Schneider's voice began to crescendo with indignation, "tampering with the school's safety alarm is a serious infraction. Both Miss Schmidt and I agree that it is of vital importance that we convey the gravity of this offense in such a way that Christian will better understand the consequences of his actions."

"Of course," Gertie replied. "I'm in complete agreement. I work in air traffic control, so I'm well aware of—"

"That's the thing, you see. We deem it necessary to suspend Christian. But in order to do so we need to ascertain that he will have adequate parental supervision."

"As I said before, his grand—"

"Frau Tischler. I understand your situation is—how should I put it—uncommon. But I do think under the circumstances it would be best if *you* were to stay at home with him. We typically find that children respond best when the mother is available to monitor behavior."

"You don't seem to understand, Christian already has supervision at home, and—"

"I really do hope you will consider taking the time off, Frau Tischler. I can't emphasize enough how important it is for your son to fully comprehend the consequences, especially at such an impressionable age. Now, if we are all in agreement here, I'm afraid I *must* attend to my next appointment."

Gertie's mouth hinged open to protest, but Herr Schneider was already on his feet, followed hastily by Miss Schmidt who had not said a single word. Holding the door open for them, Herr Schneider did not once deign to look in Gertie's direction, even as she was forced to shuffle past him on her way out.

Gertie's internal fury escalated on the drive home as she replayed the conversation in her head. Fully aware that his mother was in no mood to hear his side of the story, Christian sat in the passenger seat, eyes glued to the dashboard.

Only once she had pulled into the drive, did Gertie dare to shift her attention toward him.

"You'll go directly to your room and stay there until I tell you otherwise.

Understood?"

"Yes, Mutti," the boy replied, before opening the passenger door of her blue Citrôen.

As they climbed up the steps, the front door flew open to reveal Klaus' mother fretting on the other side of the threshold.

"Here you are. I was wondering what was taking you so long."

She was wearing a flour-dusted apron, and from the entrance Gertie caught an annoying whiff of her freshly baked cinnamon cookies.

Gertie brushed past Elke and into the vestibule, a pouting Christian not far behind.

"He's going straight to his room."

"But, what happened?" Elke stammered as she watched her muted grandson walk past her and up the stairs at the end of the hall.

Gertie hung her scarf on one of the brass hooks lining the hallway.

"I don't have time for explanations. Where's Udo Jörgen?"

"He's in the living room with Rex—"

"I need you to take him to the playground."

"To the playground?"

"Yes, to the playground," Gertie said, looking at Elke as if she were a simpleton. "Right away, please."

Elke's plump legs stood firm as she shoved her fleshy fists into her hips.

"But what if he doesn't want to go?"

"For crying out loud, Elke, just tell him he has to go with you. Make something up."

"But—"

"I don't have time to explain things. Just, please, do what I've asked."

"Fine, but I'll want to know what this is all about later. When is Klaus coming home?"

Gertie sighed.

"He'll be home in thirty minutes."

Elke removed her apron with a disgruntled huff. Nonetheless, a few seconds later she opened the door of the living room, and with a trill of feigned propriety, called out to her youngest grandson.

"Udo, darling, would you come here for a moment?"

Once grandmother and son were both out of the house, Gertie gathered up the dog's toys and belongings, and stuffed them all into a canvas shopping bag. Slinging the tote over her shoulder, she picked up the puppy and placed him in a large, open-ended box from which he was still too small to crawl out.

She carried the unwieldy container back out to the car, all the while willing herself to ignore the pathetic high-pitched whimpers and the sound of tiny claws scratching against the cardboard. Placing her arm around the passenger seat, she backed out of the driveway, thus avoiding looking up at the small, stricken face peering out from the large square window upstairs.

This time it was Klaus who was pacing the hall when Gertie returned.

"Where's Rex?" he asked, his voice simmering with rage.

"I returned him to the pet store," Gertie replied, walking past him and into the kitchen.

Klaus watched in astonishment as she opened the pantry to get herself a beer.

"What do you mean, you returned him? Why the hell would you do that?"

"To teach Christian a lesson," Gertie said, spinning toward him. With her two thumbs, she flipped open the bottle top and took a long swig.

"I beg your pardon?" Klaus asked, shaking his head. "You do realize Rex is not just Christian's, right? He's Udo Jörgen's as well. And mine. Are you trying to punish us all? You can't do that."

"I most certainly can, and I have. I wasn't consulted about this dog of yours, and you know full well the boys aren't ready for such a responsibility. Christian just proved it today. He needs to realize what it means to lose something you love. Then maybe he'll learn some respect."

"This is crazy," Klaus said.

Gertie's jaw dropped.

"Crazy? His actions caused a little girl to be injured. She could have lost an eye!"

"But she didn't," Klaus said, sifting his words carefully through clenched teeth.

Gertie steeled her eyes.

"This isn't up for discussion. He needs to be punished."

"I wasn't consulted on this punishment."

"Consider us even, then," she replied, taking another gulp from her beer.

"You're making a big mistake," Klaus said, making an effort to lower his voice, "I'm warning you."

"Warning me?"

"This sort of thing has serious repercussions. I don't know if you understand—"

Now it was Gertie who shook her head in disbelief.

"I understand that our son doesn't respect the safety of others, and I'm correcting that in such a way that he will."

"And Udo Jörgen? What did he do to deserve this punishment of yours?"

"Udo Jörgen is too young, and both are far too spoiled by your mother."

"And you call *this* showing respect? That's laughable."

"I call it being responsible," Gertie countered before changing the subject. "Where are they?"

"Upstairs with my mother," Klaus said, echoing Christian's bitter tone from earlier in

the day.

"She should go home. And tell her there's no need for her to come back tomorrow."

Klaus' cheeks reddened with renewed alarm.

"What?"

Gertie's angered eyes drilled into him.

"Christian is suspended from school for the next three days, so *I'll* have to stay home with him."

"That's ridiculous! Why can't my mother—"

"So she can undo the lesson I'm trying to impart? No. From now on, I'm looking after them."

"That's absurd. Surely you're not blaming my mother—and what about your work?"

"You don't need to worry about that," Gertie said, steaming past him to get out of the kitchen. "I'll make the necessary arrangements."

Before Klaus could get another word in edgewise, she had slammed the front door shut and had roiled off into the darkness.

For the duration of his school suspension and well into the following week, Christian refused to speak to his mother.

Udo Jörgen, on the other hand, was inconsolable.

"Where is he?" he asked again and again over the dinner table the following night. "Why couldn't we keep him?"

Klaus glowered at Gertie refusing to say anything.

"As I told you before, the two of you aren't old enough to have a dog."

Elke, likewise, did not take well to her daughter-in-law's sudden termination of her duties and refused to come over to the house. On the night of Rex's banishment, she had expressed her outrage in full to Klaus upstairs—about the dog, about Gertie's cruel punishment and the gall of not allowing her to take care of her grandsons. This time, Klaus could not and would not come to Gertie's defense.

In the first three nights that followed, Klaus attempted to change Gertie's mind, at first with continued remonstrations and then through a desperate plea. "Think of what this experience might do to them!" But Gertie reacted to both tactics with a mute and hardened countenance. On the third night he mobilized his charm still hoping her rash anger would pass and that she would see she had acted too harshly.

Getting ready for bed in their upstairs bedroom, Klaus watched as Gertie undressed with mechanical precision, folding her clothes into a neat pile before pulling a sleeping gown over her head, somehow impervious to the effect her nakedness still had on him.

"Gertie," he said softly as he walked up behind her and placed his hand gently on her shoulder. He felt her flinch at his touch and with a reflex removed his hand.

"I hoped you might reconsider. For my sake."

Slowly she turned around to look at him. In her eyes he saw a foreboding reflection of fear that unsettled him. Still, he tried to reach out to her.

"What's wrong?" he asked.

"What's done is done," she replied, looking like a frightened child. "We should all just move on now."

With each endeavor frustrated, Klaus began to question Gertie's sanity and whether he really knew this woman who, right before his eyes, was estranging herself to him and to everyone else around her. He no longer felt he could touch her, her coldness toward him a growing barrier he could not surmount.

The Sunday before Christmas, after the boys had excused themselves from the breakfast table, Klaus finally lost his patience as Gertie chewed lifelessly on a morsel of black bread, her eyes fixed on an empty space in front of her.

"I can't allow you to do this. This has got to end. It's hurting our family."

"And you don't think it hurts me?" she asked, as she stood to clear the dishes. "That it's easy being cast as the fiend?"

Klaus took another sip from his coffee and watched her walk over to the sink.

"There is a way to remedy that."

"I see," she said, staring through the plate glass window at the neighbor's leafless maple tree. "So even you are convinced I'm a bad person, when all I'm trying to do is make sure that our sons learn the consequences of their actions."

"You've more than made your point, Gertie. Show a little mercy, for God's sake. It's Christmas!"

She turned to look over her shoulder, her hands still sunk in the soapy lather of the sink. "What are you suggesting I do, then?"

"You know very well what I think you should do. Allow the boys to have

Rex back. And while you're at it, apologize to my mother. Let her take care of them. You know it's the sensible thing to do, and I'm sure your boss isn't thrilled with the current arrangement either."

"So, you're suggesting I completely dismiss what happened."

"My God, Gertie, how heartless can you be? And how am I married to someone who would do this to her own family?"

Gertie snapped.

"If that's how you feel, perhaps you shouldn't be!"

"Don't do this," Klaus said, lowering his voice with a calculating coldness.

Gertie glared back at him in silence.

"Fine then," she replied with a vengeance. "Your mother or the dog."

"What?"

"You can choose. Your mother or the dog."

Klaus pushed back his chair with a jarring screech.

"You're out of your fucking mind," he said, jostling hard against her in the narrow passage between the table and the sink.

Her hands still in the water, Gertie returned to the dishes, washing each one in rapid succession, as a steady stream of tears flowed down her cheeks.

Christmas Eve turned into the wreck they had long been hurtling toward. Gertie refused to come downstairs to celebrate, and Klaus, seeing no point in staying in such a morose household, packed up the boys and went over to his mother's where he had kept Rex hidden this whole time.

It wasn't until the day after Christmas that Gertie managed to garner enough strength to go around and give the boys and Klaus their presents. As she stood outside of Elke's dark bungalow, weighed down with a bag full of gifts, she drew a deep breath and rang the bell. On the other side, she could hear her mother-in-law's clipped footsteps hitting against floor tile before the hefty wooden door hinged open.

"*Grüß Gott*," she said, maintaining her distance.

"I'm sorry, Elke. I don't know what came over me. Please accept my apology."

Her hand still braced against the doorjamb, Elke looked down at Gertie. "Won't you come in?" she declared after an excruciating moment of silence.

As they entered her mother-in-law's over-heated living room, Klaus and the boys turned to face them. Udo Jörgen, relieved to see Gertie, jumped up from his seat and bounded over to greet her.

"Merry Christmas, Mutti," he said, wrapping his small arms around her narrow hips. "Are any of those for me?"

"Yes, for all of you," she said, putting down the heavy parcel and tousling his freshly washed hair.

In that moment, the palpable antipathy in Klaus' eyes softened and began to dissipate.

After they each took turns opening their presents, Gertie and Klaus excused themselves to take a walk, leaving the boys to play with their new spoils.

For a while they both drifted along in silence beneath a row of linden trees covered in a thin layer of fresh, fallen snow.

"I know I overreacted," Gertie said, as Klaus reached up to grab a thin branch set to fall.

A light shower of snowflakes fell over her.

"And I don't mind if the dog comes over to play, but I would prefer if he stayed at your mother's."

Klaus sighed as he snapped the branch in two.

"That's fine," he said. "She prefers to have his company."

"Does she still want to watch the boys?"

"Of course. Does that mean you'll go back to working full time?"

"Yes. Right after the New Year."

"I'm glad to hear it. It would be pointless for you to sacrifice your career when my mother loves nothing more than looking after them."

They walked a little further.

"So, it's settled then?" Klaus asked. "We'll be able to put this behind us?"

Gertie stopped in her tracks as if to steady herself.

"Yes. I promise I won't talk of it ever again."

9

Caway - February 1999

A year after her arrival in Caway, Anja woke up from a week-long struggle with nausea to determine she was pregnant. She could not bring herself to believe it at first. Although she had stopped taking the pill one month earlier with the explicit intention of trying to conceive *sometime*, she had labored under the assumption that it would take much longer for the birth control to lose its effect. After all, she had been taking it since her early twenties, and didn't it take women her age much longer to conceive? If she was honest, a small part of her had not imagined it possible. Not this soon anyway.

She and Andreas were still at the height of their honeymoon period, and although they had briefly discussed the possibility of a child, she had not yet told him she had stopped using contraception.

She knew she needed to break the news to him, preferably before the dinner rush, but she felt suddenly unsure of how he might react, or how he would interpret her one-sided decision. Would he feel betrayed?

"Andreas," she said, raising her voice in agitation as she so often did when confronting uncomfortable situations. "I have to tell you something."

Andreas looked up from his post in the kitchen where he was chopping onions.

"What's the matter?" he asked, a wave of concern rolling across his face.

Moments before Anja had seemed calm—if not a little fatigued—as she rolled the restaurant's silverware in paper napkins, creating a neat stack on the Stammtisch.

"Can you just come here for a minute, please? It's important and can't wait."

"Okay," he said, wiping his hands on a dishtowel, and walking over to sit across from her. "What is it?"

Anja's sense of guilt mounted as she looked into Andreas' eyes, recognizing just how much this man trusted her, so different from her past experiences with live-in boyfriends.

"I have to know. Do you want to have a child with me or not?"

"What?" he asked, taken aback by her sudden sense of urgency.

"A few months ago, you said you would be happy to have a child with me. But did you mean it?"

"Anja, what's come over you? Why are you so upset? Did I do something?"

"Can you just answer the question, please?"

Andreas took a deep breath.

"A child. Well, if that's what you want, yes, of course."

"No, that's not what I'm asking. I'm asking if *you* want a child. Another one. With me."

With a mischievous grin he replied, "You know I'm always happy to try."

"I'm not joking here. Bringing a child into this world, well, it's no laughing matter."

"I'm not— never mind. Since I'm not saying it right, why don't you just tell me what's going on."

Anja threw up her arms.

"I'm pregnant, that's what's going on!"

"You're pregnant?"

"Yes," she replied, her body trembling like a leaf caught in a whirling breeze.

"Then why are you so upset, that's fantastic news!"

"Fantastic?"

"Yes, aren't you happy about it?"

Anja let out a loud sigh, releasing the pent-up tension in her body.

"I thought you'd be upset with me," she said, sniffling.

Andreas reached over to cradle her face with his hands, mirroring back the look of gratitude and love in her eyes.

"But can we afford it?" she asked, once the moment had passed. "My paintings haven't been selling as well, and with a baby to take care of, well, I don't know how much time I'll have to paint on top of everything else."

Moving halfway across the world, Anja had, in many ways, lost her connection to the art world. While Patrice had made good on the sale of her initial set of Central American paintings, his health had begun to fail in recent months, and the interim gallery director, Pascal, was not particularly responsive to her newest proposal. Not that Anja felt terribly compelled to continue her association with *La Sauvage Moderne.* Pascal had been a contemporary of hers in art school and someone with whom she shared very little, if anything, in common. Having settled into her new life in Caway with only a modest amount of savings to cover emergencies, she had subsequently formed more convincing arguments for helping out with the restaurant and the *cabinas* than to sit down and paint for long stretches of time.

Andreas chuckled.

"Can we afford it. What kind of question is that? Life here is not as complicated as the one you left behind, Anja. All we need are some diapers and a good hammock."

"So, you really want this?"

"Yes," he laughed. "Our child is growing in your belly, what more is there to discuss? I'll have to call *Mutti* in the morning to tell her. She'll be knitting little socks before the week is out. And no more coffee for you," he added, taking the cup with him as he walked back toward the kitchen. "It's no good for the baby."

Contrary to Anja's hopes and fantasies, it was a pregnancy plagued with severe morning sickness and exacerbated by increased levels of water retention fueled by the tropical heat and humidity. At first, she tried to ignore just how horrible it made her feel, "It's nothing to worry about," she found herself saying to Andreas over and over again, but the denial just added to her already increasing apprehension that something was not quite right. It wasn't until the seventh month, however, that she developed the more detectable symptoms of preeclampsia attributable to her advanced maternal age and predisposition to high blood pressure.

Though her symptoms were not severe, since the condition posed a potential threat to both baby and mother, she was confined by doctor's order to monitored bed rest at the nearby clinic in Edge Creek. The rural facility was outfitted with a small ward for those ill enough to require inpatient observation but not in such dire condition to merit the long-distance transfer to the hospital in Limón.

Anja and Andreas' financial situation necessitated keeping the cabinas and restaurant open for business, and for this reason Anja found the bed rest particularly burdensome since Andreas could not visit her as often as she would have liked. When she wasn't suffering from headaches, she occupied herself with reading, but she much preferred having visitors. She begged Andreas to send friends and acquaintances, anyone who could stop by and spare a few minutes to distract her from the exasperating monotony of lying in bed all day and night. For the most part, neighbors were eager to comply, and as a happy consequence, she was able to forge much deeper bonds of friendship with people she had only known superficially up to that point.

The one person she was truly surprised to see, however, was Gertie who one day arrived at the tail end of the afternoon visiting hours.

"Gertie," Anja said, glancing up from a novel to find her visitor looming over the foot of the bed. "What a surprise."

"I don't want to disturb you," she said. "It's just that Andreas—"

"You're not disturbing me at all," Anja said, gesturing to a metal folding chair sandwiched between the bed and the window frame. "Please, take a seat."

Gertie appraised the chair skeptically then leaned her back against the window sill.

"I brought you some books I've finished," she said, unpacking the bulky canvas bag hanging from her shoulder.

"Thank you. I can't seem to get enough to read in here. If it's legible and on paper, I've been devouring it."

Gertie narrowed her gaze.

"Are they taking good care of you?"

Anja's face was flushed as if she had sat in the sauna too long despite the hypnotic hum of the fans above her.

"They check in on me a lot, try to make me comfortable. Overall, I can't complain. Pregnancy in the tropics isn't something I'd wish on anyone, especially at my age. I keep fantasizing about snowstorms and cold gusts of wind," she added with a laugh.

Anja reached across the bedside table for a glass of water sitting next to an ice-filled pitcher sweating out cold beads of inviting moisture.

"Are you thirsty?"

"I can't imagine not getting up," Gertie said, ignoring her question. "When I was pregnant, I only slept a few hours at a time. Lying still was impossible. I had to get up and walk, especially toward the end."

"I only wish I could," Anja said, looking over the rim of her glass. "I didn't realize you had a child. You've never mentioned it."

"Two boys," she said, pursing her wrinkled lips together.

"Where are they now? In Germany?"

"Yes."

Gertie often resembled a pillar of ice, on the surface transparent yet at the same time impenetrable. Given her terse response, Anja was at a loss as to what to say next. She did not want to offend her by prying too much, but at the same time she was curious about this maternal side she had not thought possible.

"It must be difficult to be so far away from them."

"Not really. They're both grown and making their way in the world. As it should be."

"Do they come to visit?"

Gertie turned her gaze out the window.

"They're far too busy with their lives to travel this far. Plus, they're not fond of the heat."

"Still, you must miss seeing them."

Gertie spun her head and glared at Anja.

"Letting go is part of the process of parenting. The earlier the better. You'll see."

Not wanting to debate her, Anja changed the subject.

"Do you know Marco very well?"

Marco was Andreas' son from his first marriage. Anja had only seen him a handful of times so far and almost always in the company of his mother or father. He was a courteous boy but tended not to say much in front of her.

"Well enough, I suppose," Gertie said, wrinkling her nose at the strong scent of disinfectant wafting through the air. "He was just a little boy when I arrived. I don't see that much of him now. Just when he visits."

"Do you think it will be difficult for him to adjust to another sibling?"

"I don't think so. Ticos are used to big families. Lots of brothers and sisters and cousins around. They love children."

She spoke this last sentence so defiantly Anja wondered if she thought Europeans did not.

"Well, I don't see myself having another baby after this, so I hope they get along."

"It's a big age difference."

Anja looked down at her swollen belly.

"Yes, ten years. We'll have to rely on the local children to play with this one."

"Well, there are plenty around," Gertie said, looking agitated. "Do you need anything? I'm off to the store to buy some cigarettes."

"No, I'm fine, thank you. But please feel free to stop by again. I could use the company."

In lieu of a wave, Gertie raised her hand as she turned to walk away.

"You won't be here that much longer. They do eventually come out."

Daniel Luís Freyer took his first breath at 4:10 the following morning after the doctor concluded that Anja's blood pressure was far too high to keep her at the clinic a minute longer. After an emergency transfer to Limón, the one-month premature baby was delivered via Caesarian section. Despite the difficult birth and his early arrival, Daniel was quick to stabilize and determined to be in perfect health. Anja, too—a fear of progressing eclampsia notwithstanding—soon regained her health and began to nurse the child who in the next few days put on the required weight before mother and son were allowed to finally go home.

Andreas, meanwhile, had constructed a nursery in the large open area of their apartment. After helping them both up the stairs, he showed off the wooden basinet he had also carved and placed in the center of the room.

"It's absolutely beautiful," Anja said, overwhelmed.

As she walked back toward their bed to lie down and nurse, she noticed a large cardboard box closed up with the words "Anja's paint supplies" scrawled across the top. She felt an almost imperceptible twinge of loss but looking down at Daniel puckering his lips in greedy anticipation, the fleeting emotion soon vanished.

For the first three months, Hyacinth—who continued to work the evening shifts—moved into the small cabina attached to the main building. While she helped Andreas attend to the guests in the mornings, her primary role was to help initiate Anja into the nuances of baby care, having served as both a midwife and doula for many of the local women.

Gertie, too, pitched in by volunteering to attend to the laundry that now required even more vigilant attention, particularly when one had to rely on the sun to keep the mildew away. The family did not own an extensive wardrobe, and the cloth diapers, too, needed continuous rinsing and washing in order for enough to be on hand, day to day, hour to hour, especially in the tropics where "dry" was a relative term.

The four of them, all in all, worked well together. That they could manage this challenge with so little gave Anja newfound respect for her adopted community, some of whom would stop by unannounced with plates of coconut rice or stew and for a chance to hold and fuss over the blonde-and-brown-eyed addition to Caway.

Seeing Gertie smile and coo over Daniel—in and of itself a remarkable transformation to behold—Anja found a place for Gertie in her growing affection, albeit one that still tended to rub together and blister at times.

The weeks and years after Daniel's birth charged past without respite. Each day was filled with child-rearing in addition to the fluctuating needs and desires of a successive wave of tourists. Out of necessity, Anja learned to rely more on the help of others just as she in turn did her best to provide for the impromptu needs of friends and neighbors. Somehow not a waking moment passed by unattended and alone.

Unlike the more Americanized Pacific coast, Caribbean tourism was small, family run, and often operated at minimal profit, if any. What their rustic community lacked in hard cash they would often make up by lending a hand. Of course, petty, competitive squabbles would arise—some lingering longer than others—but on the rare occasion when a severe storm or flood hit leaving everyone in the lurch, neighbors would find a way to set aside day to day differences and pool whatever resources were needed to clear the roads, fix the bridges or gain access to running water again. The primary currency in Caway—at times unspoken—was one of providing favors in kind.

After Daniel turned five, the director of the private international school up the road from *Quixote's* approached Anja and asked her if she would volunteer to further develop the arts program. The Integral School, as it was called, had been established a few years back by a Swedish expat, and was hard-pressed to meet the growing demand for a more rigorous curriculum better suited to multi-lingual proficiency.

"We don't need anything too elaborate," the director assured Anja, "but enough to give the students a basic grounding in the arts and broaden their understanding beyond what they might otherwise encounter here in Caway. We could even build in a field trip to the art museum in San José if you like."

Anja leapt at the opportunity. After all, when was the last time she had even thought about painting? For a moment she imagined her neglected watercolors, still tucked away in an unopened box gathering dust beneath her bedside, the pigments separating, hardening and cracking into petrified relics. Was this the sign she had been waiting for to revive her own waning practice? She allowed herself to fantasize for a few moments before her more pragmatic reasoning came back to the fore: whatever her involvement and contribution, *this* was the opportunity to ensure Daniel's chances at enrollment, even if it meant pinching every *céntimo* they had, and then some, to make sure he could attend. Soon enough, her late mornings were scheduled with preparatory meetings, requiring her to seek out a babysitter and one preferably free of charge.

Having already played the role of eccentric auntie throughout Daniel's toddlerhood, Gertie was the most obvious choice. Whether Anja liked to admit it or not, Gertie seemed to enjoy spending time with her son, going out for walks along the beach or watching him from a distance as he played in the small, makeshift children's area Anja had carved out of the restaurant's main dining room. As long as Gertie had something to read and her beer and cigarettes close at hand, her needs were more than satisfied.

It was during one of these caretaking sessions that Gertie introduced Daniel to the game of Ringer. She had purchased a bag of marbles on her last bus trip to Limón and was eager to show him the basics. Taking him out in front of the restaurant, not far from the road, she drew a circle with a stick on a smooth patch of dry, sandy dirt. As Gertie knelt in front of Daniel explaining the rules and showing him how to flick the marble forward with his thumb, Ms. Adina, a heavy-set woman and one of the matrons of Caway, ambled up with Treven. Eleven years old but already tall and muscular for his age, he walked a few paces behind his grandmother, weighed down by the heft and volume of their groceries.

"Irie, Ms. Gertie, what you got there?" Ms. Adina said, in her sweet, out-of-breath voice as she stopped in the shade of the canopied archway to look down at them.

In her heavy, German-accented English, Gertie replied, "I'm showing Daniel to play Ringer."

Ms. Adina furrowed her large, expressive brow.

"What's that now?"

"A marbles game, grandmother," Treven said, placing the heavy bags down on the ground and holding his hand out to Daniel in expectation. "Let me try."

Ms. Adina slapped the back of Treven's head. Her strength had diminished with age, so the jolt landed more as an embarrassment than a wallop.

"Where are your manners?"

Treven rephrased his request in a more modest tone.

"I'm sorry. May I play with you?"

"Of course," Gertie said, picking up the large onionskin shooter and handing it to him.

Treven smiled to himself as he bent down over the circle.

"This sure is a nice one."

"It was a gift from a school friend. Now watch, Daniel. See how he holds it with the crook of his finger?"

Treven shot the marble, and they all watched in silence as one of the targets rolled a few inches past the perimeter of the circle leaving the shooter well within its confines.

"Ja," Gertie cried. "Just like that."

Ms. Adina harrumphed and shook the halo of white hair surrounding her plump, caramel face that was peppered here and there with tiny brown moles.

Reluctant, Gertie stood up and smoothed out the creases of her wrinkled sundress.

"That was a beautiful memorial for Mr. Hudson," she said, attempting to make small talk.

"Yes, that's right," Ms. Adina said, looking Gertie over with an approving smile, happier to be talking about adult matters instead of some foolish boys' game. "You were there, too."

"Is that typical for funerals?" Gertie asked, picturing the flower-laced canoes floating by like a royal procession down Horner's Creek. Just behind it a much larger fishing boat had traveled all the way from Limón carrying Mr. Hudson's casket covered in an elaborate arrangement of hydrangeas and lilies.

"For the fisherman, yes," Ms. Adina replied. "But Ole Mr. Hudson, he was special, you see. That's why so many boats come and pay their respect."

"I've never seen anything like it. All those boats floating, so quiet and peaceful and everyone standing on the riverbank."

Ms. Adina nodded her head in remembrance.

"He restin' now, God bless. His days of hard work are behind him."

She spoke this last sentence as if she, too, awaited the moment when her days of toil would end.

"You knew him well?"

"Everyone in Caway know Ole Mr. Hudson. He looked after folk. Always bringin' medicines and school things back from Limón. He was always findin' ways to help, Mr. Hudson."

"And his family?"

"He was a widower. His Mary died young with yellow fever after she visited her people in Panama. Left him three boys, and he took good care of them. Teach them to fish. They all fishermen, now. Make them father proud."

"Not many like him," Gertie said, looking out across the dirt road in the direction of the sea where she could hear the steady, soothing sound of the waves breaking against the coral rock. She couldn't see the ocean from where they stood because of the hedgerow and the seven-foot wooden gates the newest ecolodge had erected a couple of years back, but she could still picture the view. The Colombian owners seemed unconcerned that the lodge was in violation of the fifty-meter maritime rule, but no matter. This was Caway, and no one governing in the Central Valley seemed to care too much about the goings-on of this backwater hamlet.

"Me and Mr. Hudson—" Ms. Adina chuckled, the skin of her cheeks quaking in happy recollection. "We have some good times together. My man, he died young, too, you see, workin' for them *bananeros*. The plantations was all the way up the Star River, and I didn't see too much of him after that. I had the children here. But I always set a place for Mr. Hudson and his boys when they come back from fishin'. I make a coconut stew so good, well, you don't want to be eatin' anything else after that!"

"I can only imagine," Gertie said.

Despite her many years in Caway, Gertie still found the Caribbean fare too flavorful for her taste. Not to mention the endless use of rice and beans. She had grown up on potatoes and meat and had not developed much of a palate beyond that.

"And how is Ms. Anja?" Ms. Adina asked. "She's lucky to have herself a good man. Hard workin', that Andreas."

Gertie raised her eyebrows.

"Busy as ever," she said. "That woman wouldn't know to keep still if she wanted. Always getting her nose stuck somewhere."

"Like the Bible say, idle hands are the devil's play," Ms. Adina countered. "We best be goin' now, Tre."

"Just one more go, grandmother, please?"

Ms. Adina shook a thick, cracked forefinger his way.

"I'm not tellin' you twice."

"You can come back and play some other time," Gertie said, as she watched Treven continue to stare at the colorful glass marbles lying on the ground.

He nodded to her in polite acknowledgment but with a distanced reservation.

Gertie started to place an awkward hand on Treven's shoulder as he picked up the heavy groceries again, but then thought better of it.

"Daniel will want to play with someone other than me," she added. "Once he learns how to play the game as well as you."

When Anja returned from her meeting, Gertie was perched near the children's table, drinking a Pilsen and immersed in a crossword as Daniel constructed a fort out of large and discolored Lego blocks.

"I'm sorry I'm so late," Anja said, putting her purse on the Stammtisch and walking over to her son. "We completely lost track of time."

"No matter," Gertie said, not bothering to look up.

Anja kissed the top of Daniel's head before admiring his handy work.

"And he wasn't too much trouble?"

Gertie bulged her eyes out at the puzzle in front of her.

"He's no trouble at all," she replied.

"He'll start school next year, so you'll have your days back to yourself soon enough. I promise."

"I've already said it's no trouble. No use you pretending otherwise. False sentiment doesn't suit you, Anja."

"False sentiment don't be ridiculous. I was just trying to be thoughtful of your time!"

Gertie stood up and stared at her like a bull whose territory was under imminent threat.

"All I have is time. And I don't need your help looking after it."

10

Kirchheim / Munich - 1983

In the New Year, Gertie threw herself into her work, rarely returning home before seven in the evening, long after Klaus had relieved his mother of the childcare responsibilities. Klaus had assumed that at some point Gertie would reach out to him again. That she would not—*could not*—choose to exile herself from his touch for the long term.

All these years—despite the stress of work and children and his mother's increased presence in their lives— they had managed to keep their sexual relationship alive, healthy. In fact, it was their deep, physical intimacy that had made it possible for Klaus to overlook his wife's aloof and idiosyncratic tendencies. Seen through the kaleidoscope of sex, he had found her quirkiness endearing, and on its own, quite titillating in that he alone was privy to this other side of her that she kept hidden away from everyone else. But the Rex incident had inexplicably changed things, so much so that she had seemingly lost all interest in being touched, let alone having sex. Yet something inside him no longer dared approach her.

In front of the boys they each put up a tolerable pretense, but once their sons had gone to bed, Klaus would invariably make a bee line for his study, leaving Gertie to tidy up the kitchen in her own silence. Afterwards, she would go into the living room to read, sometimes well into the night, until she could no longer keep her eyes open and at which time a vague and resigned sense of duty would compel her to climb the stairs and crawl into the bed beside him, noiseless as a mouse.

Simone stopped in her tracks on the pedestrian walkway near *Marienplatz*.

"Klaus Tischler. My God, it's been ages! How are you?"

It was the first, sun-drenched afternoon in March, and Klaus was in Munich running errands for the Easter weekend.

"Simone. You're looking good. As always."

"You're not looking so bad yourself," she replied, jutting out her hip. "A bit preoccupied, perhaps."

Klaus' eyes stopped to linger for a moment on the snug fit of her blue-gray satin blouse.

"Yes. Too much work I'm afraid."

"How about a drink?" she offered, "Do you have time? I'd love to hear what you've been up to all these years, and my local pub is just around the corner."

"I was just heading back to the lab." he said, stepping back on a raised cobblestone and losing his footing. His face flushed with embarrassment.

"*Ach*, why the hell not," he said, recovering his balance. "It's not every day you run into an old friend, is it?"

"Cheers to that," Simone said. She hooked her arm beneath his and led him toward a side street with comparably little foot traffic. "A little *Gemütlichkeit* will do us both good."

They turned into the entrance of a cavernous, early twentieth century building and walked through until they reached an open-air courtyard in the back. Turning right, they veered down a narrow stairwell with an elaborate wrought-iron railing. At the bottom, in the shadows of a recessed archway, they encountered a black door with art nouveau lettering that announced their arrival at *Cabaret*.

Inside, the dark parlor was furnished like a 1920s speakeasy, sparse except for an array of whiskey barrel tables that lay scattered across the low-ceilinged space. The lounge was empty at this hour apart from two men who sat steeped in animated conversation near the small stage crammed like an afterthought in the back.

Simone walked with purpose toward the bar where a young, dark-haired attendant stood polishing glasses in a tuxedo vest and tie, the forearms of his white, pressed shirt rolled up with meticulous care.

"Hallo *Kätzchen*," he smiled.

"*Grüss dich*, Markus" Simone said, leaning over the counter to kiss him on the cheek.

"The usual, I presume?"

"Yes. And whatever Klaus here is having."

"A *Paulaner*," Klaus said, avoiding the bartender's eyes.

Markus tipped his chin down in prim acknowledgment.

"With pleasure."

Simone pulled a pack of cigarettes from her purse and offered Klaus one.

In response, Klaus grabbed a box of matches from the counter.

With a confident flourish he struck one before leaning into the fragrant halo surrounding Simone and watched as the hissing flame lit up her face with an inviting glow. By the time they had each taken their first intoxicating drag, their drinks stood ready and waiting in front of them.

Grabbing her wine glass, Simone pivoted away from the bar and walked toward a nearby table. Taking a seat and crossing her long legs encased in well-fitting designer jeans, she busied herself with the ashtray until Klaus made his way to sit beside her.

"So, tell me, Klaus, where have you been hiding yourself these days?"

He recounted the chronology of his life since they had last seen each other. Simone, through the grapevine of mutual friends, had heard about his marriage to Gertie, but not about their sons or their subsequent move to Kirchheim.

"Somehow, we've managed to make it work," Klaus said, before finishing his beer. "But it hasn't been easy."

"Better you than me," Simone smiled. "As you know, I'm not cut out for that lifestyle."

"And you? What's keeping you busy besides the freewheeling, single life?"

"Continuing my life's calling, of course. Right now, I'm working a freelance gig for *EMMA*, covering the social welfare beat."

"Emma?" Klaus asked, furrowing his brow.

"Short for emancipation. I'm writing on reproductive rights. Women in the workplace, that sort of thing."

"So, let me ask you this. What about men's liberation?"

Simone raised one of her shapely brows making it that much harder to deny the stunning allure of her presence.

"And what do you mean by that?"

"You place so much emphasis on the social oppression of women. What about cases where the opposite is true?"

Simone laughed.

"Now, now Klaus. While I'm sure such cases do exist—and it's without a doubt a component of the capitalist class structure as a whole—it's still mostly women who suffer at the hands of the existing patriarchy, not the other way around. There's no denying that."

Having finished her drink, she glanced over at Markus and with a knowing smile, lifted two fingers to indicate another round.

Klaus shook his head.

"I'm not so sure about that."

She peered into his eyes as if trying to divine a secret.

"Are you trying to tell me something?"

"No," he scoffed, circling the rim of his glass. "Of course not. It's just that you make it sound so extreme. As if a man's point of view doesn't matter."

"What's really bothering you, Klaus? You seem inordinately agitated by all of this."

He stalled for a few seconds, unsure whether to continue or not.

"Things between me and Gertie are strained at the moment. I'm seeing a side to her that quite frankly concerns me."

"She's an odd one, alright," Simone said, leaning back in her chair and recrossing her legs. "But you knew that already."

Klaus shook his head.

"It's not her quirks that bother me. It's the way she behaves toward the boys. And lately, toward me."

"And how's that?"

"She's not affectionate. It's like the roles are somehow reversed, and I have to play the nurturer."

"That's not such a bad thing, if you ask me. It's good for men to get in touch with their feminine side. It helps to balance things out."

"Feminine side? I wouldn't say *that*. Not that I have a problem with affection. What I do have a problem with is Gertie's coldness and cruelty. We haven't had sex for months, and I think she's withholding as a—"

Klaus cut himself off not wanting to reveal too much of what had happened over Christmas, but he could feel the anger rise up in him again as he replayed the memory in his mind.

"Well, it's like she's punishing me."

Sensing the rawness of his emotions, Simone put her hand over his.

"Sometimes the past repeats itself," she said, with a softness he had not counted on but that felt like a cushion for his aching confidence.

"Gertie carries a heavy burden, Klaus. One she refuses to discuss. But sadly, she's not the type to seek out help. I think you know that."

Klaus' eyes bored into hers, recalling that Simone had known his wife much better than he had ever cared to admit. Their one night together had obscured the part she had played in Gertie's life beyond what had transpired at the party.

"Yeah. I think you're right about that."

"I never had a chance to say anything to you after that night," Simone said, stroking the back of his hand. "I realize I didn't handle the situation well, but I did very much enjoy your company. Much more than I would have cared to admit."

"Me, too," Klaus said, taking her hand between both of his. "Me, too."

Klaus and Simone's love affair began casually enough. After finishing their drinks in *Cabaret*, she had led him back to her apartment, an unspoken invitation.

"So, what happens now?" he asked after they slept together.

"What do you mean?" she said, propping herself up on her elbow, her tousled blonde hair cascading down her chest.

"I'm married. I shouldn't be here."

Simone laughed.

"Stop giving yourself such a hard time. It was only a fuck, and a good one at that."

Having received the affirmation he sought, Klaus allowed himself to absorb the full form of her naked body, the one she had allowed him to take without inhibition for the last hour and a half.

"I'd like to see you again," he said, reaching for her hand.

"I don't see why not," she replied, looking amused. "At least now you know where to find me."

Stepping into the dusk outside her apartment building, Klaus wondered briefly whether he would see Simone again. He could already feel a regretful sense of déjà vu weighing him down, yet unlike their one-night stand so many years ago, where he had drunk enough to feign a convincing degree of incapacitation and ignorance, he now felt more sober than ever, and happily so. In between the flashes of guilt, he would hit the replay button in his head, making him for a giddy instance want to go back to Simone's for more.

In the past, he had felt truly awful about his betrayal of Gertie. She was the only woman he had met who not only engaged his scientific mind but also satisfied his sexual cravings without the frustrating and time-consuming games that were usually involved in the pursuit of the opposite sex. What he had so loved about Gertie was her easy relinquishment of any pretense. He had been her first, and with that had come a fierce loyalty and a natural and willing inclination to explore one another's bodies devoid of the usual complexities he had encountered with women far more experienced. With Gertie it was as if he had won the lottery. In that way, her sudden frigidity had felt like a punch in the face, a brutal punishment in light of the physical closeness they had cultivated over the years.

But even more maddening was the fact that she did not seem to miss their sex life at all. Not one bit. It was as if she had turned off a switch inside herself, and her lack of need in this regard angered him even more, propelling him to rationalize his actions and come up with excuses for why he would need to go to Munich more often. After all, she had known all along how important sex was to him.

Still, the guilt was not as easily dissipated as all that. There were the boys to consider, and of course, his mother, who, despite her dislike of Gertie, still believed wholeheartedly in the sanctity of marriage through thick and thin. While he and Gertie did not share Elke's religious beliefs or her piety, he had absorbed enough of his mother's ethics to know he was treading on dangerous ground.

And yet, what about Gertie's deceit? Couldn't he argue that she had also acted unfaithfully? Had she not, in her own way, through her silence and avoidance, first rejected him?

He tried to recall when he had last seen that fearful look in her eye, the one she had given him when he tried to reach out to her in their bedroom. It had been just a few weeks before she had given birth to Christian, and he had found her in the nursery, sitting alone in the rocking chair, crying silently.

"I don't think I can do this," she had confessed as he knelt down beside her, placing a hand on the fullness of her belly. He had tried to comfort her, but his words only agitated her more, so that the panic in her eyes turned to anger, and she began to lash out at him with her fists.

"You don't understand this. You'll never understand!"

Through the shock of hearing the piercing anguish in her voice, he had allowed her to keep hitting him, until eventually her energy failed her, and she was left sobbing uncontrollably in his arms.

That night he had carried her to their bed, where she had lain the next two days as if in a fugue. He had cared for her like a sick child, bringing her soup and tea, until eventually, the emotional fever broke, and she came back to him in more recognizable form.

She had later apologized, claiming she did not know what had gotten into her and making him promise that they would not speak of it again. He had nodded his head in agreement, but his reservations regarding her unusual behavior did not dissipate until after Christian was born, and she had taken to caring for the newborn like a natural, smiling and cooing, as if motherhood was the most wonderful thing in the world.

Klaus had almost forgotten the incident, until the day six-year-old Christian, on Elke's birthday, opened the back door of their sedan while they were driving up to Oberammergau along a curving, mountainous road.

Moments before, Gertie, who was seated in the back seat with their sons, had chastised Christian for interrupting her as she was trying to teach Udo Jörgen how to count with his fingers. Unhappy that his brother was getting all her attention, he began to play with the door lock, flipping it up and down, until Gertie told him to stop. In a show of obstinacy, he had then reached for the handle, and gleefully pushed the door open.

Panicked, Gertie had thrown herself over the boys.

"Christian, what the hell do you think you're doing? Pull over, Klaus!"

Once Klaus had stopped the car and given his son a firm scolding by the side of the road, he went over to soothe Gertie who had worked herself into a shivering frenzy.

"Are you alright?" he had asked.

"Why did he do it? Why?"

"Boys test limits, but I can assure you, he won't be doing it again."

"Limits? But he could have died!"

"But he didn't. He's fine, Gertie. There's no need to panic."

She had not had another incident until Christian pulled the fire alarm at school, and as far as Klaus was concerned, this time it had sent her reeling to the point of losing all reasonable control. In the months that had followed, however, she had somehow managed to rein it back in again, to hide it under that cool and impenetrable mask of hers, where no one else could reach her, not even him.

While Klaus felt guilty about the fact he was betraying Gertie, he justified his actions by telling himself that he could not go the rest of his life without sex, and as far as he was concerned, this was all he and Simone had between them.

But as they began to meet, first once a week, and then twice, and by the beginning of the summer as often as he could manage, it became clear to him that he and Simone were becoming much more to one another. He was finding it more difficult to be apart from her, their discussions regarding the importance of personal freedoms grew more engrossing and more meaningful over time.

Simone had touched something deep within him. Something he had always fought hard to ignore through his deliberate attempts to live up to what was expected of him, to make good on his potential, as his mother and father had always told him, not only as a husband and a father, but as a worthy contributor to the sciences, and therefore to society as a whole. That was the youthful aspiration he had shared with Gertie, the bond that had brought them together.

But having gotten that much closer to nearing the finish line and of reaching the youthful goals they had set, the feelings that arose in him now were not those of equanimity and contentment, but rather of failure and dissatisfaction.

By all counts he and Gertie were at the forefront of what was meant by success in the twentieth century. They had a comfortable home, two children, two cars, and two unassailable career paths that were only now beginning to flourish. Together, they had achieved far more than many of their peers. Yet, he felt empty inside, his marriage a farce in terms of the happiness it was meant to provide him, and the woman he had fallen in love with was now a complete stranger.

Running into Simone again, the part of him that was slowly perishing was reawakened and given new life, not just physically, but mentally and emotionally. He began to seriously consider whether Simone's theories were right after all, that the institution of marriage was indeed just a form of self-inflicted bondage, slowly suffocating the life of its hosts in order to serve the so-called greater good and to ensure the next generation of compliant citizenry.

"We need to talk," Klaus said, as he took a seat beside Gertie on one of the cushioned lawn chairs in their backyard. He had just dropped the boys off at Elke's for their Friday night sleepover, and not a moment too soon since the transition to fall was bringing on one of his seasonal migraines.

Gertie slowly lowered her book. Unlike him, she was immune to nature's antagonism, and was lost in some fiction-induced trance.

"Do we?" she asked. "I'd almost forgotten what that was like."

"We can't go on like this," he said.

She turned her head toward him, meeting his gaze with an obstinate silence.

"It isn't working, this marriage of ours."

"So, what do you propose?" she asked.

"A separation. I'll move in with my mother that way it won't change my involvement with the boys."

"I see," Gertie said, sounding deceptively calm. "And Simone? What role will she play in their lives?"

Klaus blushed like a boy caught stealing from his mother's purse.

"What?"

"Did you really think I didn't know?" Gertie asked. "She made the mistake of calling here a while back. And your clothes reek of her perfume."

"Why didn't you say anything?"

"Because I thought it would pass."

Klaus doubled over in his seat, cradling the top of his head.

"Anyway, you haven't answered my question," Gertie said, ignoring his dramatics. "As their mother, I have every right to know."

"For Christ's sake, it's not like I've introduced them!"

"Good. That would have been premature."

"And what's that supposed to mean?"

Instead of answering, Gertie locked her eyes on the sky above them awash in a vivid spectrum of bright oranges and dark, violet clouds.

Klaus looked over at her and then stood up to go.

"We can meet tomorrow to discuss the arrangements," he sighed. "For now, I'll just pack a few things and go."

"And what will we tell the boys?" Gertie asked, her voice quivering. "You haven't told them yet, have you?"

Klaus turned toward her again.

"No, of course not." The fatigue in his voice was palpable. "I wouldn't do that to you."

That night, unable to bear the constricting emptiness of their home let alone sleep, Gertie camped out in the yard, looking up at the stars and contemplating what had just happened to her. She knew she still loved Klaus—could not conceive of loving anyone else—yet she was incapable of imagining there might be a way to win him back.

By the time Gertie had deciphered his transgression, the summer break had already begun. Klaus had claimed he was far too busy with an important experiment to go on their usual vacation, so during her scheduled time off, Gertie had made a special effort to organize day-long trips for the boys, taking them on swimming excursions to the nearby lakes and recreation areas. The summer weather had proved spectacular, and as far as she could tell, the boys were unaware of the significant change that had taken place. Their exuberant reports to their father each night at the dinner table helped alter the prevailing mood between them, leading Gertie to believe that this would help Klaus see she was not such a bad mother after all, and that the current impasse between them could likewise be overcome. She continued to hold out hope that Klaus' fling with Simone would fizzle out. That she would grow tired of him—as she had of so many of her lovers in the past—and that it would just be a matter of time until he came to his senses and rejoined his family.

Gertie had not in any serious way considered the affair could end their marriage. She had assumed instead that this was just a rough patch, that they would eventually find a way through it. Now she faced the real possibility that a separation would lead to divorce, a thought that filled her not only with dread but a forlorn panic.

The following afternoon Klaus and Gertie sat down across the kitchen table from one another while Christian and Udo Jörgen played in the yard with Rex.

To Gertie's relief, Klaus had not spent the night at his mother's which no doubt would have peaked Elke's curiosity and tipped off the boys. As things stood, Gertie preferred breaking the news to their sons with some semblance of unity and restraint.

Gertie was determined to take the high road and to do everything possible to keep the peace and thus minimize the toll on their sons' lives. Klaus, having braced himself for the opposite reaction, was shocked by her ready compliance and her seeming lack of anger which in turn helped to soften his own tone and response.

They agreed that the least amount of change to the routine might lessen the blow for the boys. This meant allowing Elke to continue caring for them at the house, where Klaus would visit them in the late afternoon prior to Gertie's return from the office. The weekends would be split, meaning the boys would sleep over at Elke's on Friday—already a common occurrence—and every other Saturday night, returning home on Sunday morning to allow Gertie to have a full day with them. Vacation times would be negotiated at a later date.

Having settled on the easier of the two agenda items, they were left with how exactly they should break the news to their sons.

"You should be the one to tell them," Gertie said. "The separation is your idea."

Klaus nodded, knowing he had no choice but to agree.

With a sigh, Gertie pushed herself up from the table and walked over to the large picture window looking out on the yard. Just beyond the oak tree, in the open expanse of lawn that stretched out to the neighbor's fence, she could see Udo Jörgen and Christian taking turns throwing a ball to a tireless Rex.

"What will you tell them?"

"The truth. That you and I need to spend time apart."

"Is that all this is?" she asked, turning toward him.

The question had come out sounding hopeful, yet Gertie could feel her stomach tightening.

"I don't know," Klaus said. "Let's just get them used to this arrangement first."

She nodded her head and then looked away.

"Listen," he said. "I'm not rushing into anything, but at the same time I don't want to give you false hope. These last few months, they—"

"I love you," Gertie said.

Even with her back turned he could see she was trembling.

Klaus sighed.

"I still care about you, too," Klaus said, breaking the painful silence he had allowed to follow. "But I can't do this, and there's just no point in forcing it anymore."

The air inside the living room felt dense and claustrophobic, and the boys, each seated on the edge of the couch, were looking up at their parents with expectant dread.

Klaus leaned forward in his seat.

"What I'm about to tell you is difficult," he said. "But your mother and I have decided it would be better if we spend some time apart, so I'll be moving in with your grandmother for a while."

The boys kept silent while their father continued, though the expressions on their small faces revealed the tumult of their internal reactions. While Udo Jörgen's eyes and mouth kept dilating in suppressed panic, Christian's entire countenance was clouding over with animosity.

Udo Jörgen's immediate response was a flashback to the Rex fiasco.

"Why, Papa?" he whined, after Klaus had finished. "Why can't you just stay here?"

Christian, ignoring the convulsive fidgeting of his younger brother, continued to stare straight ahead in a stubborn muteness resembling his mother's.

"It's not a matter of not wanting to be with you. It's just that your mother—"

Christian interjected.

"It's her fault, isn't it?"

Hearing this, Udo Jörgen began to whimper and wail.

Klaus stood up to comfort him, but instead the boy ran sobbing to his mother, collapsing on her lap. Gertie, in shock, could do nothing but stroke Udo Jörgen's head with a slow and mechanical motion.

"No, Christian, your mother isn't forcing me to leave. It's just that we've —"

Christian erupted without warning.

"I don't mean, Mutti! I mean that other woman!"

Klaus looked into his oldest son's eyes, now ablaze with condemnation.

"What are you talking about?"

"The tall blonde I saw you with!"

Udo Jörgen stopped his blubbering for a moment to peer up from his mother's lap. Now it was Gertie's turn to look over at Klaus in distress.

Klaus cleared his throat to steel his resolve.

"Yes, she's a friend of mine, but she's not the reason I'm—"

"Some friend," Christian countered.

Infuriated, Klaus stormed toward his insolent son wagging his index finger.

"I will not have you talk to me that way!"

"Klaus, please," Gertie pleaded.

Nostrils flaring, Klaus watched with astonishment as Christian assumed a posture of glassy-eyed indifference.

"We realize this is difficult for you to comprehend. But it doesn't mean we won't continue to behave as a family."

"Yeah, right," Christian muttered, staring out into nothingness.

"What did you say?"

Without a word, Christian rose from his seat and turned toward his younger brother who was staring up at him in awe.

"C'mon Udo. We're going upstairs."

In a fury, Klaus grabbed Christian's shoulders and shoved him back down on the couch.

In an instant, Gertie was on her feet and between them.

"That's enough," she said, locking eyes with Klaus. Gertie waited until she could see the realization sink in.

"You have to let them go now."

11

Germany 1983-1986 / Greece - 1988

In September of the following year, at the one-year mark of their separation, Klaus filed for divorce. Gertie, having lost any reasonable hope of repairing the marriage, did not contest.

With Klaus' reluctant admission of the extramarital affair, Elke, in a strange and unexpected turn, softened her stance toward her daughter-in-law. A few days after Klaus' departure, she showed up on Gertie's doorstep, pledging her on-going support.

"I know you and Klaus have had your difficulties," she said, after Gertie had poured her a cup of coffee in the kitchen. "Nonetheless, I thought I had raised a better son than that."

Her remorse was palpable as if through some hereditary osmosis, Klaus' guilt had become her own. Sighing, she placed her plump hand on top of Gertie's slim one.

"It's always some damn temptress who lures them away," she said. "Still, we'll have to make the best of it, for the boys' sake. While Fritz was on the front, I couldn't have gotten by without my mother-in-law. I hope you'll at least allow me to do the same for you."

Despite Gertie and Klaus's attempt to minimize the disruption, the three years that followed proved tumultuous for their sons. Klaus, having exchanged his freedom for a guilty conscience, soon forgot his promise to drop by each day after school, leaving Elke to attend to the boys alone in what was now referred to as Gertie's house.

Gertie had few expectations where family was concerned and had resigned herself to her new fate with much less hesitancy than the others. As her responsibilities at home were increasingly taken up by her crusading ex-mother-in-law, she found herself dedicating more and more time to the advancement of her career, a decision she justified easily with the breakdown of her marriage and the need to provide for her sons otherwise uncertain future.

Elke did her best to support the household. And while her relationship with Gertie continued to defy friendship, they nonetheless endeavored to show one another the respect necessary to manage the challenges and upsets wrought by Klaus' erratic lifestyle with Simone.

The boys, unsurprisingly, resented any and all of the imposed changes. Where before they had enjoyed the sleepovers at their grandmother's house, it now felt like an obligation rather than a treat. To make matters worse, they were expected to adhere to a strict schedule of shuttling back and forth between the two houses in order to see their father on the designated weekends. Much like the boys, who were oftentimes itching to go back to their own rooms, by the time Sunday morning rolled around, Klaus, too, seemed relieved when it came time to go their separate ways.

Gertie's increased independence, meanwhile, suited her well. She was soon promoted to a senior position in her firm and given additional responsibilities to oversee the installation of air-traffic control systems at a number of regional airports throughout Europe and North Africa. During the course of these expeditions, she developed a close camaraderie with two of the lead engineers, Matthias Schmidt and Karsten Oberst, and for the first time since the dissolution of her marriage, Gertie found herself enjoying the company of others.

Over the course of the next two years, her relationship with Matthias and Karsten morphed from one of collegial camaraderie to friendship. Although they each led considerably different lives, the colleagues grew to confide in one another with the knowledge that what they said around the work site camp stove would not reverberate back to Munich.

And it was during one of these nighttime confessionals while stationed in Kalamata, Greece, that Gertie brought up the specter of her mother's suicide and the unspoken suspicions she had never dared mention, not even to Klaus.

It had been a scorching July day with waves of dry heat shimmering off the tarmac. An hour after sunset, they had set aside their work in the stuffy confines of the control tower to gather in front of their tents and eat an evening meal of cold cuts and feta swimming in a cool bath of salt. Amidst the wafting scents of pine descending the Taygetus mountains and a nearby jasmine bush whose sweet fragrance dispersed into the air with the drop in temperature, they would catch the occasional whiff of diesel from a truck roaring past.

They had just finished their second round of beers and were beginning their third when Matthias—who considered himself an amateur historian—raised the subject of the Axis occupation.

"The Nazis made it down here, too, in the spring of '41. The locals tried to fight them for a couple of days, with the help of the Brits and New Zealanders, but the *Wehrmacht* was too much for them. Still, the locals weren't afraid to cheer when they marched the POWs along the streets on the way to the prison camps. A tough people, these *Kalamatianoi*."

"How do you even know about that?" Karsten asked, licking his fingers after eating a stuffed grape leaf. "It's not like you've made it into town much other than to buy groceries."

Matthias shook his head.

"It's important to know the history, man, especially when we're down here working. And to answer your question, I don't go into town much because I don't want to trouble the old people. I'd like to think I'm doing what I can now to restore things, but, no, I don't want to see the hostility in their eyes. Your parents, they were obviously too young to have been involved."

"Why, was someone from your family here?"

"Perhaps? But you know how the older generation is, they don't talk about it.

It's like they have selective amnesia about the whole thing. That's why it's up to us to learn as much as we can. It's our duty to make sure it doesn't happen again."

Listening to them, Gertie had fixed her gaze on a seemingly ancient grove of olive trees that lay on the other side of the highway. In the shadows she could see the dry and twisted trunks giving way to clusters of thick, leafy branches spreading themselves wide but still within a ladder's reach. At present they were weighed down with dense baubles of fruit that during the day darkened beneath the unrelenting sun.

"Matthias is right," Gertie said. "They're not going to tell us anything they don't want."

A cloud hung over them as they recalled what she had revealed the previous night regarding the tragic, suicidal deaths of her mother and brother.

"I was only a child, but there was something about my father's inability to talk about what happened, to even acknowledge it, that made me feel as if he and the war must have played a part, but I have no proof."

Karsten looked over at Gertie with an anguished sympathy.

"Did you ever ask him about it?"

At the time of Gertie's confession, they had both responded with a respectful, acknowledging silence, not wanting to say anything that would further contribute to her pain. But now that she was raising the topic again, they felt compelled to talk about it, to ask questions, in an attempt to help her navigate the murky channels of her past.

"No, absolutely not. Unless it was related to chores or homework, my father wouldn't talk to us about personal matters. It was understood we were not to speak our mother's name."

An uneasy stillness followed.

"There must be someone you could talk to," Matthias said. "Maybe someone on your mother's side who was around back then?"

"We weren't in touch with extended family. My father's parents were killed during a bombing raid, and I know almost nothing about my mother's side. My older brothers were too young to remember the war. The one time Thorsten brought it up, my father completely lost it and stormed off to his study. Not another word was said. We just assumed he was upset because of how his parents were killed."

"Do you think Thorsten might have a suspicion?" Matthias asked.

"I doubt it. And even if he knew something, I can't imagine him saying anything to me."

"It might be worth a try. You never know. Sometimes it's better to bring these things out in the open, for your sake at least. Germans, we all have these skeletons in our closet. How could it be otherwise?"

"One of my great uncles was in the SA," Karsten said. "Still denies it to this day even though there's a photo of him in his uniform. We don't see too much of him. He keeps mostly to himself. And what would be the point, eh?"

Gertie looked at Karsten intently for a while, as if weighing out his unwitting advice. Then she turned back toward Matthias.

"Maybe you're right. But when I start to think about it, I feel like a small child again. Paralyzed."

"How old were Thorsten and Uwe when your mother died?"

Gertie sighed as she tried to remember. Somewhere in the distance, she could hear a goat's bell ringing.

"It was 1956. I had turned seven so that would make Thorsten sixteen and Uwe thirteen."

"Old enough, then," Matthias said. "They must have some idea, Gertie. It's impossible to keep secrets from kids that age. Believe me, they have their own ways of figuring things out. For your own peace of mind, you should ask them. Before it's too late."

Kirchheim/Munich September 1988

Two months after Gertie had returned home from Kalamata, Matthias' suggestion continued to churn in her mind. A part of her felt queasy at the thought of raising the topic with her brothers, but her yearning to know the truth, to stop the endless looping of possibilities, won out over her physical discomfort.

She called her brother Uwe who just so happened to have business scheduled in Munich the following week and so they agreed to meet. Of the two brothers that remained, Uwe's temperament was the more self-possessed one, and although they shared little in common, Gertie sensed he had a softness for her, albeit one he kept at arm's length.

He had chosen one of the finest cafés in the city as their meeting place, thereby establishing a certain level of formality and decorum. When its doors first opened back in 1888, The Luitpold had been dubbed the Palace-Café of Munich, and, with only a few years of closure during the war and after, it had continued to retain its status as one of the noblest and largest coffeehouses in all of Europe. It had recently undergone renovation, and in anticipation of a start-of-the-weekend crowd, Gertie had called ahead to reserve a table with adequate privacy.

On the day of their appointment, Gertie arrived twenty minutes early. She was already seated at one of the white clothed tables behind a pair of the café's imposing faux Corinthian columns when the maître d' escorted Uwe over.

Gertie stood, allowing Uwe to give her a customary kiss on the cheek before they each settled into their chairs.

"How well you look, Gertie," he said in an admiring tone as he opened the menu. "I trust the summer is treating you well?"

"That's kind of you to say. I've been busy with work which involves a great deal of travel. I've just come back from Greece."

Uwe raised an eyebrow as if to say, *my, haven't you come up in the world.*

"It suits you. And the boys, how are they?"

"Growing like weeds. For the most part they're getting high marks in school, although not doing as well in their German lessons as I would like. I suppose that runs in the family."

"Yes, I imagine on both sides they're doomed to a life of science. We certainly didn't escape our fate as far as that was concerned."

"No, I suppose not. And how is Margareta?"

Uwe's wife taught chemistry at the local Gymnasium. For reasons unknown, they did not have children.

"Same as ever. We go out hiking now and again, especially now that Greta has time off from school. We joined a rambling club, so that keeps us busy and fit when we're not working."

"That's great," Gertie said, distracted by her thoughts.

She could feel a familiar hesitation rising in her. She and Uwe were not in the habit of entertaining small talk. It felt stilted and awkward. Thankfully, the waiter arrived just then to take their order. Only after he had gone, did Uwe look over at her in a more probing manner.

"Niceties aside, what compelled you to call? There must be something on your mind."

Gertie stalled a moment to catch her breath.

"I wanted to talk to you about Adelina."

"I see," Uwe said, careful not to show any emotion at the mention of their mother's name.

"I suppose you would be curious. You were still so young."

"As you know, we weren't allowed to talk about her."

"No, I suppose we weren't," he said, stopping the conversation to allow the waiter to arrange the coffee service along with two pieces of *Käse-Sahne-Torte*, the cheese and cream cake specialty of the house. As he began to pour, the strong bouquet of a dark-roasted blend rose up to greet them.

Once the waiter had made himself scarce again, Uwe sunk his fork into the delicate pastry, and in an abrupt manner asked, "What is it that you want to know?"

"Everything. I know nothing about her."

Uwe took a sip from his coffee. Placing the porcelain cup back on its delicate saucer, he inhaled deeply.

"Our mother was a very unhappy woman. I don't know what you remember, but I can't recall a time when she expressed any sort of—*joy* in her life. She would try, at times, to feign a pleasant demeanor, particularly with you and Christian. She was quite fond of both of you, more so than with Thorsten and me. But it wasn't heartfelt, you see. We all knew that."

"Why do you say that? About you and Thorsten? What was so different?"

"I imagine it was because of the war. You and Christian came after. A fresh start, so to speak. With Thorsten and me, she was alone most of the time. Our father wasn't around, so she had to make do on her own. She was young with two small children to worry about on top of the war. I think she must have resented it."

Gertie paused to take a sip of her coffee.

"And her family? Did you meet them?"

"Her family."

Uwe's curt response was not lost on her.

"Where were they? Why couldn't they have helped her?"

"Gertie," he said, turning his attention back to his cake. "I'm not sure this is the best place to discuss these things."

"I need to know, Uwe, to understand why—"

"What could there possibly be to understand?" he said, his face stricken. "She was a sick woman. There's nothing we can do about that now."

"But there's a reason why she chose what she chose. And I need to know what it is."

"And what good would that do? There is no sense —no *reason*— in what she did."

"But don't you think that has something to do with what happened to Christian?"

"Nonsense. Christian never got over finding her the way he did. He was traumatized. And for the same reason there's no point in you digging into it. It will only hurt you in the end."

"Well, if you aren't willing to say more, I'll have to speak with Thorsten. Or with Papa."

"You're making a big mistake. There are some things best left alone."

"Uwe, I don't need you to protect me. I have as much of a right to know as you."

"Believe me, Gertie. If I could erase my mind of any of this, I would do it in an instant. I'm only warning you for your own sake."

"Was it because of our father? At least tell me that much."

Uwe looked into Gertie's eyes with a stern warning. An endless minute of excruciating silence passed between them.

"You'll have to ask him yourself," he said, folding up his napkin. "I wasn't there."

Gertie's coffee with Uwe ended with a half-hearted pledge on his part to help her set up a meeting with their father and Thorsten. He had refused to provide her with any second-hand information, as he called it, and planned to "stay out of it" if her ill-advised questioning met with resistance.

The Obermeier reunion took place in late October at Thorsten's apartment in Bobingen, a small commuter town fifteen kilometers south of Augsburg. This was the first time since Gertie's small wedding that the four of them had gathered in the same room. On the rare occasions that Gertie had seen them since her marriage, it had been either just Thorsten and her father at the family home in Augsburg or Uwe and his wife somewhere in Munich, usually at a café or restaurant.

Thorsten, as the eldest, had taken it upon himself to act as primary caretaker to their father, who at seventy-seven was in declining health although loathe to admit it. Thorsten made a point each morning of driving the extra 15 minutes to check on Werner before going downtown to work at RENK—a longstanding local enterprise leading in the development of propulsion technologies. At the end of the day, he would drive back to their father's house for their ritual afternoon coffee and cake, taken either inside the parlor, or weather permitting, in the garden.

Unlike his siblings, Thorsten had never married and had continued to live the bachelor's life in a large and comfortable apartment near the town center not far from Singold Park. He tended to keep the details of his life private though he and Uwe maintained regular contact by meeting once a month at their favorite pub, the Zeughaus, a popular Augsburgian haunt from their youth. Apart from the obligatory birthday call, his relationship with Gertie was for the most part nonexistent. She was nine years younger, so unless something crucial came up related to their father, she would not hear from him, nor he from her. Since Werner was averse to religious holidays, it had not been their habit, once they had gone their separate ways, to spend time with one another on those particular occasions.

At Uwe's request, Thorsten had reluctantly agreed to host the unusual family gathering not wanting to put their ailing father on the spot. When Gertie arrived, Thorsten and Werner were already seated on the balcony enjoying a glass of beer in the early afternoon sun.

"Is there anything I can do to help?" she asked, noticing the table setting.

"No," Thorsten said with a cool dismissiveness. "The housekeeper made *Sauerbraten*, so we just have to wait for Uwe."

He handed Gertie a beer as she took a seat facing the park, while Werner asked tactfully after his grandsons' wellbeing.

Uwe arrived not long after, so they busied themselves with eating lunch, keeping the conversation focused on what each of them had been doing the last few years in their various lines of work.

Having broken the ice and fallen back into old family patterns, they recessed for a stroll in the park, taking turns walking beside their father before returning to the apartment as the sky began to darken.

Back inside, Thorsten invited them into his spartan living room, where the walls were painted a dark gray and decorated with a collection of nondescript geometric drawings. Along with the austere, black leather seating, the room revealed close to nothing about the apartment's inhabitant other than his strict adherence to both symmetry and neatness.

"I'll put the coffee on," Gertie said.

Thorsten followed her into the kitchen.

"Uwe told me what you're up to," he said, in a not unthreatening way. "He won't like you dredging up the past."

Gertie sighed.

"We're all adults now," she said, unpacking the pastries she had brought. "I can ask him whatever I want."

Thorsten and Uwe sat opposite the sleek glass table in the living room immersed in awkward silence. They held their coffee cups close and watched their father as he decided which pastry to try first.

Gertie knew this was likely her only chance, so she forced herself to speak despite the opposition she felt emanating from the guarded postures of her older brothers.

"Papa?"

"Yes?" Werner said, his attention hovering over a piece of Black Forest cake.

"I want to speak to you about a sensitive topic."

"Does it have to do with the boys? I know how difficult it is to raise children on your own. You must be patient."

"No, Papa, it's not about the boys," she said, watching him take a large bite out of the rich, chocolate confection. "I wanted to ask you about our mother."

Werner let out an exaggerated moan and bowed his head.

He put his plate down, then resting his hands on his thighs to brace himself, he lifted his pale blue eyes in her direction. Still piercing but grown milky with age, they commanded her obedient attention.

"Now, Gertraud. Why would you want to bring that up, especially after we've all had such a nice afternoon together?"

Gertie steeled herself.

"I know it's difficult to talk about, but I seem to be the only one who doesn't know anything about her. And that causes me grief. I need to understand why she did what she did."

Having voiced her concern, she watched as Uwe turned an indiscriminate eye toward the wall art. Thorsten, meanwhile, had begun a furious examination of his fingernails.

"We did it for your own good," Werner said. "Not telling you."

"Yes, but not knowing I can only imagine the worst."

Werner shook his head.

"After what happened to your brother, why would I want to risk another tragedy?"

"Wait, are you saying that you told Christian—?"

"No, but that's why I kept it from you!"

Thorsten glared at Gertie. Ignoring him, Gertie allowed her father's words to sink in as she deliberated what to say next.

"Papa, I understand you want to protect me. But Christian was young then. Inexperienced. I'm thirty-seven now. Old enough to know."

A few moments passed in bristling silence as she stared at the top of his scalp, covered with a thin layer of white, side-combed hair. Werner was a large man, but hunched over as he was now, he seemed almost to collapse in on himself.

"Her age," Werner said finally, his voice cracking.

"You don't have to answer her," Thorsten said. In his anger, he looked every bit like their father when he was his age.

Werner looked up at his oldest, revealing a lightning flash of contempt at being coddled.

"No," he said. "If Gertie wants to know, I'll tell her."

Thorsten's jaw dropped to ready his defense, but just as quickly he clenched it shut again.

"Adelina," Werner said, as if calling out her name. "Adelina Marie Gertz. That was your mother's full name, and you have her eyes, Gertraud."

For a moment, Werner's gaze wandered back in time.

"She was seventeen when I met her. Her father didn't like me at first. Thought I was too bookish. But I loved your mother, see? And she seemed to feel the same about me, so I persisted. I asked her to marry me after her eighteenth birthday. I was twenty-seven at the time, gainfully employed, so her father relented. We married in the autumn of 1938, and Thorsten came two years later. By that point the war was well under way. It was a difficult time for your mother. I wasn't home much. Too much work to be done. Quotas to be met. Then Uwe came, and we had to make do the best way we could."

"Did our mother have siblings?" Gertie asked. "What about her parents?"

Werner looked toward the window and frowned.

"She had two older brothers. Both soldiers. They fought on the Western

Front first, but in '41 they were reassigned to Poland. Their father was an *OrPo Kommandant* by then, so he made sure they were assigned posts of his choosing. In '43, they all relocated to Kraków, and Adelina never saw them again."

Werner paused, giving Gertie a moment to process what he had just told her.

It was a known fact that the *Ordnungspolizei*, or *OrPo*, were responsible for rounding up the German Jewish population and transporting them to the concentration camps where they were then worked to the bone and systematically slaughtered. Kraków, one of the Third Reich's seats of power after the German invasion and occupation, was not far from Auschwitz.

"They were Nazis," Gertie said, her voice as hollow and distant as the sound of the neighborhood children playing out on the street. The small part of her that was not withering inside wished she could go out and join them, escape the putrid silence that now threatened to choke her, its tendril-like fingers quietly wrapping around her neck.

"Your mother," Werner's voice was shaky and hesitant, "She didn't know. Not until after the war."

"That doesn't make any sense," Gertie said, as an uncontrollable furor rose up in her. "How could she not know?"

Werner's face crumbled.

"You don't understand—"

"No, Papa, I don't!"

"But don't you see? It wasn't until she saw those horrible pictures that she—"

"That she realized what they were doing to them?! What did she think was going to happen when they were being shipped off like cattle?"

"That's enough," Thorsten said, rising to his feet.

"And what about you, Papa?" Gertie said, ignoring her brother's attempt to diffuse the situation, "what was your excuse?"

Werner looked down again.

"Who was doing the work at your factories? Are you going to tell me that you didn't know anything either?"

Werner's knees began to quiver.

"I didn't betray anyone," he said, his voice shaking. "I swear. I kept to myself. To my work. Your mother, she was with the boys. We were all afraid of what could happen. They kept telling us the Bolsheviks would—"

Thorsten stood up and marched toward Gertie, yanking her up by her arm.

Startled by his sudden grip on her, Gertie broke free and backed away from him.

"Don't you dare put your fucking hands on me!"

Thorsten glowered at her.

"I think we've had more than enough of your intrusions for one day."

Uwe, already standing, put a hand up as if to signal a truce.

"I was just about to drive to the station," he said. "I'll take Gertie with me."

Uwe gathered up their coats, placed a guiding hand on his sister's shoulder and walked her toward the foyer.

"I'll visit soon, Papa," he called out, as he held the door open for Gertie. In her muted anger she left without so much as a glimpse back.

Uwe and Gertie settled into the front seats of his Mercedes sedan without saying a word. As he drove, Gertie stared straight ahead, her energy focused on the sound of the driving rain bursting against the windshield, and the ruthless rhythm of the wipers trying to sweep it all away.

"Are you OK?" Uwe asked, glancing over in her direction. "I can drive you home if you prefer."

Gertie could hear a dark echo of fear in his voice, poorly masking his concern.

She ignored his offer and confronted him instead.

"Tell me how Christian found out."

Uwe sighed and then waited a moment.

"I'm not sure exactly. He was always trying to dig up more information about her. It bothered him that no one was around from her side of the family. Papa's parents, as you know, were killed in an air raid. As it is, we rarely saw anyone from the Obermeier side, and less and less as time wore on."

Uwe stopped at a red light and took a deep breath before continuing.

"He suspected there had to be someone, somewhere. Anyway, he went looking. He knew her name and started asking questions at town hall. Then he asked permission to read through the newspaper archives.

Before graduation, he confronted Papa. Like you did today. Except he was hysterical. Thorsten was home at the time. He said he had to restrain Christian, that he was accusing Papa of being a sympathizer and that he wanted to hit him, beat him, in fact. Thorsten was rattled and Christian accused him of being a sympathizer, too. That he always knew there was something wrong with him. That he had protected our father somehow. It was crazy.

"But Thorsten only knew because he had overheard her talking to Papa the night before she killed herself. Talking about her father and brothers and how she couldn't take it anymore.

"After Christian's death, Papa took us aside. Made us promise not to tell you. That losing Christian proved the cost of knowing about the past was too high."

Gertie looked over at him, her eyes as hard as granite.

"And did Christian find something out about Papa?"

Uwe shook his head.

"No, Gertie. Our father's only crime is that he looked the other way. Bought into the fear, just like everyone else. He wasn't *in* the party. He didn't participate. Not like her family anyway. In fact, he took Mutti away from all of that. But it wasn't enough in the end."

A long silence passed between them, with only the sound of the windshield wipers to mark the time.

"Are they alive?" Gertie asked.

"Who?" Uwe said, taking a right-side exit off the Autobahn.

"Her family."

"We only know her parents killed themselves in Kraków. Cyanide."

"And the brothers?"

"I don't know. Papa didn't follow up after she died. He wanted absolutely nothing to do with them. They were never a part of our lives, and as far as he was concerned, never should be."

Uwe pulled up to the entrance of the train station.

"Here we are," he said, sounding relieved.

Gertie looked over at him in dazed recognition.

"Thanks for telling me."

Uwe's eyes were full of sorrow.

"I can still drive you home."

"I'll be alright," she said as she opened the door and stepped out. "I always am."

12

Germany / Caway - 1995

Christian did visit Gertie in Caway, three years after she left Germany and not long after installing Udo Jörgen, then seventeen, in a village boarding school just outside of Munich.

Christian himself was enrolled at the Technical University, their parents' alma mater, and about to start his first semester, when her notice arrived in the mail:

My dear boys,

I am writing to let you know that I have decided to sell the house and to take an early retirement. I realize this news will come as a surprise; however, I could not think of another way to spare us all the grief of having to talk about a decision I have already made. Though you may find this difficult to understand, and though I cannot find the right words to explain it, know that for me this is a necessary step.

With respect to your future upkeep, I have set aside enough money for both of you in the form of a trust. I ask only that you pursue your respective career paths with as much vigor and self-determination as possible. You are gifted students—as I know your father would agree— and you have a bright future ahead of you.

While I do not know yet where I will eventually settle, I am making my way to

Central America. I will, of course, send letters when I can. In the meantime, do not worry. You know your mother can take care of herself, and she knows you are both more than capable of doing the same. Love, Mutti

This, of course, was typical Gertie. Consistent with her obstinate, controlling nature, *she* would be the one to determine the flow of communication, leaving them no choice but to wait for her to reach out to them.

Udo Jörgen, meanwhile, was beside himself.

"How can she be so fucking selfish?!"

Christian had taken the first afternoon train out to Schondorf to see him. He and Udo Jörgen were standing at the forest's edge just as the sun was about to set, well out of view of the dormitory's entrance so Udo Jörgen, with his long, stringy blonde hair, could smoke without being hassled.

"No one does this at her age," Udo Jörgen scowled. "She's been planning this for months. It's just like the time she found out about the affair and kept it to herself, remember?"

After their parents' divorce, they had watched their mother soldier on as if nothing had happened. Not once had she complained to them about the sudden change in their life. Sure, she had traveled a lot for work, which meant leaving them in their grandmother's care, but when she was home, they had gotten along fine enough. In fact, she had seemed more at peace as a single woman, one who seemed to thrive on the constant challenges of her work. It was odd that at the height of her career she would suddenly choose to cut the cord and vanish.

"Does Klaus even know about this?" Udo Jörgen asked, holding the creased letter in front of him with disgust. After the divorce, he had only referred to their parents by their first names. "How do we even get a hold of this trust she's talking about? It's not like she included any specifics."

"There's no point in getting so worked up. She's probably just going through menopause or something. The divorce wasn't as easy for her as she likes to pretend."

Udo Jörgen lit up his third cigarette.

"Menopause? And what? We're supposed to rely on *him* now? That's a laugh."

Udo Jörgen's noxious exhale began to drift toward Christian's face.

"Fucking stop doing that," he said, waving the smoke away from his lambswool sweater. "Anyway, Oma will know what to do about the money."

"If she didn't tell us anything, why the hell would she tell her? Gertie doesn't like Oma that much. And certainly not when it comes to money."

"Don't be ridiculous. She let Oma run everything in the house when she was at work."

Udo Jörgen gave him one of his crooked side glances. In the span of just a few years he had transformed from a mama's boy into a skinny and cynical bastard.

"When are you going to get it through your thick head that she doesn't give a fuck? I mean look at where she's stuck me."

The small town of Schondorf was situated on the banks of the *Ammersee* lake with spectacular views of the Bavarian Alps. Taking in the forest air not to mention the idyllic view, Christian had to laugh.

"Is it too much for you to have to go sailing on the weekends? Is that it? I would have given anything to come here."

"That's not what I'm talking about," Udo Jörgen replied with a huff. "The point is I didn't have a say. She kept talking about how this would get me into a good university, and that it would be crazy not to go, but what she really wanted was for me to get the fuck out of her hair, so who cares if it looks nice! The people suck, and because I'm the new one, I have to sit with the rejects and freaks every fucking meal. I fucking hate it here."

Christian shook his head.

"You'll get used to it soon enough. Anyway, after that you can do whatever you want."

"Yeah, right," Udo Jörgen said, grinding the cigarette out on the heel of his Doc Martens. "I'll believe it when I see it. With strings attached, no doubt. Just wait and see."

To Christian's annoyance, Udo Jörgen was right. Oma knew nothing about Gertie's disappearance or the money she had allegedly left behind. It had come as a complete shock when they told her.

It was not until a few days later that Christian received a call from their Uncle Uwe. As it turned out, it was this estranged uncle of theirs whom she had entrusted with her financial affairs. Over the phone he let Christian know in his succinct, matter-of-fact voice, that he had set up a time for his lawyer to meet with them to go over the mechanics of the trust. He expressed his regrets at not being able to join them.

"I'm away on unavoidable business, you see."

He had wished them well in their studies while at the same time not leaving a single opening in the call for any follow up questions. And, the lawyer had, in fact, set them at ease with respect to what they would receive from the trust each year, which was more than enough to fund their tuition and living expenses. But when they asked about their mother's whereabouts and when they would see her again, the lawyer could only shrug.

It was at that point that Christian decided to just wait her out. He assumed that once Gertie's mid-life crisis had passed, she would no doubt return to Germany. But when she did not, he reluctantly packed up his bags and set out to find her.

The journey to Caway exhausted him. Christian had booked the least expensive flight he could find to San José which meant a ten-hour layover in Miami until his midnight connection.

Tired of wandering around the airport's halls, he made use of his English to hail a cab to Little Havana where he was told a street festival was in full swing. As soon as he stepped out of the air-conditioned car, Christian was immediately struck by the extreme heat and cacophony of the place. People were speaking in Spanish against the blaring of car horns and live music, the young and old spilling off the sidewalks and into the streets, some even daring to dance between the still moving cars.

Never before had Christian felt so out of place, and it made him wonder how his mother was getting on. He had never traveled outside of Europe, but he could not imagine Gertie blending in much better.

Landing in San José felt equally disorienting. At 3900 feet, the temperature was pleasant enough, though he soon realized he could not get by on his school English alone. He was constantly looking up words in his Spanish-German dictionary, though the answers he received from the locals were, to his ears, just as indecipherable.

With the help of another tourist, he eventually found his way downtown only to have to face the disappointment of having to climb into a decrepit bus that provided little in the way of comfort. Still, despite the cramped seating— Christian, like his father, was a towering six foot two—he soon fell asleep. The wear and tear of the long-haul flights coupled with severe jet lag was enough to inure him to the bumpy roads and the constant shifts in air temperature.

Leaving behind the smog and dust of the Central Valley, he woke only twice, once to close the window against the rain as the bus heaved itself up a foggy incline and then again as they descended into a vast, coastal plain, where the suffocating tropical heat and humidity had forced his eyes open, if only briefly, so he could take off his sweater.

It was the jostling of the other passengers that alerted him to the first stop in Limón as he entered the 36th hour of his journey.

In his stilted Spanish, he asked the driver, a short, compact man in his forties, how much further to Caway and was told it would take another forty minutes, at least. In the ten-minute break before departing, Christian purchased a coffee and pastry from the terminal *cantina* and then tried to make sense of the unruly landscape. He had no personal frame of reference for what he saw around him, and he could not imagine why Gertie had ever come here in the first place.

Most of the ramshackle houses and storefronts were in serious disrepair, and even the people on the streets looked neglected. He had read somewhere that the population here was mostly of Afro-Caribbean descent, and as they pulled out of the ragged, old port, with its endless array of Hapag-Lloyd, Maersk and even Hamburg Süd shipping containers, he was reminded of a novel he was required to read in his last year at prep school. *Heart of Darkness* it was called, and though his academic focus was on math and science, the oppressive tone and ominous setting had stuck with him. He imagined the

Congo was not much different than what he was seeing outside his bus window.

And to think that Gertie now called this place home.

As the bus finally pulled into Caway, Christian realized, to his utter dismay, that he had forgotten to pack Gertie's letter, the one where she had mentioned the name and phone number of the restaurant she lived next door to. He stepped off the bus and asked the man taking tickets where he might find the post office, assuming they might know where to find her.

The General Post Office, as it turned out, shared a small space with the local police. On the outside it looked like any of the other rickety houses he had seen along the main dirt road, made of rough-hewn planks and not much in the way of paint. The only distinguishing feature was a hand-drawn police emblem just to the side of the open door. Christian felt alarmed at the air of casualness exuded by the two officers, who, apart from what little light came in through the windows, were sitting in the dark.

"*Disculpe*," he managed to stutter as he pulled a photograph from his wallet. "but I am looking for this woman, Gertraud Obermeier."

The younger officer, who was standing behind the counter, examined the photo with feigned interest.

"*Conoces a esta gringa?*" he asked his colleague who was sitting behind a shabby desk eating his lunch. The older officer chewed his food as he took turns looking at the photo and then at Christian.

"*Es la alemana flaca que vive al lado de Andreas,*" he said, focusing his attention back on his plate. "*Quién es este chico?*"

The young officer turned back toward Christian.

"I'm sorry, but who are you?" he asked with an apologetic smile.

"I'm her son," Christian said, pointing back in the direction of the bus terminal. "I just arrived, but I don't know how to find her house."

The older officer sat up.

"She expect you?"

The man spoke English after all.

The muscles in Christian's stomach began to tighten.

"Yes. I sent a letter, but my flight left before I could hear back. She doesn't have a phone," he added, wondering if they could refuse to tell him where she lived.

"*Tranquilo*," the officer said, standing up. He pointed out the side window as he approached him. "Her house is down this road. You walk two and half kilometer to *Quixote's*. She live in the yellow house next to it."

Christian let out a sigh of relief.

"*Gracias*, very much," he said.

The gnawing sense he had made a terrible mistake began to slowly subside.

Christian stepped out into the tropical haze and paused to take a long pull from the water bottle he had purchased in San José then began his walk along the pitted coastal road. The dilapidated homes he passed were clearly still occupied, and a good many people were dressed in what appeared to be second-hand clothes. Strangely, they seemed unaware of their plight, and he sensed in their easy-going gait a self-assuredness that did not square with his preconceptions of poverty. In fact, they seemed amused by his stares. A young woman about his age looked so directly into his eyes as they passed it unnerved him. He felt his cheeks go red as he quickly cast down his glance prompting a beguiling laugh on her part.

He continued ambling along for what seemed an eternity, encountering fewer and fewer people along the way. Crossing an intersection, he spotted a hand-painted sign nailed to a tree. *Quixote's* it read with an arrow pointing straight ahead.

Here and there he would catch a rare glimpse of the ocean, the waves crashing hard against volcanic rock or the occasional stretch of thin, black sand. For the most part, however, the thick vegetation growing on either side obscured his view. He imagined the poisonous plants and snakes that lurked just off the road, not to mention the many insects of astonishing size. Even the sea, that would normally have called out to him for refreshment, looked perilous. This was not the waterfront he knew, with combed beaches and an endless array of umbrellas and sun beds. No. Everything here was wild and unattended, and even the driftwood consisted of entire lengths of coconut trees haphazardly strewn about the seaweed-littered shore.

About the time Christian felt like giving up, he saw a posting for "*Cabi-*

nas". Walking past it, he caught a glimpse of the restaurant, convincingly camouflaged by tall, flowering bushes out front and a thick canopy of trees on top.

With eyes now peeled, he made out the distinctive mesh of a metal fence that was covered in ivy. He arched his fingers so as not to touch the leaves and pushed open the gate to reveal a narrow, pebbled path leading up to a yellow house. His broad shoulders relaxed at the sight.

Christian walked up the couple of steps leading to the main entrance on the right, took a deep breath, and knocked. After the reverberations of his strong rapping faded, he stared blankly at the wooden door as if willing it to open.

Surely he hadn't come this far for nothing? he thought. The only rustling he heard came from the surrounding trees.

He knocked again, but soon resigned himself to the fact no one was home. He did not have any energy left to go look for her, nor did he care to try. Instead, he slid down onto the top step and allowed his weary eyes to close against his propped-up backpack.

He woke with a start when he felt a light hand resting on his shoulder.

"It's just me," Gertie said, appearing like a specter against the setting sun.

"*Mutti*," he heard himself say.

His arms had fallen asleep, and as he looked around at the growing shadows, he tried desperately to shake them awake.

"How long have you been waiting?"

Christian turned his wrist and realized he had not set his watch to the local time.

"Since half past three?"

"You must be hungry then. Let's get you inside, and we'll figure out something to eat."

To Christian's surprise, Gertie simply pushed the unlocked door open.

He shouldered his bag and followed her.

Gertie gestured for him to take a seat.

"Do you want something to drink?"

"A beer would be nice," he said, lowering himself into an old, brown leather sofa.

As Gertie busied herself in the kitchen, Christian stared out through the large picture window, watching the garden fade into an overwhelming darkness.

Gertie came back into the living room and turned on the lamp.

"Don't scratch those," she said, handing him a bottle of Pilsen. "It will only make them worse."

She sat down beside him to take a closer look.

"What are they?" he asked.

In the sickly, yellow light they looked like blisters about to pop.

"Ach, don't look so worried," she said, laughing. "They're only mosquito bites, and they haven't had dengue here in years."

"Dengue, as in the fever?"Just the thought of it was enough to throw him into a panic.

Gertie threw him one of Udo Jörgen's contemptuous side glances.

"Like I said, you have nothing to worry about. But if you scratch them, they'll get infected. So don't scratch."

"Don't you have something I can put on them at least?"

"Sorry, no, they don't bite me. But if you want, I'll pick something up for you tomorrow. How long are you planning to stay, by the way? You didn't mention that in your letter."

She kept a watchful eye on him as she took a long swig from her bottle.

"I don't know." Something in the tone of her voice had made him feel inadequate.

"I bought a flexible return, just in case."

"You can stay as long as you like, of course," she said, lighting up a cigarette. "As you can see, there's plenty of room. I just wasn't sure what to expect. Are you hungry?"

"Starving. Except for some sort of meat pastry in Limón, I haven't eaten since the plane."

"I don't have much here, but I can get you something next door. My friend Andreas makes an excellent hamburger. Would you like to go over there, or should I just bring it back?"

She stretched her arm across him to reach the side table ashtray. Christian didn't remember her being quite this thin.

"I'd rather stay if you don't mind. I'm exhausted."

"Suit yourself," she said, straightening back up. He was surprised to hear a slight hint of disappointment in her voice.

"You should make yourself at home. There's a spare room upstairs, and I'll put the bedding out before I go. Whatever you do, though, don't flush the toilet paper. The pipes can't handle it. Throw it in the bin instead."

"Will it take long?" He felt oddly unnerved by her house set so close to the jungle.

"It might," she said, returning his penetrating stare. "It's a one-man operation, so it depends on how many customers he has. No such thing as fast food here."

Before leaving, she handed him a stack of bed linen and towels, still the no-nonsense mother he remembered. She had never been one to fawn on him or Udo Jörgen, not like his friends' moms who would sometimes invite him to stay during the semester breaks. They had always looked at him pityingly, incapable of comprehending his peculiar situation.

Christian's skin prickled as he peered up the dark stairwell. He found the light switch tucked inside an adjacent bookshelf, but once lit, the bare, incandescent bulb scarcely illuminated the rickety steps.

He encountered a small bathroom at the top of the wood-paneled landing, and to the left, what he assumed was Gertie's room. In the gloomy light, he recognized the distinct contours of her favorite blue vase standing atop a low-lying bookshelf. He overcame his childish fear of entering her private space and stepped inside to take a closer look. Apart from a sliding glass door leading out to the balcony, the room felt austere with only a few belongings and her paltry change of clothes hanging in an open closet. More disturbing was the fact that there were no covers on the bed. Not even a pillow.

The guest room beside it was equally bare. The furnishings were a drab, gray mattress on a box frame, and beside it, a red plastic lamp and an oscillating fan perched on an unfinished wood table. The only decorative element was a circular mosquito net hanging from a metal hook in the ceiling, its long, gauzy drapes gathered in a knot just above the bed.

Christian noticed a small spider's web in one corner and made a mental note to ask her for a broom. The room felt hot and uninviting, but at least he had a clear view of the wooden floor.

He opened the two window shutters and was surprised to find there was not a pane of glass or even a screen to protect him. Immediately, two giant insects flew past him toward the light, prompting him to close them shut once more. Clearly, he would have to make do with the fan alone.

He went to the bathroom to take a piss and feeling tired again, made up the bed and lay down. In a moment he would get up and try to figure out the shower.

"Christian!" Gertie was calling him from the stairs. "Your food is ready!"

He raised himself up on his elbows and noticed a few more welts on his arms.

"I got bitten again," he said, after taking a seat at her small kitchen table.

"They like to come out after dark. You'll want to sleep under the netting."

She placed the burger and fries down in front of him along with some mayo and ketchup. The tomato, on its dark bed of lettuce, was redder than any he had ever seen before. Popping a couple of golden fries into his mouth, he began to assemble the sandwich to his liking.

"It's delicious," he said, with his mouth still full. Apart from the close-cropped blonde hair Christian had inherited from Gertie, he had Klaus' eyes and nose, not to mention his build.

"The best money can buy," Gertie said, as she popped open two Pilsens she had taken out of the fridge. "I had one yesterday."

"I made up the room on the left," he said, taking one of the bottles from her. "But I wasn't sure which bed was yours."

She stared back at him amused.

"I don't sleep in my room," she said. "I sleep outside. On the terrace."

"Outside?" Christian said, scrutinizing her while he chewed. "Why?"

"I prefer sleeping beneath the night sky."

"But aren't you worried about the insects and wild animals?"

She took another sip from her beer keeping the bottle close to her mouth. "No, not really."

"But they have venomous snakes and spiders and who knows what else here. What if one of them falls on your head while you're asleep?"

Gertie laughed making him realize how few times he had seen her smile.

"Yes, I suppose that *could* happen, but it hasn't so far. I'm not too worried about it."

Christian shook his head.

"Well, you should be."

Christian did not recognize this Gertie. All he remembered of his mother were the sensible suits and shoes she had worn to work. She had spent a lot of time reading in the garden on weekends, but he didn't know her as this adventurous sort. Not in the least.

"You sound like your father, you know. You have his voice."

"Why did you come here?" he asked, ignoring her comment.

"Is that why you're here? To find out?"

"I came to see how you were doing. You left *us*, remember?"

"Don't be ridiculous," she said, reaching for her cigarettes. She was smoking an off brand now, something local. "You're grown men."

"*Mutti*, Udo was only seventeen! Anyway, you haven't answered my question."

"I don't have to have a reason for being here."

Her tongue was still as sharp as he recalled.

"No, but it's not every day someone gives up on their work and leaves the country."

"I didn't give up my work. I chose to retire. It's different."

"But why here? Why not stay in Germany, or even Europe? Why go all the way around the world to settle in some godforsaken jungle?"

"Godforsaken. Give me a break. It's beautiful and peaceful here."

"Peaceful?"

He shoved the empty plate out in front of him.

"I don't have to explain myself, Christian," she said, standing to clear the table. "You can either accept my decision or not. But I have every right to do as I want."

Annoyed, Christian stood up, too. The backs of his thighs were sticking to the seat. How could anyone bear to live like this, he wondered. Though the kitchen windows were open—the only ones with screens apparently—the air just would not circulate.

"You know it left Udo in a state, don't you? And that's why he doesn't write you back? He couldn't understand why I would go looking for you."

"So why did you?"

She was bent over the sink, washing his lone dish.

"Why must you make things so difficult? Why can't you be like other mothers?"

"Because I can't, that's why, and you should know that by now."

"But why didn't you at least say something?"

She looked up at him, her eyes stricken.

"What good would that have done? You would have tried to stop me. Told me it wasn't a good idea. Blah, blah, blah, blah!"

"Is that all we are to you? Blah, blah, blah, blah?"

"Of course not!"

Their eyes locked for a moment. He could almost hear the metallic ticktock of the bomb that was about to go off inside her, but she refused to say another word.

Instead, she came over and grabbed her cigarettes from the table.

"You know this isn't normal, right Gertie?" It felt good to call her by her first name. Why hadn't he done it before? "That parents don't just disappear?"

Her lips pursed into an almost invisible line.

"It would have been nice to think that you cared enough to at least tell us."

"I *do* care about you," she said, walking toward the living room and leaving a thin trail of smoke behind her.

"Well, you have a strange way of showing it."

"I know I'm not much of a mother, but I did what I could after Klaus left."

"I'm not questioning that!"

Why did it always come back to this? he thought.

She spun on her heel to face him.

"So, then what?"

There was a desperation in her eyes he had not seen in a very long time.

"I just don't understand this," Christian said. "Things were going so well."

She turned away from him again and was at the door now, her hand visibly shaking.

"I'm going out for a walk," she said. "Don't wait up."

The next morning, Christian found her in the kitchen making coffee.

"Here," she said, handing him a plastic bag. "I got you insect repellent and sunscreen."

"You were in town already?" he said, still rubbing the sleep from his eyes.

She ignored him and poured the coffee into two large mugs.

"Did you sleep alright?"

"I'm not sure what's worse. Being bitten by mosquitoes or sleeping beneath that damn net. How can you stand it?"

She shrugged her shoulders.

The coffee, at least, was nice and strong.

"I heard a strange noise at around four. They don't have baboons here, do they?"

She looked at him and laughed. At least they were back on decent footing.

"Those are howler monkeys. There's a troop that passes by here early mornings."

"Are they dangerous?" he asked, his blue eyes peering up from his mug.

"No. They're about the size of a small dog. They're folivores."

"They're what?"

"They eat leaves and berries. Maybe an egg on occasion. They don't bite. At least not if you leave them alone."

"Well, I don't know how you can sleep through all the noise."

"I manage," she said, before taking a sip from her coffee and flipping through a booklet of puzzles.

"So, what do you do around here, when you're not out communing with nature?"

"I look at the birds. Read. Do the crosswords."

He looked at her perplexed.

"That's all?"

"Pretty much."

There was no point in pushing her any further.

"Would you like to go to the National Park? It's better to go in the early morning if you want to see the animals, but it's nice now, too."

"No, that's ok. I think I'd rather stay here."

"Suit yourself," she said. "When you get hungry, there's bread and cold cuts in the fridge. Or we can go to the restaurant if you prefer."

Christian finished up his coffee, ate the two pieces of bland toast Gertie had popped in the toaster for him, and then went upstairs to do what he could not do before, it being a personal policy of his to avoid public toilets whenever possible.

The toilet in Gertie's small, utilitarian bathroom was much lower than what he was used to at home, offering a direct view of the curtainless shower stall and not much else. The large tiles she had used throughout were a dark, speckled green, a choice he would find suspect under normal circumstances, but knowing Gertie, they were no doubt spotless.

It was the plastic shower head, however, that caught his interest. An odd-looking contraption, it had the heating element built right in and was attached to the wall with a crude looking electrical wire. It looked both laughable and dangerous, but Gertie had already explained to him how it worked, and he was far too desperate to bathe to worry too much about it.

Shaking his head, he wound the meager, damp toilet roll around his hand.

Why the hell didn't she invest in an air conditioner, he thought.

Given the climate she could have easily justified the cost, but strangely she seemed unbothered by the excessive heat and humidity.

Christian finished his business, peeled off his shirt and let his pants drop to the floor. It was only as he turned to flush the toilet that he realized, with revulsion, what it was he had forgotten to do.

The wad of soiled paper he had just used was floating above his shit.

"Fuck!"

Christian watched with horror as the soggy pulp drifted, threatening to make contact with what had felt like the biggest release of his life.

"You have got to be fucking kidding me!"

Looking around in desperation, he saw nothing to fish out this ridiculous threat to his mother's pipes. *Surely it couldn't matter just the once, could it?!* But given the shoddy state of how everything was rigged around here, there was no way Christian could be certain, and knowing Gertie there would be hell to pay for not following her instructions.

Panicking, he grabbed what remained of the toilet roll and wound it again and again around his hand until it felt thick enough to act as a glove. He let out an involuntary retch as he leaned over the bowl, and as his hand dipped into the brown, murky water. Once in, though, he had no choice but to finish the task. Clasping onto the paper with his now soaked fingers he slung both wads into the open trash bin beside him.

"Brraaaggghhhhh!"

How could she make him do this?!

He had to twist his body to turn on the sink.

"Fuck, fuck, fuck!"

He let the tepid water run over his hands as he scrubbed them furiously with soap.

Never again, he told himself. *Never again.*

Christian spent the next two days sequestered on the couch, biding his time reading through Gertie's well-leafed detective novels. She would come and go at times, but apart from making sure that he was watered and well fed, they exchanged little else.

The following day, restless and bored, he accompanied her to the restaurant where he ordered yet another burger and fries, steering clear of any dishes that came with rice, beans and coconut sauce. Gertie did much the same, availing herself of two Pilsen's from the refrigerated case behind the counter.

Sipping their beers, they sat in silence at the large, communal table, the only nod to her hippie friend's German past. Apart from the hand-built wooden chairs and tables, the rest of the décor was comprised of tropical detritus: coral rocks and conch shells. There was even a bird's nest not to mention a small shrine to Bob Marley, Caway's only evident patron saint.

When Andreas finally brought out their food—they were the only customers he had but he took his time nonetheless!—he sat down to join them with his own bottle of Pilsen, just far enough away that he felt comfortable lighting up a cigarette while they ate.

"So, what do you think of our little paradise?" he asked.

Despite the deep creases cut into his sunbaked face, Andreas' eyes sparkled with the taunting mischief of perpetual youth.

Christian wiped his mouth with a cheap paper napkin.

"I suppose it's nice, if you're into this kind of thing," he said.

"And you're not?"

"It's a bit too hot and damp for my taste. And there are too many insects."

Andreas laughed and gave Gertie a look that seemed to say, '*he's one of those*'.

"Your mother tells me you're finishing up your studies. What will you do once you've graduated? Take a little tour of Europe, perhaps?"

"I have an internship lined up with Siemens. If it goes well, they'll offer me a job."

"Oh, that sounds important. So, do you work with the computers, like your mom?"

"No, not informatics. My interests are in hardware and software design."

Andreas' gave him one of his hippie-go-lucky smiles.

"Hey, if that's what makes you happy," he said.

"And you?" Christian asked. "You like this life? Doesn't it get dull after a while?"

"This?" Andreas stretched his arms out as if he were embracing the jungle. "It's my own piece of Eden. I wouldn't trade this for the world. I prefer life outdoors."

"It's a little too much outdoors if you ask me," Christian said.

"And what will you do with the rest of your time here? Tortuguero is not far by boat."

Christian took another bite and chewed his food. If anything, he had to admit Andreas was an excellent cook.

"I'm leaving at the end of the week," he said. "Just as soon as I can confirm my flight."

"So soon?" Andreas said, looking over at Gertie, but she had her nose buried in a book.

"I only came here to check on her. No offense, but this isn't my idea of a vacation."

"It's just that you've traveled so far. Might as well see something while you're here."

"I have to get ready for my move to Berlin. Plus, I should probably spend some time with my brother before I go."

This last jab was directed at Gertie who just sat there, pretending not to hear.

"All the same, it's nice you came for a visit," Andreas said.

"Yeah, well. It would have been different if she felt the same way."

At this, Gertie lifted her head and frowned.

"C'mon! It's obvious you can't wait for me to leave so you can get back to—I'm not really sure what—but why not just admit it?"

Gertie shook her head.

"That's not it at all."

"Yeah?" Christian turned to face Andreas. "As you can see, it would be pointless to stay any longer. Gertie much prefers her own company, as I'm sure you already know."

Gertie pushed herself up from the table.

"I'm not going to listen to this. I'll see you back at home."

Christian laughed.

"Home? And where is that?"

He watched as her pencil-thin outline cut across the empty dining room and walked down the side steps. In a matter of seconds, she had disappeared.

Andreas turned to look at him.

"That was a bit harsh, don't you think?"

Christian narrowed his eyes at him.

"You don't really know her, do you? I came here to give her another chance. To explain herself. But Udo is right, she doesn't give a damn about her family. And if this is what she really wants, I'm certainly not going to keep her from it. But I'll be damned if I'll try again."

Andreas shook his head vigorously and let out a sigh.

"Man, she loves you more than you can understand. It's Germany that's no good for her."

"Germany?" Christian laughed. "Where she had a comfortable, modern home and a well-paying career?"

Now it was Andreas' turn to grimace.

"No. You don't understand what it was like for us growing up right after the war. Your mother did the best she could for you and your brother, but she couldn't stay there any longer."

Christian shook his head.

"Listen, I'm glad she found a friend in you, really. You must be the only one. But as you can see, my mother isn't good at love. And quite frankly, she just isn't well. Never has been. But like she's said, it's time to get on with our lives. Leave the rest behind."

Two days later, Gertie saw Christian off at the station, though they hardly said a word to one another on the taxi ride over.

It was only when he took a step to board the bus, that she put her hand on his forearm.

"I'm sorry," she said, as he jerked his head back in surprise. "I know I can't expect you to understand this."

He looked down at her sun-worn face and saw the tears well up in her eyes.

With one arm slung around his heavy backpack, he placed the other around her frail shoulders, and on an impulse, knelt down to kiss her head.

"Take good care of yourself," he whispered, holding back the catch in his throat.

She nodded quietly and then stepped aside to let the other passengers go through.

Christian found an empty window seat towards the back, but as the bus pulled out, he could no longer see her.

Had she already left, he wondered? A second later, however, her small figure reappeared.

She was standing alone and waving at him, mouthing words he could no longer hear.

13

Caway - May 2005

On a sunny, mid-morning in May, a tall, wiry man in his forties skulked up to the kitchen counter of Quixote's. With a lit cigarette dangling from his mouth, he asked if he could get a beer.

"Pilsen or Imperial?" Anja asked, after setting Daniel up with his crayons in the play area near the entrance of the dining room. She crossed over into the kitchen to get a better look at the newcomer's face, recognizing in an instant the telltale signs of hard living beneath his matted and unkempt black curls.

"I'll take a Pilsen, or what the Ticos pass off as one."

Anja opened a bottle and handed it to him through the kitchen window.

"Are you staying nearby?" she asked. She had seen his type before and tended toward a more cautious approach.

The man took a long swig.

"You could say that," he said, looking around Quixote's through bloodshot eyes. "I've just moved up the road. Arrived about fifteen minutes ago."

Anja pointed across the garden.

"The Old Smith place?" she asked. "That makes us neighbors then."

"Yes, it does," he said, studying her as he leaned against the split-log countertop cattycorner from the Stammtisch.

Perhaps she had judged him too soon.

"I'm Anja," she said, and then gestured toward the dining room.

"That's my son, Daniel. My husband Andreas should be back any minute now. He's just picking up some guests and supplies in town."

"How old is he?" the man asked, tilting his chin up in Daniel's direction. "He looks about my daughter's age."

Anja tried to imagine this man as the father of a young child.

"Six. You should bring her by to play sometime. So, what brought you to Caway?"

He took another hefty pull from the longneck.

"The sun and the quiet. We were staying outside of San José for a while. Up in the mountains. Too cold and gray there so we thought we'd try our luck on the Caribbean. Should be cheaper, too."

"It's certainly much quieter here than in San José, that's for sure. I take it you're Dutch?"

"Amsterdam born and bred. Sure as hell don't miss the cold. Getting too old for that shit. And you must be German," he added, not bothering to hide the smirk on his face.

"Yes, but soon to be naturalized," Anja said, keen to not let him define her. "Just one more year. Andreas has his citizenship already. And Daniel, he was born here."

The man's unruly eyebrows raised up a notch.

"We won't be doing any of that. Too much trouble if you ask me. Plus, we get our pension from The Netherlands which should be fine for a decent enough life here."

Anja ran a cloth over the kitchen's stainless-steel countertop.

"That's most of the expats here, but you seem a bit young for retirement."

He narrowed his eyes at her.

"Oh, I've earned my time off. After the hell I've gone through I'm lucky to be alive to enjoy what's left."

"Sorry to hear that," Anja said, aware she had struck a nerve. "I didn't mean to offend."

Just then they heard the straining of a car engine pulling into the driveway.

"Like those crazy Amis like to say, 'life's a bitch'. Not so many of them around here, though, eh?"

Anja wondered what his beef with the Americans might be.

"Only a few. They prefer the Pacific side. Around here it's mostly Europeans."

"Well, it could be worse," he concluded, putting down his empty bottle.

"Andreas, come meet our new neighbor," Anja said, spotting her husband coming up the stairs toward them. "I'm sorry, but I didn't catch your name."

"Nicolaas," he said, eyeing Andreas carefully. "But you can call me Nico."

Andreas raised his hand in greeting, his easy-going smile releasing the tension that had built up between Anja and the Dutchman. Then he introduced them to the English couple coming up behind him.

"Can I offer you something to drink before I take you to your cabina?" Anja asked, turning her attention toward their new guests. "A juice, coffee, beer?"

Noticing the empty bottle sitting at the bar, Andreas asked Nico if he would join him for another. Nico's face lit up with a nicotine-stained grin.

"I don't see why not."

"Take a seat," Andreas said pointing toward the Stammtisch.

He returned from the kitchen with two bottles and a fresh packet of Derby's, then took his seat at the head of the table. He let out a groan of exaggerated fatigue.

"I've been up since six this morning," he said with a smile as he pulled at the thin, plastic tear tape.

"You and me both," Nico said, accepting the first cigarette Andreas tapped out. "We had to take the first bus from San José."

Andreas lit each one of them in turn.

"You're staying at the Ole Smith' place. You like it?"

"It's not exactly luxurious, is it? But it will do for now."

Anja, who stood eavesdropping in the kitchen, shook her head.

Later, as she led her guests behind the restaurant and down the garden's gravel path—pointing out the red ginger flowers, or *bastoneras* as they were known locally—she could just make out an echo of the laughter she had left behind. She wondered about this new neighbor of theirs. She had encountered Nico's annoying conceit and derisive tone in other expats who had come before him, but something about his disconcerting energy left Anja feeling on edge.

Anja came back up to the restaurant to find Nico and Andreas still talking and making their way through yet another round of beers.

"Feel free to invite your wife and daughter over," she said, as she walked past them and into the kitchen. "I'm sure the children would like to play."

Nico waved his hand as if shooing a fly.

"I'm sure they're sleeping now."

Anja found his attitude flippant but knew better than to press any further. Still, she thought it odd he would leave his family on their first day here to go out drinking.

She went behind the counter to pour herself a glass of cold water and spotted Treven, Ms. Adina's grandson, walking through the gate. He was cradling a cinched burlap sack.

"*Irie*, Ms. Anja," he said, placing his bundled goods on the corner of the Stammtisch.

"*Irie*, Tre," Anja beamed, making her way toward him. "What have you got there?"

At twelve, Treven was already resembling a young man with his broadening chest and bubbling biceps. His father was living and working in Limón now, having left his three boys with Ms. Adina after his wife was killed in a motorcycle accident.

"My grandmother made coconut oil," he said, opening the bag. "She says to give you some."

He handed her a jar of the aromatic liquid.

"Oh! That's very nice of her, but far too generous."

"You must take it. She says it's for your help with my schoolwork."

"Well, tell her thank you from me, and that she really shouldn't have. I can't believe she's still making it at her age."

Treven nodded in polite acknowledgment but kept his lips pursed.

"What will you do with the others?" Anja asked, seeing he still had quite a few jars left.

"I will sell them to the Chinese," he replied, cinching the sack.

He was referring to the long-standing, family grocery store located on the main road. Despite competition from a national chain that had opened in the newer shopping center near the bus terminal, the family that owned it still managed to do a brisk business with the residents. The Freyers shopped there almost exclusively.

"What's that?" Nico asked, finally noticing Treven's presence after Andreas excused himself to go to the restroom.

"His grandmother makes coconut oil by hand," Anja said. "She husks and grates it, then cooks it in the milk over an open fire until the water evaporates. It's rare to find someone still doing this."

Nico arched his eyebrows.

"How much do you get for it?"

Not missing a beat Treven asked, "How much do you want to pay?"

"Oh, no," Nico said, putting his hand up as if to stop traffic. "That's not for me. We don't cook in this way."

"You can use it for other things. For the skin and hair. Not just for cooking."

Nico laughed.

"And step out in this sun? I'll fry like a chicken, and my hair is greasy enough as it is."

At this Treven laughed, too.

Nico pulled out a cigarette from the pack Andreas left on the table.

"Hey, at least someone here gets my sense of humor."

Irked, Anja ignored him and turned her attention back to Treven.

"Make sure you get a good price. Your grandmother works much too hard to make it."

"Yes, ma'am."

"Would you like something to drink before you go? A juice or a soda?"

"No. I best be going now," Treven said, picking up his wares.

"Tre!" Andreas called out to him as he walked back toward the table.

"*Irie,* 'Dre," Treven said, a broad smile spreading across his face.

"What Miss Adi wantin'?"

"Some red snappa?"

"You come pick it up on the way back." Andreas said. "I have it ready."

Crossing paths at the gateway, a few tourists from the hotel next door trickled in to ask about the likelihood of an early lunch. Andreas, reluctant to move but happy for business, took leave from the Dutchman and went into the kitchen to start cooking. It was only then, without a renewed offer for yet another round, that Nico decided it was time to head home.

Anja and Andreas did not meet the Van de Steegs until the following afternoon as a tropical storm rolled in. A few of their guests, including Gertie, had taken shelter inside of Quixote's dining room where they could watch the cloudburst pass while reading or playing games with cold refreshments at hand. Beneath the corrugated tin roof, the rapping of the torrent reverberated more as a steady mantra—a benign recitation—and not a threatening force of nature beneath the open sky.

The Freyers had already served the small lunch rush and were just finishing their own mid-afternoon meal when Nico, carrying his spirited young daughter on his shoulders, ducked under the open threshold. His wife, bent over, followed close behind, all three of them soaking wet.

"*Dag,* Anja, Andreas," Nico said, blithely lifting the laughing little girl and placing her down before them. Her long blonde hair was pasted to her forehead and cheeks, and her sopping red sundress clung to her, exposing her still childish, plump limbs.

Anja and Andreas, surprised by their arrival in the pouring rain, stood up to greet them.

"That's Nina," Nico said, tilting his head toward his wife. "And the little one here is Magdalena, but we call her Lena for short. We sure could use a beer after being out in this piss, *mijn God.*"

"Let me get you some towels so you can at least dry off," Anja said. "I'm surprised you're not half-drowned. Will you get the beers, Andreas?"

As she returned from the storage closet, Anja noticed that Nina, though visibly younger than Nico, was also quite gaunt. Unlike her husband and daughter, she did not look at all pleased to have been caught in this downpour.

"Can I get you something to eat?" Anja asked, as Nina toweled off the head of her still giggling daughter.

Nina winced as if the thought of food had turned her stomach.

"No, thank you. Just a beer, please."

"And the little one?"

"Do you have ice cream?" Lena asked, her eager and sparkling sapphire eyes searching Anja's face intently.

Anja knelt down to her level.

"Chocolate, vanilla or strawberry?"

"Chocolate," Lena said, her cherubic face rounding out into a dimpled smile.

Hearing this, Daniel ran in from the dining room.

"I want some, too!"

"OK, now, no need to yell. Chocolate is Daniel's favorite, too, Lena. Why don't I prepare two bowls, and after that the two of you can play together, sound good?"

The two children appraised one another for a shy moment then turned toward Anja nodding their heads in unison.

"Daniel, why don't you show Lena your toys?"

While Anja busied herself in the kitchen, Nico and Nina, having dried themselves as much as possible, took a seat opposite Gertie, who was perched at the far end of the *Stammtisch*. She had nodded to the Dutch as Andreas had introduced her but had quickly turned her attention back to her book.

"Gertie has read every book you can find in Caway," Andreas said as he distributed the beers around the table.

"That's one way to kill the time," Nico said, raising two fingers toward his wife for a cigarette. Nina passed over the crumpled pack she held in her hand then returned to sitting with her shoulders hunched.

Anja set Lena and Daniel up in the dining room and rejoined the others.

Nina looked up at her briefly as she took her seat. Anja could see Lena's eyes were like those of her mother's except that the child's buoyant vibrancy was replaced with a subdued apprehension that made the blue radiate out like a warning.

It was obvious Nina had once been a great beauty, and judging by her height and proportions, quite possibly a model. But her confidence and composure seemed to have eroded, and her outward appearance resembled more the cast away shell of a creature that had long since abandoned its moorings.

Half-listening to the conversation Nico and Andreas had picked up from the previous afternoon, Anja sensed that in a strange, and perhaps disturbing way, Nico and Nina were well matched, like a pair of lone survivors after a terrible shipwreck. To her mind, it was a wonder they had managed to produce such a beautiful and animated child, one who on the surface appeared to be perfectly happy and healthy.

Anja turned toward Nico who just then was complaining about Dutch politics.

"If you don't mind my asking, what did you do before coming here?"

Nico looked at her with the popped-out eyes of a cartoon bulldog.

"I was a war correspondent."

"Oh," Anja said, feeling once again as if she had put her foot in her mouth. "I can see now why you would want your peace and quiet. What got you into that line of work?"

"Can I have another one of these?" he said, lifting up an empty bottle. "Idealized stupidity, that's what."

Just then a sheet of rain came gushing down, its glimmering translucence masking the tropical landscape.

"That's rather harsh, don't you think?" Anja said, raising her voice so she could be heard over the din. "Where would we be if we didn't have someone like you reporting on what's happening out there?"

"Pffft. Most journos are embedded now. They stay on base and are given media sound bites by the brass so they start thinking they're part of some fucking Rambo squad with 'specialized training'. They travel with the convoys and patrols, eat and shit with the soldiers, so, what type of stories do they file? Who are their sources? It's a fucking joke."

Anja handed him another bottle.

"Were you embedded, too?" Andreas asked.

"The Dutch didn't start that shit until Iraq," Nico said, rolling his eyes. "I embedded once, but in the beginning they had no problem with you going out on your own and filing at your discretion. That's all changed now. And it sure as hell was never the case with the Amis and the Brits."

Nico took a moment to light up another cigarette.

"The Brits have had theirs on a leash ever since the Falklands, and the Amis, well, they just psyche everyone out, as in 'don't be surprised if you're mistaken for an enemy combatant' or some such shit.

"Me, on the other hand, I always worked on my own or with other freelancers. We took risks. Not like these fucking cowards too afraid to get out from under mama commander's wings. No, we talked to civilians, ate with them, slept in the same shitholes. We got into the middle of it. That's what reporters are supposed to do."

Just then the children came running in from the dining room.

"Don't be such a baby," Lena said to Daniel, looking annoyed.

"Mama, she won't let me go first even though it's my game!"

"Now Daniel," Anja said, exasperated. "Just let her go first, please."

Daniel scowled.

"But why?"

"Because she's our guest. Now go back and play."

A triumphant smile crossed over Lena's face.

"C'mon," she said, grabbing Daniel's hand and leading him back to their game. "You can go first the next time."

Nico smiled at his daughter.

"These kids," he said. "Too bad we're not more like them."

"So why did you choose war?" Andreas asked, leaning back in his seat.

One of Nico's eyes started to dart side to side.

"It was Bosnia," he said. "I'd just finished my studies. Had a young daughter with my girlfriend at the time, and I figured, hey, why not? I'd done my military service, grew up in a rough neighborhood, too, so I knew how to take care of myself.

"It was a fucking nightmare, though. You want to think you know what you're coming up against, but it was pure fucking chaos. Snipers everywhere. Didn't know who to trust. They forced us out fast enough. Then Srebrenica happened. A total shit show between the UN and the Dutch force, and the shame of the Netherlands, if you ask me."

Just then, Nico caught Gertie's eyes peering up over the edge of her book. Nina, meanwhile, was still hunched over her beer, looking out into the rain as if in a trance.

"Back home, people were up in arms wanting to know what the hell happened. After that, I got back in. Worked with a film crew for a while, tried to piece it together. In between that I went to Rwanda which ruined my family life, that's for sure. It's hard to come down off the adrenalin. The crazy things you see and hear."

"Sounds like you've been through hell," Andreas said, looking at Nico. "Respect."

"Well, I wouldn't be here if it wasn't for her."

Nico's eyes softened as he reached over to squeeze Nina's hand.

"Saved each other, didn't we, girl? Now we'll take it easy. Just have to find a school for Lena, and take advantage of this *pura vida* life."

Anja glanced over at Nina, sensing her discomfort.

"There's a private school up the road where most of the expats send their kids," she said. "And it's where Daniel goes, too. I'm on the advisory committee, so I can introduce you, if you like."

Nina raised her eyes for a hopeful moment in Nico's direction.

"Expensive?" Nico asked. "We don't have that much money."

"By European standards, no," Anja said. "And there are scholarships depending on the situation."

"That would be great," Nina said, her voice cracking from her long-held silence. "Nico's grandmother said she could help with the tuition."

Nico furrowed his brow at her.

"If it's within reason, yes."

The moment the rain stopped, the Van de Steeg's—along with everyone else—stood to take their leave. By that point, Nico was well past tipsy and Nina well on her way.

"They're an unusual couple," Anja said, clearing the table of the cigarette litter and empty beer bottles.

Andreas took a last drag from his cigarette before getting up to stretch his sinewy limbs.

"How so?"

"I don't know. They just seem a bit odd, that's all."

Andreas laughed.

"More so than anyone else living here? You're not so 'normal' yourself, you know."

Anja grimaced, a look of concern clouding her eyes.

"That's not what I meant, and you know it. There's something wrong with those two."

"Wrong? I think you're reading too much into things. You heard yourself what he's gone through. That's enough to drive anyone crazy. If ever a man needed a break from all that shit, it's definitely him."

"I know, I know. But it's not just that. There's something funny about Nina. The way she just sits there."

"Well, they're our neighbors now. Better to accept them as they are than to make them feel like they don't belong. That's not what we're about here."

"I wasn't suggesting that. I just think we should keep an eye out, that's all."

Out of nowhere she heard Gertie's bitter cough.

"*Ach*, just leave them be."

She was standing near the front entrance readying to leave.

"The last thing they need is someone like you getting in their business."

14

Amsterdam - November 1997

"*Hey,*" a voice called out.

It was well past two in the morning, and a full moon hung low in the sky. Nico teetered back on his heels.

He had just returned from an assignment in Algeria and the images still bloomed like red algae in his head. To obliterate them, he had stepped off the plane at Schiphol, dropped off his bags and made a beeline for De Wallen, the city's red-light district. At a string of bars, he had flung himself into an unabashed bender.

"*Hey!*"

This time the voice sounded more urgent. He looked over his shoulder, at first mistaking the call as a solicitation, but instead he saw a well-dressed young woman leaning against the brick wall of the alley, just opposite the *Achterburgwal* canal.

"You 'kay?" Nico said, stumbling toward her. His long shadow, cast from the incandescent glow of the corner streetlamp, trailed behind him.

She looked up, and her head swayed as if in a dreamy haze.

"I'm ok. But you, you were 'bout to fall in the canal."

Having said that, her long, dark lashes drifted in slow motion toward the alabaster of her cheeks.

Nico looked around disoriented, his comprehension lagging far behind the staggering amounts of alcohol he had drunk.

"Oh, that one," he said, and then laughed. "Issa a good thing you saw me, then, m*ijn god.*"

Turning back to look at her, his tone shifted to one of concern.

"So, what about you? You're not planning on sleeping here, are you?"

"Oh no, I'm just taking a little rest," she said, closing her eyes and leaning back against the wall.

Nico looked down at her. She was only wearing a pair of well-tailored jeans and a diaphanous blouse.

"*Issa* fuckin' cold to rest here, no?"

Nico rubbed his hands together, waiting for her to respond.

"Hmm, but I have my coat right here."

The woman's other worldly beauty reminded Nico of a character from one of the bedtime stories his young daughter had often insisted he read out loud.

"Where?"

She opened her eyes to appraise herself and realized her coat was nowhere to be found.

"Oops," she said, sounding like a child.

"Well, you can't just kip here," Nico said, extending a shaky hand to help her up. "Whadya say we go to mine?"

The woman attempted to furrow her brow but seemed to grow tired of it.

"No," she replied, shaking her head. "I'm not like that."

"Neither am I, but it's too fuckin' cold," Nico said. "You jus' saved me from the canal, lemme at least save you from catching your death. My place isn't far, and you'll be better off on the couch."

She eyed him with suspicion but then nodded.

Nico leaned forward and braced himself against the rough brick. He reached out his hand again and then pulled her up with such unintended force that she almost went flying in the opposite direction.

"Follow me," he said, still holding her hand. "You keep your eyes on the canal. Make sure we don't fall in. 'kay?"

"'kay," she replied.

Nico led the way, and the woman glided beside him like a swan in moonlight. Meanwhile the movement of the water ricocheted light from the wake of her dark, long hair.

He gazed up and saw her lips move. Then he closed his eyes and sunk into a deep, impenetrable stillness.

Nico awoke with a start face down on the sofa. His head throbbed. His mouth felt parched. He pressed himself up to a seated position and recoiled at the thought of bringing his lips together. They felt dry and ready to crack.

He placed his feet on the cool, parquet floor where he allowed them to rest for a moment. Then, testing his wooziness, he rose to a low, wobbling stance.

Slowly, he zigzagged down the hall and toward the kitchen. Once there, he leaned his weight against the sink and turned on the faucet, grasping fistfuls of water into his mouth. Spotting the one clean glass by the sink, he filled it to the brim and drank it down. He refilled it and wandered back into the studio's living space, only then noticing that a strange woman was lying fully clothed in the middle of his bed.

With measured steps, he drifted toward her, careful not to make a sound. Seeing that she was still fast asleep, he sat down on the corner of the bed to take a closer look.

Through the fog of memory, he recalled her saving him from falling into the canal. But that was all he could remember.

He had not slept with her, that much was clear, since they were both fully clothed, and she still had her shoes on. Nico felt a pang of regret. Maybe if he had not drunk an entire bottle of vodka, he would be in bed beside her. Or, at the very least, know her name.

He took a cautious whiff of his armpits and realized he was in desperate need of a shower, and that it would be best to take one before she awoke. He was not sure what type of impression he had made on her before blacking out.

He padded back into the kitchen and threw open the window to circulate the stale air that had permeated the apartment. Then, he put on the coffee maker.

Next, he visited the bathroom. After taking a long piss, he stripped off his clothes and popped a few aspirin. In the shower he turned the hot water up as high as it could go, only stepping out again once he felt his humanity restored.

He wrapped the towel tight around his waist, looked in the mirror and decided to shave.

No use looking like a thug, he thought.

With care he opened the bathroom door so it would not let out its abominable squeak and was relieved to find he still had clean underwear stuffed in the bottom of the armoire located at the far end of the entrance way. He dressed quickly, then slipped out of the apartment to pick up pastries at the bakery next door.

When he returned, he saw she was already sitting up in bed, a look of discomfort on her face as she took in the now sun-drenched contents of his large, but shabby room.

It was two in the afternoon.

"Hi there," he said. "Care for a cup of coffee?"

He held up a paper bag filled with baked goods.

She nodded, looking somewhat uncertain as she pulled the duvet up to her chest.

Nico ducked into the kitchen. He smoothed down his hair before pouring the coffee into two large mugs. He grabbed a couple of mismatched plates from the cupboard and placed everything on a woven carrying tray left behind by the previous tenants.

"Milk or sugar?" he called out. He hoped she would not want either since he doubted the milk was any good and the sugar would require him to hunt down a takeout packet buried somewhere in the scattered mess of his cutlery drawers.

"Black's fine," came the merciful response. Her voice was low and gravelly but still strangely refined.

He brought the tray in and placed it on the living room table, opposite the couch.

"Pastry?" he asked, bringing one of the mugs over to the bedside.

"Just the coffee for now," she said, eyeing him carefully as she took the cup into both hands. "But thank you."

Not wanting to crowd her, Nico walked back to the sitting area, took a fresh roll from the plate and sank down into his beat-up leather recliner. As he chewed, he returned her quiet stare.

"I'm sorry," she said. "But I don't remember much from last night."

"That makes two of us. What's your name?"

"Nina," she said.

"Well, Nina," he smiled. "I'm Nico, and since I don't remember from before, it's a pleasure to meet you."

The caffeine was starting to kick in a little, helping to restore his confidence.

Nina glanced over the bed, distrustful.

"Did we—"

"No, no. I woke up on the couch. I think we were both pretty plastered when we got here."

She gave him a short, almost imperceptible nod before focusing on her mug and taking a few sips from her coffee.

"You saved me from falling into the canal last night. That much I can recall."

"Oh?" she said.

"Given the state I was in, I doubt I would have survived a cold swim."

"Yes," she said, though her mind was clearly elsewhere. She was scanning his apartment again, her eyes a bit panicked.

"You haven't seen my coat around, have you?"

"No, but now that you mention it, I think that's why we came here. I remember now asking whether you had one or not. When I saw you, you were propped up against the wall on the *Barndesteeg*. Dressed just like that."

She groaned and clasped her hands to the sides of her temples.

"Shit! I must have left it."

"Would you like me to try and find it?" Nico asked. "It's still very cold outside."

A worry line formed across her forehead.

"The problem is, I can't remember if I might have—"

"We'll retrace our steps. In the meantime, you can borrow one of mine."

"I'm afraid it's too late," she said, sounding none-too-hopeful. "I had my money in it. And my keys. Plus, Max—"

"It's still worth a look, though, isn't it?" Nico said, anxious to make her feel better. He could see her agitation mounting.

"I'm not so sure it's a good idea for me to go over there right now."

Nico paused a moment, letting this information sink in. It dawned on him she might be in trouble.

"You're more than welcome to stay here," he said. "And feel free to take a shower if you like. That might help clear your head."

"That's kind of you," Nina said, looking down at the duvet as if ashamed.

"It's no problem at all. I'm happy to help."

Nico could see a few tears tracing a path down her cheeks.

"Hey, are you ok?" he asked, leaning forward in his chair.

"No," she said, not looking up. "I don't think so."

"I want you to know you're safe here, ok? I'm not going to hurt you."

She began to cry without a sound, her body trembling.

Nico walked over to the bedside and placed a tentative hand on her shoulder. Nina, meanwhile, covered her eyes with her hands.

"I'll get you some tissue," he said.

He walked back to the bathroom and retrieved a half roll of toilet paper.

She mouthed a silent thanks then dried her eyes and blew her nose.

"I'm so sorry. I'm sure this is the last thing you expected."

"I wasn't expecting anything, so nothing for you to feel sorry for."

"I won't stay long. I just need to pull myself together and then—"

"Hey, I'm just glad you're here, and not out there. Really."

"You won't be once you get to know me," she said.

"For Christ's sake, Nina, you saved me last night. I'd be a right bastard to throw you out now," he added, trying to lighten the mood. "Take a shower. It'll make you feel better. In the meantime, I'll go out and get us some real food, alright? Just stay here and relax."

She nodded her head.

"A shower would be nice. Can I borrow something to wear?"

"Let me see what I can find," Nico said, as he walked back toward the armoire. He rifled through the top shelf and managed to find a clean t-shirt.

"Will this do, for now? In the meantime, I can put your clothes in the washing machine. Looks like I need to do mine as well. And while I'm out, I'll pick up a few things."

"I don't want you to go to so much trouble on my account."

"It's no trouble at all," he said, handing her the wrinkled tee with a sheepish grin. "There should be another towel in the bathroom. I'll be back before you know it."

He turned away from her, grabbed another pastry and strode toward the door. He wolfed it down and put his jacket on, not daring to look back. Despite the awkwardness of the situation, Nico could not help but feel a slight flutter of happiness.

Back on the street, Nico lit a cigarette, pausing to let the nicotine take its effect. The late November light was starting to wane, and a bank of clouds was rolling in from the North Sea. As he watched the darkening sky, his mind was a jumble of opposing forces. Nina was clearly troubled or in trouble or both. He suspected heroin, although she was clearly a cut above your typical junkie if that happened to be the case.

Objectively speaking, the situation reeked of a potential disaster in the making. He already had a daughter and an ex to support on top of just barely eking out a life of his own. At the same time, he had not felt so attracted to a woman in years. But then again, who wouldn't be?

Nina's was a rare type of beauty, the kind that left you stunned by its sheer implausibility. Still, what he was feeling in his chest was indicative of more than just a primitive lust. Her vulnerability had stirred something in him long buried beneath a growing mound of disillusionment.

As he neared his building on the *Jodenbreestraat*—one of the few historic structures still standing in the heart of the old Jewish ghetto—his thoughts turned to his own situation.

Carla, his ex, had left him two years ago, taking their six-year-old Sonja with her. They lived in Rotterdam now with her—as she liked to put it—more *reliable* dock worker boyfriend, Henk. Carla had grown tired of Nico's constant travel, not to mention his irregular hours and income. His tendency of drinking to excess—especially after one of his arduous overseas stints—had put her well over the edge. She had accused him of setting a poor example for Sonja, and of being an endless disappointment to her. She was sick and tired of his apologies and his sorry excuses, so after repeated warnings, she had finally left him while he was still on assignment. He had returned to find their flat completely emptied out apart from some of his scattered belongings dumped here and there in her haste to move out. That and a final notice for their six-month overdue rent.

After an overwrought drinking spree that lasted close to a week, he had packed up his possessions and moved into the cheapest studio he could find that was still within walking distance of his most reliable editor. To counter the otherwise unbearable pain of his loss, he would often bury himself in work, only coming up for air to visit Sonja or to blow off steam at the local bars.

Nico did not mind spending time with Henk. He was not the one who gave him trouble. In fact, they would often have a beer together in the kitchen while they waited for Carla and Sonja to get back from whatever "urgent" errand happened to need running whenever he wanted to see his daughter. Despite her newfound *happiness*, Carla had a way of making him pay no matter how long they had been apart and no matter how much money he provided for Sonja's upkeep.

He had only been with a handful of women since Carla left him. None particularly memorable except the Romanian with whom he had had a month-long affair, and as it turned out, she was only keen on him to help ease her visa situation. Apart from that, he would on occasion hook-up with an old high school girlfriend, but that situation, too, had grown tiresome. It was clear that their paths had long diverged, and apart from the sex, they had little else in common. And here he was, once again placing himself in a situation where the odds were stacked against him, and where his means were of more immediate concern.

"But fuck it," Nico thought, as he fumbled with his keys. "What else have I got to lose?"

When he entered the flat, Nina was on the couch, smoking one of his cigarettes. Her hair was wet, and she had his t-shirt stretched over her knees with just a pair of narrow, sock-covered feet jutting out.

"I hope you don't mind," she said, holding up the burning ember. "I don't have any of my own."

"Help yourself," he said, tossing one of the shopping bags in her direction. "I got you some undies and a tracksuit. And I picked up a curry and some beer as well."

"Thanks. I went ahead and put the clothes in the washer. It's warm in here, so I don't think they'll take too long to dry."

He went into the kitchen to grab some plates and to give Nina a chance to change.

"Let's eat something," he said, bringing the food out. "You must be starving by now."

Nina was standing at full height now —his height—in her new sporting attire. The grey cotton material seemed to just barely cling to her hips before draping down over her maddeningly long legs.

He went back into the kitchen to open the beers. He took a long swig from one of the bottles before returning to the crowded table that doubled as his desk, and where Nina had already taken her seat near the window.

He handed her a beer and sat down on the corner beside her.

"*Proost!*"

"*Proost*," she said, sounding a bit preoccupied.

Having found her appetite, she sunk her fork into the plate of chicken tikka masala and began to eat with slow and deliberate gestures.

"Where are you from?" Nico asked, reaching for one of the vegetable samosas. "If you don't mind my asking."

"Leiden. But I've been in Amsterdam for five years now. And you?"

"I'm Bos en Lommer bred. Do you study here?"

"Sort of," she said, turning her eyes toward the window. "I've taken some courses at the *Hogeschool.* English education mostly. But I came here to model."

"Aha," Nico said. "I have to admit that doesn't come as a surprise. But women like you must get that a lot."

"Yeah, well, to be honest, the profession is quite fucked. I don't do it anymore."

"I can only imagine," Nico said, taking another swig from his bottle.

"I made good money. For a while anyway. But you can't really get away from the drugs. They're everywhere, and there's a lot of pressure to take them. Anyway, that's how I started."

Cautiously, she looked up from her plate to gauge his reaction.

"Is that what you were on last night, heroin?" he asked, casually preparing another bite so as not to put her on the spot. When he looked up, she was nodding.

"I'm not one to judge," he said. "But you have to be careful with that shit."

"I know," Nina said, hanging her head.

"Do you want to stop? I mean, are you ready to?"

"Of course, but it's not that easy."

"The key is to disconnect completely," he said, with a measured air of detachment. "It's too hard when you're around others who are doing it."

"Yeah, well," she said, as if he would not understand. "I don't really *want* to go back to that. The problem is, I don't have anywhere else to go."

Nico narrowed his eyes.

"And the keys in your coat? What are those to?"

The cerulean blue of her eyes met his for a moment.

"To the flat where I stay. With Max."

Nico felt his stomach tighten.

"Is he your boyfriend?"

Nina averted her eyes.

"Was. But he lets me stay anyway."

"And he's the one who has your coat?"

"I think so. It's hard for me to remember exactly."

Even with a concerned expression on her face, she seemed otherworldly and perfect.

"Yeah, I'm pretty sure," she added. "He was really upset with me. He threw me out of the flat. I'm starting to remember."

"Is that where your stuff is? At his place?"

"What I have left. Yes."

Nico could feel his apprehension turn to anger.

"I'll get it back for you. You just have to tell me where to go."

Nina looked at him sharply.

"Why are you so eager to help me? Just so you know, I'm not a sex worker."

Her rebuttal stopped him short.

"I wasn't thinking you were," Nico said, trying not to sound defensive.

"Well, I'm not."

"Listen, Nina, I just want to help, ok? Sure, you're gorgeous. There's no denying that. But I'm not *that* kind of guy. Even if I do look a bit rough."

"I just want to be clear, and it's not because I don't appreciate your help, it's just that—"

"Listen. You want your stuff back, yeah? And you want to get out of this situation?"

Nina nodded.

"Then the sooner I do this the better. All I need is the address. If he's as upset as you say he is, your stuff might not be there much longer."

"It's just that...He has a tendency to overreact."

"Believe me, In my line of work I've dealt with much worse."

Nico grabbed a nearby pen and a scrap of paper, pushing it toward her.

She held his eyes for a moment, and then picked up the pen.

"He's not going to let you in," she said, shaking her head.

When she handed him the address, he pushed his chair back and stood up. The building was not far from where he had met her the previous night.

"I'll see you when I get back," he said. "Just hang tight and try not to worry."

The icy wind stung Nico's face. He pulled the hoodie up over his wool cap and with a brisk, forward-leaning motion, walked toward *De Wallen* as he had done the day before though more sober this time.

Max's apartment, as it turned out, was in a recently renovated building near the *Nieuwmarkt*. Nico pressed the buzzer for the 3rd floor and shifted his weight back and forth as he waited.

"Yes?" a nasally voice answered through the distorted intercom system.

"Nico here. I'm a friend of Nina's."

There was a long pause before the man replied.

"She isn't here."

"I know. I'm just here to pick up her stuff."

The intercom went silent.

Nico buzzed again, but this time there was no response. He waited a minute and then rang each of the other buzzers in turn. Soon enough he heard the welcoming click of the front door lock disengage. His years of beat reporting had taught him there was always at least one person too lazy to bother asking who was there.

Nico took his time as he climbed up the polished stairs, stubbing out his cigarette halfway up and flicking it behind him. On the third floor landing he waited patiently for another five minutes before knocking.

A thin, blond man opened the door, who by the look of him, liked to spend his weekends out partying.

"What do you want?" the man asked.

Nico put on his best smile.

"Like I said, I'm here to pick up Nina's stuff."

"Not my problem. You're not wanted here."

"Look, Max. The sooner we can get this over with, the sooner I'll be out of your hair."

Max jutted out his chin.

"Why the fuck should I give you anything? Or let me guess. You're her new uncle? I always knew she'd eventually turn," he added with a snort.

"I don't have time for this," Nico said, as he grabbed Max's shoulders and drove him forcefully into the apartment.

"Hey, what the fuck!"

Before he knew it Max's legs were out from under him, and in the next instant he felt his head crash against the coffee table.

Max let out a groan, but Nico ignored him as he looked around the living room.

He left Max to writhe in his misery, marched into the bedroom and threw open the closet door. He spotted an empty duffel bag and began to fill it with whatever female attire he could find before moving on to the chest of drawers.

He went back into the living room and found Max now huddled on the couch.

"Is this everything?" Nico asked, as he grabbed her coat from behind the door and then slung the duffel across his shoulder.

"Not all of that stuff is hers, you know," Max said, as he touched the back of his head and looked up at him with the eyes of a wounded child.

"You'll want to put some ice on that," Nico said, before turning to go.

"You're a fool to get involved with her," Max cried out behind him, but Nico had already closed the door.

As Nico carried the duffel bag back to his apartment, he could feel the damp cold seeping up from the cobblestones and into his shoes.

He was angry with himself for having overreacted with Max who was clearly just a privileged junkie, and it troubled him because he could see just how fucked up this whole situation was, and yet he could not stop himself from getting involved.

Who was Nina, anyway, and what the hell happened to her?

She had the type of beauty women envied, and he had no doubt they must have paid her well for it at the agency, but he did not believe that it was just the drug use that had caused her to stumble. Sure, things had not worked out with wealthy, young Max, but what else could they possibly have in common? Nico imagined not much apart from a mutual tendency toward self-destruction.

A part of him debated whether he should just ask her to go as soon as he could and forget his attraction to her.

But when he opened the door and felt the warmth radiating from Nina's presence in his studio apartment, his resolution faltered. He saw her appear at the other end of the corridor and watched as the apprehension in her face melted. She bounded toward him.

"Thank you," she said.

Nico let the bag drop on the floor and let himself be overwhelmed by her embrace.

That night they fell asleep next to one another with Nina's back pressed against Nico's chest and stomach. Nico had not rested so deeply in years.

Only when the first rays of sun started to pierce the studio's bare, white walls, did Nico's eyes begin to flutter and stir. He leaned on his forearm and watched as Nina continued to sleep, her face as soft and composed as Sonja's after he had read her a bedtime story.

The peaceful moment, however, did not last long once Nina awoke.

"I don't feel well," she told him, her pupils unveiling the darkness of her discomfort. "I think I'm going to be sick."

"Can you make it to the bathroom?" Nico asked, his brow furrowing.

She lolled her head back and forth before pitching over to the side of the bed.

"No, my legs ache."

"Hold tight. I'll get you something."

Nico grabbed a nearby trash can and placed it on the floor beside her. Helping her roll forward, he held her hair back so she could retch.

When she was finished, she wiped her mouth with the back of her hand, looking up at him like a misbehaved puppy.

"I'm sorry," she said.

"It's ok. Let's just get you through this."

Nina hung her head.

"Why don't you lie back down, ok? I'm going to get you some tablets to help with the dehydration. Can you manage alone until I get back?"

She leaned back again and grimaced. All the color had drained from her face.

Nico was no stranger to the effects of opiate withdrawal. He had helped his friend, Niels, detox while they were still in their twenties. At the time he had fooled around with the drug himself, but Niels' subsequent overdose had sobered him up to heroin's lethal potential. Now in his thirties, Nico limited his binging strictly to alcohol and hash.

At the Albert Heijn convenience store down the street from him, he bought some Imodium, effervescent tablets, *knäckebröd*, instant oatmeal and rice. Carrying the basket down the frozen food aisle, he threw in a few ready-made pizzas for himself before making his way to the cash register. He popped into the Video Odyssee on his way home to pick up a few new releases to help get them through the crucial days Nina would need to stay cooped up indoors. He had already braced himself to play the role of nurse maid, and fortunate for him, his work would not get in the way. He had vacation days owed, and about a three-month reprieve before his next overseas assignment.

The next five days nursing Nina played out like clockwork. Her worst symptoms emerged the following evening when the achiness and restless-ness kept her from sleep. Nico, who was used to going a couple of days at a stretch without, tried to coach her through the worse of it distracting her from the cravings and focusing her attention elsewhere when he could.

She only buckled once, when at the height of her delirium, she had scratched at his arms and chest in an attempt to break free of her forced confinement.

He had held her down for the good part of two hours as she had continued to thrash and volley threats, all the while keeping quiet himself. Eventually her voice and body grew limp from the effort, causing her to vomit and collapse.

Over the next four days her symptoms subsided, and on the fifth, Nina emerged from her tempest, pale and weak but not vanquished.

To celebrate, Nico cooked up a *stamppot*, a vegetable and potato mash with sausages, a meal his mother used to make. It was meant to both comfort and nourish Nina after her bleak diet of dry toast and rice.

Nico was pleased to see her appetite return once he placed the food in front of her.

"I didn't realize you could cook so well," Nina said, arching her eyebrows, still glossy and wet from the shower.

"I have a few tricks up my sleeve," he said, his face flushed from tending the stove. "But don't get your hopes up too high. This plus eggs and toast about covers my repertoire."

"I can't remember my last home cooked meal. Not that I should have expected this."

"And why not?" Nico asked, as he loaded up her plate with another ladleful. She was looking at his freshly shaved face and tamed locks as if seeing him for the first time. He cleaned up well when he made the effort.

"I would have thought the last few days made it clear. I'm a complete mess."

"You're not a mess, Nina, just an addict. And you're well past the worst of it now. At your age, this is just a minor blip in the road."

"M-hmm," she murmured as she chewed. "And you're ok spending all this time with an addict? Not many people are."

"You forget, I've been around longer than you. When you scratch beneath the surface, you'll find most people are fucked up in one way or another. We just find different ways to cope is all. Me, I drink. You, however, stumbled on a killer of a drug."

His blunt assessment made Nina flinch.

"So, why do you drink?"

"I already told you. When you do the type of work I do, it's almost impossible not to."

"But do you like your work? Wouldn't it be easier to just report on things here in The Netherlands?"

"I'm good at what I do. Not many people can handle a war zone. Plus, I'd need a lobotomy to cover a regional beat. Too boring and predictable. That's why there's so much drug use, Nina. In some ways, we have it way too good here in the West."

Nina narrowed her eyes at him.

"So, what is it then? Are you trying to save the world or something?"

"Pffft. I'm not *saving* anything, just showing the world it has an asshole, that's all. Holding up a mirror to reflect the horrors lurking beneath the façade. Shame can be a powerful deterrent at times. To those who wield power anyway."

"Well, I can relate to the part about the mirror. I can't stand the damn things."

"You shouldn't be too hard on yourself. Believe me, compared to what I've seen, you're practically an angel."

"Ha! Clearly, you don't know me."

"I know enough to see the person you're hurting most is you. Listen, whatever shame it is you happen to be dragging around with you, it isn't worth it. You can start again, you know. Many people do."

"Yeah, well, I'm not so sure one can undo what's already been done."

"What could be so permanent?" he asked, watching as she averted her gaze. "You're young. You have a good head on your shoulders. Obviously, you're attractive."

"I'm sick and tired of being attractive. It's a curse."

He waited until her eyes turned back toward him again.

"You told me before you were studying English," he said, holding her gaze as gently as he could. "Do you want to teach?"

"I thought I did, but I don't think I'd make a good teacher now."

"But you must have other interests."

Nina looked around the flat for a moment as if she were seeing it for the first time.

"Animals," she said with a sigh. "I like animals. I get along with them just fine. I had cats and dogs growing up. And when I lived in Leiden, I worked at a stable on the weekends, brushing and feeding the horses. I learned a bit about training them as well."

"Why not try to get a job as a vet's assistant? The Holland Riding School is not far from here, you know."

"Yeah, but I'm not really qualified now, am I?" she replied, her tone dripping with sarcasm, a sign she seemed to be warming up to him.

Nico shook his head. His concerned expression revealed a hint of tenderness.

"No one is ever qualified at the beginning no matter how many courses you've had," he said, as he stood to clear the table.

"If you're willing to do the grunt work and aren't too proud, you'd be surprised how far along you can get."

"I suppose so," Nina said, not sounding convinced as Nico walked their empty dishes back to the kitchen. He returned a few moments later with another round of beers.

"Why don't I ask around for you?" he said.

"Would you?"

"Of course. There's no harm in asking."

"At this point, what have I got to lose, right?"

"To new beginnings, then," Nico said, touching the top of his bottle to hers.

"To new beginnings," she replied.

After dinner, Nina curled up on the couch while Nico pushed *Se7en* into the VHS player. Nico sat down beside her on what had become his usual spot, pressed play, and wrapped his arm around her as she leaned back against his chest. In the last three days they had developed a ritual of watching films together as Nina had continued to detox. To their mutual amusement, they had found they had similar tastes, often drawn to thrillers and certain kinds of horror flicks, the darker the better. As the film progressed and Nina grew tired, she would lean her head against Nico's shoulder, or lie on his lap while he caressed her hair, the soothing action calming her otherwise agitated nervous system.

Although these moments of intimacy taxed Nico's desire, he sensed that making a move would threaten his chances with her. Under the circumstances, he was pleased to discover he could act more or less the gentleman, and that time had wrought its advantages over his much younger and heedless self.

As they watched the exposition of each of the deadly sins in turn—Gluttony, Greed and Sloth—Nico could feel Nina nestle more deeply into his side, until finally she looked up at him, her eyes pleading.

"Everything okay?" he asked.

She nodded her head but said nothing.

Nico hit the pause button.

For a moment, she remained motionless, searching his eyes as if trying to fathom something. Then she pushed herself up, her lips parting, as she brought her face to his.

The next morning, Nico awoke to the smell of coffee.

"I thought I'd make breakfast for a change," Nina said, walking back from the kitchen carrying their two mugs of coffee. She was wearing one of his t-shirts again, her legs uncovered except for a pair of wool socks that sagged helplessly around her narrow ankles.

Nico smiled at her. He was still too groggy to talk. He took a few sips and watched as she brought in the tray stacked with fresh slices of toast, butter and jam and a plate of cheese and cold cuts.

"Did you mean that last night?" she asked, arranging everything on the table. "About helping me find a job?"

"Of course," Nico said, watching as she proceeded to make up a plate for him.

"Listen, I know you've only known me for a little over a week, and I probably seem like an old man to you, but if you're wondering what the catch is, there isn't one. Maybe this is all going too fast for you, but it makes me happy to have you here."

"You're not an old man," Nina said with a smirk. "Experienced, yes, but not old."

Nico laughed.

"Seriously, though," she added, her demeanor changing as she prepared her own plate. "I'm not used to trusting men."

"I can see that."

"I do like you. Very much, in fact. I feel calmer and at ease here, and I'm not used to that."

"Well, I'm happy to hear it," Nico said, smiling at her.

They ate in silence for a while, listening to the rustling of the wind and the leaves through the cracked open window.

"After we eat, I've got to go to my editor's office for a while. I'll see what I can dig up from the want ads while I'm there. In the meantime, is there anything you need?"

He knew better than to offer her any money at this stage of her recovery, and she seemed to know better than to ask.

"No, I'm fine for now. I'll just stay here and clean up. Probably read a while. Maybe later we can do the shopping? I'll try my hand at making dinner this time."

"Great," Nico said, before heading off to the shower. "I'll be back at around three and then we can go out. I'll be curious to see what you can cook in that closet of a kitchen."

"You'd be amazed by what you can make in one pot," she yelled after him. "Especially when it's just spaghetti carbonara."

After Nina detoxed—already a full week into December—Nico was happy to find that they had settled into a calmer, domesticated routine. He was relieved of all housekeeping by Nina, who, without discussion, took over the cooking and cleaning. On the limited occasions when Nico needed some privacy to finish up work from home, she would go outside to take a long walk.

At first, her protracted absences left him unsettled. Would she come back, he wondered? But each time she returned looking more refreshed than when she had gone, so that before too long, Nico felt confident enough to entrust her with their shopping.

In the evenings they continued to watch films, but since the Christmas festivities were well underway—the city a bustle of craft markets and mulled wine—neither could resist the urge to go out for a while. Though estranged from family and lacking in religious belief, when December 24th rolled around, they, too, went out to gawk at the lights, not unlike the hordes of tourists who had traipsed from near and far to admire the relics of Amsterdam's Golden Age.

Each morning Nico woke up beside Nina he was struck by the dumbness of his luck. She seemed fonder of him with each passing day, often squeezing his hand or giving him a kiss on the cheek when he was least expecting it, and to his surprise, their sex life continued to develop. It was only when he was facing her that he noticed an odd tendency of hers, at times, to lock her eyes on the ceiling above them. For the most part, though, she preferred to take the reins, which pleased him all the more.

Meanwhile, to encourage her hopes at landing a new career, he brought home books—both bought and borrowed—related to all manner of animal training and welfare. Books she seemed to devour throughout the course of the day, and that they would discuss over breakfast and dinner.

When their first month anniversary rolled around, Nico had found an immediate opening for a receptionist at a nearby vet's clinic. They spent the weekend preparing her for the interview, and on the following Tuesday, Nina was offered the job. Elated by the good news, they celebrated the New Year by going out to a Thai restaurant and popping open a bottle of sparkling wine.

Money had gotten tight in the last few weeks, but Nina had gained some much-needed weight, and overall she looked healthier and happier.

By the time Nico needed to travel for work again, she had developed enough confidence and dedication to her job that he knew she would do just fine without him.

15

Jodenbreestraat - Late Winter - 1997-98

Nina found the separation from Nico more difficult than she had expected. Coming home to an empty flat, she could feel the weight of her old depression starting to wrap itself around her again, constricting her breath. They had been together for almost two months, and a day had not passed without them seeing one another. With Nico gone all of a sudden, Nina realized how much she depended on his encouragement and comfort.

To calm herself, she went on long walks in *Vondelpark*, passing through the upscale neighborhoods surrounding the Museum Quarter and marveling at how anyone could afford to live there. One day, catching sight of a billboard showing off a former colleague's legs styling a pair of heels outside a high-end designer boutique, she was reminded yet again of the opportunity she had squandered when she had thrown away her modeling career for drugs. Not that she missed the tedious work. She had hated every minute of it apart from her earnings, but for the first time in her life, she had lived on her own, far, far away from the dysfunction of her family.

Then she met Max.

Funny but sad Max who had introduced her to the temporary bliss that was heroin. Max, whose only demand was that she be *seen* by his side while they secretly made fun of all the ass-kissing imposters desperate to cling on to the tailcoats of wealth and beauty. After that, she had not bothered to look back. Max came from old *Van der Bijl* money, so it had not mattered whether she worked or not. It was only when he had raised the prospect of using needles that the trouble between them began. She had resisted, which made Max resent her, seeing her refusal to shoot up with him as a form of betrayal.

Now sober but relying on Nico for support, Nina could not shake the residual guilt and anxiety that her past failures provoked in her. It was only when she wandered along the paths and ponds of the English gardens, that her nerves would start to calm again as her lungs filled with the moist, cool air.

Her work at the veterinary clinic, of course, was also a welcome change, a way for her to fill her days while she waited for Nico. And for once, her looks did not play a role in how she made a living. At least not in an overt way. At the clinic, everyone, including her, wore loose fitting scrubs. The focus was on the immediate care of their furry and feathered patients.

As the weeks progressed, Nina had learned more about how to prepare each animal for examination, a task she cherished for the close contact she would have with these small creatures, many of whom she seemed to bond with instinctively. Marie, a matronly woman, and one of the assistants she got along with well, had even gone so far as to encourage Nina to sign up for some veterinary courses.

"You're a natural," she had told Nina. "When you're ready, I'll help you with the application."

Only once during Nico's time away had Nina felt a strong urge to give in to a quick fix, just a little something to get her through the loneliness of returning to the cavernous emptiness that greeted her each night. Instead of going straight home after work, she had walked to *De Wallen* to see if she could sniff out one of Max's dealers. But when she crossed over the frozen canal on *Kloveniersburgwal*, her recollection of meeting Nico had stopped her in her tracks. Mid-bridge she had turned back and instead gone into a kebab shop to pick up dinner. She had spent the rest of the night watching films she had already seen with Nico, reliving their happy memories from the not-too-distant past.

Nico, meanwhile, was living through a form of hell requiring his absolute focus if he hoped to make it back to her alive. In the two weeks he had been away, Nico only managed to phone Nina twice, and even in those brief calls, she could hear the tension in his voice masked only by the relief of hearing hers.

"No matter what, just promise me you won't give up, alright?"

"I promise," she said, restraining her sadness. "But please come back soon."

"Believe me," he said, his voice crackling over the poor connection, "the thought of seeing you is the only thing getting me through the day."

Nico arrived home from Algeria, dropped his luggage in the entryway and said nothing. The dullness in his eyes and the haggard lines marking his face revealed more than he could express in words.

Nina felt a small tremor of shock at seeing this unsettling transformation. This was not the same man she had met four months before. Nonetheless, she knew what she needed to do and went into the kitchen to retrieve three beers.

In the living area, she handed him an open bottle.

Nico took a long swig and then began rummaging through his dusty backpack.

"I want to show you something," he said, pulling out a video recorder.

Nina placed the other bottles on the living room table and sat down on the couch while he finished connecting the video recorder to the television set. He pushed play and sat down beside her, gripping his beer.

The television screen displayed the footage he had taken—not the gruesome outtakes he had turned into his editor—but personal excerpts from the outdoor market in Bouiret Lahdab, where one of the recent massacres had taken place. As they watched, he explained to Nina that because of the on-going civil war, hundreds of people in the outlying areas had fled their villages and set up refuge in the commune there, and that just a few days earlier, dozens of women and children had been killed by men wielding axes and knives.

"Why are they so calm?" Nina asked, astounded as she watched a crowd of mostly women dressed in a range of light to dark colored *hijabs* winding their way through makeshift vegetable stalls. On the opposite side, collections of dusty wares were spread out on the parched, ochre ground opposite the main road. "They're shopping as if nothing happened. How do they even dare to go out?"

"They have no choice," Nico said, as he stared at the screen, his eyes vacant. "They have to do what they have to do to survive."

As the camera panned to a patch of ground covered with dark stains in front of what looked like a municipal building, Nina reached over and squeezed his hand.

"It happened there," he said. "Most of them were just small children. Babies."

"But why don't they leave?"

Nico shook his head.

"Where would they go? This is all they know, Nina. In a way, still going about their lives becomes its own form of resistance."

The camera's view had shifted and was now climbing up the tattered walls of the adobe structure, framed on one side by an azure sky.

"And the government does nothing?"

"Government, as we know it, doesn't exist there. The culture is tribal. They adhere more to *asabiyah*, as Ibn Khaldun called it. A kind of group solidarity that can shift dependent on the circumstance. If you are on the wrong side of those wielding the power in the moment, well..."

"I can't believe they send you to such places."

"If we don't record it, the world doesn't see it, acknowledge it, and then what?"

They continued to watch in silence until the tape turned to static.

Nina hit the pause button as Nico continued to stare straight ahead as if in a trance.

"Are you going to be ok?"

"I need something stronger than this," he said, lifting up an empty beer bottle.

"Let's go out then," Nina said.

He had warned her about this, and there was nothing left to say.

After Nico shut off the videorecorder, they went to the *Café de Vriendschap* on *Nieuwmarkt,* a tiny tavern shrouded in darkness apart from the flickering flame of glass-encased candles at each table. Nico knew the bartender, Jan, a war veteran who had served in Bosnia, and someone who well understood Nico's need to obliterate memory. Jan had eyed Nina with suspicion at first as they took their seats at the cramped bar where the low-hanging lamps emitted a red-tinged glow. But once Nico introduced her as the girlfriend who had saved his life, Jan was more than happy to keep the drinks flowing. If anything, he was relieved to have someone else there to keep an eye on Nico.

And sure enough, after a few rounds, they were interrupted by an Englishman who had caught sight of Nina's overwhelming good looks.

"Excuse me, darling, but are you sure *he's* the company you're after tonight?" he called out with a cocky laugh. "I can guarantee we'd make a much better offer than he ever could."

Nina froze in her seat, only daring to stare straight ahead at the bottles lined up behind the bar. Nico looked at her and then turned blurry eyed towards the well-tailored suit with the stylish gray hair and his much younger acolyte.

Nico stood and walked toward them, a smile spreading across his face.

"You think that get-up makes you king here, eh?" he said.

The man gave him a look of mild amusement mixed with disdain.

"Well let me tell you," Nico said, as he stepped in closer. "You wouldn't last a minute where I come from, because you'd be bled out on the street."

The man took a step back without saying anything while the acolyte stretched his hand back to reach for his jacket.

"You see, the problem with you finance types," Nico said, unphased, "is that you think you've got it all figured out, when, in fact, you've *not got a fucking clue* at the suffering you create with those *fucking* spreadsheets of yours. And with that suffering, you see, comes a *helluva* lot of anger. Anger in places where they don't have any respect for, what is this, Armani?"

The older man flinched but did not move.

"And sure, you think, 'I don't have to deal with this riff raff. I'm here, they're there. That's someone else's problem.' Well, think again, friend."

Nico was now standing a nose's width from the older man's face.

"Because a time is coming when you'll wish you had, and no amount of back room dealing is going to save your ass when they tear you limb from limb, just for that gold watch of yours."

Without a word, the man ducked around Nico and walked out, leaving the younger man to gather up their things and follow on his heels.

The incident, which had caught everyone's attention, provoked a loud round of laughs from the few remaining people in the bar.

"Good fucking riddance," Jan said, lifting a bottle of vodka with a wide grin. "For that, you get another round on the house."

At first Nina was taken aback by Nico's ostentatious confrontation. But seeing the heavy toll his work took on him, she understood the source of his anger. She knew the other women before her had had no tolerance for this drunken, nihilistic tendency of his, but in a strange way, she now felt even more drawn to him. She could identify with his angry defiance, even though she was reticent to express her own.

In celebration of the suits' defeat, they drank until no other customers were left, freeing Jan to join them for a couple of rounds. And when they could no longer sit up, let alone see straight, Jan walked them to their building, where once again Nico and Nina crawled up the stairs to the studio and passed out on the bed, an unconscious commemoration of their first night together.

They did not stir again until the following afternoon, when they showered and dressed before going out for a late brunch. Despite a persistent chill, the sun shone bright through the cloudless March sky, so they opted to sit outside a favorite waterfront café, sipping Bloody Mary's with their coats and dark sunglasses on.

"It's not such a good idea to follow in my footsteps, you know," Nico said to Nina, looking across the water as he massaged his throbbing temples. His black, curly hair—still somewhat damp—had grown long over the winter months.

"I like your company," Nina said.

He looked at her over his glasses, his eyes rimmed red.

Unlike him, Nina looked as radiant as ever with her silky, black hair wafting in the wind. Her skin was immaculate.

"Well, this company's no good, Nina. Some would say I'm leading you down a wayward path, just taking a longer, more tedious route."

"I'll be the judge of that," she said. "And anyway, at least you get me."

He lit two cigarettes before handing one over to her.

"Just so you know what you're getting yourself into. I'll admit I was surprised you didn't walk out on me last night now that you've seen what a bastard I can be."

"You're not a bastard, just brutally honest, and not many people can handle that. What matters is that we look out for one another. We're both misfits, just in different ways."

"So, you're willing to stick it out with me? Through sickness and health? Good and Bad? And all the bullshit in between?"

Nina laughed.

"If that's meant to be a proposal, I wouldn't say no."

Nico smiled.

He was looking out on the water again, nodding with satisfaction.

"She's the spitting image of you," Nico's grandmother exclaimed one year later when she saw Lena for the first time in the maternity ward at the OLVG Hospital in *Oosterpark.*

Magdalena Sofia Van de Steeg had howled her way into the world earlier that day, Shrove Tuesday, after a difficult labor that had lasted almost 24 hours. Nina, exhausted, had held the baby girl only a few moments before handing her over to her proud father.

Nico and Nina had been married just a few months when she realized she was pregnant. Unsure of how she felt, she had embraced her new condition only after Nico had persisted in his jubilance at knowing he was, once again, an expectant father.

Nico soon found them a much larger apartment and took on even more work assignments in anticipation of the needs of their growing family. Nina, meanwhile, continued to work at the veterinary clinic though her ambitions of becoming a certified assistant were soon put on hold.

Apart from the company of a newly adopted German shepherd named Wuodan whom she would take out for long walks before and after work, Nina had spent most of her pregnancy alone.

In the early months she had suffered from acute nausea which had made it almost impossible for her to be around cigarettes let alone continue to smoke herself.

As the pregnancy wore on her physical intolerances grew to include beer, strong-smelling foods as well as most cleaning agents so that the months leading up to her delivery constituted the most ascetic of her adolescent and adult life. However, not until she felt the baby kick did it truly dawn on her how her life's trajectory was irreversibly altered.

Fortunately, when Nico was at home, he managed to dial back the drinking and smoking which he now only indulged out on their terrace. His happiness at starting a new family with Nina acted as an antidote to the violence he was so often subjected to at work, and despite his still dim view of the world, he could not wait for his new child to arrive.

All in all, Nico and Nina felt as if they had somehow stumbled upon that elusive portal leading to domestic contentment. Nico's estranged mother had died in a car accident three years earlier, so it was Nico's grandmother, the Oma Arend, who had joined forces with them to assist the young family, particularly after Magdalena's birth.

Nina, who did not have any contact to her own family, soon came to rely on the Oma as one of the few people with whom she could discuss her pregnancy outside of work. Over the occasional cup of tea while Nico was away, they had found a way to bond over their mutual love of animals, and when Nina's belly began to grow, it was this wizened 78-year-old woman who guided her through each and every concern with calmness and pragmatic encouragement. It was with great gratitude and remembrance that they eventually named the child after her.

When mother and baby arrived home, it was the Oma who stayed for three weeks, dutifully attending to the cooking and cleaning while Nina focused her attention on learning how to breastfeed, a practice that did not come easily. Nico, meanwhile, kept busy attending to Wuodan.

They both took advantage of their parental leave, though in practical terms, they needed Nico's income far more. He returned to work six weeks later, leaving Nina to juggle the baby and dog with the occasional visit from the Oma to help relieve her.

Lena rarely fussed, but on the exceptional occasions she would not be mollified, Nina would pack her into the stroller and put Wuodan on his leash. The fresh air and the rhythmic perambulations soon put Lena to sleep, but even more so, they restored Nina's need to feel human again and not like an automaton made only for feeding and changing her daughter.

By the end of the third month and feeling as if she had almost mastered her new routine, Nina began to enjoy her young motherhood, delighting in the ever-expressive nature of this tiny and helpless human. Though Lena looked more like Nina, she also exhibited—through some mysterious biological alchemy—Nico's more lovable quirks and gestures. This never ceased to amaze Nina, and she grew fond of cataloguing these traits to share with Nico at the end of the day, and on phone calls when he was traveling.

Only on one occasion did Nina run into an old acquaintance from her modeling days outside of the Hermès boutique on the *P.C. Hooftstraat*.

"*Mijn God*, is that you, Nina?" Isa said, looking both incredulous and slightly put off. "I almost didn't recognize you with that stroller. What happened?"

Nina shrugged and smiled.

"I got married. Had a baby."

"I can *see* that," Isa said, raising an immaculate eyebrow. "Is it Max's?"

"God, no. Haven't seen him in ages. I'm with someone else."

Isa murmured and crossed her arms.

"And does this someone make good money?"

"Good enough," Nina said. "He's a reporter."

"Really?" Isa said, as she tapped her stilettoed Jimmy Choo. "I guess that means you're off the runway then."

"Yes. Can't say that I miss it."

Isa took a moment to appraise Nina, looking at her from head to toe.

"It's all nappies and milk bottles now, I suppose, but, hey, at least it doesn't matter if you let yourself go. *Me*, on the other hand. Well, you know how it is."

Nina replied with an icy silence.

"Anyway, I have a lunch date so I *must* be off," Isa said. "It was nice running into you, *doe-doei!*"

Once, in the early days of her career, Nina had made the mistake of confiding in Isa, mistaking Isa's curiosity about her life as genuine care. Not long after that Nina noticed a change in how the other models treated her, and how they whispered behind her back and kept their distance. Nothing had changed. Isa was still malicious and above all, competitive, and Nina felt relieved to never have to work alongside her again.

After a six-month leave, Nina returned to work part-time, dropping Lena off at daycare on her way into the clinic and picking her up at lunchtime. They spent most afternoons walking in the park—rain, drizzle or sunshine—to let young Wuodan run off-leash and tumble in the grass with the other dogs. Lena, in her stroller, would either look around in wonder at the trees and passersby or fall asleep, oblivious to the sound of ringing bicycle bells or the shouting from a nearby football field. Back home, Nina would play with Lena until it was time to bathe and feed her then put her to bed. The child slept through most nights, which allowed Nina to wind down and fall asleep herself, already worn out by the day's endless activity.

Nico would join them for their walks when he could, content to stroll along in the waning summer light while Nina recounted their daughter's newest achievements. On other days they would work through the logistics of managing their daily lives, a never-ending task that somehow pulled them forward in time with ever increasing acceleration.

Nico disliked that his interactions with his young family were so limited and dependent on the prevailing needs of his work. He tried his best to minimize his overseas assignments, succeeding on rare occasions to negotiate shorter stays thanks to one editor's preference for his many years of experience. Still, he was away far more often than he would have liked.

When he was at home, he would relieve Nina of the childcare, taking his infant daughter into his arms, singing to her and making her laugh while her mother got around to doing whatever it was she could not do otherwise. He tried to go along with Nina's household preferences, even going so far as to adopt certain childrearing practices he would have scoffed at while he was with Carla. After a rough assignment he would still go out on the occasional drinking binge, returning home the same night and not as blindingly drunk as in the past. Though Nina no longer joined him, she understood his need to vent, and as long as their daughter was not affected, she had no problem accommodating him. Nico was, after all, very loyal to his young family, and although he was not as pleasant of a drunk for others to be around, he did not turn his anger toward those he felt obliged to protect, especially after growing more estranged from his first daughter.

Roughly once a month Nico would drive to Rotterdam to visit Sonja, at times with the whole family, which would give Sonja an excuse to dote over her half-sister like a living doll. Nico struggled with the recognition of the distance that had grown between him and his oldest child, particularly when Carla would not make herself scarce. But having Nina and Lena by his side seemed to lessen his grief.

When Nina did accompany him, however, he could sense the tension in her rise as they drove past Leiden. Her eyes would dart back and forth and her hands would fidget with her handbag as if at any moment she expected to encounter some dreaded ghost from her past.

Once Nico had made the mistake of stopping for gas just outside the city limits.

"What the hell are you doing?" Nina had asked. "We can't stop here."

"But we've got to get gas. It'll just take a minute."

"Well, a minute is too long."

"Can you at least tell me why this gas station is off limits? I understand you don't want anything to do with your family, but what's the likelihood they'd be here anyway?"

"Nico, this is all I ask from you when we make this trip. I'm happy to spend time with Sonja and put up with Carla's bullshit, but I don't want to be anywhere *near* Leiden. Not even for a second. I've told you this so many times!"

Nico had rolled his eyes and thrown up his hands as if dealing with a crazy person before steering the car back toward the highway.

"Fine. If you can't talk about it, I won't ask."

"There's nothing to talk about. I don't want them in my life, and I sure as hell don't want them in Lena's. Ever. And that means no stopping. Not ever."

Of course, this had only piqued Nico's curiosity about Nina's family all the more, but he knew better than to push her. He had his own guarded secrets to conceal. Ones he intended to keep at arm's length, not only from his family, but from himself.

"The past is the past," Nina had told him. "Mucking around in it only sullies the present."

Plus, a search for Nina's name yielded nothing apart from the obvious work references. Nico could not find even the remotest mention of a life in Leiden.

It was a brilliant, mid-September afternoon when Nina packed seven-month-old Lena in her stroller, placed Wuodan on his leash and headed out to *Oosterpark.* They wound their way along the lakeshore, Nina lost in thought as she watched the slender, swaying willows while Wuodan paced beside her, keeping an ever-watchful eye on a raft of ducks preening themselves in the shallows.

At first, Nina did not respond to the man's voice yelling after her. It was only when she heard her former name ringing in her ears that she turned with alarm to see who it was. Sensing the sudden fear rising in his mistress, Wuodan began to growl and bark, assuming a protective stance between Nina and the strange, white-haired man standing just a few feet in front of them.

"Joanna," he said with triumph as he peered into the stroller. "Is that your little one?"

Nina resisted an impulse to let Wuodan off his leash.

"What are you doing here?" she said, looking around wildly.

"Just out for a walk."

"I mean, what are you doing in Amsterdam?"

"Your mum's at NKI. Lung cancer, I'm afraid. You should go and visit her. She won't be around much longer."

Nina flashed him a look of absolute hatred, her heart pounding in her throat and every one of her nerve endings twitching in a desperate desire to flee. She could smell the acrid sweat forming in her armpits, but she forced herself to stay put until she could formulate a way out without Piet following her.

"Anton is here, too," Piet said, leering at her and licking his lips with his fat, bilious tongue. "Been a long time since you've seen him, eh? In fact, I'm on my way to meet him now. In *de Wallen*. Why don't you come along? For old time's sake."

"I'd rather put a bullet through your head," Nina said.

Wuodan crouched down and snarled at him, waiting for Nina's command.

Piet stepped back with a crooked smile.

"Now, that's no way to talk to family."

"You're not family," Nina hissed, doing everything she could not to scream and wake her daughter. "You're the scum of the earth, and I want nothing to do with you."

Nina let out the leash so that Wuodan could lunge for Piet's ankles.

"Hey now!"

Piet looked at her stunned as he stumbled back.

"I'm warning you. You either get away from me, or I'll have him rip your balls off."

Piet narrowed his eyes.

"What you need is a good fuck, you stupid bitch."

Nina could feel herself shaking, her firm grip on the leash and carriage turning her knuckles white.

"What?" Piet said, picking up on her fear. "You think leaving just changes things, Joanna? It sure as hell doesn't change the fact you're just another worthless slut. And one day, you'll see. You'll come crawling back to us, begging. Because I'm telling you, no one is going to keep a washed-up basket case like you around for long. I can guarantee it."

Shaking, Nina watched and waited until Piet walked far enough away that she could get a sense of where he was headed. As soon as he was out of sight, she darted into a nearby neighborhood, repeatedly wrenching her head to look over her shoulder. The only thing keeping her from devolving into complete hysterics was Wuodan's protective vigilance.

Lena, meanwhile, continued to sleep, blissfully unaware of the threat they had just faced.

Spotting a nearby pay phone, Nina walked toward it, and with shaking fingers, dialed the office. She knew Marie would pick up the phone, and right now she could not bear the thought of calling Nico on his mobile.

"Marie, you've got to help me," she said, after hearing the older woman's calm and melodious voice on the other end.

"Nina?" Her concern was palpable. "What happened?"

"I had a run-in with someone in the park," Nina said, in between panicked gasps for air. "I had to get away from him, and now I'm lost."

"My God! Are you alright? Do you need me to call the police?"

"No, no! I have Wuodan and Lena with me. I just need help figuring out where I am."

"Is there a taxi near you? What street are you on?"

Nina looked through the clear glass panes shielding the phone booth.

"*Transvaalplein*," she said, just barely making out the street sign on the corner.

"*Transvaalplein*? Let me get the map."

Nina could hear the shuffling of papers on the other end of the phone line as she surveyed the quiet residential street. Her breath was short and shallow, and her heart was still pounding in her chest, but the motion of rocking Lena's stroller to and fro helped to soothe her, as did the sight of her dog at her feet, his ears perked and eyes attentive.

By the time Marie picked up the phone again, Nina was no longer gasping for breath.

"Nina?"

"Yes?"

"You're on a circular. If you walk around, you'll hit *Transvaalstraat*. Take a right, and you'll come to *Linnaeus*. If you go left it takes you back to *Oosterpark*. Are you sure you wouldn't be better off in a taxi? I'd offer to pick you up, but Carl has the car."

"No. I'll be fine from here, thank you. I just needed to know where to go."

"Call me when you get home, ok? I want to know you made it back alright."

"Ok."

"Please be safe, Nina. Talk soon."

Nina followed Marie's directions but could not get over the feeling that Piet could still come after her. She kept looking behind her as she walked, scanning the streets for a sign of the man her mother had married, and who had grown old and unkempt in his splotchy, pale skin. The man who had brought his oldest son, Anton, to live with them, a beast if she ever knew one.

They turned onto *Balistraat* where they lived, and Nina lunged for the door of her building. In her haste, she ran into the young woman who lived on the second floor. A blue *niqab* concealed her face. The intensity of her kohl-lined stare was arresting as she held the door open so Nina could pass through with Wuodan and the stroller. For a brief second their eyes locked, and Nina felt an unsettling shudder of recognition.

Once they were safe inside the vestibule, the veiled woman stepped around them without a sound, closing the door behind her. Nina waited to hear the click of the lock engage then dropped the leash so Wuodan could run ahead of her up the four flights while she pushed the baby carriage into the narrow lift.

Inside the sanctity of their home, Nina scooped Lena up from the stroller, carried her into the living room, and holding her tight like a shield, collapsed on the couch, grateful she had forgotten to raise the blinds earlier that day.

Nina lost track of time as she lay staring at the ceiling. The contours of the white molding high above her and the undulating curves provided her with a sense of visual comfort as she fought to suppress the storm raging in her head.

She had propped Lena up with pillows on the far end of the couch so the child could play with her rattle and a collection of colorful plastic rings, but after a while Lena began to fuss, so Nina turned on her side to breastfeed her.

It was only when the phone rang that Nina startled as she realized the afternoon had already slipped into twilight and left the room gray.

"*Van de Steeg,*" she answered, listless.

"Nina?"

Marie's voice brought back the rush of terrible images from earlier in the day.

"I was just calling to make sure you made it home alright."

"I'm sorry. I was so tired when I got here, and it just completely slipped my mind."

"It's ok," Marie said. "What matters is that you're alright. You sounded rattled when you called. Do you want to talk about it?"

Nina paused before answering.

"I'd rather not. I've got to feed Lena and put her to bed. Plus, there's really nothing else to discuss. It was just an unpleasant experience."

"Did this man try to hurt you?" Marie asked, sounding unconvinced.

"No. It wasn't like that. Just a verbal confrontation. I'm fine now. Really."

"Well, if you feel like talking later, just call me. We can get a coffee or a tea. Whatever you like. Alright?"

"Thanks, Marie. I appreciate it."

"Anytime, love. And give little Lena a good night kiss from me."

Nina hung up the phone and went through the motions of changing Lena's diaper. Once she had fed her again and put her to bed, she lay back down on the couch, exhausted.

"You wouldn't believe the shit I had to go through today to access the archives," Nico said, as he walked through the front door. He put his shoulder bag down in the hall and walked toward her. "Hey, did you forget to take Wuodan's leash off?"

"What?" Nina said, her voice small.

Nico leaned down to pet the dog who was circling around his feet.

"Or were you about to go out again? He's dragging his leash around."

"No. I must have forgotten."

"That's not like you," Nico said, as he unclipped the leash. "Are you ok?"

Nina pushed herself up from the couch.

"No, I'm not feeling well. I think I should go to bed. Lena's on the couch."

She avoided Nico's eyes, got up and walked down the hall toward their bedroom.

"Have you eaten?" Nico called out after her, before leaning down to greet his daughter.

"No, you go ahead. I'll eat something in the morning."

"Nina. You have to remember to eat. Otherwise, you'll be a mess when you have to nurse again. Go to bed. I'll bring you some take out in a bit."

But Nina did not respond to Nico's attempts to wake her later.

Early the next morning she pried herself up from bed as Nico handed her Lena who was fussing and eager to feed.

"You slept through her crying last night. How are you feeling? I gave her some formula, but she wasn't happy about it."

"I've felt better," Nina said, lifting her t-shirt.

Nico placed his hand on her forehead.

"You're not running a fever."

Agitated by his touch, Nina shook herself free.

"It's not the flu."

"Are you going into work?" Nico asked.

"Yes," Nina said, impatient. "I'm fine. Now can you leave me alone?"

"Well, you're not acting fine," Nico said. "What happened yesterday? You've barely looked at me."

Nina exhaled loudly and fixed her eyes on the creases of the duvet.

"Did I do something?"

"No."

"So, I didn't do anything, but I'm still getting the cold shoulder? Can you see how I might find that a bit irritating?"

"Can you just leave me alone, please? I don't want to talk about it right now."

"Does this have to do with Lena?"

"No. It's got nothing to do with you or with Lena. Now can we stop talking about it?"

"But that's the point. You haven't actually said anything. You're obviously upset, and now I'm upset. You were fine yesterday morning when we said good-bye, but something changed. I'd just like to know what it is."

"I told you. I'm not feeling well."

"Ok," Nico replied, a tad too sarcastic. "Do you need to go to the doctor?"

"No, it's not like that."

Nico held his tongue for a moment, not wanting to say anything he might later regret.

"So, what would make you feel better?"

"I just need some time alone."

"Fine, I'll take Lena to day care. You take Wuodan."

Nina looked up at him startled.

"Wuodan?"

"You can at least take him for his walk, can't you? Or do you want me to do both?"

Nina hadn't thought through the implications. The thought of running into Piet again filled her with a renewed sense of panic.

"What's the matter?" Nico said, picking up on her distress. "Did something happen during your walk yesterday? Is that what this is about?"

Nina shook her head no, but it was already too late. Nico knew she was lying. Her inability to respond or even look him in the eye confirmed it. Now it was just a matter of getting her to admit it. He had no intention of leaving until she did.

"Don't lie to me, Nina. It's clear something happened, and now I'm worried. Why are you anxious about taking the dog out?"

Nina placed Lena on the bed then looked up at Nico.

"I—"

She broke down sobbing.

Nico tried to put his arms around her.

"Don't touch me," she stuttered, pushing him away.

At a loss for what to do next, Nico picked up Lena who was becoming agitated at the sound of her mother's inconsolable weeping.

"Nina," Nico said, repeating her name softly.

"I'm so sorry. I don't want to hurt you, but, please. Tell me what I can do. Tell me what happened."

"You. Don't. Want. To know." She could barely get each word out.

"Yes, I do. I'd rather know than go nuts wondering what the hell is going on here. Whatever this is, I can handle it. After all the crazy shit we've gone through, you can give me that much credit."

"I should just go," she said, shaking her head.

Nico startled.

"What? Why?"

"You won't want me here if I tell you. You just won't."

"That's crazy. Of course, I will. I love you. You're the mother of my child, for Christ's sake!"

He looked down at Lena for a moment, then turned back to her.

"Did you have sex with someone? Is that it?"

Nina's crying jag renewed with force.

"Nina, whatever happened we'll get through this," Nico said, leaning over her as she wept onto her pillow. "But if someone hurt you, I'll crucify him."

"No, that isn't it," she said, her voice barely audible. "It's what happened before."

"What do you mean, 'what happened before'?"

"When I was in Leiden."

Nina's head hung so low that Nico could not see her face.

"Who, Nina? Who did this to you?"

"You don't want to know." she said again.

Nico reached his hand out to her, and this time she did not push him away.

"Please," Nico said. Lena, who was perched on her father's shoulder, looked over at her mother, quizzically.

An excruciating silence passed between them as Nina fought with her convulsing body to regain control.

"It was my mother's husband," she said at last. "And his son. I couldn't stop them. I didn't stop them."

Nina threw herself forward on the bed, shielding her face in the covers.

Nico felt a flash of anger overwhelm him. He wanted to destroy these two monsters masquerading as men.

Instead, he put his daughter down on the other side of Nina and then sat next to her on the bed. Instinctively, the baby reached out to her mother with chubby fingers and gurgled some incomprehensible condolence.

Nico, who was incapable of saying or doing anything else, leaned his elbows on his knees and clutched at his forehead.

Once the silence grew too overwhelming, Nina muttered to him through the duvet.

"Do you want me to leave now?"

Nico did not say anything at first, still too shocked by what she had told him.

"No," he said at last. "This doesn't change how I feel about you, Nina. It just makes me want to protect you more."

16

Balistraat - Indische Buurt - Amsterdam 1999

Nico and Nina spent the next few weeks walking a maze of broken glass within the narrow confines of their apartment. Nina admitted to having seen her stepfather in *Oosterpark* but refused to give Nico any additional information, and all Nico could work out was that she had changed her name before moving to Amsterdam. Her surname before their marriage had been of Frisian origin, Jelckama, meaning that under Dutch law she could have changed it based on ancestral heritage. In his attempts to learn more about her, Nico had not found anyone else by that name living anywhere near Leiden.

Nina was adamant about not sharing the history of her family name, and the more he pushed her on the subject, the more recalcitrant her silence.

Nico, his eyes tired and bloodshot, looked into hers beseechingly. "Nina, please, let me help you. I'll make sure he never—"

Nina turned away from him.

"This isn't something you can fix. I've buried them, and they're dead to me. I don't need you digging up their graves."

Her encounter with Piet, however, had left Nina with a heightened degree of agoraphobia that had turned their lives upside down. Nico had begun to walk her to and from work, taking on more and more of the responsibility when it came to exercising the dog and attending to Lena. After an agonizing week, he convinced Nina to see a psychiatrist, who put her on Clonazepam, an anti-anxiety medication that left her feeling drowsy but allowed her to still function day to day. Unfortunately, the drug left her lethargic and unsteady, and not even their child's innate charms seemed capable of lifting her spirits.

Their sex life, too, came to a crushing halt. What Nico had on some subliminal level intuited about Nina at the beginning of their relationship was now the named albatross that inhibited affection. Neither could bear to discuss it let alone initiate that level of intimacy.

Mercifully, once the medication and treatment started to take effect, Nina's aversion to being touched at all relaxed somewhat. Nico, meanwhile, sought solace in caring for Lena and marveled at her resilience in light of the catastrophe that had sideswiped their family.

"She hasn't arrived yet?"

In dismay Nico repeated Anette's words, the day care provider who had just called him. It was mid-afternoon Thursday, already an hour and a half past the time Nina was supposed to have picked Lena up.

"Did you try calling her at work?"

"We called thirty minutes ago, but the woman who answered said she left on time. We assumed she was running errands. We've gone ahead and fed Lena."

"Of course," Nico said, his mind racing to come up with an explanation.

"We can keep her longer if you like," Anette said. "That's not a problem. We just thought you should know in case there's been some sort of incident."

"Thank you. I'll be there as soon as I can."

Nico hung up the phone and dialed home. No answer. Then he called Marie from the clinic as well as a couple of his old friends who had gotten to know Nina, but no one had seen or heard from her. After finding out if there had been any reported accidents in the area, he hurried to the day care center to pick up his daughter.

Anette and the two other women greeted him warmly as if somehow *he* was the one in need of assurance and comforting. Nico took Lena into his arms and did his best to hide his worry, stressing to them that something unavoidable must have come up. That this was not like Nina at all, but that he appreciated their call. Nina, after all, did not have a mobile phone, a situation Nico meant to remedy as soon as possible.

Nico felt Lena's body go limp as she started to drift off to sleep in his arms, so he placed her in the stroller and pushed her home as fast as he could.

"Nina," he called out as he opened the door. The only response back was a whining yelp from Wuodan who was wagging his tail in impatient anticipation. Nico scanned the kitchen and living room for a note. Some sign that Nina might have returned. But he found things the way they had left them that morning, except for a deafening stillness that in Nico's mind echoed a previous foreboding: "*You won't want me here if I tell you.*"

Nico stirred up the sediment of his memory, sifting it for some desperate clue as he checked Lena's diaper. Then he let her crawl around on the floor as he busied himself fastening Wuodan's leash. Ten minutes later, he was back downstairs, the dog lead in one hand and the stroller in the other.

First he walked toward *De Wallen*, stopping off at *Wertheimpark* to let Wuodan sniff and do his business. Then he remembered the street where Max, Nina's ex, had lived. He walked to *Nieuwmarkt* and located the building, but the name on the buzzer had changed. He pressed it firmly nonetheless, until an older woman's voice answered a few seconds later.

"Is Max there?"

"No. No one in this building by that name," she replied, in a pleasant but certain tone.

Nina stepped out of the *Oostenburger* Canal Veterinary Clinic and looked around. The sky was gray with haze, and she could feel a light drizzle on her face. She was certain Piet was just around the corner. The last hour behind the reception desk, she had felt like helpless prey. She had spotted him twice, *she was sure of it*, peering at her through the textured glass doors, each time ducking away as she turned her head.

When it had come time to leave, she had exited through the back door, all the while feeling his caustic breath burning against the back of her neck. *Don't panic*, she said to herself, *Whatever you do, don't panic.* She walked as fast as she could across the *Czaar Peterstraat* overpass and then began to zigzag, winding her way through residential side streets until she got up the nerve to look over her shoulder. From her limited vantage point on the *Entrepotdok* footbridge, he was nowhere to be seen. Still, he could not be too far behind, so she heeded her inner voice to run.

Nina sprinted to the main entrance of the Artis Royal Zoo in less than a minute. Nico had given her a year-round membership pass for her birthday which she flashed impatiently at the young attendant who waved her in with a look of annoyance. She wound her way around the animal exhibitions until she spotted the entrance to the library.

Her intuition was telling her that Piet had picked up her scent again, and that Anton was with him now. She needed to hide somewhere and fast. Panting and out of breath she approached the front desk. She showed the white-haired attendant her permit and asked in a frantic voice where the toilets were.

"Up one flight of stairs and to the right," he answered, narrowing his eyes in suspicion. She was sweating profusely.

With Wuodan pacing just a few feet ahead of him along the patterned brick of the pedestrian walkway, Nico pushed Lena's stroller alongside the narrow *Achterburgwal* canal until he reached the alley where he and Nina had first met. A heartfelt pang of nostalgia was soon followed by a shudder running down the length of his spine as he stared at the brick wall considering the possibilities.

Nico was aware that her doctor had recently altered her medication. Was she going through some form of withdrawal, he wondered? Had she gone out looking for a substitute? In a flash of delayed comprehension Nico realized that she might have gone to see her doctor. But wouldn't she have called to let him know? Parking the stroller and leaning his back against the wall, he forced himself to push his doubt aside as he dialed Dr. Van den Broek's number.

The brusque but efficient assistant picked up the line only to put him on hold within the span of a few seconds.

"Van den Broek," a deep, sonorous voice answered a minute later.

"Did Nina come to see you this afternoon?"

"No. Not today. Why? Has something happened?"

"I'm afraid so," Nico said, with an air of reprimand. "She went to work as usual and left at the normal time. But she didn't pick up our daughter from day care. She hasn't been home since, and I'm out looking for her. Normally, she would have called me."

"I see," the doctor said in a cold but considerate tone. "Is there anyone else she might have gone to see? An old friend, perhaps?"

"I've already made the round of calls," Nico said, impatient. "It just doesn't make any sense. The last few weeks she's hardly gone out. You of all people should know that."

"Is Magdalena with you?"

"Of course!"

"Mr. Van de Steeg. I understand this is disconcerting for you. Unfortunately, some patients react poorly to a reduction in benzodiazepine, the Clonazepam. Have you contacted the police?"

"No, should I?!"

"No, no. The best thing you can do right now is to go home and take care of your daughter. There's a very good chance Nina will come home soon. She may, in fact, already be there. But if for some reason she isn't, we will need to wait the requisite 24 hours before contacting the authorities. You say she was last seen at work today?"

"Yes," Nico said, the annoyance in his voice palpable. He was well aware of the official protocol for missing persons. "But can't they make an exception in this case?"

"I'm afraid not. When the time comes—if it comes—I can alert them on your behalf so they can be aware of the possible side effects. Of course, I would also provide them with my contact information. You must keep in mind it is more likely that Nina will come home first. She feels safe with you. If she has had an unusual episode, she'll want to be at home once it passes. The best thing you can do for her is to wait for her there."

"And what are these side effects, if you don't mind telling *me*?"

"They can vary from patient to patient, Mr. Van de Steeg. It's not possible to predict the outcome so there's no point in speculating. But please understand, we will do everything we can for her. Of course, I'll want to see her as soon as possible to make an assessment."

"Jesus Christ, then why did you change the dosage? Maybe this wouldn't have happened!"

"Clonazepam is a very effective treatment for acute anxiety. However, due to the potential for dependency, it is not a drug we administer long-term."

"There wasn't some other drug you could have put her on instead?!"

"Nicolaas, please know we are doing our best for her. Nina has endured an acute trauma. We are using the best-known methods to treat her condition."

"Fine," Nico shot back. In unconscious retaliation he had bounced the handle of the baby carriage much harder than necessary, waking Lena.

"So, you'll go home now?" the doctor asked.

"Have I got a choice?" Nico said, leaning down to comfort his daughter by placing his hand on her cheek.

"Good. Then please call me at this number as soon as you hear from her. The emergency service will patch you straight through."

Nina ran up the exposed stairs of the library's modern vestibule, keeping her footsteps light and doing her best not to attract any further attention. Seeing the sign for the restrooms, she dashed across the light-filled landing as if her life depended on it, and closed the door only to discover, as she reached down, that the lock she had counted on was missing. Instinctively, she pushed her back up against the entrance until she could get her bearings.

A quick glance around confirmed that no one else was in the stalls. The three compartment doors were wide open, and apart from her breathing, a hollow silence filled the space. Spotting a round metal garbage bin beside the two sinks, she pushed it over with some effort to block the entrance. Then, she walked to the furthest stall, locked herself in and climbed on top of the toilet seat to make sure her legs were not visible beneath the hanging door.

Squatting beneath the weight of her winter coat and hat, she could feel the heat rising in her body, but she did not dare move a muscle. Cornered, she waited, still and petrified, her nostrils flaring.

After a while, she felt her sweat turn cold and her body temperature drop. Her breathing was no longer audible, but the heavy pounding of her heart rung loud in her ears. She tried to muffle the sound by hugging her knees to her chest as she cradled her head and clenched her jaw to keep from screaming in terror.

An indeterminate amount of time passed as she sat shrouded over the toilet seat, her eyes squeezed shut trying to eliminate the clouded images of Piet and Anton still flickering at the frayed edges of her psyche.

Then, with a startling, metallic clang she heard the bathroom door knock against the trash can. Panicked, she placed her feet on the white tile floor. Her legs, not having moved for some time, felt heavy as stones.

"Is someone in there?" she heard a man's voice yell out after the banging had stopped. No doubt the attendant she had spoken to earlier from the lower floor.

"Please open the door. I don't know what you're up to in there, but you should be advised that I'm alerting the building's security right now!"

Nina shook then stamped her feet until she could feel a numb, tingling sensation coursing through her legs. She slid the lock open, stepped out of the stall and used her body's strength to shove the metal bin out of her way. She peeked out first to see if anyone was lying in wait in the hall and then crossed over to the double glass doors leading to the library's upper stacks. She walked quickly and quietly across the lofted gallery until she reached the vestibule on the opposite side. Then she ran down the stairs to the ground floor, hoping the attendant had gone up in the opposite direction.

The sun had begun to set, meaning she would need to leave soon before the gates to the Royal Zoo were closed for the night. She made her way to the nearest exit but could not get a good sense of where Piet and Anton might be. Nonetheless, she was certain they must be waiting for her somewhere. And if they knew where she worked then they knew where she lived.

She dug through her purse, until her frenzied fingers opened the zipper of a small side pocket where months before she had deposited a key for safekeeping. Relieved to feel the serrated metal edge, she gripped it firmly in the palm of her hand then shoved it into the folds of her coat pocket. Following her instinct, she wound her way west to the only place in Amsterdam she knew she would feel safe.

With the afternoon light starting to fade, Nico walked Lena and Wuodan home but without any intention of staying put as Dr. Van den Broek had advised. Instead, he called up the babysitter they had used on a couple of occasions and offered an emergency rate that made it well worth her while to reschedule whatever plans she might have.

Before she arrived, Nico put in one last call to his grandmother to gauge whether Nina—on an off chance—had gone to see her.

"Nico, it's been ages since I've heard from either one of you! Are you trying to break your grandmother's heart? How is Lena? I haven't seen her in months."

"She's doing well, *Oma*, and I promise we'll bring her over for a visit soon. We've just had a run of bad luck lately getting ill and such. We didn't want to expose you."

"Rubbish. I'm as healthy as a horse. You should have told me sooner. I would have brought over some soup."

"I know, I know, but listen. I need to go out and run an errand now. I just wanted to give you a quick call to let you know we're thinking of you."

"Don't make me wait too long, Nico, or you'll find me on your doorstep unannounced."

Nico hung up the phone feeling agitated. He had exhausted all of Nina's known contacts and felt guilty about deceiving his grandmother, but the last thing he needed was another person worried sick while he tried to fix a situation where he already felt at a complete loss.

As Nico wrote down his number on a scrap of paper, he briefed the sitter on Lena's needs for the night and how much to feed the dog. Heading back out into the cold, he had no idea where to look for Nina, but he was determined to unearth every urban hellhole to find her.

With the sun set, the temperature dropped, and the winds flared up again. Nico, however, could only feel the stoked rage still burning inside of him since he had learned about Nina's abuse at the hands of her stepfather and his son. Every night after Nina had gone to sleep, he had imagined killing them both, each fantasy a variant of some clichéd torture he had seen on film or television or in the killings he had had to report on for his work. Nico had experienced his share of violence and growing up had had to dole it out on occasion, but up until now his adult life had been dedicated to exposing murder, not participating in it. Now that his own family was affected, however, he could not help but identify with this impulse.

It frustrated him that Nina refused to tell him their names and where they lived. But given her fragile condition, he had no choice but to spare her the anguish. Still, he could not comprehend why she would want to protect them, why she would not want to see them punished and instead continued to punish herself.

If Nico was not going to be given the satisfaction of beating those rabid animals to a pulp, he sure as hell was not going to allow them to ruin his life. For the next few hours, fueled by his rage, and with a photo of Nina in hand, he scoured the streets and asked shop owners and pub keepers if they had recently seen her.

At half past midnight, feeling both fatigued and discouraged, Nico went into the *Café de Vriendschap* for a much-needed break. Someone other than Jan was tending bar that night, so he ordered a pint and posted himself at the edge of the counter to keep a look out on the street. When the young barman brought over his beer, Nico showed him the photo and asked the question he had posed a hundred times already.

The bartender looked at the image and then back at Nico, sizing him up.

"Does she live around here?" he asked.

"Used to."

"Then I'm pretty sure I saw her on my way to work. Going into a building on the *Kloveniersburgwal*."

"Are you sure?" Nico asked, surprised. "Was she alone?"

"Yeah, she was letting herself in."

"She had a key?"

"Yup. Seemed out of sorts, though. Kept looking over her shoulder."

"And what time was this?"

"Would have been around six o'clock."

Nico thanked him, left a large tip, and in one gulp finished his beer.

Back outside, an icy drizzle had begun to fall. Nico pulled up his hoodie and walked back across the tree-lined canal a few hundred meters from where he had just been sitting.

For the second time in less than twelve hours, Nico stood in front of Max's old apartment building and began to ring the buzzers at random until someone finally let him in. He knew that Nina could not be in Max's old flat, so she was either in someone else's apartment or hiding somewhere in the common area. He suspected the latter, so he made his way past the staircase and toward the back courtyard but found nothing beyond the usual collection of garbage and recycling bins as well as row after row of parked bicycles. Coming back into the vestibule, however, he could see that a small storage area was built into the back of the stairwell, and that the low wooden door obscuring it was closed shut.

"Nina?" he called out, approaching the storeroom slowly. "Are you in there? It's me, Nico. I've come to take you home."

He heard something rustle behind the door, which both relieved and concerned him. He waited to see if she would say something, but as the silence settled, he braced himself for what he would find.

"It's just me, Nina. I'm going to open the door now, ok? Don't be frightened.”

He heard a small gasp from the blackened recess. As his eyes adjusted to the darkness, he could just make out her outline. She was crouching down in the far corner, the toes of her boots visible across a faint line of light cast through the open door.

“Please don’t be afraid. No one is going to hurt you. I just want to take you home where you’ll be safe, ok?”

Nico went down on his knees and crawled closer until he could see the rounded reflection of fear in her eyes.

“Nina? Do you know who I am? Just nod if you’d rather not say anything.”

To his relief, she signaled her recognition.

“Would you take my hand, please? It’s cold, and Lena misses you. I promise you’ll be safe.”

Nina stared at him, reluctant at first to accept his proposition, but seeing that he was not going anywhere without her, she resigned herself. Cautiously, she placed her gloved hand in his and allowed him to help her crawl out of the awkward and musty space.

Once they were standing, Nico tried to lead her toward the front entrance.

What if he’s out there waiting?” Nina asked, not daring to take a step further.

Nico turned toward her. On the outside he appeared both calm and confident but inside he felt a pang of utter devastation.

“He’s not here, Nina. I promise you.”

Outside the street was empty apart from an old man and his prancing cocker spaniel. Nico squeezed Nina’s hand to reassure her then led her toward the *Nieuwe Doelenstraat* where he could hail a cab. Once he had managed to coax her inside, he gave the driver their address and leaned back in the leather seat, exhausted. Other than the constant purr of the diesel engine, they rode home in silence, Nina’s hand tightly gripping his as they each stared out the windows at the slumbering cityscape.

It was almost two in the morning when the taxi dropped Nico and Nina off.

Before opening the door to their apartment, Nico reminded her about the babysitter's presence.

"Just go straight through and into the bedroom, alright? I'll deal with her."

Nina nodded in wide-eyed, silent acquiescence.

Nico turned the lock, and in a matter of seconds they could hear the babysitter begin to stir from her sleep. She greeted them with a drowsy "good evening" as she sat up to switch on the lamp.

"Sorry to wake you," Nico said hurriedly, trying to draw her attention away from Nina as she walked right past them and into the bedroom, her eyes cast down.

"No problem," the babysitter said, looking over at Nico, her face an open question mark. "Lena and Wuodan both had their dinner, and Lena's been fast asleep since eight o'clock." Leaning in she added, "Is everything ok?"

"Yes," Nico said, averting his eyes as he fumbled for his wallet. "Thanks again for coming on such short notice. We really appreciate it."

"Of course! Any time."

An awkward silence ensued as she took the large sum of money from Nico's open hand.

"Lena was a perfect angel. No trouble at all."

Nico walked her to the door and helped her with her coat. The day care center had recommended her, and apart from the day care's small staff, they knew no one else in common.

Relieved, Nico closed the door behind her but wondered what he should do next. Dr. Van den Broek had insisted he call right away. But at this hour of the night it didn't make any sense.

In the darkness of their bedroom, he found Nina lying still on the bed, her back toward him and enveloped in an air of despondency. Nico took a deep breath as he walked around to face her, unsure of what he should say. He breathed a sigh of relief when he saw that she was breastfeeding Lena who lay cradled in her arm looking up at her, her little sock-covered feet stamping with delight.

Lena slept between them for the few hours they were able to lie in bed together, defying sleep. When the first rays of impossible sun began to filter in through the shades, Nico was face up and staring at the ceiling.

"Dr. Van den Broek wants to see you right away. He thinks you may have had a reaction to the withdrawal of your medication."

Nina continued to lay still.

"I'm not crazy," she said at last.

Nico turned to his side.

"I know that," he said. "It's the world that's crazy."

Nina turned to face him, resting a hand on her sleeping daughter's back.

"I was sure that he was following me," she said, shaking her head in disbelief.

That they both were."

An impregnable silence followed as Nico stared into the clear, blue depths of her eyes. He felt a sense of deep melancholy but also relief to see that she was here with him, mentally.

"Do you feel safe now?" he asked.

"Yes," she replied, without a hint of hesitation. "It just felt so real, you know? I can't really explain it."

Nico nodded, his brow furrowed. After another silence passed, he asked, "Are you up for seeing him today?"

Now it was Nina's turn to look up at the ceiling.

"In a little while, ok? I just want a little more time with Lena."

"Of course. I'll call work and let them know we won't be in. We'll all go together. You, Lena and me."

The sun shone bright that afternoon, the air light and refreshing, as if an early spring had arrived to take away the young family's despair. Nina pushed Lena's stroller as Nico walked beside her, and apart from their sleepless eyes obscured behind dark sunglasses, they appeared like a typical family out for a lunchtime stroll.

When they arrived at Dr. Van den Broek's office, the assistant whisked

Nina away behind the closed doors of the consultation room. Nico, meanwhile, sat in the waiting area with Lena who he placed on the floor so she could play with a set of wooden blocks he had uncovered in a play chest next to the magazine rack. Nico was grateful for the distraction and watched with a tired smile as Lena knocked over the small towers he built for her, never tiring of the surprise. In that moment he wished she could always remain like this, happy and ignorant of what transpired in the lives of her parents, blissfully untouched by the invisible scars that marred them both.

After half an hour, the heavy door of the consultation room opened again, and he and Lena were summoned inside by Dr. Van den Broek, an impeccably dressed man of commanding stature who gave off an air of gravity that belied his still youthful looks.

Placing Lena between them on the gray, mid-century sofa opposite the doctor's well-worn leather chair, Nico took note of the well-crafted bookshelves and the displays of erudition. Scattered throughout the room were discreet but evocative *objets d'art,* no doubt meant to signify a tacit recognition of the mind's interminable complexity. It was here where the modern alchemist worked his unruly magic, straddling the esoteric and tangled realms of consciousness that made up the minds of his patients.

Nico sighed.

"I was just speaking with Nina about the change in her medication, Nicolaas. We both agree it would be best if she could come and see me every day for the next two weeks, so we can keep an eye on how she's adjusting. Nina was hoping you could accompany her here and back. Would that be something your schedule can accommodate? Looking at my calendar, I would suggest 2 or 4 PM."

"I can make either time work," Nico said, his tone firm and his face stoic.

"2 PM it is then. I also suggested to Nina that she take at least the next week off from work. That will give her some time to recover in peace without the stress of additional obligations."

"And Lena?" Nico asked. "Should she still go to day care?"

"Yes, I would suggest you keep to your regular schedule as much as possible."

Nina remained silent throughout the brief discussion, continuing to look straight ahead although Nico was aware that she was doing everything in her power to keep her eyes from welling up. It angered him that she looked like a prisoner, as if she needed to appear calm and rational so that she would not be considered a potential threat to herself or to Lena.

In that moment Nico understood just how exposed she must have felt. It was an inherent paradox of the mental health system. On the one hand it functioned to alleviate the suffering of the "unstable" while on the other hand, it pronounced heavy judgments and at times, severe consequences. It infuriated Nico to know that somewhere out there Nina's stepfather and stepbrother were no doubt still abusing women while Nina alone continued to endure the anguish of their unpunished crimes and transgressions.

The winter holidays swept over them in a peaceful blur of timeworn observances. With Dr. Van den Broek's close monitoring and a refinement of her medication, Nina soon re-stabilized, and within two weeks Nico came home to find that she had placed the ornaments on the small fir tree he had bought and was lighting the candles to Lena's wide-eyed delight.

On the twenty-fifth, dressed in their finest, they visited the Oma who had insisted on cooking a traditional roast duck. She teased and berated them for putting her off the last few months and marveled at hearing her great granddaughter's wide-ranging gurgles and intonations.

""She's twice the size of when I last saw her," she exclaimed. "*O-ma*, can you say it?"

Carrying Lena over to the Christmas tree, the Oma sat her down on the floor, and like a princess, delivered one by one, the many overdue *Sinterklaas* presents she had both bought and made for her.

Back home in their apartment and once Lena was fast asleep, Nico received the gift of a timid resumption of their marital affection that seemed to coincide with Nina's newly renewed interest in her outward appearance.

A week later, they rang in the new century in the quiet, candle-lit comfort of their living room, watching the televised fireworks display and sharing a bottle of champagne. Despite the circulating Y2K rumors and a heady mix of *fin de siècle* anticipation, the New Year felt both calm and hopeful.

On the cloudy and gray afternoon that followed, with just enough chill in the air to keep Wuodan feisty, they took a long walk together through *Flevopark*. At its furthest edge, the park gave way to the *Niuwe Diep* lake, formed by the creation of the *Diemerzee* dike, built in the 13th century to protect against rising sea levels.

"I miss the ocean sometimes," Nina mused as she gazed out onto the choppy water. "That's the only part of my childhood that I look back on fondly. It was the only place I felt free from everything else. Free from myself."

"We should take a beach holiday," Nico said, taking her hand. "Lena is old enough now. Where would you like to go?"

"As far away from here as possible."

"Let's go to Costa Rica. Cas just came back and can't stop raving about it. He says it's super laid back. And it's about as far away as you can get from here."

Nina met his eyes with kindled curiosity.

"I've never traveled outside of Europe. Is it very expensive?"

Of late, Nina had started to worry about their finances.

"The flights perhaps. But once we're there, it's a hell of a lot cheaper. Don't worry about that. We've got some savings set aside."

Nina's face lit up in a way he had not seen in months.

"Let's do it," she said, her tone definitive. "For Lena's birthday."

17

Amsterdam - Spring 2000-Fall 2001

Greeted each day by the cold north wind, Nico cursed his way through their first few weeks back in Amsterdam. Not even the tropical nostalgia of their trip was enough to sustain him through the bleakness that had crept back into their everyday life. Having returned to the heart of Nina's most recent trauma, Nico watched with dismay as she reverted to her more familiar, melancholy self. With something akin to religious fervor, he had hoped that their visit to Costa Rica would change her and even restore her mental health, and for the time they spent there it did.

During those three rapturous weeks without a care, he had witnessed a transformation in Nina. She had laughed often and without hesitation as they had walked along the rain forest trails and long stretches of semi-deserted beach. With Lena on his shoulders and the sun-kissed waves lapping at their feet, he had watched Nina's limbs relax and turn golden as if she had been rightfully restored to her goddess-like height. In the early mornings she had woken up hungry for his touch so that each day Nico had fallen more in love with her. Plunging into those strange new depths with her full of warmth and vitality, he could not believe his restored fortune. Their connection to one another and even to themselves had never felt more potent.

Yet the moment they set foot in The Netherlands, the pulsing ember they had kindled turned ashen gray. In the days that followed their return, Nico watched as Nina's anxieties took hold of her, wrapping themselves around her like a tight-fitting cocoon. Before long she was reaching for her medications again, clinging to her doctor's visits as if to a life preserver.

Nico's disillusionment and sense of helplessness could not have felt more profound.

Added to that, the situation with Nina's work did not help matters. Her emotional hiccups prior to their trip had not gone unnoticed at the veterinary clinic. Her many absences had made it unlikely she would be offered a chance to advance beyond her part-time position.

In a way, Nico could not help but feel abandoned, as if the woman he had discovered on the beach had somehow slipped away from him with the outgoing tide. On their vacation they had spent almost every minute outdoors, rarely interacting with other people, but even when they did, she had seemed relaxed and at ease. Now, back in their crowded, urban landscape, Nina grew increasingly resistant to leaving the apartment which in turn amplified his own sense of breathless claustrophobia.

The family's financial burden was now his to bear. In the year and a half that followed, Nico felt compelled to seek out more consistent work which in turn translated into even longer periods of time spent away from home. He justified his long absences, both to his anxious wife and to himself, by pointing out that even though he was a veteran war correspondent, his pay was no longer increasing but the competition was. What he did not tell Nina, of course, was that he found a sense of relief in being able to leave her on occasion, even as his work environment became more hostile and required him to watch his every step.

His reputation among some of his younger colleagues had developed a corrosive edge not compatible with the now less forgiving work conditions, and it was starting to eat away at his ability to infiltrate certain key sectors and sources. More disturbing, however, was the degree of resistance he was encountering among a newer wave of editors who seemed more concerned about their paper's return on investment than the substance of certain undeniable and hard-hitting facts. Nico found himself having to bite his tongue, toggling back and forth between the exhaustion of needing to work on an even tighter budget and the frustration of having to wag his tail while still adhering to what he understood as the meat and potatoes of journalism: the dirty, raw and unfiltered truth.

"A plane just flew into the World Trade Center in New York."

Anselm, Nico's editor, swiveled in his chair, unmuted the large TV behind his desk and switched the channel to CNN.

Nico leaned in for a better view.

At first, all they could see was the top of one tower. A large, black, gray mass of smoke was billowing ominously behind it, and a smaller plume was rising to meet it from a crooked gash about twenty odd floors below.

"What the—"

Anselm lifted his hand signaling Nico to keep quiet.

The live feed was playing a patched through call between an off-screen anchor and a CNN executive who had a direct view from a top floor office about a mile away.

"What can you tell us about the situation?" the male anchor asked.

"A plane hit the top of the north tower head-on," said a gravelly, matter-of-fact voice.

"Was it a propeller plane?"

"No. A two-engine jet. Maybe a 737."

"To repeat: are you saying this was definitely a large, commercial jetliner?"

"Yes. A passenger, commercial jet. It was teetering back and forth—wing tip to wing tip— when it flew into the tower."

"Did it go all the way through?"

"No. It appears to still be embedded, somewhere inside the building."

Through the black smoke, Nico could make out the dark-tinged glow of an orange wall of flames emanating from the jagged steel rip across the building's top floors. In Nico's mind it recalled the fantastical image of some hideous, sci-fi, monster's grin.

"It looks like multiple sides of the building are on fire," a woman's voice said out of nowhere. The newscast had switched to a WABC affiliate broadcasting out of Battery Park City. *"There's a lot of debris fluttering down, like leaflets."*

"Did you see what happened?" another disembodied anchor asked.

"No. I felt it. It was like a gigantic sonic boom. The television went out. I could feel vibrations along the windows, and when I looked up, the top side of the tower just...exploded."

The live footage was now showing a view from the opposite side showcasing a row of blown out windows stretched across the entire width of the building, the licking flames visible throughout. Heavy clouds of black, gray smoke continued to rise, growing denser by the second even as the prevailing air currents tried to shift them east toward Brooklyn.

The broadcast switched back to the original voice of the CNN anchor now speaking to a street level bystander patched through on his cell phone. As they spoke, the live camera image held steady on the north face of the tower, pulled back enough to reveal a partial view of its 110-story twin to the left. The man on the street, Winston, was describing the burst of flames he had just witnessed as another plane entered the live camera's field of vision to the right. It was flying well below the gash, and as Nico lifted his finger to point at it, it disappeared again hidden behind the inferno.

"What the fuck was that?"

For a long second, the image on the screen blanked out and in the moments that followed, Nico and Anselm witnessed a spectacular, red-flamed explosion just behind the north tower.

It was 9:03 AM in New York, and what Winston had just described was happening once more.

Did you see that?!" Nico was still pointing to the right of the screen, dumbfounded.

"The building is exploding right now!" Winston yelled through the phone. *"You've got people running up the street! Ok, the whole building just exploded!"*

The off-screen anchor and one of his colleagues, still talking, failed to realize that a second plane had just hit. They thought the plane stuck in the north tower had generated the secondary explosion.

Nico could not believe what he was seeing.

"OK, now one of our producers is saying that perhaps another plane might be involved. Let's not speculate, but now it's the second twin tower that's on fire."

"No shit," Nico murmured.

"The second twin tower is spreading much more debris. Is Winston still on the line?"

Furious, dark clouds began to form as the smoke from the two buildings combined. Most of the discernible wreckage flew through the air on screen looked weirdly like white papers fluttering, much like what an earlier eyewitness had described on the phone.

Beyond this spectacular burst, a much uglier truth was *not* visible to them. The desks, the furniture, the computers, *the people* who were there moments before, were now gone. All that was visible was the eerie sight of the explosion's aftermath and the scattering of this white debris. Nothing else.

"Another passenger plane has hit the World Trade Center," the anchor repeated to his invisible, worldwide audience. *"We just saw that a plane deliberately hit the south tower. Two planes... These are just frightening images."*

Anselm's phone began to ring. He moved to the opposite side of his desk and picked up the line. "I'm watching it now," he said, as Nico's eyes stayed fixed on the monitor.

"Have you got Jansen there?... He's in New York now... You've got to get him live on this.... Yes. Whatever it fucking takes. Get him taping audio, video, whatever he can get his hands on."

"Perhaps because of the angle, it looks like the towers are leaning," the unembodied anchor was now telling them. *"Someone who is a witness is now saying that the towers are leaning."*

Smoke rose from the second tower in a straight, vertical column as it met the more horizontal exhaust still billowing from the first explosion. The camera zoomed back to show the entire, southern half of Manhattan. It was dwarfed from above by a threatening black mass that created an apocalyptic haze as it drifted east toward Long Island.

For the next 50 minutes, as Anselm continued talking on the phone, Nico watched as the buildings burned on screen and as the broadcast switched back and forth between live footage and replays of the second blast caused by United Flight 175.

One minute before the top of the hour Nico and Anselm watched, incredulous, as the south tower collapsed before their eyes. What before was a rush of smoke rising was now a runaway train of fury turned in on itself, churning downward. Dark, gray clouds filled the screen as the shattering rubble folded in on itself, concealing any sign of a structure.

On the streets below, people in southern Manhattan were running for their lives, pursued by the onslaught of ash and debris as tall as the skyscrapers surrounding them.

At 10:28 AM, in geminate destruction, the north tower collapsed. An astonishing glow of orange smoke obfuscated everything on screen.

It was only a few days later that Nico viewed the more disturbing images. The shocking video deliberately kept off the air that day, September 11th, 2001. Captured by a French film crew that happened to be on location, people could be seen gathering along the serrated edges of the north tower's 90th some odd floors. As the camera zoomed in, Nico watched in spellbound horror as one person, and then another, fell out of the building.

But no.

It was so much worse than that.

They were jumping. The people were deliberately *jumping*.

Nico rewound the film to watch it again. To see if what he was interpreting was correct and at the same time hoping to God not. But each time he watched, slowing down each frame per second, unable to stop himself from doing it over and over again, the visual conclusion was unavoidable.

The tremendous heat from the still burning jet fuel. The lapping flames closing in on them. Suffocating them. They were choosing instead to jump from the building.

Without a doubt it had been impossible to breathe in that inferno. Or to even think. Instinct must have driven them toward the windows. Toward fresh air and toward the cloudless blue sky of what had started out as a glorious, late summer morning, scrubbed clean of the previous days' humidity and metropolitan grime after an early evening thunderstorm the day before.

They—the ones atop the north tower—the ones who had survived the plane's initial impact—had chosen the certainty of catching one last, clear and crystalline breath, one last view of *their* Manhattan over the horror of staying in that blazing death-trap—one that only moments before had symbolized the top of the world.

In the days that followed, one man in particular haunted Nico's dreams. In the close-up footage, the man appears to approach a shattered window shrouded in darkness and just below the scorched floor above him. For a brief instant, he squats down, and then, like a gymnast, his arms extend out, and with a graceful swan dive, he flies.

As the fallout from 9/11 continued to cloud the world's vision, Nico knew that all hope for the immediate future was suspended. Walking home that night, having watched the western hemisphere's most imposing structures crumble like desiccated leaves in the hands of some maniacal monstrosity, it was impossible not to feel it: the visceral, inescapability of mankind's fear stripped bare of protective pretense and left to cower in some desolate and exposed corner.

Within a month of watching the World Trade Center collapse, Nico found himself packing his gear for Islamabad. Along with other NATO allies, the Dutch were soon contributing their own air, land and sea support to the trademarked Enduring Freedom campaign, particularly the ISAF operations near Kabul. In the twisted logic of his profession, Nico knew he would be milking this for all the steady, long-term work he could get. At the same time, however, he was aware that the consequences had just ratcheted up to an even deadlier degree. Having reached center stage under such an ominous spotlight, he knew that serving *his* side—and after watching the towers fall there was no doubt where his loyalties stood—meant practicing a de facto journalism of attachment. Any and all overtures toward neutrality had just been obliterated as pie-in-the-sky fantasy, and no self-respecting journalist could reasonably deny that.

Three weeks later, Nico stepped off the UN chartered flight at Schiphol and made a beeline for the Café Rembrandt in the Arrivals hall. Bleary eyed and on edge, he could not face going home straight away, so he downed three bottles of Grolsch and drank another two standing at the corner bar opposite his apartment building before resigning himself to the stumble home. It was the first alcohol he had had in weeks, and he had never felt more grateful.

As soon as he opened the door, he heard Lena's pitter patter steps running toward him. "Papa!" she squealed. It was well past her bedtime, and by the weary look on Nina's face, it was clear she had defied her mother's wishes by waiting up for him. Nico knelt to embrace his daughter, her round and childish face lit up brighter than a Christmas tree. In a matter of seconds, he felt her joyful, little arms surrounding him. It was hard for him to believe that in just two months she would turn three.

"Did you bring me candy, Papa?" The innocence of her question was almost too much to bear, and before he knew it, his eyes teared up.

Nina stood back a few paces.

"I thought you were arriving much earlier," she said, unable to mask the twinge of hurt in her voice. Glancing over, Nico recognized the nervousness at play in her eyes. She had never seen him weep like this.

In truth, she had never seen him look so shattered. He had lost so much weight that his clothes barely clung to his body. His eyes, too, looked different, the pupils more dilated than usual despite the alcohol. Something else had happened to him in Kabul. Something that had changed him.

They did not speak much until the following evening. Claiming that he could not sleep, Nico had passed out on the couch but not before he had downed half a bottle of gin. He slept straight through the morning and well into the afternoon. Then he woke and picked up the bottle again.

His mouth loosened by cocksure inebriation, he began telling her what it had been like over there, but this time Nina found it impossible to listen. She now associated his far-off tales with the falling skyscrapers she had seen on television, the ones that still haunted her dreams. It unsettled her to hear him talk like this, so she tuned him out.

"Are you even listening to me?" Nico asked. They were seated at the small kitchen table, two bottles of beer between them, having just put a cranky Lena to bed.

Startled, she blurted out her 'yes' one second too late.

"Yeah?" Nico's eyes flared at her with indignation. "Then tell me what I just said?"

She stared at him, her large eyes pleading for forgiveness.

Nico tore his face away from her.

"I don't know why I even bother. I'm going out for a while. Don't wait up."

He slammed the door behind him as Nina withdrew back into her numbness. The tears she had shed the first few times he had left her were no longer accessible. She reached over for his half-empty beer and without thinking, finished it.

"I'm sorry if I upset you the other day," Nina said, fidgeting with her dessert spoon. "It's just disturbing to me, the work you do."

They were sitting in his grandmother's dining room, having endured most of their Christmas meal in silence. From the moment they had arrived, Nina had been antsy and on edge, trying her best to play happy family for Oma's sake, but failing miserably in light of Nico's disregard for her charade. Oma, of course, had seen right through their trouble, and had judiciously kept herself out of it by attending to Lena's childish needs and by piling repeated portions onto Nico's plate. Only in the kitchen as they had prepared the dessert plates had she shown Nina her sympathy by patting her on the back.

"Disturbing," Nico said, as if weighing out the meaning, his eyes focused on his brandy glass, preparing to drink up the remaining dregs.

"Yes," Nina said, looking over at Oma for support, but her eyes were cast down as she stood to clear the dishes.

"It's just that with Lena, I can't let myself—"

Nico raised his hand.

"It's ok."

He could not take another minute of her anguished moping. It had been going on for days. "You have your secrets, and now I'll have mine. For Lena's sake, it's probably better if we don't talk about it, yeah?"

Nina nodded, which only fueled his anger more. What had happened to the woman who would stand by him? Who understood the sacrifices he made every time he went out on assignment? Who would listen to him when he needed to talk about the horrors he had just lived through?

"I certainly wouldn't want *you* losing any sleep on account of *me*," Nico added.

Nina swallowed hard.

A part of him could not help but smile at her defensive reflex. She was never going to share herself fully with him, and in that moment, he realized it was just as well.

Forcing a laugh, he stood up on wobbly legs to refill their glasses.

"Let's have a toast then."

She looked up at him startled, but then raised her glass.

"To our fucked up little secrets, Nina, may they serve us well."

By spring Nico almost welcomed the flaring up of Mid-East tensions. Most of what he had shot in Afghanistan had put him back on the editors' A list so that soon enough 2002 was passing him by in a flurry of work that had him flying back and forth from Kabul. All of this meant, of course, that he had too much on his hands to spend time worrying about the state of his marriage. He was providing for his family, and that was all that mattered.

Nina, knowing this, played her part by caring for Lena which seemed to keep her on an even keel. At least that is what Nico told himself when he would catch her still popping the pills that Van den Broek prescribed.

Whatever her mental imbalance, she was at least taking good care of their daughter. Nico could not fault her for that, and secretly he was glad to leave her psychic care to somebody else. He had tried to break through to her, but it had never worked. And as long as they kept to their agreement—barring the occasional slip up, of course—they managed to get along just fine. Not that he stayed put for long. He would play with Lena while Nina was cooking and would help get her ready for bed, but once she was fast asleep, that itch to go out for a drink would take over. He would be out the door again, leaving Nina to do whatever it was she did on her own at night without him. She was usually asleep by the time he came home.

By year's end the focus of his work had shifted to the looming crisis in Iraq. To assuage any lingering feelings of neglect, Nico booked an extended family holiday to the Canary Islands, where for a few days, at least, they rekindled the fleeting joy of a temporary, beach-side escape.

18

Baghdad - March-April 2003

Along with the Grand Ishtar, the Palestine stood proud and prominent against the Baghdad skyline. Built like a 1980s, Soviet-bloc relic, the 18-story hotel had a plethora of fortified balconies that looked out across Firdos Square and the Tigris River toward what would soon be renamed the Green Zone. Most of the international press had set up camp at the Palestine, heeding the Pentagon's warning that to do otherwise would endanger their lives.

As expected, the top floor lounge was packed that night. The bombing was set to begin in less than 48-hours' time, and plenty of open Chivas bottles were making the rounds. Beneath the low ceiling, the lighting was dimmed to a dull red, but it did not take Nico long to spot two of his Spanish cohorts from his most recent tour in Afghanistan. They were seated at a table with two people he did not recognize.

"You made it," José said, getting up from the table to give Nico a one-armed embrace.

"No way I would miss this," he said, pulling up a shoddily upholstered seat. "After Kabul, this place is fucking paradise. We've got beds, sheets, the cooks aren't trying to poison us. What more could you ask?"

The table laughed in response, and José made the necessary introductions. Carlos, meanwhile, signaled the waiter for another round. They were throwing back bottles of Farida lager at his table along with a local chaser tasting of anise. It was an odd mix for Nico's taste but after his enforced teetotaling in Afghanistan, he was not about to turn it down.

Over the first set of drinks, they compared notes on logistics: where to get food, water, cigarettes, etc., but soon enough the topic of conversation turned to the war itself.

"When you think about it," Carlos said, "Baghdad isn't that different from most cities. Nico's right. It's no Kabul. The people are guarded, yes, but it was the same during Franco. And it feels a hell of a lot safer than Afghanistan. For sure more civilized."

"Yeah, they're not as anti-Western as people think," the ruddy-faced Swede sitting next to him said. "I mean, look around. Apart from the *hijabs* and whatnot, it's clear they want the same sort of things we do."

Nico rolled his eyes.

"We'll see how long that lasts once the bombs drop. From the look of it, they're completely unprepared. Like they don't think this is going to happen."

The British brunette sitting next to the Swede nodded her head as she poured herself another shot.

"Rumor has it the Pentagon is targeting independents this time around," she said. "*Inadvertently*, of course."

As part of the much smaller contingent that had opted out of the embed programs, quite a few of them seemed concerned about getting hit by "friendly" fire. They were all keeping tabs on the military talking heads, alert to any veiled warnings regarding safety and the prevailing needs of military personnel.

"The Amis aren't that stupid," Nico said, and took a long pull from his beer bottle. "I ran into a woman from Reuters who said a U.S. spook told her to move here from the Al Rashid. They wouldn't be doing that if they had an ulterior motive. Hitting a hotel full of international journos would crucify their chances of consolidating European support."

José shrugged.

"No point in getting paranoid now. We're already here."

"Anyway, who would want to damage such a fine example of late '80s architecture?"

Carlos laughed as they raised their bottles.

Unsurprisingly, the Swede and the Brit got up to leave before they ordered another round. They had been inching toward one another all night, which left the Spaniards and Nico to discuss matters much closer to their hearts: American cult films. José, like Nico, was a big fan of David Lynch, and even after Carlos bid them good night at 2 AM, the two men stayed up talking and taking turns drinking straight from the arak bottle.

"They're all fucking crazy," José said, after they had finished a detailed survey of Lynch's female leads. "But it takes one to know one, right? I mean that guy is the king of uncomfortable."

Nico nodded.

"So how do you think he gets them to perform like that?"

"Hell if I know, but to me it's like they're all hiding something. A secret. And you can see it in their eyes, right? They're mysterious. Alluring. Then Lynch puts them in these stressful situations where it's going to force them to reveal the secret somehow. But they resist, and *that's* how he builds the tension. Anything can happen. Seems to work, too, this push and pull, because they do whatever he wants."

"So, if you had your chance—forgetting about the wife and kids for a moment—who would it be?"

"What do you mean?" José asked.

"Who would you want to fuck?"

José laughed.

"Wait a minute, are we talking fictional characters or real women?"

Nico shook his head.

"Does it matter?"

"Of course it fucking matters! It's not like they're that crazy in real life."

"But I thought you just said they were," Nico said. "All right. Fine. We'll make it more interesting. Which character would you rather fuck: Dorothy Vallens in *Blue Velvet*, Lula Fortune in *Wild at Heart* or Alice Wakefield from *Lost Highway*?"

"Dorothy," José said without hesitation. "Hands down."

"Really?" Nico laughed. "I would have pegged you as a Laura Dern type. All wild at heart and weird on top. Maybe just the weird on top bit."

José laughed, too, but his cheeks turned bright red.

"And you?"

"Oh, I'm an Alice man," Nico said, turning serious. "She's mine alright."

Their coverage of the non-stop bombing began bright and early on March 20th and continued over the course of the next three weeks during which Nico's bond with the Spaniards was further cemented. Without the material support of an embed program, the men spent a not insignificant amount of time working together to secure their basic needs.

On April 8th, it was Nico's turn to go downstairs and scrounge up something to eat. Just before noon he made his way back up to the 14th floor where he had left José on the balcony taking skyline footage of the on-going battle.

As Nico approached the door to their room carrying a plastic bag filled with flat bread sandwiches, a reverberating blast threw him back against the corridor wall.

The Palestine, whose English insignia was clearly visible in the noon day light, had received a direct hit from an American tank positioned across the al-Jumariyah Bridge.

Nico's world went black.

When he regained consciousness, he reached up to touch his head. He took a moment to assess the extent of his injuries, but apart from a throbbing headache and minor cuts to his hands and arms, he was more or less okay.

Dazed, he used the wall to push himself up to a standing position. A wave of nausea overtook him, but he forced himself to stumble forward.

José and Carlos were still in the room, and if they were still alive, he needed to help them.

The door to the room had been knocked off its hinges, and all that was visible through the threshold was a cloud of acrid dust and smoke that forced Nico to cover his mouth to keep from coughing. Peering in, he could see rays of dust-diffused sunlight pouring in through the cracks in the external wall.

"José, Carlos!" he called out, as he crossed the threshold. The bathroom was just to the right of the entrance, and he could see Carlos on his hands and knees, bleeding from a cut on his forehead. He had been showering just moments before.

"You ok?"

Carlos waved him off.

"Check on José," he coughed. "He's outside!"

The room was covered in a cloud of dust and debris. Nico had difficulty at first making out the balcony, but as he moved closer, he could see José's foot sticking out, the heel of his sneaker facing up to the sky. As he reached the mangled door frame, he looked in horror at José's back, pinned down by a large chunk of cement from the balcony above.

"Fuck! Carlos, come quick!"

Half-dressed, Carlos was just a few steps behind him. They looked up to make sure nothing else would come crashing down on them and then tested the stability of the floor before maneuvering around José's body.

"José, can you hear me?" Nico asked. "We've got to get this fucking thing off of him!"

Instinctively, they grabbed hold of the jagged cement.

"On three, lift and move to the right," Nico ordered. Straining with effort—the block was much heavier than it looked—they managed to place it down a few inches away from José.

"He's breathing! We need an ambulance."

"It's too dangerous to keep him out here," Carlos said. "They might fire again."

Nico weighed out their options. Moving José without a back brace could kill him.

"We need a board. Something to keep him straight."

Carlos went back into the room, and while Nico checked to see if José was bleeding, Carlos dragged the fallen door toward the balcony.

Taking pains, they slid José on top of it and carried him out to the hall only to find that the elevators were not working.

"Damn it! Stay with him. I'll get someone to help."

Nico took the stairs to the lobby. Descending the fourteen flights, he had to use the handrail to keep his vertigo at bay. His head throbbed. He was concussed, but compared to José, it was nothing.

The lobby, meanwhile, was in total chaos. Rattled and outraged reporters were demanding answers from frightened staff who were likewise confused by what had just happened.

"Do we have to evacuate?" Someone was yelling. "How bad is the damage?"

The thought of possible building collapse was foremost on everyone's mind, but with a battle raging outside, going out on the street was tantamount to suicide.

Nico scanned the floor for the hotel manager to whom he had ingratiated himself by speaking the little Arabic he knew. Spotting him, he ran over and interrupted his conversation with another journalist.

"You've got to call an ambulance. We've got a wounded journalist on the 14th floor. He could die any minute. I need to get him out of here, now."

"Ambulances are coming," the manager said, as he tried to gulp down his fear. "We have a lot of casualties on the 15th floor, too. If you and some others can bring him down, it will be faster."

"We can't take him down those stairs. His back may be broken. We need an elevator, man!"

"We've been ordered to halt service until the damage is assessed, but let's see if we can get you on the staff elevator. Follow me."

On the way, Nico stopped two German reporters and grabbed them by the arms.

"You've got to help me. C'mon!"

On the ride up the elevator he explained the situation.

"You're not looking so good yourself," one of the Germans said. "Your eyes—"

"The blast knocked me out."

"Looks like we'll have to keep an eye on you, too."

"Yeah, well, first things first."

The ambulance, a battered van with a stenciled red crescent on the side, took far too long to arrive. By then the international correspondents who had moved the most injured to the lobby could do little else but listen to their colleagues moan in pain. Any illusions they may have harbored regarding journalistic immunity had shattered into pieces along with the blown-out balconies above them.

For Nico it was too painful to even look at José. His face was turned at an angle to breathe while the rest of his body lay splayed out and motionless on the splintered door. Had they paralyzed him just by moving him? No one dared touch him again, but there was something inhumane about just watching him lie there on that battered and unforgiving surface, unable to offer him any means of comfort.

A dull, throbbing anger consumed Nico as he sat on the floor next to José. He had seen gruesome, limb-wrenching trauma before, but it had never been quite like this. Not where a presumed ally had suddenly morphed into the aggressor.

And in his mind's eye all Nico could see was himself standing watch on that balcony just a few hours earlier while José and Carlos slept. It could just as easily have been him lying here with a broken back. He had taken so much for granted, and for the first time, Nico could feel the cold tendrils of fear wrapping tightly around his neck.

They were fooling themselves to think that covering this war would somehow make a difference. The type of journalism that had moved people to protest had disappeared along with any lasting memory of what had happened in Saigon. The world truly had gone to shit, Nico realized, and this newly minted quest for Enduring Freedom© was proving it.

José died not long after his surgery at Saddam City Medical Center, one of the few hospitals left unlooted in Baghdad. When they got word from a Russian reporter who had made it back to the hotel, Nico and Carlos were not so much shocked as saddened. They had known all along what the outcome would be, and in a way, the news had ended the slow torture of not knowing what else was happening to their friend.

Still, despite their own injuries and the prevailing need to bring José's body home, they were forced to stay put a few days longer until a handful of emergency flights resumed take-off from the recently liberated airport.

Nico flew back to Madrid with Carlos to attend Jose's funeral on the sprawling grounds of the *Almudena* cemetery. Standing amid the densely packed tombstones and towering monuments, Nico could feel his claustrophobic anger begin to surface again. They had just lowered José's coffin into the ground, and although he was standing toward the back of the crowd, Nico could see the rippling anguish skittering across José's widow's face. Until then, she had kept the steady flow of tears in check as her two young sons stood beside her. In that moment a howl tore out of her. Struck by its force, the six-year-old child began to wail uncontrollably, while the older one, the spitting image of José, stared straight ahead in a stoic rage.

Nico shook his head in helpless fury and then walked away. All he wanted was to find those fucking soldiers, grab them by the balls and then—

"Hey, man," Carlos called out to him. "You ok?"

Nico had just crossed beneath the imposing *neomudéjar* entrance, his eyes adjusting to the contrasting shade produced by the stark sunlight.

Carlos walked up beside him.

"Sorry. Religious ceremony is no good for me."

"That's ok, man," Carlos said, reaching up to put his hand on Nico's shoulder, "Let's get a drink."

Carlos led them north into the *Pueblo Nuevo* neighborhood before stepping into an old and rundown pub on the corner of *Hermanos Goméz*. The ragged white awning read *Bar Asturias* and looked to have been hanging there since Franco's days.

"It doesn't look like much, I know, but no one will bother us here."

Nico took a seat at one of the rickety wooden tables in the back while Carlos got them each a bottle of beer and a whiskey. Apart from a couple of day laborers having their lunch, there was no one else in the place.

"To José," Carlos said, raising his glass.

"May the bastards who did this to him die an equally slow and painful death," Nico added, before throwing back the shot.

They drank their beers in silence and stared straight ahead at the sunlight trying to come in from the entrance.

"I can't do this anymore," Nico said, after a long silence. A cloud of stale, smoky air hung in front of them like a shroud.

"I understand, man," Carlos said, before signaling to the bartender for another round. "You've got a wife and kids. You can't afford to carry this around with you. In this job you gotta stay focused every minute to stay alive."

They paused a moment to finish their beers.

"He felt a lot of guilt about leaving them, you know?" Carlos added. "But the thing is, José didn't know anything else. That camera was his life, man. As strange as it sounds, he was living his dream."

Nico lit a cigarette in response.

Carlos narrowed his eyes.

"What will you do when you get back?"

"I'll take medical leave. Milk it for what it's worth then try to get my family out of Amsterdam. Nina's not well, so a change of scene would do us good. Live somewhere cheap for a while. Central America maybe."

Carlos smiled at him as he stood to retrieve the drinks that the barman had laid out for them on the counter.

Nico watched as he walked over to the bar. Carlos had just lost his best friend and colleague, and yet here he was, comforting *him*. Like Nico, he had not really slept the past few days, and there was a distinct cheerlessness to Carlos' gait.

"So Central America, eh?" He put the shots and beers down on the table. "There's still some fucked up shit going on there, man. Not exactly las *Islas Canarias.*"

"Pfft. Getting away from Europe is the whole point," Nico said. Something inside of him was tightening against the sadness. "Anyway, the Costa Rican economy seems good enough, and they've got no army. The people may not have much, but they're not destroying the place, either. And right about now I could use some of that *pura* fuckin' *vida.*"

To this they raised a glass again.

"Europeans are too soft," Nico said, starting to sound more like his old self. "Not much different than the Amis, really. We're well off, but all we do is bitch about how it's not enough. The petrol's too expensive. Not enough money to buy a second car. Can't win the lotto, blah, blah. People have no fucking clue how the rest of the world lives, or just how fucking desperate it is out there, and I'm fucking bored with it. I will say this much about Spain, though, at least the people here haven't been completely neutered. Not yet anyway."

Carlos laughed.

"Ok, *amigo*, but after living in sleepy little Costa Rica for a while, don't you think you'll get bored, too? They have some nice *mamacitas*, but, what else?"

Nico drew his eyebrows up with a haggard effort.

"I'm getting too old for *mamacitas*, my friend. The one I've got back home is more than enough for me."

"Well, here's to a few good adventures anyway. I can't imagine you sitting on your hands for too long, that's for sure."

19

Amsterdam - April 2003–November 2004

"I think you should see a doctor," Nina said, as she nestled against Nico's gaunt abdomen and as the sun filled their room with a dull, gray light. It was the first time they had been intimate in months but seeing the bruising on Nico's back and upper arms had alarmed her. Until now it had not been possible for her to comprehend what the bombing in Baghdad had meant.

Nico pulled her close.

"I just need some rest," he said, suppressing a yawn.

But Nina could not sleep anymore.

"Your eyes are cloudy, Nico. You don't look well."

Nico sighed and turned on his back.

"You shouldn't worry so much. It's nothing a little time won't cure. But sure. I'll go."

"It's just that—"

"What would help me more is if you could just relax, ok? It's over. And anyway, looking as bad as I do works in our favor. It'll mean I'll get maximum disability, and then I can figure out how to get us out of here. Between the savings and what we'll get each month, it'll be more than enough to live on, assuming we keep things simple. We can live at the beach or up in the mountains, whatever you prefer. The most important thing is we'll be together."

Nina was sitting up now, leaning on her elbow to get a better look at him.

"What are you talking about?" she asked, her brows knitting together.

"Costa Rica, remember? When we were there you said you would do anything to stay?"

Nina's head and neck tilted back.

"Yeah, ok, but we're not really in a place to do that *now*."

"Of course we are. It's time we start living our lives the way we want."

"But what about Lena?" Nina asked, pulling up the duvet. "What about her school? And it's not like we speak any Spanish. Why would they let us stay there?"

"You're worrying again," Nico said, rolling his eyes. He reached across her for the cigarettes lying on the bedside table. "I thought this was what you wanted."

"Ideally, yes. But right now? I'm just worried about you. You haven't been yourself, and I think we should wait."

"What, and drive each other crazy cooped up in this apartment?" He took a long drag from his cigarette before letting out a cloud of smoke. "I thought you wanted to get the fuck out of Holland."

"I do," she said, sounding defensive.

"So, what's the problem?" he asked, flicking ashes into his palm.

"Let's just have you go to the doctor first, ok?" She took the cigarette from him to take a pull. "After that we can talk about leaving."

"Wait. Are you saying what I think you're saying?"

"What?"

"You think I've lost it, don't you?" Nico laughed, the sound a bitter echo in her ears. "You've been spending way too much time with those shrinks of yours. I mean, did you even *eat* while I was gone?"

Nina crossed an arm in front of her.

"Don't start with me." she said, taking another drag.

"Fine. We won't talk about what the hell is going on with *you*. But let me tell you, no amount of pill popping is going to help us keep our shit together. Changing this situation will."

He took what little was left of the cigarette away from her.

"Now, I'll go and see those little men in the white coats, and they can prescribe whatever the hell it is they want if it means we'll get our money. But I'm sure as hell not going to let them brainwash me into thinking I should just loll around here waiting for death to come. We're getting out of here, damn it. I mean, look at you. You're ten years older than when I left."

The dam of tears she had been holding back suddenly burst.

"If that's how you feel, then why don't you just fucking leave again!"

"No, no," Nico said. "That's not what I meant."

After about a minute he dared to put his hand on her arm to comfort her.

"All I'm saying is that we need to go somewhere else."

His voice sounded calm again. Gentle.

"Things aren't working out here. I think you know that."

Wiping her cheeks, she nodded.

"I want the old Nina back," he said, wrapping his arms around her again. "The one I married. Okay, so we have a few lines on our faces, who cares? All that matters is that I love you, and I just want us to get out of here before it's too late."

Nina knew it would not be that simple. It never was. A part of her wanted to believe Nico, to believe that he really was okay and that this was nothing more than a temporary setback. But everything about him was so different now. And what shocked her most was that he could not see it.

She had noticed the change after his first trip to Kabul. After they had agreed not to talk about troubling things. The haunted look in his eyes had scared her. It had felt too dark and at the same time too eerily familiar, and all she had wanted to do was push it away.

To complicate matters, she was not sure she could still trust Nico. His behavior was more erratic now, and his moods indecipherable, especially after that call he had received from The Hague. And though she was loathe to admit it, she was still angry with him for having abandoned them just as the world had felt its most threatening.

Yes, she was drinking more at night to calm her nerves, but she had nonetheless managed to do what was necessary to take care of herself and Lena. The last thing she wanted now was to leave the safety of their home, however imperfect.

"This MRI shows you've suffered a substantial blow to the head, Mr. Van de Steeg."

The neurologist had his back turned and was pointing to an image of Nico's brain projected on the wall-mounted display behind his desk. He was a short man, but his girth more than made up for his height.

"Can you see the bruising here? I'm surprised you didn't come in earlier."

"I had my hands full covering the war," Nico said. "But now that I'm home, I can't seem to concentrate for shit."

"Any other symptoms?"

Nico glanced over at Nina, the corners of his lips turning up. *If it's a head case he wants*, his eyes seemed to say, *that's what he'll get.*

The doctor turned back toward them.

"It's like I'm in a fog all the time," he said, touching his hand to his forehead. "There's a constant, dull pressure. It never quite goes away."

"And at night? Are you sleeping?"

Despite his matter-of-fact tone, the doctor looked genuinely concerned.

"More or less," Nico said, sounding like an impudent schoolboy. "I don't feel like getting up most mornings."

"He's more sensitive to the light now," Nina said. "He can't stand it when I open the shades. That used to not bother him."

Nico's lips drew down.

"I'm not surprised," the doctor said, as he dropped back down into his chair. He had not bothered to turn on the overhead lights.

"We'll need to keep you under regular observation. Given the severity of your symptoms, I'll go ahead and write a letter for your leave of absence. What you need now is time to rest. I would also recommend you start seeing a psychiatrist."

"Is that necessary?" Nico asked.

"As you just pointed out, you've suffered a significant injury in a combat zone. We'll have to monitor you for any signs of post-traumatic stress disorder."

"Okay," Nico said, looking displeased. "but I'm pretty sure I'm not going off on some rampage, if that's what you're worried about."

The doctor looked up sharply from the note he was scribbling.

"I'm not suggesting anything of the kind, Mr. van de Steeg. It is, however, standard procedure in a case like this."

"Right, well, I'll go and see Nina's shrink, then. We've had a few chats in the past. If there's anyone to convince you I haven't lost my marbles, it'll be him."

"Why are you so bothered about seeing a psychiatrist?" Nina asked him later, as they rode their bikes home through the drizzle along *Wijttenbach-straat*. They had left Lena and Wuodan with the babysitter, and this was one of the few moments they had had alone.

"I'm not bothered if it helps my case," Nico said, his eyes shielded behind the dark glasses he now wore when he had to go outside. "But I'm telling you, there's nothing wrong with me. Not like that."

At home things were calm for a while, but Nico's behavior remained inconsistent. He slept very little at night and would often doze off in the late mornings or afternoons. Apart from the appointments he was forced to attend, he declined to participate in any form of therapy or to even fill the Prazozin prescription that Dr. Van den Broek had prescribed for the PTSD.

He would walk Wuodan and pick up the groceries, but for the most part he spent his time surfing the internet. *Making plans for our future*, he would assure Nina. Sometimes he would share the things he had learned about Costa Rica, but for the most part, she could not help but keep her enthusiasm in check. It was hard enough adjusting to Nico's constant presence in their lives which had, in some ways, made it more difficult to manage Lena's outbursts.

Nico had always been her favorite, and now that he was home for good, Lena had learned to play up the advantage. *But Daddy said I could!* had turned into her defiant new catchphrase, one meant to put Nina in her place.

What occupied Nico most, however, was finally reading the Srebrenica Report that had been issued the year before just a few weeks prior to the assassination of the controversial parliamentarian, Pim Fortuyn.

The Institute for War, Holocaust and Genocide Studies (NIOD) had published the findings after the government had appointed them to investigate and analyze the circumstances surrounding what the International Tribunal for the former Yugoslavia would later classify as genocide: the massacre of over 8000 Muslim men and boys by Serb forces at a time when Dutchbat was serving their third tour of duty as part of the UN Protection Force. NIOD had taken seven years to complete the study, but once published, the results were damning, forcing Prime Minister Kok and his Purple Coalition to resign within a week, the same body, in fact, that had commissioned the report.

With so much time on his hands, Nico spent weeks obsessing over it, mining the 4000 pages for details that would help him write his memoir since coverage of that war had jumpstarted his career.

In conversation with Nina over dinner, and long after Lena had gone to bed, Nico was drawn more and more to steep himself in the past, as if by recounting the bitter details, he could somehow make more sense of his situation. Tonight, he had come into the kitchen talking non-stop about the lead up to the war in Bosnia.

Nina set down their plates and took her usual seat opposite him at the small kitchen table. It was a mild, summer evening and the windows next to them were wide open, letting in the occasional breeze and the diffused, white glow of the fading sunlight. It reminded her of the meals they had eaten before Lena was born.

"Van den Broek lobbied hard to send our troops into Bosnia," Nico said, in between bites of the mashed potato and sausage she had piled on his plate.

Nina's brows furrowed at the mention.

"The foreign minister, not your shrink," Nico clarified, slicing through the taut casing of a *braadworst* about to burst.

"The UN was still pissed that The Netherlands had pulled our battalion out early after Israel invaded Lebanon in '82. I've told you about that. It's where I was shipped after basic training. A fucking bloody mess.

"Anyway, the Dutch called the follow-up rotation back early, a damned good decision if you ask me. But now we're on the UN Secretariat's shit list, right? Van den Broek—that self-righteous twat—he couldn't handle that. Felt it was high time The Netherlands proved its military worth and restored its rightful place among the international elite. He was practically begging them to take our battalion.

"But the UN declined his offer. Told him the Serbs had accused the Dutch of bias in the conflict. Well, no fucking surprise there. Everyone in their right mind knew the Serbs were the aggressors. And you would have thought that would have settled things, right?"

Nina nodded her head even though she was barely following.

"But no. Van den Broek and Kok had something to prove, so they offered up the battalion again. By that point the UN wasn't about to decline a second time—not after fucking Croatia anyway—so where do they send them? To the fucking backwaters of The Balkans.

"I mean, even in Tito's heyday they had left that place to rot. The population was mostly illiterate, and they were barely subsisting off whatever it was they could grow up there. The river is what divided them. Serbs to the east, Muslims to the west. So once the war started, you can well imagine the tension. When Tito died, all that was left was the hatred they still had for one another.

"Now, can you imagine having to sit in the middle of that and try to keep the peace? What a fucking joke. Even the Canadians we replaced couldn't get their asses out of there fast enough. And the Serbs who had taken control of the surrounding area, well they sure as hell hadn't forgotten about Van den Broek. 'Bruka, Bruka!'—they called our soldiers. It means disgrace in Serbo-Croatian."

Having finished their meal, Nico leaned back to let out a loud burp, and then cracked open the second can of beer that had been waiting for him beside the first. Nina cleared the plates and replaced them with a full pack of cigarettes and an ashtray.

"While I was still stringing for *Trouw* in '92, I made it as far east as Visegrad before the Serb paramilitaries made it clear I better get my ass back to Sarajevo if I knew what was good for me. They had just taken over from the JNA, the regular army, and they weren't letting journos or international aid groups through anymore.

"What little I did get to see, though, was disturbing enough. It's what it must have been like under the Nazis. Muslims being rounded up, their homes and possessions confiscated. We'd already heard of the ethnic cleansing going on in Bijeljina and Zvornik, and there was no mistaking the message in Visegrad either. Sure enough, the proof is in the report. The ones they didn't deport were later killed in concentration camps."

After a moment, Nina cleared her throat in response to Nico's sudden silence. Something was driving him to talk to her about this right now in spite of his usual wariness.

"You never told me about that," she said, her voice softened to offer encouragement.

Nico raised a wary eyebrow. *Can you blame me?* it said. But she held on tight to his gaze until she could see his shoulders give way.

Nico lit up another cigarette.

"I wasn't surprised Srebrenica happened. For fuck's sake the Serbs are known to have collaborated with the Nazis back then!"

Just then an aberrant clap of thunder jolted their eyes toward the window. The sky above the courtyard had turned a rich shade of violet gray.

"What I couldn't wrap my head around was why Karreman's battalion did absolutely nothing to stop it. Don't get me wrong. I had reservations about our troops being sent there to begin with. The Bosnians needed humanitarian aid and all that, yes. But no one—not the EC, not the UN, not even our own fucking government—wanted to own the responsibility of it. Half-measures all around," he added, shaking his head in frustration.

"The situation was fucked and sending our troops was tantamount to putting them on a suicide mission. But Jesus, once you're actually there? I sure as fuck would like to think I would have gone out fighting."

As he said this, a cooling mist wafted in. For a brief second, Nina hesitated. The light touch of water against her skin felt like a consolation, but it did not last. She managed to jump up just in time to close the windows as the rush of rain began to thump hard against the glass.

"I'm not sure I understand," Nina said, sliding down into her chair like a student kept after class. "What were they supposed to do exactly? Wouldn't it have caused more of a problem if they had returned fire?"

Nico jerked his head back involuntarily.

"That's just it. They weren't allowed to shoot except in self-defense. And the fact is, they were already mentally destroyed. The Serbs had tightened the noose around them nice and slow. Starting in February, '95, no more fuel trucks, and in May, no more food. For two months they ate nothing but emergency food rations, meanwhile they were about to reach a critical point with the diesel. The troops they had sent on leave six months prior weren't allowed to come back, which meant everyone else had to pick up the slack without any chance of reprieve. They were already hostages themselves—though no one at the top wanted to admit it—and when Mladic finally attacked, he took 30 of them as collateral.

"Meanwhile, back in their cozy offices, the UN bureaucrats and the Dutch ministers were all wringing their hands, theorizing what it would mean to pull the Dutchbat out, how it would *look* to the outside world. They thought they could still negotiate with Mladic, a war criminal and a mad man who had already steamrolled over their so-called safe area. They thought they still had a leg to stand on, but Colonel Karremans was already suffering from Stockholm syndrome.

"In the end, it didn't fucking matter. Mladic wouldn't allow anyone *other* than Karremans to negotiate withdrawal. By that point he'd had his hands tied for so long, had been denied air strikes for so long, he'd forgotten any sense of mission. Plus, his battalion, *his* countrymen, were up against a wall. A complete fucking shit show. The brass had spent *months* watching the situation in Srebrenica deteriorate while still telling him he wasn't authorized to do anything beyond self-defense, so in the end, that's exactly what Karremans did. He saved himself and his boys, shook Mladic's hand after the man basically threatened his kids, and let the Serbs slaughter 8000 Muslims right beneath his fucking nose."

Neither of them spoke.

After a while Nina lit two cigarettes along with a white, long-stemmed candle that stood alone at the table's edge. As they sat there, the two smoky coils mingled with the flame's yellow glow, forming a somber tableau that mirrored itself in the wetted windowpanes.

"I tried to make a difference you know, after what happened in Kabul," Nico said, his voice now cushioned against the darkness. "I turned my film over to those bureaucrats in The Hague."

Nina reached out and put her hand over his.

This was the most he had ever said about it.

He let out a small, contemptuous laugh that contrasted sharply with the creased lines of his face.

"In the end, though, I suppose I'm not as brave as I thought. I could have tried to stop them from hurting that boy, but I didn't. I had you and Lena to think about. That was all that was supposed to matter."

Over the course of the next sixteen months, Nina tried to make sense of what Nico was saying. But as time wore on, she found it more and more difficult to follow. Talking about the wars of the past seemed to lessen his depression somehow, but he tended to walk in circles around certain topics, growing increasingly agitated with each successive turn.

To Nina it was an odd preoccupation, one she felt was unsuited to getting over his most recent trauma. But it did, at the very least, hold his attention. Since his return home, his short-term memory had begun to fail. Even when she spoke, he would sometimes lose the thread of what she had just been saying.

"Did you pick up the bread?" she asked.

Nico had just gone shopping but had walked right past her in the kitchen.

"What?" he yelled back through the corridor. He was making his way to the living room to sit in front of his computer again.

Frustrated, Nina walked out to confront him.

"Did you pick up the bread I asked for?"

"The bread?" he looked up at her with a scowl.

"Yes, the bread. That's why you went out, remember?"

A brief blur of confusion ran past his eyes before he could rearrange his features into some sort of feigned recollection.

"Oh, shit. I forgot. Sorry."

"You didn't forget the beer," she huffed, grabbing her coat off the hallway rack. "And where's Wuodan? Don't tell me you forgot him, too."

Nico jumped out of his seat to trail after her.

"I didn't take Wuodan with me," he replied. "I left him here with you."

"But you did take him," Nina reprimanded in earnest. "I handed you the leash and held open the door. Where is he?"

Nico opened his mouth to say something, but then froze.

Trying not to panic, she implored him again.

"Did you leave him tied up outside the store?" It took another moment for him to respond as his eyes darted around, helpless.

"I must have," he replied, a little shaky.

Nina kept her own voice steady.

"You stay here with Lena. I'll go and find him."

Nico nodded with his hands on his head, not daring to look up at her.

Walking as quickly as she could, she tried not to let her anger overwhelm her, focusing instead on her labored breath.

At first, she could not see Wuodan anywhere near the entrance, but just as she was about to let out a flurry of curses, her loyal dog came bounding around the bend, the silver-haired store manager right behind him.

"There you are," he called out to her. The look of relief on his face felt much like her own. "I called out to your husband, but he couldn't hear me for some reason. Must have been listening to those walkmans. He looked very intent."

Handing her the leash, he added, "Sure had us worried there for a moment, though. A dog this size isn't that easy to forget."

"You're up already?" Nina asked.

Nico had pushed open the kitchen door. It was half past eight in the morning, and she was pouring herself a cup of coffee. Just moments before, she had stood in front of the window and watched as the wind whipped the fallen yellow leaves of the elm tree in the courtyard below, a few still clinging lifeless to the stripped, bare branches. It was a typical November morning in Amsterdam, gray and cold.

"I couldn't sleep," Nico replied. "Thought I'd get the papers."

Nina filled a second mug and handed it over to him.

"I'm not going in today," she told him. "Lena's pediatrician appointment is at 10:30."

"I can take her if you want. I don't know why you didn't ask me before."

"I didn't think you'd want to," she replied, looking at the dark circles beneath his eyes. "Besides, you've never gone on your own. You wouldn't know what to ask."

"What would I need to ask? Aren't they the ones who are supposed to tell you if there's something wrong?"

Nina stared back at him, not bothering to answer. In the past week, Nico had not left the apartment other than to take Wuodan outside. She had wondered if he was falling back into his depression.

"You can come with us if you like," she said. Nico had not talked about their plans to move for well over two months, and she was starting to suspect he might have given up on the idea. It had seemed unlikely, but the thought of it had cheered them up at times and brought them closer together. It was something to fantasize about during those dreary days when the headlines seemed filled with non-stop talk of war and terrorism.

"No, that's alright," he replied. "I've got some things I need to do."

She followed him into the living room where Lena was sitting beside Wuodan on the couch watching *Sesamstraat*.

"I need to change the channel, Lena. Papa wants to watch the news." Surprised to see him up at this hour, the girl did not protest. Instead, she crawled into his lap and watched as he surfed the channels before landing on *NOS journaal*.

Finishing their coffee, they listened to a recap of the world headlines followed by some heated speculation regarding the U.S. election scheduled to take place later in the day.

"We can only hope that they get rid of that idiot this time," Nico said, standing up. "C'mon Wuodan. Out we go."

While he was out, Nina showered leaving Lena to eat her breakfast in front of the television. When she heard the door open again at a quarter to ten, she was already dressed.

"You were gone a long ti—Jesus, Nico, are you alright?"

He was standing in the hall out of breath, his face gone a sickly, gray color. Wuodan, meanwhile, kept trying to lick at his hands.

"You can't go out," he said. "Not now."

"My God, do I need to call you an ambulance?"

She walked over to him to place a hand on his forehead. She could smell the strong stench of his sweat.

"No," he said, forcing her to follow him into the kitchen.

"What happened?" she asked. She could already feel her stomach tighten.

"Theo van Gogh's been killed. Shot and stabbed on Linnaeus Street."

"What?"

"I just saw him," Nico looked catatonic. "It just happened. The police went running after the guy. He tried to cut his head off and pinned a letter to his chest."

Nina put a hand over her mouth.

"He was just riding his bike to work," Nico said. "Like anybody else."

In her nightmares Nina had been waiting for this moment, and it had finally struck.

"You're going to quit your job," Nico said. "And we're going to pack our bags. We can't stay here anymore."

Later that night she and Nico sat close to one another in front of the television, Lena cradled fast asleep between them.

Van Gogh's latest film, *Submission,* had just aired on public television, a collaborative project with Ayaan Hirsi Ali, the right-wing MP who had also written the script. The film had incensed the fundamentalist Muslim clerics who had been outraged by its depiction of women with the text of the Qur'an written in henna across their naked bodies, a symbolic protest of sexual abuse.

Just then the camera cut to a live feed on the central square. Huge crowds of demonstrators had formed, and the mayor, Job Cohen, was addressing them:

"Today an Amsterdammer was murdered. And we are filled with horror and dismay. That is why we are here together on Dam Square – a symbol of our freedom – to say loud and clear what we think of this cowardly and heinous murder.

As we are here, we differ in many ways, but we are one in our anger and our grief. One in our belief that the freedom to say what you think is a foundation of our society. That foundation has been questioned. Van Gogh was gagged and silenced.

This is a gross violation of the standards that we, in Amsterdam—and that goes for all of us whoever we are and wherever we have come from—in our mutual movement to uphold that which is necessary for a decent living together in this city. We resolve differences of opinion through dialogue, and in the last instance, in court. Not by taking the law into our own hands. That we do not accept.

All the people in the Netherlands, in Amsterdam, may, within the limits of the law, say and write what they want. This is at the root of our constitutional state. Theo van Gogh made bold use of that right to freedom of expression, as a writer and a filmmaker. He made a lot of people quarrel with me. That is allowed in this country. At the same time, he was for the right of others to disagree with him. He often cited, in the spirit of Voltaire, the following statement: "I am all that you say you disagree with, but I will continue to fight for your right to say it. To continue to fight, we won't gather for a moment of silence, but to say loud and clear: freedom of expression is dear to us, and it must continue."

20

Caway - 2005

In the four years since they had last visited Costa Rica, not much had changed on the way from San José to the Caribbean. The buses were updated castoffs from *El Norte*, but it still took a good four hours to get from the capital to the port city of Limón and then the dusty depot in coastal Caway.

As Nico pulled their heavy luggage from the hold, Nina's eyes landed on the bright murals covering the back of the small shopping center that had grown around the town's only source of public transport.

"Mama, look," Lena said, pointing a chubby finger at the cartoon-like image of a sloth hanging from its technicolor tree.

"Do you remember seeing one of those?" Nina asked.

Lena shook her blonde curls, looking every bit the poster child of good health.

"You saw a real one when you were still a baby. Now we'll see them in our garden."

Lena wrinkled her small nose.

"Are we going to live *here*?"

"Not here, in town," Nina said, averting her eyes from an older, indigenous woman with a limp making her way slowly toward the bus. "But this is where we'll do our shopping."

"Do I have to speak in Spanish?"

"Of course."

Lena jutted out her chin and scowled.

"English, too," Nina said, with just the touch of disciplinary inflection she tended to reserve for public outings. "But at home we speak Dutch."

Lena crossed her arms.

"But it's too hot here!"

"You'll get used to it soon enough," Nico said, cutting her outburst short. He had broken out into a heavy sweat stacking their suitcases on the tile floor in the sheltered terminal area. "Now, go and help your mother find a taxi. I don't want to have to carry all of this out front."

Nina grabbed hold of Lena's sticky hand and led her down the corridor between the bus depot and the shopping center. They walked past the open-air storefronts, the barber shop situated next to the butcher's and followed by the video arcade. Nina could already feel the stares pivoting in her direction. Like a magnet, her unusual height and good looks had always drawn male attention, but here it could feel lewd and even threatening at times. It was a side of her newly adopted home she had grown to despise, and that made the darkness of her past immediately cloud the present.

"Stop dragging your feet," she said, tugging at Lena's arm.

"I'm going as fast as I can, Mama!"

Passing the pet-store and veterinary clinic, Nina felt a pang of regret. They had left Wuodan behind in Holland, and the heartbreak of it was still painful and raw. Nico had insisted they could not take him, saying it would raise unnecessary questions at customs, and they had, at least, managed to find him a good home with a trusted neighbor. Still, Nina had cried for days, and she could not forgive herself for not fighting to keep him.

On the corner in front of the bank Nina spotted two unmarked vehicles idling. The driver of a sun-blotched 1980s Honda Civic was already negotiating with a young couple she had seen on the bus, so Nina waved her hand to attract the attention of the older, Afro-Caribbean man sitting in the beaten-up microbus.

As he stepped out of the driver's seat, Nina could see that his graying dreads extended down below his waist, and that his faded t-shirt displayed the red, green, black and gold of his Rastafarian allegiance.

"Yah, *mamí*," he called out to her. "Where yuh go?"

"My husband has the luggage," she said, pointing in the direction from which they had come. "Over there, where the bus pulls in. Can you drive us back there? It's a lot to carry."

The Rasta shook his head, his eyes weary.

"Nuh miss, not allowed. Best, yuh wait here," he added, as he ambled down the corridor.

Nina stood beneath the shaded steps in front of the bank and watched as Lena played hopscotch beside her. She had forgotten about the languid pace here, so different than San José and even the small mountain town where they had lived the first few months.

Though closer to the capital's cosmopolitan amenities, the mountains had proved an ill match for them, especially during the rainy season. The daily downpours had only heightened Nina's depressive moods, and the perpetual chill of their drafty rental on cloudy days was too reminiscent of what they had left behind in Amsterdam. It had not taken much prompting to agree that they would be better off near the beach, so Caway it was.

When their driver returned with Nico and their luggage, Nina was surprised to see the older man carrying the heavy load.

"Where to?" he asked, as he packed the luggage into the back of the van. Despite his age, he made the work look like nothing. Nico, meanwhile, was drenched in sweat.

They stopped first at the Chinese grocery to pick up supplies, and as they each piled back into the van with a cold drink, the driver confirmed with Nico that they were headed out to *de ole Smith place*, as he called it.

The drive itself felt as slow as walking, but they could at least feel a slight breeze coming off the water. Soon they could go for a swim, Nina thought, tasting the tang of salt at the edges of her lips. The car radio was tuned into a local, Reggae station and the steady, thrumming beat helped recalibrate her senses.

"So, I take it Mr. Smith is well known around here?" Nico asked, striking up a conversation from the front seat.

The Rasta nodded.

"His family was one of the first to settle here."

"I was reading about the Jamaican workers who came to build the railroad for the United Fruit Company, the one that used to run from San José?"

"Yeah, my father work for them. But Mister Smith, his people live in Caway a long, long time before that. Fisherman they was. Come from Panamá and Nicaragua. Only Bribri livin' here then."

"Did they get along, the Bribri and the fishermen?"

"Yeah, they peaceful. Things only change when they come and take the land to make the banana plantation. The government up in San José give the Bribri land to *Mamita Yunai* to help pay for the railroad. Make the Bribri live more up the mountain."

Nico shook his head.

"They're not writing about that in *The Tico Times.*"

"M-hmm," the Rasta murmured. "Babylon be everywhere."

They passed a few small hotels along the way, a couple of them freshly constructed and landscaped. At *Playa Oscuro* they turned inland, and a kilometer after that they made a sharp turn onto a grass-covered drive at the end of which sat Mr. Smith's wooden bungalow.

They all helped to unpack their belongings from the minivan, after which Nico pressed the fare plus a generous tip into the older man's hand.

The Rasta gave them a short bow.

"Jah bless," he said, before driving away.

Nico read the folded note stuck in the door jamb and then wandered off to procure the key from one of the neighbors while Nina and Lena took stock of their new surroundings.

The unadorned clapboard structure was surrounded by a well-kept garden full of hibiscus and striking red spears of heliconia. Though it was midday, they could hear the loud chirping of cicadas from the nearby trees.

Lena sucked in her breath.

"Mama, what's that," she asked.

An elegantly crowned bird with striped tail feathers was grazing in the small clearing at the edge of the garden.

"A wild turkey," Nina replied in a whisper. "But they have a different name for them here. Great Currasow."

Nina and Lena watched as the majestic-looking creature made its way toward the tree-lined edge, each consciously aware of the other's location.

"We'll see a lot more from now on," Nina said, marveling at her daughter's stunned curiosity. They had made it back to Eden after all.

Fifteen minutes later Nico returned with a broad smile on his face, his gait noticeably relaxed. "Cool neighbors," he said, unlocking the door.

A musty smell greeted them at first, but as their eyes got accustomed to the cloistered surroundings, they could see that the simple furnishings were in decent enough shape, and that the house was tidy. While Nico opened the shutters to let in the fresh air, Nina walked behind a curious Lena, eager to check out the rest of their enchanted house.

As it turned out, there was not much more to see. Apart from the combined kitchen and living area, there were two bedrooms in the back with only one small bathroom squeezed in between. To Lena, though, it was a life size playhouse.

While she went off to explore her new bedroom, Nina put away the groceries and began to make some ham sandwiches. Nico, meanwhile, began to fidget.

"After we eat, I should go back into town again and find the ICE office. You know how long it took them before to set up the internet."

"Yeah, fine," Nina said, not bothering to look up from her work. "I can stay here and unpack. We can always go to the beach later, before the sun sets."

Just then, Lena came running back into the kitchen. "Papa, I want to go!"

"No, Lena, you stay here with your Mama. We'll go to the beach later like she said."

Nina already knew he would stop off at the first bar along the way. Nico's daily excursions were now a part of their Costa Rican routine, and in many ways, Nina welcomed them. She needed time on her own, and Lena was still young enough to take an afternoon nap. And even if Lena could not sleep, she had learned long ago how to occupy herself when her mother turned quiet.

Mama and I walked to our very own beach today, the magic one with the dark, dark sand. I asked her if it was because of the black people, but then she turned red and said I'm not allowed to say that. She said the sand was because of vocanos, and that Papa would tell me more when we got home. He couldn't come with us, and I was sad. But Mama said he had to go buy the internet so we can play games together.

It was hot, hot, and I didn't want to walk on that stupid long road. But then Mama found me a sloth, a real one this time, and we got to see the funny red-yellow-and-blue birds that go, "caw! caw!" Mama said they bicker like that because they're married for life, and when you're married you have to fight sometimes because if the words get stuck in your head and they don't come out, you can go crazy. She says it's good that I'm more like Papa, because when the words get stuck she feels scared, and she doesn't want me to be scared.

Mama didn't take her shirt off at the beach even though she always does, but I did. And I jumped in the waves with just my blue bottoms on, and Mama said I was just like The Little Mermaid *'cept I have gold hair and hers is red. And I said, 'Mama, look, I'm a dolphin!' and she laughed, but then a giant wave came and crashed me, and all the water went up my nose, and made me tumble.*

Mama stopped laughing, and it made me cry because she looked so scared, but then I was brave again, and I jumped in and Mama did, too. She floated me to the big waves until the sun went purple orange and we had to go back. I wish Papa could have seen me dive like a dolphin.

It was a long way back to our new house, but this time Mama carried me.

The next morning Nina woke up just as the sun was beginning to rise. She had forgotten how much her body felt inclined to adapt to the natural rhythms of light and dark here. Still groggy, she got out of bed to make coffee in the old-fashioned, Tico way, first by boiling water on the stove and then pouring it through a sock-like, cotton filter fitted to a simple wooden stand.

Normally the Van de Steeg's would have slept until eight or nine, but the coolness of the early mornings was not something one could afford to miss in the coastal jungle. Though it would take time to adjust to the nighttime chorus of frogs and insects, not to mention the clatter of canopy detritus hitting the tin roof at night, it was better to nap in the heat of the afternoon or go to bed early than forgo the sung pleasures of a tropical dawn.

The fragrant coffee tasted particularly good this morning and taking one of the enamel mugs outside, Nina immediately felt a sense of relief. In the mountains outside of San José her still lingering agoraphobia had often compelled her to stay indoors and well out of the neighbors' sight. Here, though, she could confidently linger on the porch or in the yard, protected by the thick veil of vegetation that surrounded them on all sides.

Nico shared her need for privacy, but unlike Nina, he needed far more contact with the outside world. He could easily turn on his extroverted side whenever it suited him. She, on the other hand, found it increasingly difficult to carry on a conversation outside of her own home.

"How they get anything done around here is a fucking miracle," Nico said, after he had gotten up and joined her on the back porch.

Nico, of course, had arrived too late the day before to speak to anyone about the internet service and was now suggesting they go into town together after breakfast.

"I need you to stand in line while I go to the bank and make sure our account is set up."

Since their arrival in Costa Rica, Nina had gotten used to accommodating these types of requests to keep Nico from tapping his foot and muttering obscenities under his breath. Nina was better equipped to "put up with such nonsense" as he called it, and since she would often find a way to make it into a game for Lena's sake, he had no qualms asking her.

It was noon, though, before they finished their errand. Hungry and hot, they popped into one of the open-air eateries on the main strip and ordered a *casado* each, the equivalent of a worker's lunch that included a choice of meat. rice and beans, fried plantain, and a small salad.

"Now what?" Nina asked, stripping the chicken off the bone on Lena's plate.

"I'm taking you around to meet the Germans."

Nina opened her mouth to protest.

"They've got a boy that's Lena's age," Nico added.

"But," —her voice was quivering— "I've still got unpacking to do. I'd rather wait."

"You're going to have to meet them sooner or later."

Meeting his gaze, Nina's eyes narrowed. He did not often pressure her like this.

"C'mon now, we've talked about this."

To avoid a response, she focused instead on managing Lena's plate for her and then eating her own. The rest of the meal transpired in ambient silence as they ate their food and watched the slow comings and goings of passers-by.

Dark clouds rolled in as Nico settled the bill. As they walked back, a sweet, acrid scent pierced their nostrils, and before long a flash of lightning shattered the sky above them followed by the sounds of an ominous, rolling thunder.

"We should stay put until this passes," Nina said.

"Stop being so uptight," Nico said. "We'll be fine. It will strike the trees long before it hits us. Anyway, it's more refreshing to walk in the rain, right Lena?"

She was riding atop her daddy's shoulders and laughing.

"We don't want our daughter turning into a worry wart, do we? One in the family is more than enough."

Fuming, Nina fell back behind them. There was no point in arguing in front of Lena.

Plus, in the rush of the downpour and still lagging a few paces behind, she had to concede that Nico was right. It was far more pleasant walking in the rain than being drenched in her own sweat, and for a few moments, she allowed herself to smile at them, imagining the warm shower she would take when they got home.

But when they approached their turn at *Playa Oscuro*, Nico walked straight ahead.

"Where are you going?" she called out. "We're to the left."

"I'm taking you to the restaurant," he said, not bothering to look back.

"But we're soaking wet, and I'm in no mood for this!"

"Are you ever?" Nico said, turning on his heel as Lena bobbed side to side to keep balance. "They're not going to mind. Plus, it will give Lena a chance to play with their son."

As it turned out, Anja and Andreas had welcomed them with open arms not to mention dry towels and the enticement of ice cream to bring their two six-year-old children together. Anja had done what she could to make Nina feel more at ease though her discomfort at having to socialize under such bedraggled circumstances was palpable.

By now Nina was well past the point of trying to fake her way through social situations. That part of her had withered after her last encounter with Piet. But she had hoped, at the very least, to make herself invisible, an impossible task when forced to sit shoulder to shoulder at Quixote's *Stammtisch*.

It was obvious from what Nico had shared with everyone at the table that they had run away from their former lives, so what more could she possibly add? It was embarrassing enough that they had come in looking like they had washed up with the tide, though interestingly enough, Anja and Andreas seemed to accept this about them without question. No, it was the other woman with the penetrating gaze, Gertie, who had made Nina feel awkward and ill at ease, as if she could read the secrets written beneath her skin. Nina made a point to just ignore her.

In the days that followed Nina nonetheless found herself spending more and more time at the restaurant, relieved to have found a playmate for Lena. As she grew increasingly more comfortable with Anja, they eventually discussed the school situation in more detail, prompting Nina to go ahead and ask Nico's grandmother to wire the necessary tuition money. Anja had assured them both it was the best they could do for their daughter, and Oma, of course, was delighted to hear that Lena would attend a proper, international baccalaureate school.

Filling out the application the following afternoon at one of the smaller tables in the Quixote's dining room, Anja surprised Nina by asking if it had been difficult to leave Europe.

"I imagine it was hard for your family to accept," Anja said, offering Nina a cigarette from the pack she had just opened.

Nina tensed at the question but took the cigarette all the same, careful to take her time lighting it.

She had not told Anja about her family and neither had Nico. After the Piet incident and Nina's persistent refusal to even speak their names, they had agreed, for Lena's sake, to consider her family dead.

"What matters is that we stay in touch with Oma," Nina said, referring to Nico's grandmother. "Nico has spent so much time abroad, in some ways, she's gotten used to that. Apart from her, there's really no one else."

"That's the same for me," Anja said, with a far off look in her eyes. "I lost both of my parents to cancer."

Nina nodded, eager to keep Anja talking which she did for the next half hour. Feigning rapt attention at first, Nina listened as Anja went over the details of her hometown persecution. She had grown up in a conservative southern village and had been forced to return there once her parents, one after the other, took ill. A bohemian who had always welcomed foreigners into her father's house, Anja was soon targeted and maligned as the "immigrants' whore," as she put it. After her parent's deaths, she had moved back to Basel, which had always been her city of refuge.

"That's where I attended art school, but after a while it felt too provincial and bourgeois, too much about making money. Once I met Andreas, well, I didn't see any point in going back there except to pack."

Pausing for a long moment, Anja lit another Delta until the weight of her words had visibly dissipated. Then she turned her attention back to her patient listener.

"I heard from Barbara Olsen that her assistant, Birgitt, is going back to Switzerland at the end of the month. She's going to need someone to help her out with the horses. What do you say?"

The offer took Nina by surprise.

Anja flashed her a conspiratorial smile.

"Nico told me. He's been going on and on about how great you are with animals. If you're interested, I can let her know tomorrow."

Nina swallowed hard but soon found herself saying yes. The thought of working again had not crossed her mind, and Nico had neglected to mention any of this. Technically, they were only here on extended tourist visas without work permits, but it was easy enough to just cross the border for a few days to get another 90-day extension, a common ex-pat tactic. As far as their financial matters stood, they had been getting along just fine on their monthly disability stipend. Still, to have an excuse to get out of the house and spend time with horses again, it was her lost dream now materialized as possibility.

The meeting with Barbara took place two days later at her large, American-style stucco house not too far from the town's edge. Anja had accompanied Nina to make the introductions but had cordially refused Barbara's invitation to come inside.

"You know how it is," Anja said, smiling and waving her off with exaggerated familiarity. "I have too many errands to run, and if I leave the restaurant for too long Andreas will go crazy."

Escorting Nina in, Barbara led her down an inlaid terracotta hallway and past a large, open living space appointed with elegant furniture and artwork set against a dark and polished wood floor. They proceeded through a set of open French doors that led out to a secluded and meticulously landscaped garden.

"Anja tells me you've done this type of work before, is that right?" Barbara said, pouring Nina a cup of tea. They were seated in the relative coolness of her shaded back patio, one of only a handful in the area with direct access to an ocean view and thus a breeze.

"Yes," Nina said, taking a sip of the fruity, herbal concoction. "Growing up, I helped out at the village stables after school and during summer breaks. I would have lived there if they'd let me."

Barbara smiled and nodded. Something about Barbara's open yet genteel demeanor and her soft blue eyes made it easier for Nina to relax. Nina tended to like Swedish women, thought them less complicated than most, and before long, Nina found herself speaking openly about her work at the clinic, how she had regretted not having furthered her veterinary studies but that she had always hoped to work with horses again, having often daydreamed of landing a position at the *Hollandsche Manege*, the royal riding school in Amsterdam.

Barbara laughed, connecting easily to what she meant.

"Things here are a bit more rugged than that, I'm afraid, but we make do. Obviously, we're not supplied with the newest and greatest, but we take good care of our mares, and make sure they're not overworked. We've got a couple of colts and fillies, too, but most are on the older side. All but one is tame, so it shouldn't be difficult for you to adjust. They're grass-kept, so grooming will be different than what you're used to, and, of course, there's pasture maintenance involved. But you'll learn all of that soon enough. Have you ever worked with tourists or led out a group?"

"No, just grooming and exercise, but I can clean out stables, too."

"That's not a problem," Barbara said. "We'll be going out together until you feel comfortable. You'll need to get used to the trails and what constitutes good safety in the tropics. Around here that mostly means dealing with packs of dogs, pets and strays alike. As you may have noticed, none of them are leashed."

"I have," Nina said. "Dogs happen to be one of my specialties, though. I've had a few, and of course, we saw all kinds at the clinic."

"That's great to hear because that's the one thing that makes the clients nervous, especially the inexperienced ones. The horses are used to them, but the riders don't know that. If you run into a pack, particularly the ones that like to chase *and* bark, it's better if you can distract them from the group. The most important thing is to make the clients feel that you're in charge. You'll see, once we go out. Now the big question. How are you with people?"

Nina looked down at her hands.

"If I'm honest, I prefer animals to people," she said, looking back up slowly to gauge Barbara's response. "But I think I can manage."

"I appreciate your honesty. Of course, we'll have to get you up to speed on the local color first. Some of the tourists can be quite chatty and ask a lot of questions, but for the most part, they prefer to just look around, and I like to leave it up to them to engage. If they're interested, I'll talk. But if they prefer just to ride, I'm more than happy to go in silence. The golden rule is to always be pleasant, even when they're not. I draw the line at safety, though. You do what you must so no one gets hurt. Horses included. In the end, safe riding is what we're all about."

Nina nodded, surprised that her admission had not put an end to their conversation.

"So, are you interested?" Barbara asked, leaning in as she clasped her tanned hands together. "We could do a trial period. See if it's a good fit?"

Nina let out a sigh of relief.

"That would be great. I do have a daughter just starting kindergarten, but my husband can take her and pick her up. It shouldn't be a problem."

"Yes, Anja mentioned that," Barbara said, standing up to signal the end of their meeting. "My Ingrid and Lars are there, too. Second and fourth grades. Why don't you come over Friday morning so we can get you started? We work most weekends, but I'm assuming that comes as no surprise. Tuesdays and Wednesday are slow, so if you need those off, it won't be a problem."

"Sounds perfect to me," Nina said, with a lilt in her step.

"*Pura vida*, then," Barbara said, opening the door for her with a smile. "We'll see you on Friday."

Before long, Nina was out of the house on a full-time basis. Most mornings she would leave on foot, arriving at the horse pasture by 7 AM. She looked forward to these solitary walks when her mind would quiet so to better hear the birds and animals rustling in the trees. When she neared the meadow, she was greeted first by the dewy, sweet scent of overgrown grass and then by the mares' ears perking up at the sight of her.

One horse in particular insisted on preferential treatment. Tall and white, *La Reina* towered over the others and tended to snap. Within a few days, however, Nina had coaxed *La Reina* into showing her more restrained side and convinced Barbara that the mare was ready to lead so long as Nina held the reins.

The workdays were long, but apart from not seeing Lena as much as she would have liked, Nina did not miss being away from home. It was still difficult to relax around the clients—the men in particular—but most of her time was spent with the horses. She did not miss the drudgery of her daily housework, and the way she saw it, it was Nico's turn to make sure Lena was fed and clothed and got to school on time.

With horses to nurture and take away her sunken thoughts, three months passed in quick succession. Deep down Nina could feel a hidden part of her opening up again, like the faint promise of a sunbeam gleaming through dark clouds after a brutal rain. Before Nina knew it, July was upon them, and Nico was once again chattering about having to cross the border to renew their visas.

In the privacy of their dimly lit living room, having just put an overexcited Lena to bed, Nico sat down beside her on the worn couch, a beer in one hand and a lit cigarette in the other.

"We can stay in Bocas for two days, and after that, we can head down to Panama City to check out the canal, do a little shopping while we're at it."

Seeing his excitement mount, Nina interrupted him.

"But Barbara asked me to work during the school break."

Through the gloom of the lamp's cast shadow, she could see Nico's eyes bulge out.

"What? You told her no obviously."

It took her a second too long to respond.

"Jesus, Nina," Nico said, jumping out of his seat. "We talked about this."

"Why don't you and Lena go, and I'll go after?" she asked, her eyes pleading. "It's just not a good time right now."

Nico paced the small living room.

"Because it doesn't work like that. How many times do I have to tell you? We have to go before the visas expire."

Nina sighed.

"Fine. But I have to come back right after."

Nico turned on his heel.

"Are you joking? Lena has a two-week break from school! And I want to see something new, have some fun. Remember that?"

"But how can you be so selfish when you know how much this job means to me?"

"Selfish?"

Nina turned away from him to grab the cigarettes from the side table.

"We need the money," she said. "More than you'd like to admit."

She could feel his eyes narrowing as she busied her hands with the packet.

"What's that supposed to mean?"

"My job is what's paying for your beer tab. If you haven't noticed, we're going through money a hell of a lot faster than before."

Nico shook his head.

"Why can't we just compromise on this. I'll go the first few days, and then you and Lena can go to Panama City together. Stay as long as you like."

"And when do *I* finally get some time off?"

"Time off?" Nina said, throwing her arms up. "Isn't *this* your holiday?"

"That's not what I meant, and you know it."

Nina sighed again.

"Nico. It's not like we'll have time alone in Panama."

"Don't you think I know that? I'm the one who's taking care of her."

"And is that a problem?"

"No," Nico said, his eyes darting from side to side. "What I'm saying is that I need a break."

"So, what's wrong with my suggestion?"

"Are you being purposely obtuse? I'd like *you* to help out with her. You know, spend some time with your daughter, not to mention your husband?"

"And what exactly do you think I was doing when you were off traveling for months on end? It's not like anyone gave *me* a break. And let me tell you, it was much more difficult taking care of her then."

"We came here to get away from that stress, remember?" Nico said, stubbing out his cigarette in the ashtray next to her.

"No, I came here to get away from Holland. Working, for me, isn't a problem."

Nico let out a huff of frustration.

"But what you do can be done by someone else. It's not a life-or-death situation, for chrissake."

Nina folded her arms tight, a plume of smoke emanating from her fingers.

"I told you. It's a busy time now."

"And what have you got against spending time with Lena and me?"

"Nothing. It's just that for once I'm doing what I want."

"Ach, Nina, you know damn well I'm glad you've found something to do! It just shouldn't come at the expense of our family. You barely see Lena now."

In a flash Nina was on her feet and in his face.

"Don't be ridiculous," she said in a hushed tone, trying to contain her anger. "A day hasn't gone by that I don't see our child."

For a long moment their eyes locked, neither one of them willing to back down.

"Is it that you don't want to see her more? Or that you don't want to see me?"

"You're being unfair, not to mention, cruel."

"Am I? I just want to be clear about what's happening here."

"What's happening is that I'm doing what I want," Nina said, her whispered voice now a force of calm. "It's you that doesn't want me to see it through in the proper way."

His eyes broke away from hers first.

This new demeanor unsettled him.

"You make it sound like you're saving the world, but they're just horses, for fuck's sake. And as fucked up as my work was, my priority was always the two of you. Always."

"I know that," Nina said. "But all I'm asking is to help out during the busy season. We can go for a longer holiday in September when it's slow."

"Fine," he said, as he walked toward the refrigerator to grab another beer.

"I'll take her camping for a few days so you can get back to your precious horses. But don't even think about backing out in September. We agreed things would be different here."

The next afternoon, sheltered from the sun's direct wrath if not the extreme humidity, Nico could not help but vent as he sat sticking to the red pleather covering the *Stammtisch's* wooden stools.

"The whole fucking point of moving here was to spend more time together, not less," he said to the Freyers who occupied their usual seats, Andreas at the head of the table where the built-in bench formed an L, and Anja to the right on the stool beside him. Gertie, meanwhile, sat catty-corner on the bench nearest the entrance. Her nose, as usual, was buried deep in a detective novel, a contemporary English one from the look of it.

"You have to see it from her point of view," Anja said, grabbing Nico's empty beer bottle as she got up from the table and walked back toward the kitchen. "There aren't many places to work around here. She's just making sure she can hold on to a good thing."

"Yeah, but Barbara's a mother, too, isn't she? Surely she would understand a family wanting to spend some time together when the kid's not in school."

Anja looked at them through the kitchen window as she slid open the refrigerated case. "Everyone here works during the holidays. We don't earn enough otherwise. That's the price we pay for living in paradise."

"You're joking, right? Barbara's loaded. Those horses are a hobby for her, and if you ask me, the only reason she does it is to meet men. Why should *my* family have to suffer just so she can get laid?"

Anja's eyebrows shot up in a warning, but Lena and Daniel were too deep into their Lego construction to pay much attention to what they said.

"Barbara's a friend," Anja said, placing another bottle down hard in front of him. "I'd watch what you say."

From the corner Gertie rolled her eyes, a gesture not lost on Nico.

Nico shrugged his shoulders in a haphazard *mea culpa*.

"Yeah, fine, it's just that playing house dad all day is starting to get on my tits."

Gertie let out a sharp guffaw.

"That's typical," she added.

Nico turned toward her.

"I'm sorry, but have I ever heard you speak? What would you know about raising kids anyway?"

Gertie put her book down and returned Nico's defiant stare.

"Plenty. I raised two boys on my own and worked full time."

Having said her piece, she picked up her book again and began to read as if nothing had happened.

"Oh, I get it. You think I'm some kind of chauvinist, is that it? Well, let me tell you something. I've bent over backwards for that woman, and if it didn't involve breaking her confidence, I'd make my case for sainthood right now."

"Sainthood?" Gertie peered over her book and looked even more amused. "The way you treat that woman?"

"What the hell would you know about relationships, anyway?" Nico said.

Anja and Andreas exchanged a quick look of panic before Nico laughed her off.

"My guess is you're alone for good reason."

"Okay, that's enough," Anja said, surprised to find herself jumping in to defend Gertie. "Nina carried your child for nine months. I hardly think you can top that."

Andreas nodded and having caught Nico's eye, began to fan himself in mock exaggeration. *Time to lighten things up.*

"Yeah, ok," Nico said, before taking another swig from his beer.

Andreas, meanwhile, tilted his head toward the kitchen, signaling to Anja it was time for him to start the evening's prep work.

"If it's time alone together you need," Anja said, standing up. "We'd be happy to look after Lena for a couple of days, and maybe someday you can return the favor. God knows we need to look after one another here."

After three days of relaxing on the dreamy white beaches near Bocas Town, Nina took the bus from Almirante to Guabito, crossing the Costa Rican border at the Sixaola River. It was only a 92-kilometer stretch, but with passport and immigration controls—not to mention the long wait for the bus—it took the better part of a day for her to get back to Caway.

The air was not as heavy as it had been all day, and relieved to finally stretch her legs, Nina decided to just walk home. She could still feel the nostalgic pulse of Nico's touch earlier that morning within the veiled confines of their beachside bungalow. It had been far too long since they had reconnected. She was still surfing the remnant waves, when a drunken man called after her.

"Hey, sweetness. How's about letting me see those tan lines up close."

She was still wearing the sleeveless blue sundress Nico had bought for her in Bocas, a flowing, high-waisted thing that happened to highlight the extraordinary length of her legs. In that instant she regretted not having traveled in something more practical, though so far she had managed to tune out the catcalls as she walked past the bars on either side of the main road.

"I know what you're looking for," she heard the man say with a hiss, not daring to look over her shoulder. Startled, she could sense he was now walking just a few paces behind her.

"And once I get that dress off of you, you'll be begging for more."

Nina knew better than to quicken her step. Though her heart was now pounding in her throat, she had to appear cool and unbothered. Meanwhile, her tongue had turned to sandpaper.

The unpaved road, like all the others in town, was poorly lit and the sodium-vapor lampposts were few and far between. Still, the police station was just a few yards down the road. All she had to do was keep walking, she told herself, in between stolen breaths.

It's early. People are still on the streets. It would be crazy to try something now.

"C'mon, now, don't go making me work this hard."

There was something off about the man's accent, but through his slurred speech it was difficult to be sure. The lack of certainty made her skin crawl even more, until she spotted a young, laughing couple walking toward her. They appeared to have just come from the beach, and in the instant that they were about to walk past, she flashed them a look of panic which the young man caught before spotting the man behind her.

"Hey," he said, breaking out into a toothy smile and pulling his girlfriend across the road toward Nina. "We've been looking all over for you!"

Nina glanced over her shoulder and saw the other man retreat.

"Was that guy bothering you?" the young woman said in a whisper, her face shadowed with concern.

Nina's shoulders collapsed.

"I can't thank you enough," she said, her voice shaking. "He just started following me and saying horrible things. I was walking to the police station, but then you came along."

"I could see straight away something wasn't right," the young man said. "Do you want me to go and find him?"

Nina shook her head.

"No, I just want to go home."

"Are you staying close by?"

"I live here," Nina said. She'd almost forgotten that she looked just like any other tourist in town. "I was just walking home, but I can see now it's not a good idea."

"We can walk you if you like," the young woman said.

"It's quite far, I'm afraid, and in the opposite direction. I should probably just take a taxi. There's one out in front of Akee's Bar."

"We'll walk you there then," the boyfriend said.

"Thank you. Just so you know, it's not usually like this here."

"No problem at all. We've had a fantastic time, so no apologies necessary. Anyway, I guess it just takes one drunk asshole to ruin someone's day. I'm sorry it had to be you."

"Yeah, me, too," Nina said.

They walked her back the way she had come, and sure enough, one of the regular cars was hanging out in front of the bar as expected. Having confirmed the fare, the young man held the back door open for her as she climbed into the back seat.

"Thanks again," Nina said. "I hope you enjoy the rest of your time here."

Through the open window, the boyfriend handed her a business card. "Just give us a quick call and let us know you made it home ok. You still look like you saw a ghost or something."

"Sure," Nina said, trying her best to smile back at him. "I'll be fine once I'm home. It's just been a long day."

The driver dropped Nina off in front of the bungalow, waiting until she opened the door and closed it behind her. Ashamed, she checked the rooms one by one, looking under the beds, and only afterwards did she lie down on the couch.

She needed to call Nico, not to mention the young man who had helped her, but she could not bring herself to pick up the phone. Piet and Anton's apparitions were still whirling around in her mind, and seeing a bright flash of her mother's disembodied head and her all too-familiar contempt, Nina began to sink again.

She looked up at the stark shadows cast by the anemic light, and a churning anger soon began to eclipse her fear. These drunken men who thought any woman was theirs for the taking. Not even a convent would be free from their pestilence.

She had escaped Piet and Anton's clutches though the scars remained. But these other men, she could not allow them to have the same power over her. She had to face them for what they were, pathetic beasts with no claim on her of any kind. She could not allow them to get in the way of her new life here. Not after the sacrifice they had made.

In that moment Nina realized she had allowed Nico to act as her bodyguard for far too long, leaning on him heavily these past few years, and hiding behind his male strength and intimidating veneer. If she were to tell him what happened tonight, he would feel compelled to not leave her side, which would chip away at what little independence she had finally carved out for herself.

No, she could not tell him. She needed him to believe in her ability to be strong, not only for her sake but for his as well. She was not blind to his frustrations, his sense of feeling trapped by her past paralysis, unable to do anything but cater to her needs. That dynamic could not continue. And she could see that he was much happier now that she was working, even if it meant attending to the more tedious aspects of childcare. He had burnt himself out with his work, and he needed this time to enjoy life again. Plus, the fact remained that despite his complaints and lousy housekeeping, he adored Lena's company.

She picked up her phone and punched in the number on the business card first. The call was short, but by the end of it she had recovered the stillness in her voice. Calling Nico, she sounded almost like herself again.

"I was starting to worry about you," he said, after exchanging their preliminary hellos.

"It's just been a long day," Nina said. "The line at the border took forever, and it took a while to stamp my visa. I missed the first bus back, so I had to wait."

"How did you get home from the bus terminal?" Nico asked, honing in on the one thing she did not want to discuss. As a journalist, he had developed an uncanny sixth sense.

"I took a taxi. It was getting dark already, and there were some drunks out."

"That's good. You know I don't like you going into town at night."

"Yeah, about that. When you get back, I was thinking we should get a dog again. Andreas mentioned that Lito's bitch just had a litter, and Lena would love having a puppy around."

Nico paused for a moment before answering.

"Are you sure? It's a rough life here for pets. I don't want her getting too attached."

"It would be good for her. Plus, everyone around here has a guard dog. It makes sense."

"I need to think about it," Nico said, sounding agitated.

"Hey, you're going to have to meet us at *Cruce de Frontera*. We forgot about the parental controls. They won't let us cross over without you, remember?"

"Of course. Just let me know when, and I'll be there."

"I miss you, Nina," Nico added, sounding genuinely homesick.

"I miss you, too, Nico. Give Lena my love."

A yelping German Shepherd mix puppy greeted them when they finally got home.

"His name is Odin." Nina said, with a sheepish smile.

"Is he mine?" Lena asked, her eyes widening as she dropped to all fours. In excitement, Odin licked her face inducing a wave of high-pitched giggles.

Nico looked over at Nina and shook his head.

"He'll make a great guard dog," she said, but there was no need to defend her decision. She could already see that Odin's soulful eyes had melted whatever resistance Nico might have mustered.

"And you won't have to worry about him during the day," Nina added. "I'll be taking him with me to the stables until he's fully trained."

21

Caway - Three Years Later - 2008

"Are you sure it isn't too much trouble?" Nina asked as Anja sat down for a quick smoke in between serving lunch to a boisterous group of Americans who had wandered over from the *La Divina Lodge*. Nico had just taken Lena home, annoyed by the tourists' loud conversation.

"Not at all," Anja said. "We eat at that time anyway."

In the last three years the post 9/11 economic boom had spread its wings all the way to Caway, and new lodges and hotels had popped up around town while nearby tracts of jungle were razed in speculative anticipation of increased foreign development. The steady stream of tourism and investment provided a welcome influx of cash, but with it, a more hectic existence for those still living on the margin.

"You know how Nico is about cooking, and now that Lena is walking to school on her own, I would just feel better about her eating at least one warm meal during the day."

Anja shook her head.

"Don't even think about it. It's easier to get Daniel to do his homework when Lena is here anyway. After that, they can do what they want."

"Thanks, Anja. Now that Nico's started this research project of his," Nina said, signaling a pair of air quotes with her skinny fingers. "It's almost impossible to get him away from that damn computer. The house is a total mess, but what can I do?"

"He mentioned something about that," Anja said, giving Nina a quick sideways glance in between monitoring the tables in the main dining room. "What do you think will come of it?"

Nina let out a heavy sigh, her sunken eyes dulled by fatigue.

"I don't know. It keeps him busy, which is better than having him hang around the bars waiting for Lena to get out of school."

"Do you think he's doing alright?" Anja asked, no longer looking at her.

Nina lit up another cigarette.

"As well as can be expected, I suppose. He doesn't miss Amsterdam, if that's what you mean. He's always going on about how it's turning into the United States, with people tripping over themselves to out shop one another. I can't say I miss it either," she added, exhaling.

"Maybe he's just bored," Anja said, her tone far from convincing.

Nina shrugged which only made the boniness of her clavicles that much more apparent.

"He's got the internet to keep him busy. Maybe a little too much, if you ask me, but he does keep on top of things. Knows what's going on. And he keeps Lena informed, too. That's what they have in common, that endless curiosity of theirs. Drives me a bit nuts at times, but as you can see, she's doing well in school."

"Lena's a sharp one, alright," Anja said, straightening her skirt as she stood up. An older couple had just walked in looking for an empty table. "Independent, too."

Nina took her cue and stood up as well, extinguishing her cigarette.

"Yeah, just like her dad. I would have given anything for that kind of freedom as a child. Anyway, thanks again," she added, as she gathered up her things to leave.

"Fuckin' hell, have you heard the news?" Nico said, stumbling into Quixote's, his dark curls greasy and disheveled and with a week's worth of stubble sprouting across his gaunt face.

Andreas looked up from his morning edition of *La Nación*, and held up the front page that read, *"Gigantesco banco estadounidense* Lehman Brothers *se declarará en bancarrota"*. "Aren't you glad you're living here instead?" Andreas said, grinning like a mischievous schoolboy. Despite his age and the deep creases in his eyes, he still looked like one, too.

"Fuck," Nico said, collapsing onto the stool next to him. "This won't be good for business here. The first thing to go is the vacation money."

"Yes, but at least life in Caway doesn't cost so much. Anyway, we always have the backpackers. That's why I never went for the luxury thing. Too much bother. When you live a simple life, it takes more than this to throw you off."

Nico looked at him through narrowed eyes.

"There's the kids' school to think about," Nico said.

"Pfft," Andreas said. "If Daniel can't go to *Escuela Integral* because there's no money, I'll teach him what he needs to know."

"You better not let Anja hear you say that. She'll go through the roof."

"Ach!" Andreas slapped the notion down like a pesky fly. "She likes having things to keep her up a night. Gives her a reason to make the coffee strong in the morning."

"That's what I don't get about you two. You're always *tranquilo* and smiling while half the time she's blowing her top. Just the other day she was hassling me about the tab. I told her already I'd get the money to her next week."

Andreas took a sip from his morning coffee and shrugged.

"People are who they are."

"Yeah, well, at least you know I'm good for it. But this news," he added, shaking his head. "Who the hell knows how the economy's going to react?"

Andreas peered over his mug, his sharp blue eyes probing Nico's face.

"You really worried about that?"

Now it was Nico who shrugged him off.

"Worse case we have to go back. But like you said, the living's easy here."

"I never said easy. You have to be tough to survive this jungle."

"I've got no problem with tough," Nico said, drumming his rawboned fingers on the table. He and Nina had both gotten thinner in the past year, and it was that time of the morning when his fidgeting was at its worst.

"Ach, go get yourself a beer," Andreas told him. "She won't be back for another hour or so."

"Tre, is that you?" Anja said, walking the dusty road back from a board meeting at the school. She had caught sight of Treven, a few feet ahead, making his way toward Ms. Adina's house.

"I haven't seen you in a while," she added, catching up to him.

Treven's face was still smooth and boyish, and he was sporting a head full of short, tight braids. But he had grown much taller and more muscular in the last year, resembling more a young working man than a fifteen-year-old. Rumor had it he had dropped out of high school in Bribri.

"I just came from Limón," he said.

"And how is your grandmother doing?" Anja asked.

Tre shook his head, diverting his eyes to the road ahead.

"The doctor says she'll be going Home soon."

Anja reached up to place a hand on his shoulder. Ms. Adina had been in hospice care for a few months now.

"I'm really sorry to hear that. How long are you in Caway?"

"Just today to pick up her things."

"Come and have lunch with us first. Andreas would be so happy to see you."

Staring down the road Tre gave her a hesitant nod.

Anja looked at her watch and could see it was going on eleven already. She had meant to hurry back to help Andreas prepare. Not that she expected much of a lunch rush, but the few guests who were staying at *La Divina's* had made a habit of coming over to start their day with a late brunch.

"Why don't you come at around one, ok? We should be able to eat together then."

One more hour to go with Señora Lopez, ugh! She's so boring! She's always going on about handwriting as if anyone cares. Someone should tell her people use computers now. That's another thing that drives me nuts, having to take turns in the "computer lab". They only have three and one of them is usually broken. It's such a joke. At least Papa lets me use his to play The Sims.

I asked for a Nintendo for Christmas. Daniel usually lets me play his, but he doesn't like it when I beat him at Super Mario. God, there he goes again raising his hand.

"Teacher's pet," *I whisper, as he gets up to write the answer on the chalkboard.*

"Lena, quieres ir después?"

"Sí, Señora."

Now everyone is giggling. They all know I can't stand her, but she hasn't caught me out yet. I could do these drills in my sleep, they're so easy.

Papa says I'm a natural with language, and that it's too bad they won't just let me advance, but Mama says it's better if I stay with my class. I don't really care either way. It's not like we don't all spend time together already. This school's not big enough to just stick to kids your own age.

The older girls don't really like me. They're always calling me a tomboy behind my back and making fun of how Mama dresses, as if that's any of their damn business. I wouldn't want to spend time with them anyway. All they do is sit around yakking about their hair and make-up and who looks more like Shakira. Duh, none of them! Anyway, I'd rather ride bikes or go swimming. Even going fishing is more fun, like the other day when I helped Daniel and Andreas reel in that red snapper. No, they just don't like that I hang out with some of the older boys and that Daniel's my best friend. For whatever reason they all have some crazy crush on him.

Papa says I'm too smart to care what they think anyway. That's why he doesn't mind me playing video games even though it drives Mama nuts. She's always nagging us to go outside, as if we don't live outside already! Anyway, Papa says the jobs of the future will be based on games, so it's better for me to understand how they work. I don't know if he just says that to make her feel better, but I wouldn't trade playing with him for anything else in the world. It's what I live for on weekends when Mama's at work.

On Sundays she takes me to the stables if all the horses aren't taken. Sometimes I just hang out with Odin, though, and read. Barbara usually brings me whichever Harry Potter *her kids have just finished so it's not too bad either way.*

The other day Tre came by to help her clean out the stable. He asked me if Deathly Hallows *was any good, so I just gave it to him. He was pretty happy about that. I was almost done with it, and to be honest, I already knew what was going to happen anyway.*

"I ran into Tre," Anja said, dropping her leather satchel with a thud. Her face was flushed with perspiration. "I don't understand what he's up to in Limón."

Andreas, stooped over a cutting board at the kitchen island, was regarding the small mound of minced garlic he had just prepared. He was in the early stages of coconut sauce preparation, a ritual he undertook with the measured patience of a monk.

"Time waits for no man," he said, finally looking up.

Anja moved past him to pour herself a glass of water from the refrigerated tank.

"You can say that again. He should be finishing up with school."

Shrugging to no one in particular, Andreas returned to his work.

"I've invited him over for lunch," she said, leaning against the kitchen sink. "I hope this time you can at least try to talk some sense into him."

Groaning, Andreas raised his knife in the air, catching a glint of late morning sun on the blade.

"His grandmother is dying, Anja. We have to respect the family's wishes."

"Do you think Ms. Adina would be happy knowing her oldest grandson has given up on his education? What's he going to do later without a diploma? He's smart, and I'm not going to watch him throw away his chances without saying a word. There's only so much he could possibly be doing for her now that she's in the hospital."

"You know it's not just Ms. Adina he looks after. How will you help by making him feel bad about school?"

Anja thwacked her glass down on the counter before reaching over to grab an apron from the hook.

"I should know better than to talk to you about these things. You chose this life. Tre, on the other hand, should have the opportunity to do something else."

"Not everyone's meant to be a rocket scientist, Anja."

"Ach, forget it," she said, as she stormed over to the counter to clear away the empty beer bottles. "I take it Nico was here already?"

"M-hmm," Alfred said, taking a large yellow onion from the bowl in front of him.

"That's another one you should talk to. Drinking away his daughter's tuition."

"*Tranquilo*," Andreas said, raising his hands to soften the air between them. "He told me he's getting the money together next week."

"I don't care about the when, where or how. The more he drinks, the less likely they are to pay off her bill. They're already six months behind, and you know money's tight enough that I can't go paying for hers as well. As much as I'd like to."

"The man doesn't drink *that* much, Anja. But, ok. I'll talk to him about it. Anyway, I thought it was his mother who paid the school."

"His grandmother," Anja said, rolling her eyes. "And all I'm telling you is what I know. They're behind on their payments, and I can't go asking the treasurer again to be more lenient. It isn't fair to the others."

Tre arrived shortly before one o'clock, just as the last two guests were settling their bill. He stood tentatively at the threshold and waited until Andreas caught his eye and waved him in.

"I hope you brought a big appetite," Andreas said, gesturing for him to take a seat.

Tre nodded, sitting down on the bench closest to the door while Anja brought out the woven place mats from the kitchen.

"Scoot in, Tre," she motioned with her hand. "We always eat at this end of the table. Lena and Daniel won't be coming until late."

Tre did as he was told, sidestepping his way in. Meanwhile, Andreas, carried in a steaming pot from the kitchen while Anja busied herself setting the table with plates, bowls and cutlery.

"I made one of your grandmother's favorites," Andreas said, taking a seat and filling Tre's bowl with a ladle full of rich, coconut fish stew.

"Smells good," Tre said, after an awkward silence. "She teach you to make it?"

"Long time ago, yes," Andreas replied, his voice softening as he filled the two other bowls. "It never did taste quite as good as hers, though. She never would tell me her secret ingredient. But I think I might have guessed it."

Tre put a spoonful up to his mouth and blew.

"M-hmm," he said, squinting his eyes at Andreas after savoring the first bite. "That's her recipe alright."

Andreas let out a small laugh, his eyes sparkling.

"I thought as much."

"So, what is it?" Anja asked, sinking a spoon into her bowl.

Andreas exchanged a knowing look with Tre and smiled.

"I can't tell you," he said, marking an X across his heart. "Chef's honor."

Smiling back, Tre turned his attention back to his food. For a while they each enjoyed the meal in silence. It was only after Andreas began to serve him a second bowl, that Anja dared broach the dreaded subject of school. As was her wont, she made an impassioned plea, while Tre nodded along, in between chews. It was only in the frenzy of Lena and Daniel running up the front steps that he received a respite. Dropping their book bags on the floor, they ran over to see what was on the table.

Daniel peered over his mother's shoulder and scrunched up his nose.

"Fish stew?" he said.

"Yeah, and? You should be happy you're even getting a warm meal. Sit down."

"Where?" Daniel asked, looking over at Tre who was sitting in his seat.

"Are you blind?" Anja said. "You can sit next to me."

"But that's *my*—"

"But, but! You have to learn to be more flexible Daniel."

"But he's in—"

"Sit."

Lena, meanwhile, had already moved in next to Tre.

"I like fish stew," she said, looking over at her neighbor and smiling.

"You would," Daniel said. "Because it's gotta be better than that stuff your dad makes."

Lena's eyes popped out as she nodded in exaggerated agreement. Daniel, meanwhile, broke out laughing in hysterics. Finally, having had enough, Lena kicked him under the table.

"Ouch!" Daniel grabbed his shin.

"He's such a baby," Lena said, looking at Tre and shaking her head in mock adulthood. "I barely touched him."

Daniel glared at her, the remnants of his smile turning mischievous.

"You two stop horsing around, now," Anja said, placing two bowls in front of them. "Tre's going to think you both behave like babies."

Daniel and Lena exchanged a look of dissatisfaction.

"Do you stay in Limón now, Tre?" Lena asked.

While the others waited to hear the answer, Daniel took the opportunity to bypass the stew, reaching instead for the bread and butter.

"Yeah. I've been staying at my father's."

Anja threw Andreas a worried look. Rumor had it Ms. Adina's son had gotten up to no good in Limón. This was after he had lost his job as a dockworker, having left his sons in his mother's care.

"And your brothers?" Anja asked, trying hard to sound nonchalant.

"They stay in Bribri with my Aunt Ethel." Tre replied, looking toward the exit.

"Well, you let us know if you need any help up there," Andreas said, wiping his mouth with a paper napkin. "Are you taking the 2:30 bus back?"

Tre nodded, his pursed-lip silence starting to permeate the air around them.

"I can drive you to the station if you like," Andreas said, standing up. "I just have to pick up some crates at the Chinese grocery. You can help me load them up before you go."

In the three years since they had adopted him, Odin had grown into a perfect replica of Wuodan. Other than sporting a little more golden fur, his only distinguishing feature was the ferociousness of his bark, which meant no one would approach the Van de Steeg house, and if anyone dared even step a hair too close to a family member, he would snarl until one of his people would signal for him to stop.

Nina had trained him to guard, and despite Nico's initial resistance, he now relished the fact that they had the most intimidating German shepherd mutt in town. Apart from the Van de Steegs, the only people exempt from Odin's fierce disposition were Barbara, the Freyers, and by extension, Gertie.

Only in the intimacy of their home and garden did Odin exhibit his more playful side—fetching endless balls for Lena or turning on his back for a belly rub at the foot of the couch. Most days, however, he was Nina's protector, accompanying her to and from work and waiting attentively until she was ready to go.

Odin's presence was not the only thing that changed in the Van de Steeg's lives. Nina, once so careful with her physical appearance, had done nothing to address her looks from the moment they had welcomed Odin into their home. She had taken to wearing her black hair in a rough bob, her bangs long to better hide her eyes and the fine features of her face. She no longer wore the nice clothes she had brought with her. Instead, she would fashion a daily uniform for herself out of Nico's worn, black t-shirts, the arms rolled up, and men's khaki pants, old and sagging, but still good enough to get away with at work.

"How many hours have you been staring at that screen?" Nina asked, leading Odin in by the leash and closing the door behind her. It was late afternoon on a Wednesday, and Lena was still at Quixote's finishing up a school project with Daniel.

Nico rubbed his bloodshot eyes as he turned his wiry frame to look at her.

The place reeked of cigarette smoke.

"Not as long as you'd think. I'm going to have to take this pile of junk into Limón to get serviced. The hard drive's acting up again."

Not hiding her frown, Nina undid Odin's leash and walked over to the kitchen.

"And how much will that cost?"

"Not much. The owner still owes me a huge favor after bollixing my other machine. I'll get him to knock it off the repair price."

Nina poured Odin a bowl of his favorite kibble.

"When you go take Lena with you. She needs art supplies that I can't get in town."

"Any chance you've got ₡50,000 I can take with me?"

Nina sighed then walked over to his makeshift desk.

"Fifty? Do you think you'll need that much?"

They were starting to feel the ripple from September's financial crisis, and though they were about to enter the start of the high season, construction work in the area had come to a screeching halt, a harbinger of difficult times ahead.

"Barbara's thinking of cutting back my hours. Without as many tours being booked, she's trying not to let anyone go."

"She'd be crazy to let *you* go," Nico said, fidgeting in his seat more than usual. "You practically run the place. You shouldn't give her any time for free."

"What I do with my spare time is up to me. In the meantime, you should make sure you can get paid for whatever it is you're doing on that thing, because if I do lose this job, we're pretty much screwed."

"C'mon, it's not that bad. We've still got Oma's money coming in."

"You're not touching that. It's for Lena's school."

Nico rolled his eyes at her.

"Jesus, Nina, did I say I was? Okay, so we'll have to tighten our belts for a bit, but I'll figure a way out of this."

Nina ran her fingers through her disheveled hair as she drank in the manic flickering of his eyes. She had known Nico was up to something but had dismissed his furtive behavior the way a wife might look past a stash of porn.

"Have you been using?" she asked, narrowing her eyes.

"What?"

He threw himself back in his chair as if to scramble away from her.

"Are you on something? Right now?"

Nico shook his head in protest, but he could see in the worry lines of her eyes that she was not buying it. He sighed and looked back at his screen.

"Ok, yes. I had a little snort when I was in town, but it's nothing to worry about. It won't happen again, alright? It's just that if you want to cut a deal, sometimes you have to play along, that's all."

"A deal? What kind of a deal?"

Clocking the distress in her voice, Nico let out a nervous laugh.

"It's nothing like that, Jesus. Give me some credit. I'm just trying to find a way for us to make some extra money."

"Legal money?"

Nico looked back up at her and scoffed.

"What, like Wall Street legal? We won't have to worry about the *federales* knocking at the door if that's what you mean."

"Then what is it?" Nina said, her eyes rounding in fear. "This isn't like you, and I don't like the sound of this deal one bit."

"C'mon! You know how this town works. It caters to tourists looking for a good time. And before you accuse me of anything," he added, reaching for his dwindling pack of cigarettes, "it's not what you think."

"Then tell me."

"I can't," he said, avoiding her eyes as he lit up. "Not yet."

Nina grabbed the pack and took the last one for herself.

"I hope you know what you're getting us into. We can't afford any mistakes right now."

"You do like living here, don't you?" Nico asked, handing her the lighter. Her lack of response was answer enough. "Okay then. If you want us to stay, you're just going to have to trust me."

Nina combed out Reina's coat beneath the shade of a palm tree the next morning, not sure what to think. Nico had always looked after them, however imperfectly.

She had had her doubts in the past, especially after what happened to him in Baghdad, but in the end he had made good on his promises. Adjusting to their life in Costa Rica had taken time, but Lena was happy and doing well in school, and even though Nina earned little, the work itself was a form of therapy. She could not imagine ever having to go back to The Netherlands.

Nico, on the other hand, had been pulled out by the tide.

When this had happened, Nina could not say exactly. The last three seasons working with Barbara's horses had kept Nina plenty busy, and she had not stopped long enough to consider where exactly Nico was headed.

The first couple of years he had enjoyed his life of aimless leisure, spending time at the beach most days after dropping Lena off at school. Back then their daughter's routine had kept him in check as far as his drinking was concerned. But now that Lena was older and more capable on her own, a beer was the first thing Nico reached for after shooing her out the door with a bag of chips and a juice box.

Reina turned to nudge her.

"Sorry about that, old girl. I'm a bit preoccupied today."

Nina switched out the curry comb for a soft brush and focused her efforts on removing the dislodged dirt, but soon enough her thoughts returned to Nico.

He had developed a habit of wandering from bar to bar in the past year, collecting local gossip that he would share around the Freyer's *Stammtisch* or in the evenings with her after putting Lena to bed. At first Nina had not thought much of it. He found the goings-on in town amusing, but shortly before the financial crisis, he had started spending more and more time in front of his computer again. Never one to hold his tongue, Nina assumed he had ruffled some feathers in town especially in the tourist bars. As it turned out, it was all about this hush-hush deal of his.

Of course, he had neglected to tell her *who* it was with, let alone about. Only that it would bring in some much needed money. Still, Nico's assurances aside, Nina could not shake the feeling that this would not end well.

It was a well-known fact that Colombian dealers were running up and down both coasts, and even sleepy Caway was the home of at least one known local kingpin. His children, registered under their mothers' names, were all in attendance at the *Escuela Integral*, and he was rumored to be both a doting father and a generous donor for local causes, the clinic primary among them. No one would say his name out loud, but it was understood that his 'generosity' provided a much-needed safety net in town. Yes, there were those few unfortunate souls known to partake of his wares, but these were people with whom the Van de Steeg's did not interact socially. At least not until now.

Did she trust Nico to get them through these next few months—or years even—of financial uncertainty? She was not sure she had much of a choice. Keeping secrets was part and parcel of his previous trade, and it was a long-standing habit she had not found it necessary to question, especially given her own tendencies.

But now this particular unknown was coming between them. She could feel it in the sudden waves of anxiety that made her hand jerk unskillfully as she worked to untangle the knots in Reina's mane.

Nico was going down a road not his own, and the question remained as to whether she would follow him.

"It's ok, girl," Nina said, leaning in to nuzzle *Reina's* neck and gently smooth down her coat. "I'm not planning on going anywhere. I promise."

22

Caway - Three Years Later - July 2012

"Andreas!"

Anja was standing in the middle of Quixote's empty dining room shaking her head at the wall of water gushing down on all three sides.

"Have you seen Nico? We need him to pay, and I mean right away. The tuition is due, these damn bills keep piling up, and Jesus, when will this bloody rain stop already!"

It was noon on a Monday, and the third day straight of torrential downpours brought on by César, a tropical storm so obstinate it seemed determined to drown the entire Caribbean coast.

"*Ja*, ok, *tranquilo*," Andreas said, as he continued to sharpen his kitchen knives.

"Don't *tranquilo* me, we've got water up to our ears and no customers for days!"

"It will pass, Anja. It always does."

"*Ja, Ja*," Anja said, clawing at the pack of Derby's she had left beside her late morning coffee. "But that doesn't help us with the bills. It's never been this bad, Andreas. *No one* has customers. I'm starting to really worry now."

She lit a cigarette and shuddered in a deep nicotine-filled inhale. Her body only relaxed when the smoke began to stream from her nose and mouth.

"So our belts will be a little tight this year," Andreas said with a shrug. "Next year we'll fatten up again. You'll see."

"I don't mind a tighter belt," Anja said, looking down at her much-widened midriff. "What I'm more concerned about is our son's education."

Andreas lifted his hand to pacify her.

"Ok, I'll ask him. But you know things aren't good over there."

Anja shook her head as she tapped out a cigarette for Andreas.

"There's only so much we can do," Anja said, lighting the second one with her own. "We're practically raising Lena as it is. Have you taken a good look at Nina lately? She's like a zombie. Barely eats let alone washes herself. I'm amazed Barbara still keeps her on. Somedays I half expect to see her collapsed on the road with the vultures circling."

"Hey, that's enough now," Andreas said, emerging from the kitchen so he could smoke. He sat down beside her with an open Pilsen by his side. "You know as well as I do she's not right in the head."

"I know, but I just feel overwhelmed. Between his drinking and her absence, I worry most about Lena. She's losing interest in school, and more and more she's cooped up in that house of theirs playing video games and who knows what else."

"But Nico is there with her."

"Really?" Anja asked, raising an eyebrow. "What I don't understand is why he's not more involved. He used to be, remember?"

Andreas nodded.

"And, yeah, of course he loves her, but he's losing touch."

"Maybe it's the best he can do, eh?"

"Give up, you mean? These years are critical for her. Her future depends on it."

"Stop being so dramatic. We turned out alright, and our parents weren't saints."

Anja huffed and looked away from him. She could not believe how much water kept pouring from the sky.

"Anyway, I should check on Gertie. She hasn't been by here for a day and a half."

"Can you blame her?" Anja said. "She'd wash away just trying to walk over here. That's another one who seems to think food is unnecessary. I swear I haven't seen her eat anything now for about three weeks straight."

Andreas knew better than to say anything. Instead, he leaned back to take a few sips from his beer. He had been up since six mending odds and ends in the *cabinas* and the restaurant. Upkeep on the property alone was a full-time job, and unlike his younger days, he could feel it now, the wear and tear between the sinews. He could not say so to Anja, but he was relieved not to have any customers for a while. It meant he could take his time getting around to what he had long ignored. Thirty-five years he had worked on this hard labor of love. It had worn him out already, and it showed in the deep, weathered lines of his face, but most of all in the sharp slope of his shoulders. Like Gertie and Nina, he was built ropy and lean, but he, too, now had but little fat to spare.

He stubbed out his cigarette and placed his hands on the table to slowly ease himself up.

"Ok, I'm off to see Gertie."

Anja did not bother to disguise the mournful look in her eye. Though Andreas had meant nothing by it, she could not help but feel a jilted twinge. There was nothing that agitated her more than having to think about Gertie and her antagonizing quirks, and Anja could not even remember now how long ago their relationship had frozen into this stalemate, where they would only exchange the barest of necessities and always in brusque tones.

But behind that armored exterior of hers, Anja knew that Gertie adored both Andreas and Daniel. All these years Anja had bitten her tongue with the unspoken understanding that beneath all of Gertie's stubbornness there must also lurk a small inkling of appreciation for her. Nevertheless, there was not a single soul in Caway who irked her quite as much as that diminutive Bavarian stoic.

What Anja felt most of all, though, was an endless fatigue. She had done all she could to withstand the constant stress of the past three years. Between a volatile economy that had put their small business on the brink and her ever increasing responsibilities as the longest standing chairwoman of the

Escuela Integral, Anja felt near a breaking point by the constant demands placed on her by both teachers and administrators, not to mention some of the parents.

Taking a mindless sip from her cold coffee, she tried to remember the last time she had put brush to paper. The only thing she had done in years was retouch the paint on their hand-lettered signs. Her once-upon-an-artist's life was about as remote as the European comforts she had left behind in Basel.

"Anja!"

The sheer panic in Andreas' voice startled her to her feet.

"What happened? Are you hurt?"

"No," he said, running up through the side entrance, his shirt and shorts soaked through and dripping. "But call the doctor. Tell him he has to come quick!"

"But what is it?"

"Just call already," he said, not bothering to even dry himself with the towels stacked in the pantry beside him. "It's for Gertie. I found her on the floor."

"Oh God. Go back over there and help her then. I'm calling now."

Anja ran into the kitchen to grab the phone.

"Damn it!" she said, losing the connection after just one ring. "Not now!"

A second attempt proved fruitless. She rifled through her purse and found her scarcely used cell phone. It had no charge let alone reception.

"Shit. Daniel, get down here!"

She heard a grumbling from the upstairs apartment where he was no doubt lolling away time in front of his game console.

"I mean it. Get your butt down here, now! We have a situation."

From the top of the stairs he asked, "What is it?"

"Gertie needs a doctor. I need you to go over there and tell your father I can't get through on the phone. He's going to have to drive into town somehow and get him."

"Not in this weather he's not. The car won't make it."

"For Christ's sake just do as I say!"

Daniel didn't bother to pull on his shoes. Instead, he hopped down the stairs and out the side door like a young gazelle. Anja watched him, unprepared to see the faint outlines of the young man he was becoming. It was all happening too fast.

Anja paced up and down as she dialed repeatedly, each futile attempt leaving her more frustrated than the last. All their prior medical emergencies—Daniel's broken leg and Andreas' close call with a machete—had required them to pile into the car and drive themselves into town. An ambulance, for the most part, took far too long. But Daniel was right. Their old rusting sedan would not make it out on these inundated roads. They needed four-wheel drive.

Antonio had a jeep, she recalled. He was a seasonal neighbor who lived just a kilometer and a half up the road. If he was in town, he could drive in this, no problem. Anja debated walking over there herself, but just as she was about to write Daniel a note, he came running back, visibly shaken.

"Andreas says you have to go over there. She's having trouble breathing and is in pain."

"*Ja*, ok, but I need you to run up to Antonio's and tell him what happened. Tell him to meet us here with his jeep straightaway."

This time Daniel did not protest.

Anja grabbed their first aid kit from beneath the kitchen counter and stuffed it down into her oversized purse before adding two ripe bananas from the fruit bowl. She then filled up a large water bottle. By the sound of it, she was unlikely to return home any time soon. She wracked her brain for other possible necessities, but not knowing what else Gertie might need, she took one last look around before stepping out into the endless deluge.

Gertie's situation was far worse than Anja could have imagined. She was not, thankfully, on the rooftop veranda where she normally slept. Instead, Andreas had found her sprawled out on the kitchen floor just outside the ground level bathroom. By the look of it, she had lain there for quite some time as evidenced by the wet stain on her sundress and the smell.

"I cleaned up as best I could," Andreas said, from his crouched position beside her. He had propped her head up with a makeshift pillow. "She needs another change of clothes."

"I'll take care of that, don't worry. Have you given her something to drink?"

"I tried to give her some water," Andreas said, squeezing Gertie's hand gently, "but she doesn't want to swallow. I should go and get the doctor now."

For a moment, Anja looked away. She had to make sure to keep her emotions in check. The scene was reminding her too much of her father's decline.

"I've sent Daniel to get Antonio's jeep. If he's there, he'll meet us at the restaurant. But there's no time to waste. You're going to have to take her with you."

Hearing that, Gertie's eyes opened wide, and she began to shake her head in opposition.

"We can't move her," Andreas said. "I already tried. She's in too much pain."

"Ok. But you have to be quick. She needs to go to the hospital. Tell Daniel to keep checking the phone. As soon as it's working again, he should come over here and tell me.

"Here," Anja said, handing Andreas her mobile phone and charger. "Plug it into the jeep and call us back as soon as you can."

Standing, Andreas glanced at Gertie one last time, his eyes welling up with apprehension. He took the phone and charger and walked out without another word.

"It's just you and me now," Anja said, breaking the rainy silence as she knelt beside Gertie. She had been looking around at her sparse, utilitarian kitchen with its small wooden table and four rattan dining chairs. In all these years of knowing her, it was the first time Anja had set foot in her home.

The entrance to the house was at the opposite end, where a small living area had been carved out of the otherwise large and rectangular space. It consisted solely of a worn leather couch with a side table that looked out on the secluded garden through a large picture window.

"I think you'll be more comfortable if I change you out of these clothes," Anja said. Gertie's eyes looked up to reveal her all-too-familiar defiance.

Anja had gone through this already twice before. Her father had died not long after her mother, and she had cared for them throughout each of their extended illnesses. She had always been particularly close to her father, and when his speech began to fail him in the end, they had still found a way to communicate.

Looking down at Gertie—who in the best of times was stingy with her words—Anja wondered where to even begin.

"May I?" she asked, not blinking an eye until she could see Gertie finally acquiesce.

"Good," Anja replied. "I'll go upstairs to find you something. I'll be right back."

She walked up the narrow stairs and to the upstairs landing where she found two bedrooms facing out toward the garden.

The room to the right opened out onto the veranda, so she assumed it was where Gertie would keep her things. Stepping in through the open door, Anja's eyes were immediately drawn to a glazed, cerulean blue vase sitting atop a plain, wooden bookcase. It was an unusual piece whose stark beauty fell into deep contrast with everything else in the modest room.

The bookcase itself was filled mostly with a cheap selection of paperbacks—some she recognized from Gertie's daily, all-consuming reads while sitting at their *Stammtisch*. The lower shelf, however, was reserved for two stacks of boxes.

There was not much else to look at apart from the stripped-down bed, a small closet in the far-right corner and a tall, wooden bureau sitting next to it.

Anja walked over to the closet first and pulled aside the thin blue curtain that acted as a makeshift door. She took stock of the few familiar sundresses that made up the majority of Gertie's wardrobe. She pulled out the one made of faded jean material and seeing a brown woven blanket resting on the shelf above it, took that out as well. Next, she pulled open the top drawer of the bureau. Inside she found the underwear and socks she was looking for, all neatly folded and arranged in the ample space provided. For a nosy second, Anja felt tempted to rifle through the rest of her drawers, but instead she walked over to the veranda to take a good look at where Gertie reputedly slept.

She slid open the glass door, and peering out into the pouring rain, spotted a small mattress leaning against the wall at a slight angle. Next to it was a large plastic flashlight, the kind people used when they were on the lookout for something in a dense patch of forest. Thin, blue bed sheets hung from a clothesline strung out along the balcony's edge that thanks to the heavy rain were damp to the touch. Nonetheless, the white floor tiles were for the most part dry, meaning the roof's incline provided just enough cover to make it possible to sleep out here regardless of the weather.

Squatting down, Anja tried to imagine what it must be like. There were tree branches hanging just above the veranda meaning all sorts of creatures could theoretically make their way over, a thought that made her shudder. A patch of dense, saturated clouds sat suspended above the trees meaning that on a clear night, Gertie would have a direct line of vision to a crystalline sky.

The stars and moon no doubt kept her company at night, but that thin mattress of hers could hardly have felt comfortable. Gertie's needless stoicism was something Anja could not bring herself to fathom. Living in the tropics was challenging enough without layering on additional difficulties, and now that Anja had full confirmation of Gertie's meager and monk-like existence, it was no less unsettling.

She made her way back down the stairs only to find Gertie in the same position she had left her. The only difference was that her eyes were now closed. Her breathing—though steadier than before—was still audibly strained and labored.

"I found a blanket and a change of clothes for you," Anja said, kneeling again so she could face her. "The trick will be not to move you too much, but that shouldn't be a problem."

Gertie's eyes popped opened, revealing her trepidation.

"Come now. You know I have more than enough experience doing this for my parents. I promise I'll go slow and check in with you every step of the way. If it's too much, just shake your head or blink your eyes that way I'll know when to stop. Ok?"

Gertie stared at her blankly for a few seconds before giving her a slight nod.

"Good," Anja said, taking a moment to assess her situation.

"This dress attaches at the shoulder. What I'm going to do is unfasten it and pull it down to your waist."

Gertie nodded again before squeezing her eyes shut in dreaded anticipation.

Using a light touch, Anja unbuttoned each of the shoulder straps. The dress was far too large for Gertie's wisp of a body, but in this instance, it proved a benefit. Anja pulled down slowly until she came to the first major point of resistance.

"I'm going to move each of your shoulder blades up, ok?"

Gertie's eyes were still forced shut. Whether out of resistance or modesty, Anja was not sure. She waited a couple of seconds longer until Gertie gave her the next go-ahead nod. With deft hands Anja lifted each feather-light shoulder in turn, pulling down the bunched cloth toward her waist.

"There, that wasn't so bad, was it?" Anja said, trying her best not to focus on Gertie's skeletal chest. It was difficult not to take in what little remained of her, the shock of withered skin against bone.

As if reading her thoughts, Gertie's eyes fluttered open.

"I'm sorry it has to be this way, but I'll try to be as quick as I can. I'm going to do the same with each hip now, are you ready?"

Gertie nodded with a little more confidence this time, presumably relieved by how it had gone so far or just ready for it to be over. Wanting to limit her discomfort, Anja made sure to pull the underwear down with the dress. Gertie grimaced at this more unsettling maneuver.

It was heartbreaking to see her so exposed, her undernourished limbs splayed, her skin the color of gray parchment. Anja felt a heavy weight in her chest as she gathered up the clean clothes beside her, working quickly to dress her with as much care as before. She finished by putting socks on her feet. Like Gertie's hands, they were cold to the touch.

"There. Now to tuck you in with this blanket. Shall we?"

This time Gertie's eyes showed their gratitude before her lids closed again in fatigue. Anja spread the blanket out over her, lifting shoulders and hips one last time to provide her more comfort. It was still hot in her house, but her body could no longer regulate temperature. With the added warmth, however, Anja could see her start to relax.

"I'll be right here if you need me," Anja said, pulling over one of the kitchen chairs "All you have to do is open your eyes, and I'm there."

She watched Gertie's labored inhalations until her own weariness slumped her forward in her chair. Cradling her head, Anja closed her eyes and thought of her father. How strange to have moved halfway across the world only to find herself right back here again.

Two hours passed as Anja listened to the rain in syncopated rhythm with Gertie's breath. At three, Daniel came running to inform her about Andreas' call. He and Antonio had made it into Limón and were now on their way back with a doctor. If they were lucky, they would arrive in about one hour's time.

"Have you eaten?" Anja asked her son, his head poking out of an oversized Nirvana t-shirt left behind by one of their surfing guests.

"Yeah, some bread and jam," he said, glancing over at Gertie shrouded beneath the blanket. "How is she?"

Anja pursed her lips and shook her head.

"She's resting as best she can."

"But why is she still on the floor?"

"She's very ill, and it hurts her too much to move right now. All we can do is make her as comfortable as we can until the doctor comes."

"But will she be okay?"

His look of complete incomprehension was more than Anja could bear.

"I hope so. But she may need our help for a while."

The concern in Daniel's eyes mounted.

"What can I do?"

"For now, just go back to the restaurant. I need you to keep an ear out for the phone."

"Ok," he said, letting go of his held breath.

It was four-thirty in the afternoon before Antonio and his jeep finally arrived. The young doctor, cradling a large, black medical bag, was dripping wet when Anja answered the door.

"Dr. Gutierrez," he said in a rushed tone before crouching to remove his muddy boots. As Anja led him toward Gertie, he mentioned that he had left Antonio and Andreas at the gate. They were trying to jigger loose an old, rusty lock so they could drive the jeep closer to the house.

Not wasting any time, he washed his hands at the kitchen sink and then knelt down beside his patient.

"How long has she been like this?" he asked, opening up his bag and placing a stethoscope on Gertie's chest. Her eyes remained partly closed, and she seemed not to notice him.

"We only found her today at noon. The last time we saw her was in the evening, the day before yesterday. We assumed she didn't want to leave her house in this lousy weather."

"Yes, your husband said as much," Dr. Gutierrez said, with a hint of impatience. His tone had sparked a flare of guilt in Anja's head, as if his question was meant to uncover the whys of Gertie's failing health and not her current incapacitation.

Anja sighed.

"She's as stubborn as a mule, doctor. But I guess you're right. We should have seen this coming."

"I'm going to give her some morphine now," he said, ignoring her. "We'll need to take her to the hospital as soon as possible."

"Is there anything I can do to help?" she asked, sounding far more desperate than she intended.

"Some coffee would be nice," he said, rubbing his eyes. "We need to see if they can get the jeep in closer. Then we can move her."

Glad to have something to do, Anja walked over to the kitchen cabinets, and to her surprise, found a *bolsa de chorrear*. Finding a tin of fresh grounds in Gertie's otherwise empty refrigerator, Anja put on the kettle, and then busied herself with the filter preparation before placing a white enamel coffee pot beneath it.

"Should one of us go with you to the hospital?" Anja asked, standing beside the filter, waiting for the water to boil.

"I don't think there's enough room in the jeep," Dr. Gutierrez said. "Besides, she'll be heavily sedated until we can evaluate her condition more thoroughly. We'll call as soon as she can receive visitors. Is she a relative of yours?"

"No, but a close friend."

"You'll have to contact the family, then," the doctor said, peering up at her for emphasis.

"Her family?" Anja asked, somewhat stupefied.

"Yes. Her condition is critical. She may not have much time left."

"But that's the problem, you see. They're in Germany. We don't know who to contact."

"Well, the sooner you can find out, the better. They'll want to know her situation."

Anja pulled the boiling kettle off the stove and wracked her brain, trying to come up with a suitable explanation.

"We can try and ask her, of course, but I don't think she'll tell us. You see, the situation is quite strained."

Dr. Gutierrez looked at her again skeptically.

"There's got to be a least one person," he said. "At any rate, she'll need someone who is authorized to act on her behalf. Unless she's made other arrangements, that will have to be a family member."

Had Gertie made other arrangements? Anja wondered. The only person she was even remotely close to was Andreas, and he had never mentioned anything of the sort.

Seeing that the coffee had filtered through, Anja stepped outside to call in Andreas and Antonio who had just driven the jeep into the yard and were pulling down the back seat to make room for Gertie.

Anja carried four mugs out to the front steps so the four of them could gather in the doorway for a quick conference while Dr. Gutierrez explained how best to carry Gertie out to the jeep. With the pain dulled, he explained, she was unlikely to feel too much physical distress, but at the same time they would have to provide her with as much support as possible. He had not detected any broken bones, but he reminded them that she could have sustained other injuries during the fall.

Fortunately, the rain had petered out by the time they maneuvered her onto Dr. Gutierrez's stretcher. Only a light mist clung to her wool blanket when they finally walked her out in the sinking twilight.

"Thank you," Anja and Andreas said, unsure how else to express their gratitude to both Antonio and the doctor. As the men mounted their seats and prepared to pull out, Andreas walked over to the passenger side one last time.

"Please tell her we'll make it to Limón as soon as possible," he said, looking at Gertie over Dr. Gutierrez's shoulder. "And that I keep my promise."

Once they had lost sight of the jeep, Anja and Andreas went back into Gertie's house.

"The doctor said we have to get in touch with her family," she said, making her way toward the kitchen. "Do you know how we can do that?"

Andreas shook his head before turning his bereaved eyes to face her.

"We're her family."

Anja turned away from him to pull open a drawer.

"Not according to the law. There must be an address around here somewhere. Didn't you tell me that her oldest came to visit once?"

"Stop that. You know she won't forgive us if we go through her things."

"At a time like this? I hardly doubt it, the woman's at death's door!"

"And we still have to respect her wishes. I know for a fact she hasn't contacted them. Nor have they reached out to her."

Anja crossed her arms, planting her feet in front of him emphatically.

"No, I'm sorry, but that's not how we're going to do this. Her sons have a right to know, damn it! Don't you remember their names? If anything, we might be able to find them on the internet."

Andreas was avoiding her gaze by staring down at the patch of floor where he had found Gertie.

"Christian," he said finally. "Udo Jörgen and Christian. But you have to promise me not to go through her things."

"My God! All I'm looking for is a piece of paper with a phone number or an address."

Andreas looked up at her, his eyes softening.

"She doesn't have much left now but her dignity, Anja. And that much, at least, she deserves to keep."

Anja's mouth flew open in protest, but something inside her made her stop.

"Fine," she said.

She pressed her lips shut as she swung herself toward the kitchen sink. Things still needed to be cleaned up before leaving, and the last thing she needed was to feel the weight of Gertie's spooky unspoken wrath. Like it or not, there would be no avoiding her now. Andreas had said it. They were family.

The hospital called the following afternoon, confirming Anja's suspicions. Gertie, though previously undiagnosed, had advanced lung cancer that had reached an inoperable stage. All that was left to do was provide her with hospice care.

"She'll be lucky to live out the rest of the year," Dr. Gutierrez told her.

Though he was the one to deliver the news, Dr. Gutierrez would not be her attending physician. That job would be taken over by the resident oncologist, Dr. Grunwald. Dr. Gutierrez did have a message to pass on to them. Gertie had asked them to visit the following day. The hospital would call in the morning to confirm.

"And when you come, please don't forget to bring her identity papers and social security card. We'll need those to complete her medical record."

The next day after lunch, Anja and Andreas prepared to drive into Limón. The potholes of the surrounding roads were still filled to the brim with water, but Andreas felt confident that their old car could still make it. The only snag, of course, was that they would have to leave Daniel in charge of receiving their first customers, a group of Americans due to arrive in the late afternoon.

"Remember to offer them something to drink," Anja said, pacing back and forth as she waited for Andreas to return with Gertie's papers. "Let them know we'll be open for dinner at five once Hyacinth arrives, and make sure you help her as best you can until we get back tonight. And don't forget to wash your hands."

Daniel rolled his eyes, as he looked up from his game.

"Ok, stop worrying already. It's not like I haven't lived in a restaurant my whole life. I'm pretty sure I know what to do."

Just then Andreas appeared in the door.

"Do you have her paperwork?" Anja said, not knowing where else to direct her frustration.

"*Ja, alles Gut,*" Andreas said, walking past her and toward the garage. "Let's go."

At 3 PM they arrived at *Dr. Tony Fació*, the only hospital serving the Limón and Talamanca provinces and situated on a peninsula not far from the original site of the United Fruit Company infirmary. From the windows facing south it was possible to see nearby Uvita Island, or *Isla Quiribrí*, as it was now known officially but rarely called. They were met at reception by a much older man, Dr. Grunwald, who was of similar stature to Gutierrez but of much wider girth with white hair and furrowed brows. He led them first into his cramped office where they each took a seat opposite his almost buried wooden desk. It was piled high with stacks of medical journals on both sides with a scattering of patient files in the little space left in between.

Imaging scans from a variety of sources hung on the walls surrounding them, not to mention the many framed degrees and certifications Dr. Grunwald had acquired over the length of his prestigious career.

"Doña Gertie's condition," he said, folding his chubby hands as he took his seat in front of them, "is incurable. The cancer has spread to all the major organs and an operation would be ill advised since she would be unlikely to survive the surgery. All we can offer at this point is pain management."

"What about chemo?" Andreas asked.

The doctor closed his eyes and shook his head.

"I've already informed Ms. Obermeier of this, so she is fully aware of her situation. She has stated adamantly that she does not want chemotherapy, but in this case it's not even an option. The cancer is too widespread. Chemotherapy would prove too taxing on her system, and it's highly unlikely to produce any desirable effects. I'm afraid it's just too late for such measures. They would only cause her unnecessary suffering."

The doctor paused to let the news sink in.

"I did inform her that we would do our very best to manage her pain here in the hospice ward. Afterall, we are equipped to provide 24-hour care," he said, before letting out a sigh. "But she is insisting that she wants to go home. I told her that I cannot in good conscience release her unless I can be assured she will receive adequate care."

"What would we have to do?" Andreas asked.

Dr. Grunwald looked sternly at him and shook his head.

"You have to understand. She would need around-the-clock monitoring. We could provide you with the necessary medications, but you would need a local nurse to come by each day, or perhaps every other day, to check on her. Apart from that, she would need constant care. I could have one of the hospice nurses go over the necessary procedures with you, but you will need to think long and hard and feel certain about what it will mean to take her back home. Personally, I would advise you against it. It can be an extraordinary strain for a small family, especially when you have a business to run."

"Yes, we realize that," Anja said, seeing that Andreas had already made up his mind. "But she's a close friend—more like family—and we live just a stone's throw away. I think we can manage if we all take our turn."

Andreas nodded.

"If that is what you are prepared to do," the doctor said, looking at each of them in turn. "I should allow you to discuss this with her in person. She can talk somewhat but not for long or very loudly. At any rate, I *will* keep her here for at least another week before considering a transfer. I strongly suggest you contact her family in the meantime as there will be arrangements to make."

They got up and followed the doctor down the hall and toward the cancer ward. He pushed aside a cordoned off privacy curtain in one of the rooms where they found Gertie propped up in bed. She had tubes coming out of her nostrils and others extending out from her thin arms.

"Doña Gertie?" Dr. Grunwald said softly. Her eyes, for the most part, were closed. "Your friends are here to see you."

Gertie opened her eyes more, and seeing Andreas, smiled weakly.

"I'll leave you to talk now," the doctor said. "But please. Only ten minutes. You still need your rest."

"*Hallo, Alte,*" Andreas said as they each approached her from opposite sides of the bed. "You're looking a hell of a lot better than two days ago, I'll tell you that much. How are you feeling?"

"Like someone who's bound to a bed," Gertie said, her voice still weak but defiant. "The pain is mostly gone, so that's good."

"The doc says you want to come home."

Gertie nodded.

"Just as soon as he'll let me. I don't want to be here anymore."

"Are they not treating you well?" Anja asked.

Gertie looked unspeakably frail.

"No, the nurses are good. I just can't see the sky from here."

"The doc says we have to be trained first before we can take you home," Andreas said.

"And it will take at least one more week," Anja added.

"Yes, he told me the same. I realize I'll be a burden. But I promise not to ask too much."

"*Quatsch!*" Andreas said, "Don't be ridiculous, It's not a burden at all."

"Of course it will be, but I want to go home. I don't need this much attention. I'm not a small child."

"No, but we're not going to leave you alone either," Anja said. "I'm afraid you're going to have to put up with us most of the time. And no objections either," she added, reacting to the tightening grimace on Gertie's face. "It's one of the doctor's conditions. Otherwise, we'll have to leave you here."

In mock seriousness, Andreas pulled a face until Gertie lowered her chin in mute acknowledgment. If she wanted to see out her days with a view of the garden, Anja thought to herself, she would have no choice but to rely on them and that meant playing by the rules.

"Now, Gertie," Anja said, weighing out her next words. "I know this is a sore subject, but the doctor has asked us to contact your family."

In the flash of a second, Gertie's eyes filled with anger, but her voice was still far too weak. "No," she mouthed.

The night before, she and Andreas had found a mention online for a Udo Jörgen Witzmann at the Max Planck Institute in Tübingen. They had not been as successful in tracking down the oldest son. She and Andreas had argued about sending an e-mail.

"It's Gertie's choice," Andreas had insisted, so they had waited until today to decide.

"Gertie, whatever happened before, your sons will want to—"

"No," she said again, this time with volume. "They have their own lives to live. I don't want them worrying about what's left of mine."

"But you can't actually believe that," Anja said. "It's not possible to—"

"Anja," Andreas reached across the bed to put a hand on her wrist. "You heard what she said."

"But—"

He was squeezing hard now.

"*Verdammt noch mal, lass es sein!*"

"Fine, I'll let it be," Anja said, pulling away. "We'll discuss this later."

It was then that they noticed a young nurse nearing the bed.

"We need to go now," Andreas said. "Unless you need me sooner, I'll be back to see you the day after tomorrow. And don't worry. We'll sort things out so we can bring you home. Until then, rest."

Andreas took Gertie's hand and gave it a gentle squeeze, and then with a wink, took his leave. Anja lingered just a few seconds longer.

"I'm on your side, too," she said to Gertie. "Please don't forget that."

23

Caway - August 2012

"How is she even paying for any of this?" Nico asked, slow to accept the fact that Anja and Andreas were going to take over Gertie's care. He and Nina had come over for a nightcap and had joined the Freyers around the communal table in what appeared to be an impromptu meeting of their closest neighbors.

Antonio was there, sitting next to Marienne, the French proprietor of the *La Pinta Inn* that bordered Andreas and Anja's property toward the back. Javier, from the *La Divina* lodge was there, too, though he soon found an excuse to head back across the street once the Van de Steeg's arrived.

"She has her bit of savings from the sale of the house," Anja said. "Nadine and Tom are still living in Canada, but they let her stay there in exchange for keeping an eye on the place. After all, they can only come down a couple of weeks out of the year."

Nico let out a snort.

"Shrewd move on her part. Things aren't looking so good with this Maritime Law."

"For Christ's sake, man," Anja said, brushing past Marienne as she stood up from the table to get their guests another round. "One crisis at a time."

The last thing she needed was to listen, yet again, to one of Nico's pessimistic prognostications.

"I'll believe it when I see it," Andreas said, before leaning back in his seat at the head of the table. "*Asamblea Legislativa* talks more than it likes to act."

Antonio, sitting cross-legged at the opposite end, scratched his beard and raised a weary eyebrow.

"I don't know about that. Just last week nine properties in *Puerto Viejo* were served with demolition notice. I would check in with a lawyer if I were you. This eco-tourism thing has got the government seeing dollar signs everywhere. You can bet they'll be citing 'environmental considerations' every chance they get, if you know what I mean. Better safe than sorry."

"Yeah, ok," Anja said, clinking down two handfuls of cold beers in the center of the table. "But that's a well-known party town and those places are right on the beach. We're well beyond the 50 meters, and that's what the regulation says, 'no permanent structures within the 50-meter high tide line'. Anyway, Andreas owned this property back in 1976. That was a year before the law even passed."

"And what? You think that old wives' tale about the president means you're grandfathered in?"

Nico was referring to the 1915 shipwreck off the coast of Caway that happened to be carrying with it the Costa Rican president. Grateful to the people of Talamanca for rescuing him, Alfredo Gonzáles Flores had allegedly granted the canton a certain degree of self-determination.

"No one's said anything against it," Andreas said, smacking the thought away like a persistent mosquito. "Not once in the 36 years of me living here. *Mein Gott*, this whole town almost is within the 200-meters. We already have municipal concessions for the *cabinas* and the restaurant. It's just newsmen making noise to sell papers. That's all this is."

Nico let out a derisive laugh.

"Noise? If it wasn't for those journalists, you wouldn't even know this was going on."

"And here I thought you'd had your fill of journalism," Anja said with a wry grin. "Are you having second thoughts?"

Nico narrowed his eyes at her.

"May not have a choice seeing how much the rent's gone up around here."

Of late, he'd taken to carrying his laptop everywhere he went, making a big show of his alleged and on-going "research".

"If anyone has trouble it will be Javier," Andreas said, frustrated. "He's the one right on the water. But we're here to talk about more important things. Like how we can help Gertie out."

The table went silent for an awkward moment as they looked down at their perspiring beers. With fingers fidgeting, Marienne was the first to cave into the pressure.

"I'd be happy to help out with meals," she said, her dyed blonde-hair doing little to hide the lines in her worried face. "But it's hard enough now keeping up as it is. I really don't understand why she doesn't just stay in the hospice."

"Is that what you would want?" Andreas asked.

Marienne flinched. It was not like Andreas to be so direct.

"None of us is getting any younger," she said, then flipped her head to look away from him. "And anyway, I would never have let myself go like that. Not ever."

"That's well beside the point," Anja said. "And we do appreciate your offer, Marienne. It's just that things will be a bit more challenging for a while, and we're hoping we can count on you to help us out every now and again."

Nico scanned the faces around the *Stammtisch*. All of them knew that Antonio would be working in San José for the next two months, so he was out. Nina, meanwhile, who had been sitting mute beside him, looked as if she was about to cry.

"Ok, I can't say I've ever cared all too much for that woman," Nico said. "But in exchange for a few beers? Yeah sure, count us in. Just not with the bed pans."

Ten days after being hospitalized, Dr. Grunwald released an even frailer Gertie into their care. Other than Olga, the hired nurse from Edge Creek,

Anja and Andreas were the only ones on hand to greet her once the ambulette pulled up in front of the door.

With the driver's help, they carried Gertie up the stairs and to her room which Andreas had rearranged so she could see out toward the garden from her now elevated bed. Olga walked them through their soon-to-be daily procedures of changing out fluid bags and making sure the oxygen flow was appropriately set. The toughest part was balancing Gertie's dignity with the indelicacies of care: bathing, eliminating, cleaning up after a bout of incontinence. Olga, in typical Tica fashion, showed discretion as she offered them advice.

None of this, of course, was new to Anja having done her fair share of family caregiving. But as Olga busied herself reading through Gertie's medication log, Anja wondered to herself how she had come to inherit such an awkward arrangement.

Visiting Gertie in the hospital had been challenging enough. But now, seeing her in a bed as alien to Gertie as the house was to Anja, she found herself at a loss. Taking care of her beloved parents had come second nature. Gertie had not given Anja the time of day let alone restrained herself from showing her disdain. Yet for years this woman had taken up a choice seat in their living room. *The tables have turned*, Anja thought to herself, and for a devilish second, a temptation arose. Gertie, whether she liked it or not, would now have to rely on her.

The thought vanished, however, as Anja's eyes assessed Gertie's condition, her body wracked again by a convulsive cough.

The first few days caring for Gertie proved exceedingly difficult. Gertie kept insisting that their presence was too intrusive. "You only need to come three times a day," she kept saying. But it soon became apparent that Gertie's wish for independence was not one her body could indulge. At times she would feel fine without additional oxygen, but just as quickly she would find herself gasping for air. Her pain medication, too, seemed to require an infinite amount of fine tuning.

"My back is bothering me," Gertie said to Anja after she had caved into Gertie's earlier request for an afternoon alone.

Rolling her onto her side, Anja found the source of her discomfort. She was bleeding from two spots to the right and left of her scarce buttocks.

"I shouldn't have listened to you," Anja said lashing out, but more berating herself. "We have to shift you to another position. Otherwise, you won't heal."

Gertie pulled her frown down ever further.

"But I'm more comfortable this way."

"I know that," Anja said. "But right now you have these two sores, and they're only going to get worse the more pressure you put on them. We have to move you. Now."

Gertie didn't argue as Anja shifted her to lie on one side, using the extra pillows to bolster her. Though Gertie was loath to admit it, she generally felt much better after one of Anja's adjustments.

It was then Anja realized she and Andreas would have to take turns sleeping in the room beside her. They worked out a schedule where Anja would take care of Gertie in the mornings and Andreas would relieve her in the afternoons once their son returned home from school. Daniel would then keep Gertie company during the evening rush or until one of them came back to check on her.

A week into their new routine, Anja decided it was time once again to broach the unwanted topic. The sun had just begun to set, and Andreas had gone back to the restaurant to prepare for the dinner shift.

"I realize this is difficult for you," Anja said, replacing the near empty bag of saline solution. "But if I don't say this now, I won't forgive myself."

She could see Gertie's hands begin to tighten, but taking a deep breath, she continued.

"You have to consider your sons' feelings. Whatever happened between you, it's in the past, and it's nothing compared to what you're facing now. I know they would want to know about this, and to be given a chance to speak to you."

Gertie's face was drawn from the day's fatigue, and she had no energy to fight back. Instead, she cast her sunken eyes down.

"You don't understand," she said at last, her voice heavy and sad. "My bloodline is cursed."

Anja pursed her lips.

"Cursed? How?"

"By the sins of my mother's family. My sons can't know. They would be cursed, too."

Anja's forehead furrowed. How could Gertie, who scoffed at the slightest bit of nonsense, now be muttering such superstition?

"I don't understand."

"This death thirst," Gertie said, shuddering. "It must end with me."

Was this the morphine talking?

"There won't be many more opportunities for you to say good-bye," Anja said, impatiently.

Gertie rolled her head to look away from her.

Anja grabbed a clean sheet from the top of the bookcase.

"Maybe you're right. Maybe they don't want to hear from you right this minute, but that doesn't mean they won't feel differently later on. If you don't tell them what's happening to you, how will they find closure? We all deserve that chance, no matter how painful the relationship. They're your sons!"

Gertie turned her head again, weighing out Anja's words in strained silence.

Not knowing what else to say, Anja shook out the sheet.

Only after she had finished the task of rolling her patient back and forth to change out the bedding, did Gertie break her silence.

"I'll think about it," she said in a whisper, as Anja propped her back up against the pillows so she could look up at the purple-streaked sky.

"What's happening to Gertie?" Daniel asked as Anja came down the stairs freshly showered. He had surprised her by making a pot of her late afternoon green tea before she was due to relieve Andreas.

She took a good look at her son and was amazed by just how muscular and tall he had become. At thirteen, his burgeoning maturity was no match for his accelerated growth spurt, and seeing the broad outlines of a man developing, she knew all traces of her little boy would soon vanish. Nonetheless, as he slid into his familiar seat on the worn, corner bench beside her, his eyes revealed a childlike concern that made her realize they had not yet made time to discuss the full gravity of Gertie's situation.

Anja let out a deep sigh.

"You remember me telling you about how I took care of Oma and Opa? Well, Daniel, Gertie doesn't have much time left. All we can do is try and keep her as comfortable as possible, until the time comes."

"I know that," he said, with a hint of his new teenage impatience. "I mean, what will happen to her afterwards?"

"Afterwards?" Anja looked at him confused. She flashed back to the time when he was six years old and had brought home a dying fledgling finch, and how she had had to explain to him what was happening.

"What will happen to her body and then to *her*?" he asked again.

His straight blonde hair, Anja could see, was starting to turn brown.

Anja paused for a moment, cradling her Japanese teacup. A gift from her parents, it was one of the few heirlooms she had brought with her to Caway.

She recalled the times Gertie had babysat Daniel, and how the two of them had formed, from very early on, an almost unspoken understanding. It was only when Gertie would catch sight of Daniel coming home from school that she would allow herself to smile.

"Gertie asked us to have her cremated. You know what that means, don't you?"

"Yes," Daniel said, shifting in his seat. "But where will her ashes go?"

Anja shook her head. "We haven't talked about that yet."

"I mean will she stay here or go to Germany?"

Anja wondered if Gertie had talked to him about this when he kept her company in the evenings.

"It depends. Her sons are in Germany, but she may decide something differently."

"But part of her will always stay here, right? No matter what?"

Anja took a long sip as she tried to fathom the questioning look on her son's face.

"Yes," she said, slowly picking her words. "A part of her will always be here with us, even if her remains are not."

"But if she dies *here*, then she stays *here*. Right?"

He was looking at her as if he was trying to decipher a great riddle.

"I'm not sure what you mean, Daniel."

Anja thought back on the Catholic tradition in which she was raised. Both she and Andreas, who was raised Lutheran, had rejected orthodoxy early on, but she knew that many of Daniel's friends, not to mention his teachers, were well steeped in Evangelical or Catholic practice. She wondered if their influence had touched him in some way.

"Daniel, none of us knows for sure what happens after death. But when we care for someone, when we love them, I do believe we carry them with us in our hearts. And in that way, yes, they are here with us. I know I still feel the presence of my mother and my father, so in a manner of speaking I also brought them here. And I would hope that through me, you can feel the love they would have for you. They're a part of you, too, you know, in your cells, in your DNA. And of course, when I look at you, I can see my father so clearly in your eyes."

Daniel, who had been looking at her intently this whole time, nodded.

"But will I be able to see her? To talk to her?"

"I think you will feel her presence, yes, and you can always talk to her if you want. Don't let anyone tell you otherwise. She may not answer you, of course, but you may hear her in other ways, like the way I hear my parents, especially in moments like this."

Daniel nodded again, but his lips had grown thin.

"Why isn't anyone else helping?" he asked.

Anja let out another heavy sigh.

"People have difficulty extending themselves beyond what they know. In a situation like this? When someone isn't family? It may be they're not prepared to see death up close. Sometimes people are just afraid. That's not to say it hasn't been frustrating. We're part of a small community. And at the same time, everyone else has their work to do, too. That's why we're so grateful to you, Daniel, for your help and understanding."

"But we're the only ones helping her other than that American woman." Anja shrugged.

"Yes. She's a widow, you see, so she knows what it's like."

She and Andreas had hoped for more assistance from their friends and neighbors, the surprise exception being Sandra, the American who lived two kilometers down the road without a car. Most everyone else who had known Gertie over the course of the last eighteen years had kept a conspicuous distance. Friends and acquaintances of theirs would run into them in town and make a point of asking after Gertie, but beyond offering token condolences, they did little else to help dissipate the hardship. Could Anja really fault them, she wondered? Gertie had never been one to extend herself either, so the burden had fallen on them.

Daniel, at least, was more than stepping up to his new responsibilities. He would take the initiative with their guests and for once was doing more to keep things tidy upstairs.

"I don't get it," he shook his head.

"People are complicated, son," Anja said, reaching over to tousle his hair. "What matters most is keeping an open mind, even if that means you sometimes forget to do your homework."

The reminder, at least, brought a sheepish smile back to his face.

"I should probably go and finish," he replied. "I'll see you over there at six?"

"Six it is," Anja said, shaking out one of the last cigarettes from the crumpled pack in front of her. She had just enough time for one more.

Four weeks later Anja was startled awake by the vehement screeching of two macaws in a nearby tree. It took her a moment to realize that the other sound she could hear between squawks was Gertie's wheezing.

Anja threw off the mosquito netting and staggered into Gertie's room. Disoriented, she could not locate the oxygen mask at first, then, almost in a panic, she found it lying on the side table. Anja forced herself to calm down as she placed the mask over Gertie's nose and mouth and then saw in her friend's eyes the primordial fear that the rest of her body had long abandoned.

Another wave of distress washed over Anja.

"Is that better?" she asked.

Gertie's head tilted forward. Recently, her repeated coughing spells had left her almost speechless.

"I have some good news for you," Anja said, hoping to provide Gertie with a little distraction. "I think we've figured out a way for you to see the children's parade."

Gertie blinked and then opened her eyes a bit wider.

Dia de la Independencia had always been Gertie's favorite holiday because she loved seeing the children parading and dancing in their colorful, folkloric costumes.

Anja sat down beside her and reached for hand. In the last two weeks Gertie had allowed her to do this more often.

"I knew that would please you," Anja said. "It's going to take some coordination on our part, but I think we can pull it off."

Anja steeped herself in the hazy morning silence while she waited for Gertie's breathing to stabilize, but when she leaned over to remove the mask, Anja's stomach heaved with a sudden sense of apprehension.

Gertie's small head was sunk deep in the depression of her pillows.

"I know you told me you would think about it," Anja said. "But it's time."

Two weeks earlier Anja had found a phone number for Christian in Berlin.

"I know you're not up for talking," Anja continued, "but I'd like to call him on your behalf."

Gertie said nothing but continued to hold on to Anja's hand, squeezing tight.

"I can call from the restaurant," Anja said, her voice softening even more. "But I'd prefer to do it here. And I promise, no matter what, I'll stay by your side the whole time."

Gertie's gaze was fixed on the ceiling, her head frozen in place as if to keep her thoughts in a little longer. Finally, she lowered her eyes to meet Anja's, and with her fingers, tapped the bed.

"From here then," Anja said.

With a nod, Gertie acquiesced, as her eyes filled with tears.

Anja spent the rest of the morning attending to Gertie. At noon Olga arrived to assess her pain medications, which meant Anja could return to the restaurant for a much-needed break.

She was greeted first by the sight of a drunken Nico, leaning in through the kitchen window, mouthing off in one of his usual outbursts. Nina, meanwhile, sat slumped at the top of the front steps, petting Zelig, Daniel's dog, who lay sprawled out in front of her feet.

"That second half was shit," Nico said, as Anja walked behind Andreas, who was in the kitchen too busy chopping tomatoes to notice she was there.

Andreas shrugged his shoulders.

"One team wins the other loses."

Nico let out a loud guffaw.

"What kind of German are you anyway? The only reason you don't care is because your team won."

Andreas shook his head and smiled as Anja's face turned beet red behind him.

"When are you going to get it through that thick skull of yours that he's Costa Rican now. He's only told you that about a half dozen times."

"Whoa," Nico said, putting up his hands in exaggeration. "Someone woke up on the wrong side of the bed."

Anja narrowed her eyes at him.

"You would, too, if you bothered to care about anyone other than your-self."

"Hey now, cool it," Andreas said, as Anja walked past him in a huff. She was carrying their laptop into the dining room, getting ready to set up her workstation.

"Not German," she heard Nico mumble under his breath. "You don't even know what the hell we're talking about."

Anja turned in her seat to face him.

"Excuse me?"

Seeing the defiance on her face, Nico burst out laughing.

"Andreas, man, your wife is turning tropical. Talk her down before she gives us both a hangover."

"Talk me down?"

Anja rose to her feet again. Her eyes scanned the room as she approached him, but Nina was no longer in sight.

"For your information, Nico, that's not how Andreas and I operate. And you—of all people—should try showing a little more respect. Turning tropical, *mein Gott*. And let me tell you what gives *me* a hangover," she added, poking a finger into his thin chest. "It's you coming in here and taking whatever you want from that fridge without thinking twice about paying for it. Meanwhile we're working our asses off here taking care of Gertie, and you can't be bothered to even make good on your promise!"

Nico rolled his eyes as he staggered away from her.

"Spare me the fucking martyrdom, Anja. You're not the only one having a hard time. We have enough troubles of our own without you piling on with the guilt."

"I beg your pardon?" she said, stomping toward him. "If I'm making things so difficult for you, why the hell do you bother to come around? Apart from drinking us out of house and home, that is?"

"That's enough," Andreas said, wiping his hand and coming out of the kitchen. "Time to cool off."

But Anja had already reached the boiling point.

"Could it be because we're the ones taking care of your daughter?" she asked, her eyes ablaze. "Making sure she eats decent every once in a while?"

"You keep my daughter out of this, you—"

Andreas put his hand on Nico's bony shoulder and guided him out the door.

"For your information," Anja said. "Lena is the only reason I have anything to do with you."

"Don't fucking bother then," Nico said, shrugging off Andreas' hand as he stumbled down the steps. "We don't need your charity, and Lena sure as fuck doesn't need *you*. You think you're some kind of saint?" he added, turning toward Anja, his face convulsing in a mix of pain and confusion. "Let me tell *you* something. There's no saving anyone, Anja. Ever. Life doesn't fucking work like that."

And with that, he wandered off, calling out his wife's name.

"That's it." Anja said, still simmering in her hot-white agitation. "I won't have him here anymore. Do you hear me?"

"Sit down," Andreas said, helping her to take a seat. "Calm down."

Anja leaned over and for a few moments let her head fall into the cradle of her hands.

"You need to go over there," she said finally, tilting her head towards Gertie's house. "She won't be with us that much longer."

Petting Zelig, Nina had wandered back in time to the days she had lost in their old Amsterdam apartment. In those early years of waiting for Nico to come home, it was her dog Wuodan who had stood by her side and kept her secrets safe.

Lena—still a toddler then—was far too young to understand her. But even so, Nina never felt certain. Her daughter had always possessed an uncanny ability to see straight through her. Or so it seemed. Wuodan, on the other hand, who also watched her every move, intuited what she needed without even the slightest hint of admonishment. In fact, much like the horses she had cared for in her youth, Wuodan would exude a sense of quiet calm that would allow her to forget her own role in the polluted past. Only with Wuodan had she been able to see past that version of herself to something different.

But when the fireworks went off in the restaurant behind her—No, she could not sit there a moment longer. Anja and Nico's fighting reminded her too much of her parents.

Instead, she had gotten up, and with Zelig following on her heels had wandered off toward *Playa Grande.*

On the way she noticed that the gate to Gertie's house was open. She stopped to close it but was pulled inside by a need to see the rainbow eucalyptus in the garden, the one that had so captivated her the only time she had gone to visit.

Not that she had said much to Gertie then. The increased tension between Nico and Anja had caused her to feel uncomfortable in Anja's presence. She had withdrawn into herself and gone back to only engaging when it was necessary. In other words, not often.

As a result, Nina was spending even more time holed up with Nico inside their cottage, drinking more with him just to pass the time. They had lapsed into their old patterns, but unlike the past, he no longer showed an interest in helping her.

Approaching the prismatic Eucalyptus, she placed her hand on the vibrant, smooth bark until she had worked up the nerve to go inside.

The front door swung open with little effort.

As Nina peered in, she could see the primly dressed nurse, Olga, sitting at the kitchen table at the other end of the house about to eat her lunch.

"*Buenas tardes,*" she said, standing up. "Can I help you?"

"I came to see Gertie," Nina said, looking hesitant.

Olga waved her in with an enthusiastic smile.

"Please, come in. *Doña* Gertie is resting but still awake."

"Can I go up on my own?" Nina asked.

"Of course! I was just sitting down to eat, so perfect timing. It will give me a chance to spend some time in the garden, if you don't mind, and get some fresh air."

"Not at all," Nina said, and waited for the nurse to take her leave.

Nina's pulse began to quicken as she placed her hand on the stair railing. She could smell the warm, humid air above her laden with a sick, sweet scent.

Her stomach tightened, but she forced herself to go up.

At the top of the landing, she tiptoed toward the doorway.

Nina was shocked to see what little remained of Gertie, who was propped up like a thin, rag doll staring out toward the garden.

"Gertie?" she said, her voice hoarse and barely audible.

Slowly and with difficulty, Gertie turned to face her.

Nina felt startled at first. From a distance, Gertie's face looked ashen and distorted. As she approached the bedside, however, she could see it was the nasal cannula that had made her features look alien.

"Come closer," Gertie said, each syllable an effort.

"I'm sorry," Nina said, flustered. "I shouldn't be bothering you like this."

"Don't be. Please. Sit."

Nina lowered herself onto the bed to face Gertie whose eyes immediately probed her own with an intensity that belied her otherwise visible weakness.

"I'm sorry I haven't come by sooner."

"It's ok. I know it's not easy."

Nina's eyes darted around the room.

There were stacks of linens on a nearby table and two oxygen tanks stored not too far from the bed. The venting concentrator was right beside her as well as the IV stand with its dripping fluid going ceaselessly into Gertie's arm.

"There's something I want to tell you. Something I've been meaning to say for a long time but couldn't."

Gertie nodded in encouragement as Nina let out a heavy sigh.

"I have this problem, you see," Nina said, glancing down at her weathered palms. "And I know you know about it because I can see it in your eyes, in the way you look at me."

After a pause, Nina continued.

"I was scared of you because of it. I didn't want to be marked in that way. And it really bothered me that you could see because most people try *not* to see it. They prefer to just ignore what's in front of them because they don't want to get involved. They know something's wrong, but they know better than to ask. Because when they do find out it just makes them angry. As if you're trying to hurt them by telling them the truth."

Nina shook her head as if to loosen the choked-up words.

"Because when they know the truth all they can see is the brokenness. And no matter how much time goes by, you can still see it in their eyes. That distance. That wishing that you didn't come from such a fucked-up place, but that you do anyway. You've burdened them with the knowing, and they can never see you the same way again. Even if part of them still wants to."

Gertie reached out for Nina's hand.

Exhausted by the weight of her admission, Nina's shoulders slumped forward and she began to sob.

"The funny thing is when I did tell Nico, when I didn't have a choice, I still lied. I still didn't tell him everything."

"It's ok, Nina," Gertie whispered, squeezing her hand. "It's ok."

For a while they sat in silence as the venting oxygen marked time with a mechanical sigh.

When Nina looked up again and wiped her cheeks, Gertie pointed toward the small bookshelf on the opposite wall.

"The blue box," she said, her voice soft. "On the bottom."

Nina got up to retrieve the small, rectangular case.

As Nina carried it back toward her, Gertie gestured for her to open it.

Inside lay an engraved, jade-handled dagger encased in a worn leather sheath.

Gertie opened her mouth to say something and then began to cough.

Nina looked down at the knife and then at Gertie.

"It's for you," Gertie said, when she recovered.

"But why? I don't understand."

"For protection. Even if you never have to use it, you'll know it's there, and that's all that matters."

"Thank you," Nina whispered. "Thank you for seeing me."

24

Caway - September 2012

Anja returned to Gertie's that afternoon worn out from her fight with Nico and with no desire to call Gertie's son. To buy some time, she made herself a pot of tea in the kitchen and then went upstairs to check on Gertie. She found her propped up on her bed with her eyes closed. Her breathing, assisted by the concentrator, was slow but steady. There was no sense in disturbing her now. Gertie would need all her strength for the call.

Anja glanced around one last time and seeing that the IV was still in order, she went downstairs. As she poured the tea, Anja noticed the watercolor supplies she had brought over weeks earlier and that had collected dust on the kitchen counter.

Anja had bought the high-quality sketchpad on a family trip to Panama City but had never gotten around to using it. She sipped her tea and flipped past the first few pages filled with Daniel's grade school doodling until she landed on an empty page. Guided by instinct, she went to the sink to fill a shallow bowl with water, and then picked up the colors and brushes and brought them to the dining table.

Outside, the afternoon rains had begun to pour. Dampened by the rustling sound of the trees, she could hear the pitter patter playing against the metal roof as she opened the case of pigments. She selected the larger of two round

332

brushes and immersed the sable hairs into the water until the head was fully saturated. Hovering over the cobalt blue square, she touched the tip to the compacted powder, releasing the liquid and allowing the cake to dissolve into its more pliant form.

She circled the brush within the absorbing puddle and repeated the process until the tincture reached her preferred saturation. Satisfied, she molded the tip of the brush carefully then proceeded to sculpt out her first line on paper.

Soon, Anja fell into a meditative state where only the undulating motion of her hand existed. Her thoughts and worries disappeared as her attuned senses brought to light a mix of sinewy blues and reds with each deliberate stroke. Before long, a complex blend of contours emerged bleeding in and out of one another on the cold pressed paper.

The time passed without notice, and only when the painting had reached its full expression did Anja set aside her brush.

She looked up at the clock in the kitchen.

It was a little after ten at night in Berlin.

Weighed down once more by a sense of duty, Anja climbed the creaking stairs back up to Gertie's room, and found her sitting quietly, staring out the window at the gently swaying tree branches. Billowing clouds lined by the sun's fading beams were now giving way to a deep, blue vault of sky.

"Did you manage to get some rest?"

Gertie turned to meet her eyes and tilted her chin.

"Good," Anja said, walking over to the bookcase. Admiring the delicate curves of Gertie's porcelain blue vase, she made a note to herself to bring some fresh flowers up.

"I brought my phone with me," Anja said.

Gertie cast her eyes down.

Looking at her pale, gaunt face, Anja reminded herself that there would be no better time. Still, a wave of remorse overtook her, as if she were Gertie's unwilling prison guard.

Anja dug into her skirt pocket and took out the phone and a small scrap of paper. She turned to punch in the numbers, her eyes trained on Andreas' hard-to-read scrawl. A long silence followed before she heard the familiar electronic pulse of an open, German connection. She held her breath and waited.

"Witzmann," said the resonant voice on the other end.

"Is this Christian?"

"Yes. Who's calling?"

"This is Anja Reinhold," she said, trying not to rush her words. "My husband is Andreas Freyer, a good friend of your mother here in Caway who I believe you met."

"I see," he said.

Anja could not help but detect a small hint of suspicion in his voice.

"I'm calling because your mother is very ill."

Anja paused, trying not to rush her words.

"I'm afraid she has terminal cancer, and it's gotten difficult now for her to speak."

A long silence followed.

"I see," he repeated, this time with a slight quiver in his voice.

"I know this must be hard for you to hear," Anja continued, interjecting her voice into his silence. "And I'm very sorry to have to tell you this over the phone."

"Does she know you're calling me, my mother?"

The pitch of his voice was higher now.

"Yes," Anja said. "She's right here next to me."

"And she wanted this? For you to call?"

"Yes," Anja replied.

Christian could feel his ears start to ring. He was remembering the woman's name now, a vague recollection from one of Gertie's old letters, the last of which he had left sitting in his desk drawer, unopened.

"And what does she want?" he asked, sounding bewildered.

"I'm afraid there's not much time left."

"But does she want me to go there? What is she expecting from me?"

"I think, for now, it's better if you just talk to her."

"Are you telling me she's dying?" he asked. "Right now?"

"It's hard to say exactly, but yes. Very soon."

There was no easy way to put it, and it was ridiculous to try and shield him from the inevitable.

"You're telling me she can't answer? What am I supposed to say to her?"

"It would just be nice if she could hear your voice," Anja said. "I can put the phone up to her ear. If she responds, I can repeat it for you."

"This is all happening too fast. Just a moment, please."

Christian stumbled back from where he was standing in the kitchen and sat down on a step stool.

For a few agonizing seconds Anja feared he would hang up the phone.

"Ok," he said, after another deep breath.

Gertie was looking over at Anja expectantly now, a thread of worry knit across her brow.

"Ok, I'm going to put you on now," Anja said.

Christian could hear the sound of creaking floorboards. He tried to picture his mother in her room, but all he could imagine was an empty bed, the one she never slept in.

His breath grew short and shallow as he realized she was waiting for him to speak.

"*Hallo Mutti*," he said, in the only way he could remember.

He paused and waited, finding it difficult to believe she could not answer. But then he heard her rasping voice straining to say his name.

"Anja tells me it's difficult for you to talk," he said, wiping the tears from his cheeks. "So that leaves me to carry on this conversation. Some things don't change now, do they?" he added with an anguished laugh.

"You left without any warning before, and well, I guess it's happening again."

He paused for a moment, the bitter resonance in his voice echoing.

"It hurts to hear you suffering, *Mutti*. And you must know this comes as a complete shock. I—"

Another convulsion interrupted his thoughts, his mind seized by raw emotion.

"I should tell you about Udo Jörgen," he said at last, and cleared his throat.

"He's at Max Planck in Tübingen now, working on intelligent systems design. You know, the stuff he was always going on about. He's got no girlfriend to speak of, but he's married to his work. He's a lot like you in that way, but it seems to make him happy. He's lousy about keeping in touch, but we do see him around Christmas when he comes to Berlin.

"And I have other big news," he said, as he looked down the long hall of his *Altbau* apartment at the closed bedroom door on the far end. "You're going to be a grandmother."

He could hear a gasp on the line and Anja repeating his words in a loud whisper.

"Yes," he said, smiling despite his sorrow. "My girlfriend, Esma, she's at 39 weeks now, so the baby is due to arrive very soon. We don't know if it's a boy or girl. Esma wants to keep it a surprise, but of course, we're delighted. Even Klaus is excited for us. For a while we weren't sure if—"

His voice trailed off as his mind wandered.

"I'm afraid I really can't make it to Caway now," he said. "I hope you can understand that."

On the other end he could only hear her labored breath.

"Esma needs me here, and there's no one else to help out."

He tried to picture Gertie as he had last seen her on the veranda, looking up at a dark sky, and smoking. Always smoking.

"Damn it, *Mutti*. I wish I knew what else to say, but I just can't wrap my head around it."

He began to sob out loud, no longer caring if she could hear him.

"It wasn't supposed to be like this, it really wasn't. You said you had your reasons, but you never told us why. And after all this time—

"I suppose it doesn't matter. But I don't understand *why* it had to happen. Not like this. And what I'm saying now, it's coming out wrong, but— I've missed you. I have. Even if I didn't want to admit it."

He stopped to listen once more to her arduous breathing. It sounded a bit louder to him somehow. Had he hurt her with what he had said, he wondered? He could not even begin to imagine what she was thinking. And wasn't that the problem all along? He had never had a clue.

"I hope you know I've always loved you," he said, though the words came out somewhat defiant. "Udo does, too, even if he is far too stubborn to say it. You know he's always been far more sensitive than he likes to let on."

There was a buzzing of static on the line now.

"Christian, the connection is breaking," he could hear Anja say.

"I'll let Udo and Klaus know," he said, feeling suddenly helpless. "Can I give them your number? It's the only one I have."

"Yes, of course," Anja said. "But please, she wants to say something."

There was another long pause.

"*Ich hab' dich lieb,*" Christian heard her say, the words catching in her throat.

"*Ich dich, auch, Mutti*" he replied. "*Ich dich auch.*"

An early morning shower had given way to a welcome breeze when the children's Independence Day Parade, accompanied by three musicians, wound its way into Gertie's Garden. Upon approaching the two-storied house, the mostly adolescent troupe was quick to arrange itself into four distinct rows, all within easy view of Gertie's propped up perch on the veranda above. With circular skirts twirling and sashes swaying, they began to dance to the beat of a traditional *campesino* song, the girls with their broad-striped skirts moving in undulating waves as the boys weaved through and around them, lassoing their bandanas.

For fifteen minutes they danced for the small audience of friends and family who had tagged along to cheer them on. Afterwards, Daniel and Andreas provided them with cold refreshments, while Anja remained stationed next to Gertie, watching the scene from above with pride.

"Can you see the banner?" Anja asked, pointing to two students holding up a painted cloth that read, *¡Viva siempre la paz!*

Gertie, misty-eyed, but unable to speak, nodded.

Anja waved her arms to get the crowd's attention.

"*Hola, amigos!* We want to thank you for bringing *Día de la Independencia* here with you today. Sixteen years ago, Gertie made Costa Rica her home, and watching you dance and celebrate is a very special honor for her. She wishes you all *pura vida*, and may you always live in peace."

"*Pura vida!*" the crowd replied, smiling and waving at them.

"*Vaya siempre con Dios, Doña Gertie,*" a woman's voice rang out above the rest before the parade continued on its way into town.

Gertie's eyes were closed when Anja and Andreas carried her back into her room. She was worn out from the excitement, but the contented look on her face more than justified the effort. Anja gave her hand a gentle squeeze and left her to rest.

At dawn the following morning Andreas returned to Quixote's, his face drawn in sadness. Seeing him from the kitchen, Anja put the kettle down and without saying a word, embraced him. They held one another on the threshold, silently weeping into each other's arms.

"What's the matter?" Daniel said, as he came down the stairs still rubbing sleep from his eyes.

Stepping apart, Anja and Andreas hesitated.

"She's dead, isn't she?" Daniel said, his voice leaden.

Anja nodded, wiping her cheeks.

"When did it happen?" Daniel asked, looking directly at Andreas. "Were you with her?"

"It happened while she slept," Andreas said, looking at his son with concern.

"But you were with her, right?"

Daniel's eyes were ablaze now, and without warning, his chest began to heave.

"Tell me you were there, that you didn't leave her to die alone!"

Andreas nodded.

Though Daniel was already as tall as him, Andreas embraced him as he had when he was a small child and a tantrum would overtake him. Uncontrollably, Daniel cried in his father's arms as Anja joined them, draping her arms around them until the force of Daniel's grief softened.

"She's gone, son. She isn't suffering anymore."

When they finally let go of one another, Anja could not help but think of Udo Jörgen and Christian. Would they, too, find solace in each other's arms?

Picking up her cell phone she stepped out into the garden, the fresh dew flickering cold against her feet. She took a deep breath and dialed Christian's number.

Gertie's body was cremated in Limón, her remains brought back to Caway a week later. She had rejected the idea of a formal funeral and interment. Instead, she had asked Daniel to scatter her ashes two kilometers away at Horn Creek.

On the bright Sunday morning that followed, a small group gathered at Quixote's that included Sandra, Antonio and Javier. The van de Steeg's had kept their distance since Nico's fight with Anja, and Marienne, next door, had claimed she could not leave her guests.

Around the *Stammtisch,* they shared a cup of Anja's French-pressed coffee, while Daniel sat on the front steps, tossing a blue and green onionskin marble between his hands.

When it was time to go, Anja handed him Gertie's corked, cerulean vase which had been resting at her usual spot at the end of the table.

Holding it close to his chest, Daniel walked down the steps.

The adults followed as he led them down the road toward *Playa Grande.* At the sandy path marking the entrance, he turned right. The sun was still low enough in the sky to make the long walk along the untamed beach a comfortable one.

It was a walk Daniel had made with Gertie countless times, the salty breeze a refreshing accompaniment. He could remember holding her hand as a young boy as they climbed up the steep dunes, having had their fill of splashing in the shallow tidal pools or building fortresses in the dark sand.

She had always made a point of walking all the way to Horn Creek before turning inland and following the shady path back to their home. It was part of her daily perambulation, begun usually before sunrise, but she would make an exception when Daniel asked to tag along.

She had doted on him during those walks, their special friendship a guarded secret. She loathed showing affection around others, something he appreciated having been born into a public space. On those walks she had become his one, true confidante, the person he trusted above all others. Gertie was older than his parents, but she had treated him much differently, had valued his opinions in a way they could not since they were far too busy, most times, conducting business in the middle of their home.

When they reached the wide mouth of Horn Creek, its dark, serpentine form flowing ceaselessly into the sea, Daniel found it difficult to reconcile what he was feeling. Cancer had taken one set of grandparents before he was born, and his only remaining grandmother lived more than an ocean away. Other than his parents, Gertie was the only person who had known him since he was young, and now she, too, had succumbed to cancer.

"Why do you have to do that?" he had asked his parents more than once though he knew it was pointless to try and make them stop. Their incessant smoking was one of the few pleasures in a life otherwise filled with endless work and not much left to show for it. It was one of the few times that Gertie, too, had failed to give him an adequate answer. Still, he knew they loved Caway just as fiercely as Gertie had, and as he did, too. Despite their financial difficulties, they told him they were happier here than with the life they had left behind.

He had asked Gertie once why she had left Germany, and she had flashed him a look of such hurt and betrayal that he had felt the need to apologize.

"I can't talk about the reasons why," she had told him. "But I did it to save myself and protect my sons. They can't see it that way and neither would anyone else. Some things are just too difficult to fathom, especially when you can't find the right words to explain them. But Daniel, sometimes we have to make decisions that are hard to live with because not making them will mean we won't have any life at all. Like I said, I can't explain without it causing more harm."

A cold prickling had run down his spine, and a part of him had understood what she meant without wanting to, without the need to hear it said out loud.

It was in this moment that Gertie had shown him how to be strong in a way that he knew mattered. People had found her strange and unnerving, but in her own, maddening way, she was just being honest. And it was through her eyes that Daniel had seen what the weight of a burdened past could do to a person.

Daniel led the group further upstream where a fallen log stretched across the water and where a tall, thick canopy of trees vaulted above them like an outdoor cathedral.

"This was Gertie's favorite place," Daniel said, as the others lined up beside him near the water's edge. Handing the vase to Anja for a moment, Daniel climbed up onto the bleached-out trunk. On the opposite shore a large iguana was climbing up a palm tree, a sunbeam stretching wide across its back. Daniel scanned the canopy above him in search of Gertie's three-toed sloth, but without luck. Then he turned back to Anja so she could hand him the urn.

Deftly, he swung himself up to a standing position and picked his way along the trunk's smooth edge one step at a time until he reached the midway point above the creek.

"Does anyone have anything to say before we let her go?" he asked.

Andreas cupped his hands. *"Du bist uns ewig lieb, Gertie,"* he called out, until the echo of his voice was finally silenced. It was then that Anja gave Daniel the solemn nod to carry on.

He looked out at his father and mother for a moment, surrounded by their neighbors and friends. Anja was holding onto Andreas' hand.

Further downstream he could see Nina leading a white mare up toward them. Catching Daniel's eye, she stopped short. She didn't want the others to know, Daniel sensed, so taking a deep breath, he whispered his own good-bye.

"I'm going to miss you," he said, as he uncorked the vase. "And I won't ever forget you. I promise."

Only then did he tip out the contents of the blue vase.

The air was still for a moment as the ashes burst out like a grey, white cloud suspended above the water. What the wind did not scatter the stream's current absorbed, carrying what remained of Gertie out to sea.

25

Caway - Two Years Later - 2014

Anja stood slumped over the open hood of her Nissan station wagon, her salt-and-pepper curls sticking to her cheeks and forehead.

They had purchased the used car two months earlier, and now, for the third time in a week, it had stalled. But this time, when she had turned the key there was only a single click of the ignition, followed by the bright console of lights fading to grey against the afternoon sun. The battery was dead.

"This can't be happening," she said out loud to no one in particular.

Anja had errands to run. They were low on their basic supplies for the restaurant and the electric bill needed to be paid before the new guests arrived in the late afternoon.

To make matters worse, Anja knew they would have to rely on a mechanic in Limón. Andreas had handled the repairs of their previous car himself, but he could do nothing with these electronic components that appeared impregnably sealed.

In that moment, Lena sauntered past wearing a black mesh top and a pair of shorts that revealed her long and unmarred, 15-year-old legs.

"Hello, Lena," Anja called out, relieved to see her.

Lena turned to look over her shoulder before exposing the laughing skull embossed on the front of her shirt. Her eyes were a piercing blue like her mother's, set against a bronzed face with her long, chestnut hair pulled back into a luxurious, high ponytail.

She stared at Anja with a blank expression for a moment before continuing on her way.

Anja stood beside her broken down vehicle, her lower jaw sagging in astonishment.

What had gotten into Lena? Why hadn't she offered to help?

Anja slammed the hood of the car shut.

"Verdammt noch mal!"

She had no time for this. One way or another, she had to get into town before the whole day turned into a shambles.

She grabbed her shopping bag, and then began to walk, thankful at least that Lena was already too far ahead to see in the distance.

"What are we going to do about that useless station wagon?" Anja said, looking across the table at Andreas that night. They were smoking their last cigarette before heading up to bed, exhausted. "We'll be lucky to break even this month."

Andreas took a sip from his Pilsen.

"Maybe we trade it in for something older? Something I can fix, like my Vanagon?"

Anja shook her head in exasperation.

"The Westfalia you had in Germany four decades ago? What are you going to do? Become a full-time mechanic in your 60s? You're barely keeping up as it is. I say we get our money back."

Andreas looked at her sideways.

"Get our money back? Have you been smokin' the ganja?"

At this they both laughed to keep from crying.

"I should be the one asking *you* that question," Anja said, once she had recovered. "We need to pull it together, old man. Half the time I don't know where you are anymore, and I need you *here*," she added, tapping the table with her index finger. "Daniel needs you."

Andreas leaned forward in his seat to stub out his cigarette.

"Who says I'm going anywhere? It's you who can't relax and settle down. You're more irritable lately, and it's becoming a real drag."

Andreas gathered up the empty beer bottles and pushed himself up to standing.

"I'm irritable because of this damn situation with Lena," Anja said, as she finished the last of her wine. "You know I saw her today when the car broke down, and did she bother to even say hello? After all we've done for her, the insolent girl? I'm going to have to say something to Nico, and you know how much I can't stand that man."

"You shouldn't take it personally," Andreas said from the kitchen, where he was putting the empty bottles into one of the brewery's return crates. "She can't help the situation she's in with those two. Just let it go."

"How can you say that?" Anja said. "After all the effort we've put into her upbringing, trying to salvage something for her?"

"Maybe you should convince the school board to let her continue," he said, coming back into the dining room so they could place the metal gate across the kitchen window and lock up for the night.

"You know that's not possible. I extended her enrollment for as long as I could, but with her grades dropping like they have, I can't make a case for scholarship. We can barely keep our own son enrolled, let alone chip in to help her."

Anja grunted as she and Andreas lifted the yellow metal barrier into place.

"You're the school administrator, not me," Andreas said, locking the hinges. "I'm just saying it's harsh not to let her finish out the term. Give Nico and Nina some time to get the money together for next year."

"With him leaving now to go back to The Netherlands to take care of his grandmother? You know damn well where that relationship is headed. He won't be back."

Andreas shook his head.

"So why bother talking to him?"

"Because this is about Lena, not them."

"All I'm trying to say is what good will it do?"

They went back into the kitchen and locked the door so they could go upstairs.

"They may have given up on their daughter's education," Anja said, turning off the downstairs lights. But I sure as hell haven't. Not yet anyway. I'll just have to talk to her alone."

Andreas said nothing as she followed him wearily up the stairs. The morning would be upon them sooner than they wished.

Three days later Anja ran into Lena again on her way to a board meeting at the school, the road even dustier than before.

"Do you have a moment, Lena?" Anja called out to her before she turned onto the main road.

Dressed in pink athletic shorts and a cropped, white t-shirt with the word ZEF written across it, Lena hesitated before flashing Anja a look of annoyed exasperation.

Anja walked toward her with a hurried step, while Lena stood, her narrow hips cocked to one side and her arms crossed in defiance.

"I can see you're upset with me," Anja said, standing in front of her. "But instead of playing these games, why don't we just talk about what's the matter. Ok?"

Lena sneered.

"What makes you think I have anything to say to you?"

"I just want to understand why you're so angry with me all of a sudden."

Lena stared back at her with narrowed eyes. The last time they had been on good terms was two months ago, when Lena and Daniel had been sitting behind her laptop making fun of something a schoolmate of theirs had posted on his Facebook page.

"Because you're the reason I'm going to school in fucking Bribri now."

Anja sighed.

"Is that what Nico told you?"

"No," Lena said, jerking her head back.

"You know I did everything I could to convince the board to reconsider, but your parents are almost a year behind with the tuition payments. The fact your grades were falling didn't help matters."

Anja paused, waiting for a response, but Lena just rolled her eyes and shifted her hips.

"Now listen," Anja said. "If you want to work with me after school to improve your grades, we could see about having you reapply for the following term."

"What would be the point?" Lena said, her tone turning vicious. "My Nana isn't sending us the money. Half the time she doesn't even remember who we are anymore. And isn't that all you really care about? Making sure your precious school gets all its money?"

Now it was Anja's turn to feel outraged.

"That's a ridiculous accusation. You know damn well I couldn't care less about money. What I'm offering you is a way to become eligible for a scholarship. But you'll have to earn it, Lena. We both know how clever you are, but you have to apply yourself. Then we can see about fixing this."

"Yeah, well, what you can't seem to get is that I don't want your lousy help!"

Anja could see by the fire in Lena's eyes, so reminiscent of Nico's own, that it was pointless to continue.

"Fine," Anja said, no longer bothering to mask her frustration. "If you change your mind, you know where to find me."

"Bitch," Lena muttered before taking a crushed cigarette out of her front pocket. She took a long drag as she lit up with her mother's lighter, watching Anja as she turned right in the direction of the school. Only when she had lost sight of her did Lena start walking toward town again.

Walking past Black Beach she spotted Daniel on the municipal soccer field, scrimmaging with some of the boys from school. Catching his eye, she gestured for him to come over.

After a short exchange with his teammates, he walked across the grassy field toward her, taking his time.

"What's going on?" he asked coolly, before looking over his shoulder.

"I just saw your mom," Lena said. "How do you put up with her shit?"

"Is that why you called me over?" he asked, his pimpled brow furrowed. Rivulets of sweat were running down the sides of his forehead, his t-shirt drenched.

She had known Daniel for as long as she could remember and had once considered him a close friend. They had even kissed a few times.

"She's always putting her nose where it doesn't fucking belong," Lena said, taking a last, dramatic drag from the stub of her cigarette. "I mean, you must hate that, right? Are you even allowed to do anything without her knowing?"

Daniel looked at her for a long second.

"I don't know what you're talking about."

"Oh, you know what I'm talking about."

She lowered her voice and looked into his eyes with exaggerated concern. "I mean, how are you ever going to get around to, you know, doing it?"

The blood drained from his face as she burst into laughter.

"Fuck you," Daniel said, giving her the finger before walking away.

"Only in your wildest dreams," she replied. "I don't fuck mama's boys."

"Oh, yeah?" Daniel said, spinning back around to face her, his cheeks flushed with fury. "But you'll fuck everything else, won't you?"

She looked into his eyes, long and hard.

"You're as pathetic as your lying friends over there, you know that? And you can say all the lousy things you want, but I'll be the one who finally gets the hell out of this town. You'll see."

"Motion carried, and with that we'll adjourn. When we reconvene in May, Ms. Reinhold will present a review of our prioritized projects against next year's budget proposal."

The board meeting had exhausted Anja. Though she had stepped down as chairwoman the year before, she found her new role as treasurer equally arduous. There just was not enough money to do all that was needed, and it was difficult to convince good teachers to stay for long in such a small and remote village even if they did offer a competitive salary.

It was the ex-pat parents, of course, who still expected the impossible from them while at the same time making excuses for why they could not pay their children's tuition on time. It was enough to make Anja want to tear her hair out.

She had managed to retain the core of her idealism over the years, doggedly advocating for the best in education and as much equitable access as they could provide, and at the end of each term, Anja still felt a jolt of pride knowing that they had, against so many odds, succeeded in bringing these children at least one step closer to graduation. Nonetheless, she knew that the demands of such a thankless task had left an indelible mark on her that cut deeper into her morale as each year passed.

Anja could feel the weight of her responsibility as she walked down the dry, cracked road leading away from the school compound, made up of the single-room, rectangular buildings they had managed to stitch together over the years like a quilt. With each labored step an invisible force pressed down on her, the guilt of so much work still left undone. For a moment she considered going home to rest for a while, but then remembered they needed coffee for their guests in the morning.

She forced herself to turn right at the crossroads, feeling resentful that their car was still in Limón undergoing repairs. It took her a good half hour to trudge the one and a half mile stretch into town, but as she approached the outskirts, instead of turning right on the Main Road, she continued straight around the headland and toward the entrance of the National Park.

Anja could not remember the last time she had visited. Had it been for Hyacinth's birthday party? She wasn't sure. She and Andreas preferred going to *Playa Grande* with its magnificent, solitary coastline that most tourists found "too wild". In contrast, the white sand beaches of the National Park were almost always dotted with bikini-clad visitors. The turquoise clear water set against the picturesque curvature of the cove leading out to Caway Point was as close as one could get to the images that lured people here in the first place.

Approaching the entrance, Anja caught the eye of the Bribri ranger, his black hair pulled back and his green uniform lending his otherwise youthful face an air of solemn authority. Anja pulled out her pocketbook.

"*Ish a'sh ke'ne*," she said in Bribri, before paying the nominal fee and signing her name in the registry. The young man returned her smile and nodded his head.

"I won't be long," she added, "just a short walk."

"Please," he said, waving her inside. "Take your time."

Anja walked along the path winding its way through the canopy but still within easy view of the incoming tide. She was struck by just how much the shoreline had receded in the past few years. She remembered her first visit seventeen years earlier, and how the white sand had stretched out to meet the water, leaving an ample buffer between the ocean and rain forest. Now, the waves were almost crashing into the trees.

Straying off the path and toward the water, Anja slipped off her flip-flops and waded in, leaving her empty shopping bag on top of the steep dune. Within moments her feet stumbled upon a submerged sandbar giving way to a sudden drop off. Instead of venturing further, she stood, watching and swaying as the breakers continued to batter what little remained of the berm. She wondered how much longer it could hold before the saltwater overwhelmed the embankment completely. A freshwater tributary lay just beyond the edge of the coastal forest. Once breached, it would prove disastrous for the microclimate that had established itself in this narrow swath, one of the only places where endangered Hawksbill turtles still ventured to lay their eggs. Each year volunteers intervened as desperate midwives to ensure that at least some of the hatchlings survived, their mothers working off the instinctual assumption that having laid their eggs, they had ensured their obligation to a successor generation.

We humans aren't much different, Anja thought to herself.

We assume with birth that the rest will follow. That we will strike it big, or at least hit the mark of continuing progress, assuming we even know what that word means. Education was a crucial start, but then what? Human beings clearly did not lack for intelligence, yet they seemed incapable of setting aside avarice in order to sustain the planet, not to mention the many life forms upon which they all depended.

Yet despite seeing the obvious signs of environmental degradation, Anja could not help but feel a sense of soothing tranquility as the waves rocked her back and forth.

She stepped out of her saltwater soak and wandered back into the green, shaded forest, where she could hear the piercing bird calls and the occasional rustling of falling leaves. A small brown lizard darted across her path, recognizable for just an instant before being swallowed up by its surroundings in camouflage.

Anja breathed in the briny air. She knew books were only good up to a certain point.

She allowed herself to imagine someday disappearing along with this beloved coastline. It would be up to her son and the subsequent generations to carry its collective memory forward, for this beautiful and wild place would always be his, embedded deep in the encoding of his DNA.

Forty-five minutes later, Anja had finished up her shopping at the Chinese grocer and had picked up a cold soda for the long walk back. It was a hot and arid day, but soon the rainy season would be upon them. Although Anja preferred the drier months, she looked forward to the change of season. Despite the perpetual dampness that came with it, the afternoon downpours had a way of not only marking time but also cleaning away the layers of accumulated debris, and this dry season had felt particularly grimy, the dust and sand penetrating into every pore and cranny.

A quarter of a mile out of town, Anja was forced to the side of the road by a cream-colored sedan, a new one by the look of it. It sped past only to stop abruptly, leaving a cloud of choking grit in its wake.

"Damn tourist," Anja mumbled to herself.

The car continued to idle as Anja walked past. Then a man with well-trimmed silver hair rolled down his window.

"Arcadia Lodge?" the man said, not bothering with any of the polite preliminaries. By his accent Anja could tell he was North American.

"Pardon?" she asked, leaning down toward the open window. A blast of arctic air hit her face. She could see a well-dressed woman sitting beside him, her face glued to the sleek tablet that was resting on her lap.

"I'm looking for the Arcadia Lodge," the man said, now talking into his iPhone. He looked up at her vexed. "According to the GPS it should be right here."

"The Arcadia." Anja paused to collect herself. "That's the new hotel up the road. If you just go past the next intersection, it should be on the left."

"Thanks," the man said, looking down at his phone in doubt. "The signs here haven't been clear."

"That's the charm of the Caribbean," Anja said, forcing herself to reflect back a tolerant smile. Her gesture seemed to perplex the man even more.

"If you say so," he said, as he began to close the car's window.

"Enjoy your stay," Anja added.

As the glass sealed shut, Anja could see the woman turn toward him. They were once again within the cool confines of their luxury conveyance, Anja's services no longer needed.

Anja arrived at Quixote's bone-weary only to find Andreas sitting alone with a bottle of rum. He had his head cupped in one hand and held an almost empty glass in the other. No one else was in the dining room, though the sun was about to set.

"My God, don't you think it's a bit early for that?" Anja said, more alarmed by Andreas' haggard appearance. "We'll have customers coming in soon."

"Not tonight," he said. "We're closed."

"Closed?"

Anja looked at him as if he had lost his mind.

"You know we can't afford that. Not now."

"Sit down," he said, motioning with fatigue.

"What's going on?" she said, sinking into the seat beside him. "You're scaring me."

Andreas poured another two fingers into his glass.

"You haven't heard yet, have you?"

"What?" she asked, taking the glass from his hand. She took a sniff and, overpowering her senses, drank. The sweetness burned all the way down her throat.

"The Maritime law," Andreas said, shaking his head with disbelief. "They just passed a regulation on 'existing construction in the restricted zone'. It says municipalities will charge concession fees to anyone within 200 meters, starting at 100,000 *colones* a month. That is, if they allow us to stay and don't demand a demolition."

Andreas sunk his head again and stared vacantly into the wood grain in front of him.

"I worked all my life to buy this land and build this place," he said, as he lifted his large and calloused hands. "Now they say we have to pay them to stay. On my land?"

Looking at Anja again, his hands fell limp.

"How can we afford it?"

Anja's jaw hung open as she stared straight ahead trying to process what her husband was saying. She was certain that after the passing of the 2012 moratorium the central government had realized the necessity of grandfathering in long-term residents, some of whom had been living on their coastal property for decades, the land rights passed down from one generation to the next.

"They can't do this," she said, with an air of finality. "The people won't stand for it."

Just a few months earlier a grassroots protest had ended violently with the police using teargas to break up the rally.

"I don't know. The municipality has no money and charging concession will make sure they do."

"Not if they run everyone we know out of business," Anja countered.

"But that's it. Now they have these big money investors so it won't matter about us little people. No more sleepy Caway, Anja. You know how greed works its magic."

Anja looked at him in disbelief.

"Where's your fighting spirit, old man? We can't give up that easy. You never have before. And if I couldn't change you after all these years—and God knows I tried—why this?"

A smile started to play on his lips in recollection.

"I'm a lover, not a fighter," he said. "I'm too old now for these games they play."

"Don't you give me any of that hippie nonsense," Anja said, pushing the bottle of rum aside. "What about Daniel? This place is his home, remember? And his only inheritance. We can't let them take that away."

"Daniel will make his own way when he finishes school. Just like we did. The times change, Anja, and who says he'll want to stay here? He can always go to Germany if he likes. In that way he's already a rich man."

Anja sighed and for a moment said nothing.

"He should have a choice either way. But if not for Daniel, then what about us? You may see yourself as an old man," she said, narrowing her eyes at him playfully. "But I'm still young enough."

Andreas chuckled.

"I still have that fire in me, and hell knows no fury like a menopausal woman."

"You don't have to tell *me* that," Andreas said, looking up at her with a tenderness that could only be forged from the many challenges they had faced together over the years.

"So, can we open the restaurant now, since the bulldozers aren't waiting for us at the gate?"

Andreas nodded in acquiescence before getting up from the table.

"Better call Hyacinth," he said, smiling at her with his old jester's grin. "Tell her no day off after all."

THE END

About the Author

Diana García is a writer, an information professional, an avid reader and traveler. As the daughter of mixed heritage, she grew up straddling the distinct cultures of Costa Rica and the United States, and considers herself fortunate to have gained an additional, adopted home in Germany where she studied as an exchange student. She lived and worked for 16 years in New York City and now resides in Costa Rica with her partner and two cats.

You can connect with me on:

🌐 https://linktr.ee/dianagarciaauthor

www.ingramcontent.com/pod-product-compliance
Lightning Source LLC
Chambersburg PA
CBHW031439160726
47994CB00005B/1795